'... the complexities of family, politics ... colourful, bittersweet [and] affecting novel'
Sunday Times

'Christie Watson's debut novel, set in the troubled Niger Delta, does what fiction does best, it captures place and characters so well that you feel you are also there. It is sincere, it is powerfully written, and it deserves to be read'
Helon Habila, author of *Oil on Water*, winner of the Commonwealth Prize

'Lyrical and beautifully drawn, a poignant coming-of-age tale, set in an Africa few readers will have experienced. A must-read'
Lesley Lokko, author of *Sundowners*, *Bitter Chocolate* and *One Secret Summer*

'Utterly readable and engaging and deserves to reach a wide – transcultural – audience'
Margaret Busby

'Funny, tragic and moving in all the right places. A must-read!'
Pride (Book of the Month)

'A breakthrough novel . . . Watson tells her story of culture clash without heavy messages, but the issues are sure to spark intense discussion'

Booklist

CHRISTIE
WATSON

Tiny Sunbirds
Far Away

Quercus

First published in Great Britain in year of 2011 by Quercus
This paperback edition published in 2012 by

Quercus
55 Baker Street,
7th Floor, South Block
London
W1U 8EW

Some characters in this novel first appeared in a short story entitled
'Basketball Player', published by *Wasafiri, Everything to Declare:
25 Anniversary Issue*, Vol. 24 Number 3, September 2009.

A CIP catalogue record for this book is available
from the British Library

ISBN 978 1 84916 375 0

10 9 8 7 6 5

Typeset by Ellipsis Digital Limited, Glasgow

Printed and bound in Great Britain by Clays Ltd, St Ives plc

For the Egberongbes,
who had me fall in love with Nigeria

ONE

Father was a loud man. His voice entered a room before he did. From my bedroom window I could hear him sitting in the wide gardens, or walking to the car parking area filled with Mercedes, or standing by the security guard's office, or the gate in front.

The gate had different signs stuck on it every week:

No Hawkers
Hawkers Only Permitted if Called by Residents
No Barbecues in the Gardens
No Overnight Guests: Remember,
Friends Can Be Armed Robbers Too

And once, until Mama saw the sign and had Father remove it, after he had laughed so loudly that the walls shook:

No Sexual Activity or Defecating in the Gardens

We lived on Allen Avenue in Ikeja, on the fourth floor of

a gated apartment block called Better Life Executive Homes. I loved watching the street from my window, the traders outside walking up and down the avenue, with brightly coloured buckets and baskets and trays balanced on their heads. They were always shouting: 'Chin-chin, chin-chin', or 'Flip-flops', or 'Batteries', or 'Schnapps'. Every day, no matter how many days I had looked out of the window during my twelve years, there was something being sold that I had not seen before: shoe-horns, St Michael's underwear, imported *Hello!* magazines. I loved watching the women huddled underneath umbrellas, their legs poking out of the bottoms like thick yams. Or the men with necks covered in yellow gold, sitting on the bonnets of their BMWs, and the women wearing Western-style clothes hovering around them like stars around the moon. The women visited the boutique dress shops, and all the day the men would go in and out of the bars and Chinese restaurants, one hand always in their pocket ready to pull out some more naira.

Occasionally Mama rushed in and pushed me off the window seat, opening the window wide to let out the cold air and let in the heat, and the smells of the nearby market, of sewerage from the open gutters, the fresh fish, raw meat, *akara,* puff-puff, and *suya*. The smells made me feel sick and hungry at the same time. 'Don't look at those men,' Mama would say. 'I wish they would go to some other place to spend their money.'

But there was no other place. Allen Avenue was the richest road in Ikeja, with the most shops. If you had money to spend, Allen Avenue was where you spent it. And if you were even richer, like us, then you lived there. On Allen Avenue every house or apartment had a generator. The hum they made was constant, day and night. Roads surrounded us that had no electricity at all, where people went to bed as soon as night fell and, according to my brother Ezikiel, produced too many babies. But Allen Avenue was brightly lit. People left their televisions and radios on loud all night, to show how much money they could afford to waste.

'Hey, hey you! I need soaps.'

'Best quality soap. Anti-germ. Very fine, good for skin. Will smooth you and soothe you, Mama. Very famous soap. Imported from US.'

Mama waved her hand up and down as the tall woman with the blue and white plastic bowl full of soaps walked slowly towards the security gate. She did not rush. Nobody did. Even when the other hawkers realised that Mama was buying soap. That she had money to spend. They looked up at the window and shouted out the contents of their bowls or baskets or trays: Oranges, Pure Water, Bush Meat, Alarm Clock, Petticoats, Gucci Handbags.

But from where I was sitting, I did not need them to shout.

I could see everything.

Father worked as an accountant for an office full of government ministers in central Lagos, and had to leave the apartment very early in the morning to miss the worst of the go-slow. Ezikiel woke up extra early to see Father before he left for work, even though he was fourteen years old and not a morning person. He liked to sit on Father's side of his bed next to his neatly laid out work clothes, and watch him dress, pass him his tie, cufflinks and wristwatch. Mama would tut loudly into her pillow before swinging her long legs out of the bed as Father whistled and teased her. 'It is like sleeping next to a handful of needles,' he would say, 'sharp and bony, poking me through the night.' Mama would tut even louder, and sometimes suck her teeth.

We all had breakfast together. Father ate Hot Food Only, but lukewarm, which made his Hot Food Only rule seem silly. Ezikiel and I ate cereal, or rolls with jam that Mama had stolen from her job at the Royal Imperial Hotel. After dressing in her work uniform of navy blue skirt and white blouse, and painting her lips with a tiny paintbrush, Mama would make Father's coffee, extra sweet with warmed condensed milk. Then she would kiss Father on the mouth. Sometimes twice. After kissing Mama, Father would have the same red colour on his lips and make us laugh by pretending to have the voice of a woman. Father laughed the loudest. He always laughed at breakfast time, until he had a mouthful of food, or until our neighbour, who did not begin work until nine a.m., banged on the wall with his knuckles.

After Father and Mama had left for work, Ezikiel and I walked to the International School for Future Leaders, which had floors so shiny I could see my reflection in them. My best friend Habibat and I liked to sit by the fountain at lunchtime and take off our shoes and socks, dipping our feet into the cool water. Ezikiel liked the clubs and societies: Chess society, Latin club, Science club. But we both liked school. We liked the marble floors, cool air-conditioning, and wide running field that seemed to stretch forever.

It was nearly night outside when Father arrived home. My window was shut, the air-conditioning was on full, but still, I could hear his footsteps on the path, his key in the lock, and his slamming the door. Ezikiel jumped up from where he had been reading on my bed, knocking his textbook onto the floor where it opened at a page that had a picture of a man with no skin showing his insides, and arrows pointing to the different bits inside him: descending colon, duodenum, liver.

Father's footsteps thudded across the hallway before the door burst open. 'Kids, where are you? Where are you, trouble kids?'

Mama hated Father calling us kids.

Father loosened his tie as Ezikiel and I rushed over and followed him to the parlour.

'I came top in the spelling test, and the teacher said I am the best at Latin. The best he's ever taught.' Ezikiel was breathless from talking too fast. His nostrils were flaring.

I moved closer to Ezikiel's back. Even though Ezikiel was only two years older than me he was already a whole head higher. My eyes were level with the bony part at the bottom of his neck. I could not see Father drop to his knees, but I knew that he had. He knelt every day so that we could climb onto his shoulders, a shoulder each, and he would lift us to the ceiling, and throw us into the air. He was always in a good mood when he first returned home.

Father stood slowly, pretending to wobble and almost drop us, but I knew how strong he was. Ezikiel had told me he'd seen Father lift the car with only one hand, so that Zafi, our driver, could change the wheel.

We laughed and laughed on Father's shoulders, tickling behind his ears. The laughter flew around the room like a hungry mosquito. My own laughter was loud in my ears. I could barely hear Mama.

'Get them down, for goodness' sake; they are not babies any more. You'll damage your back!' Mama came out of her bedroom wearing a dressing gown and red eyes. 'It's dangerous!'

Mama had never liked us to sit on Father's shoulders, even when we were younger. She said that she did not like the idea of us falling, of having to catch us, but I was sure that she did not want us to know about the top of her head where her weave had been pulled tight and left a patch of bald, or the high up shelf where she kept a tin of liquorice, and a photograph album that we were not meant to see.

Suddenly, Ezikiel's wheeze appeared. It was louder than the television showing a Nollywood film. It was louder than the hum of the generators. It was louder than Father's laughter. Ezikiel's body straightened and he banged his head on the ceiling. I grabbed onto his arm.

'See what happens,' said Mama, rushing forwards.

Father dropped to his knees, and I jumped off, and stood back as Ezikiel slumped over. He was already coughing and hitting the front of his chest. His breaths were coming quickly, and out of time. Mama dropped down, sitting behind Ezikiel, holding his back with her arm. The redness had disappeared from her eyes and jumped into Ezikiel's.

'Quick,' she shouted at Father, who was getting to his feet. Mama stroked Ezikiel's hair, whispering into his ear, rocking his body back and forth, back and forth.

In one movement, Father opened the sideboard drawer and pulled out a blue inhaler, flipped the cap off, and passed it to Mama who stuck it into Ezikiel's mouth, and pressed the top twice.

The inside of Ezikiel's bottom lip was blue.

'Get the paper bag on the kitchen top, quickly.' Mama pressed the inhaler again. She continued to rock.

I ran to the kitchen. The brown bag on the kitchen top was full of peppers. I looked around for another. My eyes could not work fast enough. They zoomed around the kitchen but everything had become blurry. I could hear the rasping of Ezikiel's breaths, and I could feel Mama's panic in my neck.

There was no other bag. What should I do? I had twelve years; I was old enough to know that peppers should be treated carefully. I looked at them. They were unbroken. I took a long breath, and a chance that their pepperyness had not seeped out, emptied the bag, and ran back.

Ezikiel was slumped over his inhaler, Mama was behind him holding him up, and Father was behind her holding her up. Father had his arms wrapped around both of them. When I ran towards him he pulled me into his arms, too.

Mama grabbed the brown paper bag from my hand and placed it over Ezikiel's nose and mouth. It took a few seconds before the red trees in his eyes grew branches, and his tears fell like tiny leaves onto the bag. He pushed the bag away.

Mama leant forwards and smelled the bag.

Mama gave me a look that said, 'Stupid girl.'

I said nothing.

Father leaned towards Mama, and stroked her face where her frown line cut into her forehead. 'He'll be fine,' he said, in his loud voice that sounded so sure. Mama's frown line became less deep. His arm tightened around my back.

Father was right. He was always right. Ezikiel's breathing slowly improved. The trees disappeared and the wheeze quietened. Mama sniffed the bag, then put it back over his nose and only took it away to puff some more of his inhaler in. Ezikiel's breathing became more regular and equal, his skin no longer being tugged into his throat. I watched his nostrils until they were flat once more, against his face, and his skin change colour slowly from daylight, to dusk, to night.

Father was a loud man. I could hear him shouting from the neighbours' apartment where he argued about football with Dr Adeshina, and drank so much Remy Martin that he could not stand up properly. I could hear him singing when he returned from the Everlasting Open Arms House of Salvation Church, on a bus that had the words 'Up Jesus Down Satan' written on the side. The singing would reach my ears right up on the fourth floor. From my window I watched the bus driver and Pastor King Junior carry Father towards the apartment because he could not stand up at all.

If Father did stand up, it was worse. He seemed to have no idea how to move around quietly, and when he did try, after Mama said her head was splitting in two, the crashing became louder.

We were so used to Father's loud voice that it became quieter. Our ears changed and put on a barrier like sunglasses whenever he was at home. So when we left for market early on Saturday morning and we knew Father was out working all day on some important account at the office, our ears did not need their sunglasses on. And when Mama realised she had forgotten her purse, and we had to turn back, our ears were working fine. I heard the chatter of the women at market, the traffic and street traders along Allen Avenue, and the humming of the electric gate to let us back into the apartment building. I heard our footsteps on the hallway carpets, and Mama's key in the front lock. I heard the cupboard door open when Ezikiel and I went straight for the biscuits.

And then I heard the most terrible, loudest noise I had ever heard in my life.

My switched-on ears hurt. I tried to put the glasses on

them, to switch them down, to turn them off. Father must have been home; I could hear him shouting.

Father was a loud man.

But it was Mama who was screaming.

TWO

It was a month later when the shouting reduced enough for us to hear the words that Mama and Father were saying to each other.

'I didn't mean it to happen,' Father said.

Ezikiel and I were holding hands, and listening from behind the bedroom door. I imagined Mama's expression, pinched and unforgiving, sharp arms folded across her nearly flat chest.

'You are a louse,' Mama replied, in a voice much clearer than usual.

I squeezed Ezikiel's hand and wished as hard as possible for Mama to soften, for her to forgive. But I knew Mama.

'I am going to live with her,' said Father. The smell of stale palm wine followed the sound of his voice.

A few seconds later, the door slammed. I could hear Father walking down the hallway with his too-loud walk, and pressing the lift with his too-loud finger, and swearing with his too-loud voice.

Then it was quiet.

★

It was a month after that when Mama had to stop working at the Royal Imperial Hotel. She said that the owners only employed married women. Since Father had left, I did not dare ask her anything at all.

I did not dare ask her if she was no longer married to Father.

She had always left for work at dawn, except Sundays. Even then, she got up before sunrise and complained every week that her body was Just Used To It. She had always made our breakfast. She had always kissed us on the head before she left for work, and kissed Father on the mouth, sometimes twice. But Father was gone.

First she stopped making our breakfast.

Then she stopped applying lipstick with the tiny paint-brush.

Then she stopped kissing us on the head to wake us.

Instead she shouted my name: 'Blessing!' followed by 'Ezikiel!' as if there was an emergency.

And one day, she told us that Father had stopped paying the rent and we were going to be evicted. She said that Better Life Executive Homes had high rents that could only be paid by rich men, and she was not a man, or even a woman with a job; there was no way we would escape eviction.

And because we were being evicted, we had to move to our grandfather Alhaji's house.

I did not know what evicted meant but I did not dare ask.

I had never before seen my grandparents who lived a day's

drive away near Warri in the Niger Delta. Mama had told us once that her parents had never wanted Mama to marry Father, or any other Yoruba man.

'Did you make up with Grandma?' I asked.

'We never broke up,' Mama said. She had laid out two large suitcases on the bed and was wiping the insides clean with a piece of yellow sponge. 'Essentials only,' she said, when she noticed me looking at the cases. Her hair was matted and uncombed. She looked like the women hawkers walking up and down the avenue who wore no shoes on their feet.

'But they have never been to see us. And we live so far apart.'

'No mother and daughter live apart,' said Mama, 'no matter how big the distance between them.'

'Even if you did make up,' Ezikiel said, 'Warri is not safe. And those villages outside are even worse! Swamp villages! I googled Warri at the internet café. Oil bunkering, hostage taking, illness, guns and poverty. What about my asthma? They burn poisonous chemicals straight into the air! It's not a safe place to live.'

I could feel the panic in Ezikiel's voice. It made the words sound angry.

'I grew up there,' said Mama. 'And I was safe. More than safe, actually. I loved living near Warri. It's a great place to grow up. Of course, I won't have much time for fun now. I'll be too busy looking for work. But honestly, Warri had its own vibe; it was really fun.'

'Well, it's changed then. It's dangerous. The whole Delta region. And if we don't get shot the bacteria and parasites will surely kill us.' Ezikiel shook his head, and disappeared to his bedroom. '*Dra-cunc-ul-ia-sis*,' he shouted. I peered around his door. He was reading from his *Encyclopaedia of Tropical Medicine*. '*Schis-to-soma-haem-at-ob-ium*.' The Latin words became even longer the way that he shouted them. 'Parasites! That one makes your urine red with blood! *Leish-man-ia-sis, Lymph-at-ic fil-ar-ia-sis*. "The river-dwelling parasites burrow through foot skin, enter the lymphatic system and can ultimately cause organ failure!" Are you listening to this?'

'You'll like it at Alhaji's place,' shouted Mama, eventually. 'Or, you won't like it. We have to go, either way.' She started to cry again. It was unusual to hear Mama disagree with Ezikiel. And even stranger to hear her cry. I peered back around the bedroom door, and gave Ezikiel a look that made him close his book, and curl up on his bed, wrapping his long arms around his knees.

I did not want to leave Lagos. Every memory I ever had of Father was contained in the apartment, or garden. I remember feeling a sharp pain somewhere near my shoulder. I could barely move my arm. I could hardly breathe.

'He might come back,' I said, to no one in particular.

'Is that the only reason you don't want to leave? Do you know where we are moving? It's the parasites you should be worried about. What about my allergies? That place is so bush; I doubt they even have medical facilities!'

'If we leave, we will not remember everything. About Father, I mean.'

'What are you talking about?'

'If we stay here in our apartment we can remember Father better, even if he does not come back.' I paused, to swallow the lump in my throat. I looked out of my window to the street below.

'A person becomes part of their surroundings,' I told Ezikiel.

Ezikiel rolled his eyes and sighed before putting his long arm around me.

Later, I touched the stone walls and felt Father's smooth skin that remained cool even during the early afternoon road-melting heat. I tasted his toothbrush, which I had hidden after he left in case Mama threw it in the rubbish bin. Either the toothbrush, or my mouth, was too dry. I found Father's footprint in the red dirt behind the electric gate and put my foot inside it. My foot looked too small. Everything was too quiet. I wanted to scream.

It was Zafi, our driver, who had taught Ezikiel and me to speak Izon. Before then, we had only spoken in English, and some words in Yoruba, Father's language. Mama smiled when she heard us speaking her own language. That is why she had allowed Zafi to remain our driver despite him having only one eye and only one foot due to what Ezikiel called 'poorly managed diabetes'. He was lucky that his remaining foot was so long; he had mastered the art of driving using his toe on the accelerator and his heel on the brake. Zafi had stayed with Mama after Father left. He said that Father had a new driver with two working eyes and two working feet, and that he did not require payment until Mama had found employment. But really, I did not imagine he would find another job as a driver.

Zafi coughed all the way out of Lagos. The journey should have only taken a day but the go-slow was endless and the car tyres stuck down on the road as if they too did not want to leave. Even the gearbox joined in and made third gear into reverse, and reverse into third gear. We drove all the way out of Lagos with the gear stick facing backwards, pointing at Mama, like a long finger. As soon as we left Allen Avenue the hum of the generators began to fade, and I felt the blood rush forwards in my head. My eyes hurt. My right side began to hurt. I wondered if that was my Yoruba half.

We drove past the Egyptian restaurant where some men were playing *ayo* on small tables outside, and sat in the go-slow at the junction opposite the old Radio Lagos Station, where Father used to get annoyed at the traffic. At Oregun Road, we turned towards the Secretariat and arrived at Eleganza Building. We were silent for the half-hour it took on the express until Sagamu exit, where we followed the road until Ore Road.

Father used to say Ore Road was the most dangerous road in all Nigeria. We swerved around overturned lorries, and fell into potholes that swallowed the car. The road was sepa-rated by a concrete bank, with metal barriers between the sides of traffic. But that did not stop anyone. Cars climbed the concrete, revving until they reached the top, and slid down the other side to face the traffic head on and drive as fast as possible the wrong way. Other cars swerved and crashed and slid and skidded. I could not see the faces of the drivers of the other cars; the sun was too bright, but I imagined they all had their eyes closed like Mama.

We stopped at Ore to run into the bush and urinate. I angled myself this way and that but still the urine went on my ankles. Ezikiel laughed. As we walked slowly back to the car I listened to the voices around me. The language sounded different. People were speaking Yoruba, but mixed up with words that I did not recognise. I could speak Izon, Yoruba, English, and even some pidgin English, which Mama called rotten English. But I did not recognise many of the words around me. I held on tightly to Ezikiel's arm. Everyone we walked past watched us closely. It felt like the first day of school, where even though you wanted to be invisible, everyone could see that you were new and out of place and different.

I listened carefully to the last of the loud Yoruba voices. I listened for Father. I opened my ears as wide as they would go. But he was not there.

An overturned lorry blocked the road, and we sat for hours waiting for the go-slow to lessen. I watched the men standing around, the traders selling bananas, plantains, yams and logs. Some people had left their cars on the road and walked away, which added to the wait. Everyone was shouting. Fists were being thumped onto car bonnets. Horns blasted. People were tired of waiting. But not us. It was silent in our car. Even Zafi stopped coughing. We waited and waited without even noticing how awful the waiting was.

Eventually it turned to night and the traffic cleared. I had never been beyond Ore. I had never left Yorubaland, the land of Father's tribe. As we drove away, I wanted to turn my head around and look backwards, but instead I looked at Mama, whose eyes were still shut.

I woke with a pain in my neck that stretched right up to my ear. I tried to straighten my head but the pain made it impossible, so I turned my head back towards Ezikiel. He was sleeping with his mouth wide open. His throat looked redder than usual. He was always ill. There was never a week when Ezikiel did not have an asthma attack, an allergy, a throat infection or chest infection. Mama said he was born sickly. The first time Ezikiel had eaten meat fried in groundnut oil I was too young to remember. But Mama had told me the story so often that it felt like a memory. Ezikiel had been two years old. Before then he had lived on a diet of porridge and milk. It was before the time that Mama knew she had to bring home vegetable oil and fry all of Ezikiel's food in it. Every time Ezikiel was presented with fish or meat that had been fried in groundnut oil he screamed as though his body somehow knew what would happen. But by the time he was two, Father had bought Mama an electric liquidiser.

She whizzed up some chicken that had been fried in groundnut oil, and a tiny amount of pepper, and then spooned it into his mouth. Ezikiel gulped down the food quickly. Father and Mama were laughing. I do not know where I was, probably asleep, as I was newly born. Ezikiel's face suddenly turned red, and his skin blistered. Mama screamed. She said the next things happened slowly. First, Ezikiel's face swelled up, then his arms; then his tongue became larger and larger until there was no room for air to get into his mouth. He became blue. Luckily, Dr Adeshina was home. He stuck a syringe of medicine into Ezikiel's leg. He told Father that Ezikiel had a nut allergy. He saved Ezikiel's life. Maybe that was why Ezikiel wanted to be a doctor.

It was still dark outside but the sky had changed colour. The further away we had driven from Lagos, the brighter the sky became until we were on the outskirts of Warri, and it looked bright enough to be day. The stars were the size of my hand, and seemed to move. The moon was close enough to see its uneven surface, like a potholed road in Lagos. As we neared Warri, the sky became even brighter. I saw a flame in the distance. A giant torch, which made the sky look angry.

'Pipeline fires,' said Zafi. 'They are burning the gases from the oil.' He started coughing again.

As we drove through Warri, I opened my eyes as wide as they would go, to let in all the differences. When we stopped in another go-slow I heard birds singing loudly. I looked at the sky but saw nothing except dust and air, before I realised it was not birds singing. It was people talking, low then high, then low again. They were speaking pidgin English mixed with some other language. I did not understand a single word. Even the pidgin English sounded different. We drove past tall buildings with shops underneath hanging onto the sides, and large areas of wasteland, shopping malls and markets. But as we drove through Warri, I did not see any slums, like Makoko under the main bridge in Lagos, where the smell of fish and human waste and rubbish is so strong that if it fills your nostrils it takes all day to remove. I did not see an area like Victoria Island where the white men used to go and shop, and stay in five star hotels like the one that Mama used to work in. There was no Allen Avenue where you could eat Chinese food and shop for designer clothes. Warri even smelled different to Lagos. I closed my eyes and sniffed. The air smelled like a book unopened for a very long time, and smoky, as though the ground had been on fire.

On the other side of Warri there was nothing to see except bush on either side of the road. I closed my eyes and tried to remember Father's face. It was already changing. Becoming less clear. He had a mark above his eyebrow, I remembered, of course. But already, I had forgotten which eyebrow.

Eventually we drove past a sleeping village and down the end of a potholed road, and we pulled up outside a large gated compound. The first thing I saw was a chicken, in the car headlights, marked with a splash of red paint. The chicken stopped in front of the car and made no attempt to move, then, at the last minute, it shrieked and fluttered off. A sleeping dog was by the gate, curled up like a cashew nut. It did not move or even wake up. The gate was rusted metal with sharp broken edges. Barbed wire and pieces of glass lined the top of the gate and the wall. I could hear shouting: 'Eh! Eh!'

A woman opened the gate and came outside carrying a kerosene lamp. I could see at once that it was Grandma; she had the same pinched nose as me. She had the flattest, roundest face I had ever seen. The area around her mouth was criss-crossed with tiny scars, and two thick scars either side of her lips made her smile seem even wider. Grandma was very short, but she looked tall until, one by one, we climbed out of the car.

An old man came out from behind the gate next, half the size of Grandma. He greeted Mama with a nod. He did not extend his hand at all. His face was crumpled like my T-shirt. Mama dropped to her knees and bent her head forward until he said, 'Rise.'

Mama stood and stepped backwards, her head still lowered. 'Thank you, Alhaji, sir,' she whispered back in Izon.

'You are welcome, daughter.'

Grandfather!

Grandma reached out for Mama. She squashed her tightly, and kissed the top of her head. I had never before seen anyone kiss the top of Mama's head. Mama sobbed, just once, then moved aside.

'Ezikiel,' said Grandma. 'Let me see this big strong boy.' She hugged Ezikiel and rubbed her hand on his skinny back.

I stayed by the car and stuck my hand out to Grandma. Grandma did not take my hand. She just looked at me so deeply it felt as though she could see right through my skin, and into my bones.

We followed Grandma into the house, where I could only just see that other people were sitting on chairs. I noticed a girl my own age, and wanted to ask who she was, but I did not dare speak. It was too dark. It was too quiet. In Lagos our house had only contained four people and yet it was always noisy, always busy. This place was full of people, but it was silent. There was no talking or laughing, no music, television or radio, no humming of a generator. I could hear my own breath coming out. I could hear Ezikiel's wheeze at the bottom of his back.

We walked though into a room where Grandma pointed to the plastic chairs that were around a small wooden table. On top of the table was a tray with four glasses and four bowls. Grandma took the bowls and lifted them. She opened a door to the back of the house. Balanced on a metal block on top of the fire was a pot. It bubbled like Ezikiel's chest.

Grandma picked up a large spoon from the dusty ground. She put a spoonful of soup into each pot and handed them to us. We took our bowls into the house and sat down on the plastic chairs. Grandma followed us with a tin, which she opened to take out four white balls wrapped in cellophane. Of course, we had had pounded yam before, it was Father's favourite, but this was different. We had not washed our hands in anything except a bucket of water, there was no soap, and

I could feel the dirt from the journey stuck to my fingers. I thought of Ezikiel's parasites. Grandma was watching me. I scooped up some fish stew with the yam, and put it into my mouth. My tongue burned from the pepper, and a tiny bone caught in my throat, causing me to cough repeatedly in the quiet house. I was not hungry and the food tasted strange, and my fingers were full of parasites, but I felt as though I could not leave any at all. My stomach was angry. I could not stop thinking of the dirt on my hands, the lack of soap, and the pounded yam that did not taste at all like pounded yam.

I could see Ezikiel studying the stew. The layer on top was palm-oil red, but we did not know if Grandma had fried the fish first. He looked up at Mama, and Grandma, his pounded yam ball in his hand hovering between the sauce and his mouth.

Mama nodded her head slightly. 'It is safe,' she said.

'Your mama told me you are allergic to nuts,' said Grandma, in English. 'It is not fried in groundnut oil, only cooked in palm oil. Eh! I tried to fry it in palm oil and I am nearly blind from the smoke! But the fish is extra fresh today. I paid extra. So no need for worry about illness because it is not fried first.'

Ezikiel's face dropped. He dipped his yam into the stew so slightly that only the edge became orange. I could feel the wheeze of his breath on my arm, through the sleeve of my T-shirt.

After dinner Grandma took us to our bedroom. The room smelled of disinfectant. It was empty bar the one mattress on the floor, which did not have a sheet, but a wrapper had been spread on top. I looked around the room. One mattress! I realised that we were all supposed to share the room together. Me, Mama and even Ezikiel. And worse than that, we were all to share a bed. One mattress on the floor. I felt the pounded yam leave my stomach and travel back up towards my mouth.

There was no pillow, or blanket, or mosquito net. A tall fan stood against the wall with a plug hanging over it, as if it was not going to even bother trying for electricity. I looked quickly around the room for plug sockets, and listened for the hum of a generator. But there was no hum. Surely there must have been a generator? Surely, they did not rely on NEPA? That meant days without electricity. I did not want to believe it. *No electricity!* Cold things raced through my mind: fridges, drinks, fans, air-conditioning.

I thought of all the things I had done, to cause Father to leave. I thought of the time I had complained that he worked too-long hours. I had always complained. As soon as he had returned from work. I thought of pestering him to take me and Ezikiel swimming, when he must have been tired on his day off work. I thought of Father reading my last school report where I had received a C in Maths, which was Father's favourite subject. I closed my eyes, and pinched my own arm.

When I opened my eyes, I could see that the paint on the walls was peeling away. On the wall above the bed a large golden frame, smashed at one edge, contained a picture of just one single curly word in Arabic. I could see our suitcases, which looked brand new in the room despite being at least two years old. And I could see the dust on the ground, and hear something scuttling around on it.

We all climbed onto the mattress with our clothes still on. I watched Mama's back. I lay there for a very long time, listening to Ezikiel's wheeze. Even though Mama too was pretending, I could see by how quickly she was breathing that she was not asleep either. Eventually, I crept up from the mattress and walked to the mesh-covered window to look outside. The sky was much bigger. The brightest stars I had ever seen covered the sky, and the air was blue. The garden was full of spiky shapes and shadows. But the sky was lit up. The stars were so bright that when I closed my eyes they remained there, behind my eyelids, as though my body had swallowed some of the sky for itself.

THREE

The following morning I woke at first light. Fear made my heart race and my mouth turn dry. I looked for my dressing-table with vanity mirror and clock sent from Mama's schoolfriend in America. I felt for my magazines, books and wind-up torch. I stretched a foot off the mattress looking for my rug, and two pairs of slippers: one warm for when the air-conditioning was on full, and one cool, for all other times. Then I remembered. There were no slippers. There was no torch. There was no light. There was no dressing-table, vanity mirror, or clock. There were just the first rays of sunlight streaming in the mesh window, casting criss-cross patterns on the dusty floor.

I stepped off the mattress; Mama and Ezikiel were lying so close it was impossible to tell whose foot was whose, until I saw the chipped, worn-down nail polish stains. The air around me suddenly felt hotter, and closed in; I could not breathe properly. I went to the window and sucked in the outside air. I looked through the mesh and remembered counting five different faces that had peered through during the night. I had not recognised any of them. Even the daytime sky was different. The sun had given the sky a string of yellow gold necklaces.

I crept past the mattress. Mama's face was puffed out from crying all night. She had her arm twisted around Ezikiel in such a way it looked as though she was trying to prevent him from falling. I did not see the point. The mattress was only a few centimetres from the ground.

I opened the door as slowly as possible but it still creaked. In the hallway the smell of camphor oil was strong enough to reach my eyes. The room in front of our bedroom was filled with foam chairs, all with one or two people sleeping on them. The girl my own age was curled around another girl. Their hair was braided too tightly, and had broken spiky pieces at the front. One girl wore a blanket over her body, making it difficult to see what clothes she was wearing. The other had a skirt and T-shirt in different shades of orange. The clothes were dirty. It looked as though they had never been washed. I moved slowly and watched them as I walked past. I wanted to stop and stare – I had never before seen people sleeping soundly on chairs, and in such tight plaits, or such dirty clothes – but I did not dare. I left the room and walked outside the main door onto the veranda. A kerosene lamp lit the doorway. The veranda was wide, big enough for another house, and had plastic chairs and tables on top. Steps down the veranda were wobbly and the handrail shook. The wide yard was filled with dust and trees and flowers. A spiky palm tree in the centre looked as though it had been there before all the others, and found the best place to stand. It reminded me of the girls' broken pieces of hair. I walked to the left of the main house and past the Boys' Quarters lining the side. Ten or so wood and tin shacks held together with rope and tape, they did not look like they would survive the harmattan winds, but seemed older than even the palm tree, as though they too had existed before the main house was built. Material pieces covered the doors, large spread-out ankara fabrics that smelled fiery, like they were burning. I could hear snoring and crying and grunting coming from inside each shack. I walked past quickly.

At the back of the main building the Boys' Quarters huts became smaller and smaller until there were none. By the time I reached the edge of the Boys' Quarters the sun was pressing hard onto the back of my neck, over the top of my T-shirt, and onto my head, in the lines between my corn-rows. An area of wasteland stretched out before me up to a large fence surrounded by thick bushes. Of course, I had seen compounds before, in Lagos, gated compounds where friends lived, similar to Better Life Executive Homes. The compounds I was used to were neat and managed by a gardener and groundsman, and security patrolled the fence. Cars were parked in parking spaces, and the buildings were freshly painted and well kept. The compounds I was used to were small, containing a few buildings and a small area of outside space. But Alhaji's compound was endless. I could only just see the perimeter fence. The outside space was wild and dusty and dry. Goats and skinny sheep roamed with chickens and half-dressed children. The gate did not look at all secure.

Alhaji's compound looked more like a village, with a fence around it. I walked behind the house, where I could see the small outdoor kitchen area, where a few pots were sitting on top of a plank of wood, and piles of bowls and cups and pans and spoons were in the ground-dirt. They were covered in thick dust. A large oil barrel was full of water. It had a picture of a shell printed on the side. A cup floated at the top. I hoped that the oil barrel water was not used for washing the dusty bowls, or worse still, cooking with. A thought suddenly entered my head. Water. Why would there be water in a bucket? Why not just pour it from a tap? *No running water*. Surely, that was not possible. The house was very basic, and dusty, but it had furniture and land, and an area for Boys' Quarters, and a gate, and a wide veranda. *But there was no generator for electricity*. We had washed our hands the evening before in the bucket. Could it be possible that we did not have water? Mama had told me that Alhaji was a qualified engineer. I had expected the house to be basic and dusty, but Mama had told us that Alhaji was comfortable. *No running water?* Could a house with no running water be thought of as comfortable? I stood still, thinking about the possibility of no running water, trying to tell myself that it could not be true. The sun scratched my skin, between my cornrows, and a feeling of sickness filled my stomach. It was then that I felt eyes watching me. A boy was sitting by the bushes next to the fence. I could not see him properly but I somehow knew that he was smiling. His legs were skinnier than Ezikiel's and even though he was sitting down, I could tell that he was tall. The curled-up dog was lying next to him. He picked his hand up and waved it. For a few moments I did nothing. Then I flicked my hand up just once, and crept into the house through a small door behind the kitchen area.

I found myself in cool darkness. The space between my cornrows jumped every second like the hand of a clock. The air was sweeter inside the house, and bitter at the same time, as though two foodstuffs had been mixed in the wrong way, like a sweet and sour flavour I had tried in a Chinese restaurant in Lagos. It confused my nose and took me a long time to stop sniffing. In the hallway in front of me an open door led into a large and bare room. Grandma was sitting at the table with her head thrown back and her hair weave hooked over the chair top. It looked like a dead animal, matted and patchy. Grandma's eyes were closed. I took the opportunity to lean closer and study her face. She had rounder cheeks than me, and shiny skin the colour of a cassava shell. Her nostrils flared slightly with each breath, and she made sounds in her sleep like a baby. I wondered what she was dreaming about. I crept closer. Grandma's eyelashes were so long they had curled over completely and looked very short. Her mouth was open and I could see the gap between her teeth, wide enough to fit another tooth in. She wore a T-shirt that had the word 'Tobago' written in faded pink across her breasts, which were so enormous, I had to lean from one side to the other to make sense of what I thought was the word 'Obag'. Her blue and green wrapper was covered in hundreds of trumpets facing different directions on her body. The wrapper looked so comfortable. The jeans I had arrived in were sticking to my skin.

Suddenly Grandma's eyes snapped open, as though she had been pretending to be asleep all along. I stepped backwards. Did she know I had been staring at her?

'Good morning, Blessing. How was your rest?' Grandma spoke to me in English.

'Good, thank you,' I replied in Izon.

'You speak Izon well. That is good. I am happy that your Mama has taught you Izon.'

The words 'Zafi taught us' were in my throat, but I did not open my mouth to let them out.

'I hope you carry on speaking Izon. We all speak too much English here. But Youseff's wives only speak Izon. Only one language and they talk so much! Are you finding your way around?' Grandma reached for her weave with one hand and touched my cheek with the other. Her hand felt like the bark of a tree.

'Yes, Grandma.'

'Come. Let me see you.'

Grandma pulled me towards her and looked deep into my eyes. Nobody had ever looked at my eyes for that long before, except Ezikiel when we played stare-out games. I needed to swallow but I did not want to make the swallowing noise. I moved backwards.

'Let me show you the place.' Grandma let me go and I stood as still as possible, trying not to step even further backwards and offend her. I followed her outside the room into the dark hallway and then out the door into the hot sun.

'Who are those girls?' I asked, as we crept past the girls sleeping on chairs.

'They are some of Youseff's daughters,' Grandma said. 'Fatima and Yasmina. He is our driver, with kids all over the place.'

I wondered how many kids he had. Even through my flip-flops the bottoms of my feet were burning and I had to stand on one leg, until the other foot cooled, and then the other leg. Grandma watched me standing one-legged but did not ask anything. She probably thought I was a crazy.

Grandma waved her hand at the kitchen area, and the bucket. 'We collect water from the village tap,' she said. 'I am sure you will get used to balancing water on top of your head like the village girls. You are not in Lagos now, eh? I will show you the tap in the village next week. This week you are guest, and next week you can start chores.'

No water! Chores!

I smiled.

How far was the tap? The village we drove past seemed very far away from the compound. Surely Grandma did not mean me to collect water on my head from that far away.

Away from the outdoor kitchen we walked to the other side of the building. The sweet and sour smell from the house finally left my nose and was replaced with the smell of the Lagos gutters. 'The place for your business,' said Grandma, leading me to the back of a walled area.

The smell was bad enough for me to cough, even with

Grandma there looking at me. Three small rooms with wooden doors were separated by a wall. Grandma opened each door in turn. The holes in the ground were covered with flies. 'Look,' she said, smiling widely, 'this is how we do our business here in the soak-away. It collects and then gets soaked away into the ground. Much better than those flush toilets.'

I peered into a hole. Nothing had been soaked away. I thought of our toilet at home, with the marble floor that was washed clean every day. I pictured the shiny metal handle, which pulled downwards and flushed away anything in the bowl. I had never before given that handle much thought. But I could not stop thinking of it. I could not imagine doing any business in Grandma's toilets. I would rather not eat. I would rather starve. Or go into the bushes like I had that morning.

As Grandma led me away from the stink of the outhouse a new smell reached my nose. Lined up next to the perimeter fence were long, thin wooden tables. I wondered if that was Grandma's business. Furniture-making? The tables were lined up leaning against the wire fence. They were a very strange shape. I looked at Grandma but she did not notice me. She was pushing her way past a bush. I followed her, all the time wondering what the smell was. Then I heard water.

'The water of the Delta is the blood of Nigeria.' Grandma led me though twisted red trees and scratchy bushes until we came to the riverbank and I felt the ground underneath my flip-flops soften and cool, as though I suddenly had my slippers back. 'But we must not drink this. Only in emergencies. The tap water is cleaner. But now, this water is full of oil spills, and salt, so only for washing clothes and bodies. Not for drinking.'

I looked at the river and tried not to gasp. I had seen the ocean before at Bar Beach, and looked out as far as the horizon, and tried to imagine where it ended. But this was the widest river I had ever seen. It twisted and turned and branched to the side, as if the river itself was the trunk of a tree. I could only just see the village clinging to the other side and the children waving across the water. I waved back, before I could stop my arm. Grandma laughed. Her laugh was the same as Mama's. I remembered exactly what Mama's laugh sounded like even though I could not remember when I had last heard it.

'Be careful of the crocodiles,' whispered Grandma, her face changing shape and becoming wider. 'They might bite off your leg.'

She looked back out to the water. I watched her face to see if she was joking, but I could not read it. I stared at the water. Crocodiles? The water was still in some parts and rushing in others. An area in the middle was jumping like the space between my cornrows. The water was dark, dark, dark. It looked like thick mud. Swirly patterns coloured the top. I could not see the reflection of the strange twisted trees. I peered in, half closing my eyes, but there were no reflections. Not mine. Not even Grandma's.

From where I was standing I could not see anything.

Not even crocodiles.

The river smelled like Warri, of old books that had been left in the rains. The birds chattered, and Grandma chattered, and the children in the village across the water screamed and laughed. But still, I could hear whispering.

Suddenly I could not hear anything other than a loud chanting.

'Alhaji had prayer time put back today to give you people a chance to sleep,' said Grandma. She rushed back, away from the river.

I walked behind her, without asking the questions filling my head: could a man put back prayer time? Why was Grandma rushing me back with her? Was I expected to attend Muslim prayers?

I chased after Grandma's legs until my slippers turned back into flip-flops and the smell of the old books turned into sewerage. We walked past the boats leaning against the fence and I was thankful that I had not asked Grandma about tables. Or furniture-making. She would have known how stupid I was.

Back at the compound, as we walked away from the outhouse through a cornfield and dry grasses to a large field the opposite side of the main building to the Boys' Quarters, Grandma leant down towards me. 'We must row in whatever boat we find ourselves.'

I looked at her face. I had no idea what she was talking about. We walked past our car, where Zafi was sitting at the driver's seat with his hands on the wheel, as though he was about to drive somewhere. At the back of the field, a makeshift shelter had been made from palm fronds and sheets of metal.

'The mosque,' said Grandma, pointing to the shack.

I tried not to open my eyes too wide. I had never heard of a mosque in a garden.

Inside the shack some women were sitting at the back facing me, their headscarves pulled tightly over their heads.

Outside the makeshift mosque stood an imam wearing white robes, a small white hat, a large golden chain and a wristwatch. The boy with the dog was standing next to the imam, smiling and waving, smiling and waving until the imam slapped his hand away. But he carried on smiling anyway. I thought the imam might slap the smile from his mouth but he did not. He was busy holding a loudspeaker towards us even though we were right there in front of him. I wondered why Alhaji had his own mosque. I wondered why there was an imam in the garden; where had he come from? The imam shouted into the loudspeaker, making the low chant become static, and forcing him to move away from it for a few seconds until the screeching sound stopped.

My hands automatically went up to my ears before I could stop them, and that was when I noticed Alhaji watching me. I dropped my hands to my sides.

Grandma quickly wrapped a headscarf around my head; I had to touch it to check that it was real. Mama and Ezikiel appeared from behind Alhaji. Mama too was wearing a scarf completely covering her head. Her eyes were lowered to the ground. My mouth dropped open. Alhaji pointed to the back of the mosque, and I found my feet following Grandma's, right inside.

I wanted to ask Grandma about the shack, and why there was a holy man in Alhaji's garden, but my voice would not have been heard over the sound of the loudspeaker. I wondered what the neighbours thought of the noise, as it would surely have been heard all the way from the village. I wondered what Mama thought. Most of all, I wondered what Ezikiel thought. But even though my eyes chased his, they did not catch them.

Inside the shack Grandma ushered me to sit at the back with the other women, next to Mama. I watched Ezikiel following Alhaji to the front where he sat down next to him, on a foldaway chair. I had never heard of a chair in a mosque. The ground underneath me felt hotter and dirtier. Alhaji flicked his head suddenly around as though he could read minds. His eyes burned holes into my cheeks. I wanted to run to Ezikiel and cry on his shoulder, but an invisible line had separated us.

The imam started chanting the Koran, and then he faced the front and fell onto his knees. Alhaji and Ezikiel climbed off their chairs and folded them away, before kneeling on prayer mats that had been rolled up waiting against the wall. I watched Ezikiel. He seemed to know exactly what to do. He looked as though he had been folding his chair away to kneel on his prayer mat all of his life. Of course, we had Muslim friends at school; my best friend Habibat was Muslim, but we had never been to pray in a mosque. Habibat had to leave our school to attend Islamic school. I remembered her not eating for a whole month. I remembered her wishing she had been born a boy.

I looked at Ezikiel at the front.

The imam leant forwards and touched his forehead to the ground, as if kissing the dirt. Then he rocked back and forth chanting, and we all joined in. I copied closely, but I could feel Alhaji's eyes on me the whole time, and that distracted me enough that I was kneeling when everyone else was down, and kissing the ground when everyone else was up. I had been stupid. I was stupid. I knew that Alhaji was Muslim; that is why he is called Alhaji. I knew that he was the head of the house. I knew that we were going to live in his house. I was so stupid. It had not occurred to me to ask Mama, on the journey, or ask Ezikiel before we had left.

I looked at Mama, then Ezikiel. They were both chanting with their eyes closed.

I wanted to ask them if we were Muslim now.

FOUR

Being Muslim was like being Christian, but with more rules. We had to pray five times a day, by chanting in Arabic, and kissing the ground-dirt over and over again. We had to attend the mosque every morning when it was still dark, for communal prayers, even though Ezikiel told me that Muslims only had communal prayers on Fridays. I had to wear a head-scarf wrapped tightly around my head for prayers. But it was not so bad. I could take the scarf off between prayers. And we still prayed to God, but he was called Allah.

Grandma wore her scarf most of the time.

'Do I need to wear my scarf outside the mosque?' I asked.

She looked at me and laughed. 'You should do what you think is right. There is no rule here. Only the ones Alhaji makes up!'

I quickly looked around the garden. There was nobody nearby. 'Alhaji must be a very a good Muslim,' I whispered, looking at the mosque.

Grandma followed the line of my eyes and laughed again. 'Building your own mosque does not make you a good

Muslim.' She leant towards my face and lowered her voice. 'It makes you a good builder.'

I did not have much time to worry about being Muslim. I was more worried about Ezikiel. He had been unable to eat any meat or fish since we had first arrived nearly a week before, as it was all fried in groundnut oil. Every time Grandma tried to fry Ezikiel's food in palm oil a cloud of smoke flew in her eyes and they watered all day, until she had to give up. I sat down next to Ezikiel at every mealtime, to share my food with him. When it was scrambled egg and fried plantain for breakfast, he only had a quarter of his plate covered with egg, so I tipped my egg onto his plate. When dinner was rice with fried chicken, he had all of my rice. When it was fried fish soup, I gave him my pounded yam, and burnt my fingers and mouth trying to eat the soup by itself. I picked him fruits from the trees: avocado, mango, pawpaw. I picked him corns and even took off the stringy bits. Ezikiel was getting thinner. Every time he ate, his mouthfuls were smaller until he was hardly eating anything at all.

Alhaji did not believe in allergies. 'Nigerians do not suffer with allergies,' he said in English – Grandma had been right about everyone speaking in English; since we had arrived I had heard hardly any Izon. He pointed his finger at Ezikiel's nose. Mama sighed. We were all sitting on the veranda, where we ate all our meals together.

'He is allergic to peanuts,' said Mama. 'We had him tested twice.'

'That cannot be possible,' said Alhaji. 'Nigerians do not have nut allergy. All our food is fried in groundnut oil.'

Mama sighed again. 'It is true. Unfortunately.'

'It cannot be true. Look at me,' said Alhaji. He stretched his arms so high that his vest rolled up. I did not like to look directly at him, but his eyes caught mine.

'Look how fit and strong I am. Look at these legs, these arms. Strong and fit. The key is multivitamins. The key to long life. You see?'

Ezikiel and I nodded our heads quickly. Mama sighed again.

'Yes, sir,' I said.

'Yes, sir,' Ezikiel said. He had tiny blisters on his lips that cracked and his stomach made a sound like a nearby thunderstorm.

Alhaji unzipped a bag that was next to the chair. He took out a plastic case covered in flowers, and from that produced a pot of tiny turquoise tablets. He shook the bottle, put the bottle back, then closed the case. 'I can even advise you which multivitamin will prevent allergy.' Alhaji's neck skin swayed as he spoke. His skin was loose as though he had lost a layer of something underneath. Something important. 'Follow my health regime, and you will be as strong as Alhaji, you see? I am a pharmaceutical *expert*.'

'He cannot be cured,' said Mama. 'We just have to avoid groundnut oil.'

'I always fry the meat first,' said Grandma. 'To prevent

sickness. In all Nigeria we fry meat first. Even in Lagos you must fry meat first.'

'In Lagos we fried everything in sunflower oil that I borrowed from the hotel,' said Mama. 'But the sunflower oil has run out now; there's nothing except groundnut oil here. Ezikiel will be fine having meat or fish boiled instead of fried, and cooked in palm oil stew until I can get some more. As soon as I find a job, I'll be able to get some. Especially if I find something in a hotel.'

Grandma shook her head. 'What if there is no job? Everyone wants a hotel job. We have to fry the meat or fish first,' she said. 'In groundnut oil. He will get sick if he eats meat that has not been fried.'

I could see Mama trying to smooth her face into a more relaxed one. She looked at Ezikiel and managed to smile. 'Ezikiel can't have groundnut oil. But we'll be fine,' she said. 'Even if it means no meat for a while. I have hotel experience. And if I can't find a hotel job, at least when I'm working I'll be able to buy some vegetable oil. There must be somewhere that sells it in Warri, even if it is expensive.'

Grandma shook her head. 'We use groundnut oil for everything. And we have to fry first to kill the bacterias.'

I could feel Ezikiel next to me breathing in quickly, then out in three bursts. Grandma and Mama looked at each other over his head.

No generator! No electricity! No fridge!

Alhaji stepped forwards. He ruffled Ezikiel's hair. 'Do

not worry,' he said. 'I will take you to the pharmacy and get you specific minerals. They will prevent allergy. I am a qualified petroleum engineer, it is true. And I have applied for an important position at the oil company. But I am also considered an expert in pharmaceuticals. You see?'

He held up the plastic case covered in flowers. It looked like the case Mama used for carrying make-up. 'And if the allergy does arrive, I have the perfect cure for serious illness.'

He looked around the veranda. We were all watching and waiting, except Grandma, who had her head in her hands, and was groaning softly. With one hand he unzipped the cosmetic case again and pulled out something from it, and the other hand he pointed to the sky.

'Marmite,' he said, holding up the jar, 'is the most effective cure for serious illness.'

Grandma groaned loudly again.

'Secret ingredient of yeast,' said Alhaji, leaning towards Ezikiel, who by then was hissing and shaking.

Even though Zafi was Ijaw, and had taught us to speak Izon, and said he would work for no money at all, Alhaji sent Zafi away. He knelt down to Mama before he left, as though she were the man, and he the woman. He hugged me tightly. I could smell his breakfast.

Ezikiel was with Alhaji. He did not even come to say goodbye to Zafi.

'God be with you, Zafi,' Mama said, and gave him some naira rolled up in an elastic band.

He walked away, the driver with no car, like a tortoise with no shell.

Zafi took with him the smell of Lagos, of crispy *suya*, and frangipani flowers.

I watched him until he disappeared, then I watched the space he disappeared from.

It was Youseff who drove us to market the following morning to buy our school clothes. Youseff lived in the Boys' Quarters with his four wives and seventeen children and two more arriving soon. He ignored them all; he said there were too many to bother with. The only children I had met were Fatima and Yasmina; all Youseff's other children ran away laughing when Ezikiel and I went near them. We sat in the car for an hour in a go-slow on Airport Road, as Youseff tutted and tutted and complained about having so many children. I missed the sound of Zafi coughing. The traffic was so slow it would have been quicker to walk. Fumes crept through the window, and Ezikiel wheezed and puffed, wheezed and puffed. Car horns beeped and people shouted. Entire families balanced on top of each other swerved through the traffic on *okadas*, the motorbike taxis. Hawkers came running at the car with piles of goods balanced on their heads, or in trays in front of them. One boy went past repeatedly with a tray of banana ice cream. I did not dare to ask for one. When we arrived near the market, Youseff swerved the car into the side of the road next to a shop that said 'Modern Garments', but had nothing inside except a few naked dolls shaped like women. I dropped my eyes to the ground. Youseff waited in the car as we followed Alhaji through the market and down a road. Every so often he stopped so that Mama and Grandma could look at lace, combs, tomatoes, or dried fish. The market was the same as the Lagos markets, but the people were different. I could hear people speaking English and Izon, but there were so many other languages that I did not recognise. I could hear the singing of pidgin English, but I still had no idea what they were saying. The pidgin was so different from the pidgin English in Lagos.

We found the area with materials in the market. Grandma stopped to look at the different lace, holding up each to her face and then Mama's face and then my face. But she did not buy the lace.

'The school uniform,' said Alhaji in Izon, waving his hand over the colourful patterns.

School uniform!

I looked at Ezikiel, who was smiling and had his fist closed in front of his chest. What would our new school be like?

The woman standing behind the materials was nodding and nodding every time Grandma held up a lace. When Alhaji said, 'School uniform', she suddenly stopped nodding. Her head was perfectly still when she pulled out the plain material the colour of ground-dirt and began unfolding it until Grandma nodded and held up her hand. Then the market woman cut the material with the biggest pair of scissors I had ever seen and started folding it up again before wrapping it in newspaper and handing it to Grandma.

After we had bought our school cloth from the market I thought we would be going straight back to the car. As we walked away, I wanted to ask Mama or Grandma about our new school. I had so many questions. How would we get to school? Was it a big school? Would we have lunch from home or at school? But Alhaji waved his hand for us to follow him. We walked to the side of the market and into a shop where a man with a tape measure hanging around his neck stood by the doorway as if he expected us. Ezikiel and I took turns to stand on a stool while he wrapped the measure up and down and around us. And then Grandma handed the material over to the man.

'I will send the driver for it,' Alhaji said.

The tailor nodded and watched us walk out. I wondered what Youseff would think about picking up our school uniforms. Did Youseff's too-many-children go to the same school? Would Fatima and Yasmina be in my class?

We did not walk back towards the car. Alhaji waved his hand again. The shop we followed him into was quiet and cool with air-conditioning. I closed my eyes and felt the air land on my skin. I took as many cool breaths as possible.

'I would like to speak urgently with brother Onogaganmue,' Alhaji said.

The counter man rolled his eyes. He was wearing a T-shirt with no sleeves. Thick hair grew from his shoulders. 'Not here.' He yawned. He spoke in English. I wondered if he was Ijaw.

'I need to know the side-effects and precise action of this

drug.' Alhaji shook the bottle in front of the counter man's face.

'Sir,' the counter man leant forwards and rested his head on his hands; his vest lowered enough to see that he had breasts, 'you need to wait for the pharmacist. I am only the till man.' He pressed a button on the till, it beeped, and the money tray flew forwards. Then he pushed it shut with the back of his hand.

I could not see Alhaji's face from where I was standing behind him, but Ezikiel's eyes were open wide. The cold air was tickling my throat; I wanted to cough.

'No matter,' said Alhaji after a long silence. 'I will explain to you. You ought to know the pharmaceuticals you are selling. That way, if another customer enters you can be of more help. You see?'

I wondered why Alhaji asked the counter man a question when he already knew the answer.

Every so often, Alhaji turned to check that Grandma, Mama, Ezikiel and I were still listening.

'This Robb,' he continued, undoing the top of a small pot and sticking it in front of all our noses, 'is not so good. Many people use it on cuts but I have discovered something better and more effective.' He looked around at us. We nodded at the same time, like puppets on the same string. Alhaji opened his bag and pulled something out.

'Marmite,' he said, 'is the most effective in healing wounds.'

Grandma groaned again, quite loudly.

Everyone else looked down to the floor.

When I looked back up, the counter man was standing and shrugging his hairy shoulders. 'Are you going to buy those tablets?'

Alhaji did not say any words for five of Ezikiel's breaths.

'No,' he said, at last, 'I do not require these.'

On the way out of the shop, I looked back to see the counter man scratching his head and frowning.

We were nearly back at Alhaji's when Youseff slowed the car. 'Routine federal patrol,' said Alhaji. Sharp wires were stretched across the road. Three policemen were standing at the roadside, waving their arms up and down. They laughed. Youseff leant towards Alhaji who said something to him quietly. The car stopped. Alhaji rolled down the window. I could hear far-away clapping that reminded me of a revival Father had taken us to. Father. I tried to imagine his face. It was not clear.

Alhaji smiled as a policeman came towards us. He was as tall as Youseff and as wide as Grandma. A gun was a sleeping baby on the policeman's back. A gun! It was the first time I had seen a rifle that close. I could not stop looking at it. Grandma looked straight ahead. She pressed on my arm until my head turned away from the gun.

'Papers,' he said, in English. Alhaji opened the glove compartment and pulled out some papers, which he handed out of the window. Another policeman came over and looked at Alhaji, half-closing his eyes in the bright sunlight.

'Is that Sotonye? Or should I call you Alhaji Amir now?'

As the policeman spoke, Alhaji exhaled and his shoulders dropped as if he had been holding onto a large breath. The policeman turned to the other policeman. 'This man attended my church for twenty years. A few months in the north and suddenly he is Muslim!'

I was surprised to hear that Alhaji had been Christian. I knew that Mama had grown up Christian, of course, but it had not occurred to me that Alhaji must have been Christian then. I could not imagine Alhaji without his mosque or his loudspeaker. I could not imagine Alhaji clapping at a revival. The far-away clapping was so fast, and I could not imagine Alhaji's hands coming together quickly.

'Get out of the vehicle,' said the first policeman. Alhaji laughed, and jumped out. He had to stretch his arm up to reach and pat the policeman's shoulder. Alhaji's head moved from the policemen to the area behind and to the sides of them. What was he looking for?

'Yes, it is me – Alhaji,' he said. 'How is your family?'

The shorter policeman ignored him and looked over his papers. 'You need to give a little something to help us process this,' said the large one.

'You have my papers. Really, friend, is this required?' I could see Alhaji raise his body up towards Allah instead of bowing it away from him, which made more sense to me anyway. I was still looking out of the window at the gun, and Alhaji, even though my eyes were staring straight ahead. Grandma and Mama were doing exactly the same. Ezikiel was staring straight at Alhaji, with his mouth open. With his hand he was pressing his pocket, probably checking for an inhaler. I wondered why Grandma did not press on Ezikiel's arm until his head faced forwards.

Even stretched up as far as he could Alhaji looked tiny compared to the policemen. I looked at the back of Youseff's neck. I hoped he would get out of the car and make Alhaji appear taller. But he sat still, chewing a toothpick, his hands gripping the steering wheel so tightly that his knuckles were changing colour.

'Give us something or we will have to question you further,' the taller policeman waved to a windowless hut at the road-side, 'at the station.'

The wooden hut was tiny. The windows were closed and the door had a piece of wood holding it shut. It must have been dark inside, and hotter than I could imagine.

Alhaji stopped laughing. 'Are you crazy?' he asked.

Grandma curled her little finger around my wrist and pressed, digging her nail in. The taller policeman threw Alhaji's papers on the ground, and touched the gun on his back. He waved it. My stomach dropped. I wanted to hold onto Grandma's arm but I was scared of moving. My hands were shaking. I felt light at the back of my head, as though I was falling. I wished Father was there. Father would know what to do. He always knew what to do.

'Give us something. I am not asking.'

Alhaji looked to the shorter policeman. 'Are you going to let this work colleague talk to me like that?' Alhaji spoke quickly and out of breath as if he had been running. The shorter policeman laughed, and leant towards Alhaji's face. He looked in the car, making Grandma dig her fingernail further into my skin. I kept my eyes straight ahead. Even so I could feel the policeman looking at me. My skin burned. I looked at the sun, which had dropped down in front of the car. I looked straight at it until my eyes could see nothing but light.

'Does he think he is a Big Man?' The policeman spoke to us all, so loudly that Youseff's sudden coughing could not hide the words.

Alhaji's eyes became wide and grey. 'I will be telling my friends at the Executive Club about this,' he said. Youseff stopped coughing. 'You will be in severe trouble.'

I wondered what the Executive Club was. It sounded important.

The shorter policeman laughed first. Then the tall policeman.

The shorter policeman pushed Alhaji against the car. 'How are you a Big Man?' he asked. 'Only one wife and no son!' He pushed Alhaji again.

Alhaji bounced as if the car was made of sponge. Grandma dug her fingernail so far into my wrist that the skin broke. The stinging pain made me want to pull my hand away. But I did not move. I focused on trying to keep breathing. The air was hot going into my nose. I needed to cough. Tears filled my eyes, and the light world became blurry.

Grandma reached for her bag with her other hand, and

took out some crumpled naira notes. She passed the naira out of the window gap at the taller policeman.

The far-away clapping sounded quicker, nearer. Both policemen flicked their heads around at the same time.

The shorter policeman snatched the naira from Grandma's hand. 'At least one has sense,' he said. He put it into his pocket and pushed the gun further onto his broad back. The policemen waved the car forwards. Their heads were looking all around for the clapping. Alhaji rubbed his side where he was pushed against the car. He climbed into his seat, and shut the door. He opened his cosmetic case and began to swallow tablets without any water. 'Your superiors will hear of this,' he said, quietly, as we drove away.

We had been living at Alhaji's for six days when Ezikiel dressed in a uniform of khaki-coloured shorts and white shirt, and I in a khaki dress and a small tight hat, which only just stretched over my cornrows and made elephants dance inside my head until I removed it. There was no mirror to look at so I studied Ezikiel instead. 'Do I look smart enough?' I asked him.

'You look very smart,' said Ezikiel.

Youseff was waiting in the car with the engine running. His long legs were sticking out from the driver's seat. We could not wave to Mama; she was out looking for work. Instead, we said goodbye to Grandma and Alhaji who were standing on the veranda and waving, and climbed in the back. It took thirty minutes to drive over the bumpy roads. I tried to imagine what the school would look like. I wondered if I would find new friends. Youseff was silent all the way. He kept glancing in the rear-view mirror. His eyes watched us as much as the road ahead. Ezikiel found it funny to poke my side, causing me to jump, until Youseff flicked his head right around, and stared straight at us, even though the car was going very fast. He nearly hit a man crossing the road pushing a wheelbarrow full of yams.

Youseff parked the car outside an area of wasteland next to a village. The rusty sign outside the school said 'Holy Ghost Secondary School: Strive for Excellence'. Dozens of children were running past the sign, all dressed the same, all with wide eyes and no smiles, all with swollen bellies and skinny legs. A line of boys were marching in with upside-down tables balanced on their heads. A few girls walked past carrying larger desks on their heads. My own head banged and tapped and hurt as though there was an upside-down desk on it. It felt like all the children had jumped in and were running around inside me.

There was no marble floor, or fountain. There was no air-conditioning, or running field, or smiling teachers.

The school was a flat dark building with no door. We sat still in the car until Youseff threw his eyes at us, and then we climbed out and began slowly walking. The car moved away quickly. I could see into a classroom as we walked nearer. The children all had their hands raised in the air. I could hear the smack of a ruler on a table and the screech of chalk on a blackboard. My hand found Ezikiel's. I moved closer to his body. His arm was shaking.

When we walked into the classroom the teacher did nothing but pointed to a space on the ground near the front. 'You sit there,' she said in English, looking at me. 'You,' she pointed to Ezikiel, 'in class three.' I sat down quickly and watched Ezikiel follow the teacher's arm out the door to the other classroom. I could feel the eyes of all the children lay on top of my head like a scarf. The boy I was sitting next to looked more like a grown man. The class was full of boys. Only four girls. Where were all the girls? Why did Youseff's daughters not come with us? We listened to the teacher, Mrs Tuyowe, chant the names of our government ministers and kings and queens of England, and we listened to the sounds of the children repeating back whatever she said. Everyone spoke English. I had no idea which children were Ijaw or not. English was spoken by all the children and all the teachers. Still, I felt glad to know my language, and happy that Zafi had taught us Izon well. At break-time the children poured from the classroom like water and went to the yard where they all played hopscotch or ludo or football.

All except me and Ezikiel. I found him under a tree. We sat with our backs pressed together, and let the morning wash over us, like rocks at the water's edge.

The toilets at school made the toilets at Alhaji's place seem luxurious. They were divided into two rooms, one for boys, one for girls, but the boys' toilets were always empty, even though most of the pupils at school were boys. When I first entered the girls' toilets at the beginning of lunchtime, I could not help running straight back out. A carpet of flies shone blue. There was no window. Seven holes were side by side, girls squatting over them doing their business, their private parts on full view. There was no sink. No tap. No soap. No toilet tissue. I opened my mouth outside and felt burning in my throat. I did not turn around to see if any of the girls had seen me running. I walked quickly down the corridor, which was dusty and dirty and had pieces of rubbish screwed up and thrown around. I thought of the International School for Future Leaders, which had floors so polished that you could see your refection in them. I thought of the toilets, which were clean and had flushing water, and sinks with soap, and windows with air. I held in the urine as long as possible, until I saw Ezikiel, his back pressed against a tree.

'Where do the boys use the toilet?' I asked. 'Their toilet was empty. They must be going some other place.'

He laughed. 'Hello to you, too. How was the rest of the morning?'

'I am serious. I cannot hold it any longer. Please, please, just tell me.'

Ezikiel laughed again. I bent forwards and held my lower stomach. Eventually, Ezikiel pointed to the bushes at the back fence, where I could see the shadows of boys doing their business.

'Where do the girls go?'

'Not outside, silly. You will have to use the inside toilet. Is it locked?'

'Have you been in there?' I asked. By then, I could feel wetness on my underwear. It had turned from urgency to pain.

'You are being silly.' Ezikiel stood from the tree. He put his arm through mine. 'Come on, I'll take you there.'

'I cannot use it. It is the worst place I have ever smelled.'

Ezikiel laughed again.

'I will catch something,' I said. I paused. 'That place must be full of parasites.'

'You have to use it. Just be careful not to touch anything. Come on. We are lucky to be at school. We are lucky that Alhaji agreed to pay our fees.'

Even through the pain of holding my urine, I realised that I had not considered who would be paying our school fees, or how. It did not occur to me that a school with toilets as bad as that would still require fees. How did Alhaji pay when he had no job? I knew that Mama had arrived with a small amount of money; but she had told me that she had enough to last us a short time. And even though he was a qualified petroleum engineer, Alhaji was looking for work. How did he pay for our school fees?

We walked back into the building and I ran into the toilet, pulling up my skirt and down my underwear. As I squatted over a hole, I felt the flies rise up and move over my skin. They felt soft against the back of my legs. I held my breath. The girls in the line next to me looked bored. They did not seem to notice the flies. Or even the smell. I could hear one girl moaning. She was vomiting from one end and had irritated stools the other end. It all fell around and about and over the hole. There was no way of cleaning herself up.

I held in my breath, and my tears, and my stomach.

Afterwards Ezikiel was waiting outside. I opened my mouth in the school yard and took in air, biting it as if it was hard food. I held Ezikiel's hand tightly. 'I will surely get sick,' I said.

'You are being dramatic,' said Ezikiel. But he dropped my hand and wiped his on the back of his shorts.

Lunch for us was bread, and Blue Band margarine that Grandma had scooped out from the tin and put into a small pot. Most of the children were sitting near us eating bread. We watched some of the other children go to the gates, and haggle with the vendors and the kiosk outside which was called 'Close to God Snacks', and sold Gala sausage rolls and meat pies. I looked at the Coca-Cola and Fanta bottles on display and felt the dust settle near my mouth. I wondered how those village children could afford to buy lunch. Maybe they had fathers who had jobs.

'Who is in your class?' I asked Ezikiel. He leant closer to me. Some boys were playing football nearby. He pointed to the group.

'All of them. The lessons were good. There's one teacher who has a degree in physics. His lesson was the most interesting. There are only three girls. But then, I guess when you get to fourteen …'

'Where do the girls go?' I asked. I looked around the playground. There were some girls, mainly younger, or girls my age. But there were far more boys. And grown men. That did not make any sense. 'Why do they not separate the ages?'

'People join at different times,' said Ezikiel. 'There is a man in my class who is older than the teacher. He had to repeat the year twice and he did not start school until he was fifteen.'

'The teachers all look young.'

'They are mainly youth corpers doing national service. An older boy in my class told me. They did not get the job they wanted so the government makes them teach. That is why they hate the children.'

'Why don't they just leave?'

'They have to do a year national service. Everyone does. Well, everyone who does a university degree. And you have to do what the government tells you to do. Fight or teach.'

'Well, if I get sent to teach I will be a lot nicer to the children,' I said. 'They are always caning here. One girl was caned this morning for talking in class, but all she did was ask her friend to borrow a pen.'

Ezikiel did not say anything, but lifted his mouth into a too-stretched smile.

After school I helped Grandma with the cooking. She showed me how to raise the fire by fanning the flames with a wrapper, how to rub the meat with pepper, how to slice the fish open, and pull out the bones in one quick movement. 'You cannot have too many Maggi cubes,' she said, crumbling them in one by one. 'They add good flavour. And plenty of salt.' She opened another tiny stock cube. Then, suddenly, she put the cube into her mouth. I had read the packet which said dissolve in at least one pan of water. I watched Grandma crunching the cube. Her face did not change at all. 'Mmm,' she said. 'De-lis'ous.' Then she laughed and laughed. And I found that laughter came from my mouth, too.

As we laughed we heard shouting from the other side of the compound gate. I did not hear the words but they came in a hurry. Grandma rushed up from where we were sitting and handed me her spoon. 'You finish the soup.'

I tried to open my mouth to tell her that I could not, that I did not know how to make soup, or even how long it needed on the fire. But my mouth stayed closed. And when Grandma ran past me towards the gate carrying a large bag, my mouth stayed shut even though it was full of questions.

I stirred and stirred and stirred. I popped in Maggi cube after Maggi cube. I added palm oil so frequently the fish came to the surface of the stew and opened their mouths as though they were gasping for air. The compound was empty. I could hear movement in the Boys' Quarters but I did not dare ask Youseff's wives for help; they giggled whenever they saw me. I did not want to give them something else to laugh about.

I looked at the food in front of me. The air smelled of groundnuts. I added three Maggi cubes, some pepper, tomatoes and salt to a clean pan. Then I poured palm oil over it.

I was careful not to confuse the spoons. I watched the

soups bubble and get gradually smaller. I watched the white part of the fish from the larger pan coming away from the head, and the eyes glaze over and become filmy, like Alhaji's. Then, I took the pans from the fire and set them on the ground. Everyone was waiting on the veranda when I walked through the house with the fish pan. They were sitting with empty bowls already in their hands. I must have been cooking for hours.

I ladled the fish soup into each bowl.

'Where's Grandma?' asked Mama, who looked at her bowl with her nose wrinkled up. 'Who cooked this?'

'She got called away,' I said. 'I did not ask where.'

Alhaji sniffed his bowl. 'She had to work,' he said.

I turned around suddenly, nearly dropping the pan. I did not know that Grandma had a job. I looked at Alhaji's face to see if it was open to questions, but he had scooped out some fish and was putting it into his mouth. 'Alhaji, sir. What job does Grandma have?'

Alhaji rolled his eyes and moved the spoonful of fish back into the bowl. 'A busy job. So make sure you help her around the house.'

'Yes, sir.'

Alhaji did not notice as I put Ezikiel's soup into a different coloured bowl, and handed it to him. He smiled.

'Did you cook?' Mama looked at the soup, pushing it around with a spoon.

I nodded. 'I hope it does not taste bad.'

Ezikiel smiled again. He was getting tired of eating

nothing but fruit. He dipped his spoon in the soup. It came out covered in streaks of red, like the sky when the sun was setting.

I looked at Mama. My mouth opened to ask about Grandma's job, but then shut. Mama was coughing and choking. She clutched her own throat. She leant forwards and began retching.

I looked at Alhaji, who was doing the same. He pointed to the soup.

'This soup,' said Mama, between retches, 'what have you put in the soup?'

Alhaji coughed for several minutes. 'Silly girl. Can you not cook?'

Mama stopped coughing. 'Of course she cannot cook. We always had a cook to do it for us!' She turned to me. 'How many Maggi cubes did you put in? It tastes like pure Maggi cube!'

I smiled, slightly. 'You cannot have too many Maggi cubes,' I said. But the words were too quiet and not funny.

'What are you talking about?'

'Let me call a Youseff wife,' said Alhaji. 'They can all cook.'

Ezikiel took his spoon and put it into his mouth. His eyes watered, but he did not cough or retch. He just stayed still and ate the entire contents of the bowl.

Later, Ezikiel found me sitting by the mosque in darkness. I was watching the gate, waiting for Grandma so I could ask her where she had been, and tell her about the soup. I did not realise that I was crying until Ezikiel wiped my cheek of tears. He pulled me towards him and kissed the top of my head. 'I liked it,' he said. 'It was the first soup I've had in ages. Thank you for making me one with no fish. It tasted really good to me.'

I did not need to look at Ezikiel's face to know that he was lying. His voice was higher than usual, and his words were pushed out too quickly.

Suddenly I could hear the sound of screeching. It sounded like an alarm but louder. It hurt the back of my head and made me half-close my eyes. 'What is that? I heard that before, but not so loudly.'

'Sirens,' said Ezikiel. 'Mama told me about them. It's the white men on their way to work at the oil companies. They get taken to work in armoured vans with police escorts. Then the armoured vans take them back to their locked-down compounds. Like prisoners.'

I listened to the sirens until they had gone. 'You were right about coming here,' I whispered. 'It is not safe. It cannot be safe if people need to go to work in armoured vans.'

Ezikiel turned his face away from me. He did not say anything. Maybe he did not hear me?

'It is not safe here,' I repeated. 'And this place is full of germs. What if you get sick? We are so far from Warri.'

'I won't get sick,' said Ezikiel. His words came out quickly. He pulled me towards him and turned his face back to mine. 'I will stick to your special soup, and fruits. And I will take Alhaji's vitamins and minerals. He is an *expert*.'

I leant against Ezikiel's arm. His shoulder was sharp. His skin looked dull, almost grey. I had not even smiled. My shoulders fell forward towards the ground. 'I want to go home,' I said.

Ezikiel did not say anything at all. He put his arm around me and held me so close I could smell the Maggi cubes on his breath. 'And if the tablets do not work,' he said, giggling, 'there is always the Marmite.'

He laughed, and I laughed. Ezikiel laughed so hard, his head was thrown back. His head looked too big for his shoulders.

FIVE

I became so used to Youseff's children going in and out of the Boys' Quarters, a bowl of food or a pail of water in their hands, that I did not notice them much. They were always there in the background. The only time I noticed Youseff's children was when they were not there. One day I tried to count all seventeen of them, but they were never in the same place at the same time. It was difficult to learn any of their names, as not only were there too many of them, but they all had at least three different names. They were called by each of their different names, depending on who was calling, and why. Fatima and Yasmina were also called Eneni and Layefa, and sometimes Kindness and Beauty. When I asked Grandma about all the different names, she laughed.

'We all have two names, an Ijaw name and a Muslim name, and that is enough for most people, but that man likes to feel important. He gives them all extra names. Eh! Imagine, so many kids and so many names!'

'But how do you remember them?'

'You will get used to it.'

Ezikiel tried to make friends with Youseff's oldest son, Prince, also called Mohammed and Ebike, but whenever Ezikiel called him over to play football, Prince said, 'Sorry, sorry,' and shuffled away. I wondered if they were not allowed to be our friends. They always seemed to be too busy, sweeping the floors, washing the car, washing the clothes in the river, fetching water from the village tap, which I still had not seen. Grandma said at first we would be guests, and after that we would have chores the same as everyone else. To start with I dreaded the chores. But as the week went on, I could not wait to have chores. I did not like sitting on the veranda chair while Youseff's children cleaned and swept and cooked around me. But I did get used to them.

One morning after prayers, Alhaji sent Fatima and Yasmina to me. I had learnt their Muslim names and decided those were the ones I would stick with.

'I want them to teach you how to cook.'

The girls giggled. I wondered how old they were. They spoke to me in Izon and giggled again. 'You cannot cook?'

I shook my head. I thought of the Maggi cubes and felt hotness wipe my cheeks.

'We will teach you to make pepper soup.' Fatima stopped giggling and took my hand. She led me to the fire outside the back of the house. Yasmina followed.

We squatted down. In front of us were plastic bags full of ingredients. Fatima got them out one by one to show me.

'First fry the meat then put into the pot with water and

onion. Some red pepper.' She held up every ingredient to the day. I nodded and tried to concentrate hard.

'After the meat put the fried fish and spices. This one *enge*, *arigo*, *furukana* leaves.'

Fatima held each spice to my nose as Yasmina giggled. I sniffed each spice and tried not to cough. I did not recognise them at all.

'There is so much to remember,' I said.

Yasmina stopped laughing. 'Don't worry. We can help you,' she said.

I spent all morning with Youseff's oldest daughters. They did not speak much, even in Izon, but still it felt good to be with girls my own age. While the soup was cooking I thanked them and walked through the house to the other side of the compound. Grandma was sitting on the veranda. 'Hello, Blessing.'

I sat down next to Grandma's feet. 'I have been learning to cook. Pepper soup!'

Grandma nodded. 'That is good. I look forward to tasting your food tonight. It is good you are finding your way around. No more guest soon!'

'It is difficult to learn everyone's name and who people are. There are so many people here.'

'You get used to it.'

We watched Boneboy playing with Snap at the other side of the garden.

'Is Boneboy Youseff's son?' I asked.

'No, Blessing. His parents were lost.' Grandma paused and

looked down at me as if she was deciding something. I could hear one of Youseff's babies screaming from the Boys' Quarters.

'Boneboy had parents and a village way into them creeks. But the mobile police, the Kill and Go police, came for them. They had reports of some boys there, some no good boys, but it was not true. The police came and killed the whole village. Boneboy's parents are dead. Those bloody Kill and Go!'

I stood up suddenly. 'Dead? The police killed them? But why?'

'There used to be lots of trouble in the creeks. But things are quieter now. There is no need for us to worry now. But there was lots of trouble before. Any villages who were fighting the oil company were in danger. And the different tribes fighting each other. All that fighting. But don't worry. The fighting is quieter now.'

I shook my head. 'Surely the police would not kill innocent people?' But even as my words came out, I thought of the policemen at the roadside pushing Alhaji. I thought of their windowless hut. I thought of the sirens carrying the white men through the villages.

Grandma laughed. Then she noticed my face. 'Don't look so worried. That fighting is over. It happened when Boneboy was a baby so he doesn't even remember. And we love him well. Everyone loves him well. He stays with his aunt in the village, but they are Christian, so you will see him here most of the time. Most of the people here are

Christian but Boneboy's parents were Muslim, like us. He is a good boy.'

I could not believe it! Did Ezikiel know? A village killed by the police! Boneboy's parents! I could not wait to talk to Ezikiel but Grandma must have known what I was thinking.

'We do not talk about it,' she said. 'It is gone and finished so we do not talk about it now. It will not help Boneboy to talk about sad things. It is finished. The fighting is finished.'

I looked at Grandma. She had her eyes half-closed. Her words sounded wobbly.

Suddenly the screaming from the Boys' Quarters became louder. 'Go and check,' said Grandma, nodding towards it. 'The mother is in the outhouse.'

I ran down the veranda steps and towards the Boys' Quarters. I pushed through the material door to find a small baby on a blanket on the ground. The room was full of plastic bags. I wondered what was inside them. There was no sign of the mother. I picked up the baby, who by then was screaming in bursts, and rushed back towards Grandma.

On the way back I slowed down, and felt the baby curl into me. The screaming became less and less until it stopped. By the time I had climbed the veranda steps, the baby was watching me with wide-open eyes. The baby smiled.

Grandma smiled too, then laughed. 'That is his first smile,' she said. 'You are a natural. It is a sign.'

I looked at the baby and smiled back. I was not sure what a sign was, but it felt good to see I had made the baby smile.

He felt light in my hands, and hot, as if I was holding some midday air.

It was the very first baby I had ever held.

That evening we all came together. Alhaji, Mama, Ezikiel, Grandma and I sat on plastic chairs on the veranda. Boneboy and Youseff's children sat around the bottom or sides of the veranda. The oil lamps had been lit and the sky was full of moving stars. We ate the food that I had helped to cook. I held my breath while everyone slurped and chewed. I waited.

'This is very good,' said Alhaji. 'You see? Very good! Our Blessing is a good little cook now.'

I looked at Mama. She nodded. 'It's good.'

Ezikiel did not have fish pepper soup. I felt sorry for him, but I had to fry the fish and meat first, and I did not have time to make a separate one containing no fish. But still he nodded as he dipped his pounded yam in palm oil as though I had made the palm oil itself. All I had done was to add salt. 'It is excellent,' he said, smiling.

I looked at Fatima and Yasmina. They were not eating. They ate with their mothers in the Boys' Quarters. I did not know if Youseff's children liked my food. But they were smiling and nodding and giggling.

I ate some soup from a spoon. It tasted exactly like pepper soup. Exactly. If someone else had served me it I would not have questioned it at all. It tasted exactly as it was meant to taste!

I could not stop myself from smiling.

After everyone had eaten at least two bowls, except Ezikiel, who smiled even without the soup, Grandma sat back in her chair and Youseff's children crept closer. I wondered what was happening.

'It is time for a story,' said Grandma.

Alhaji sat up and stretched. 'Good, good. I will stay this evening. I have no important business to attend to.'

Grandma began to speak in Izon. Her words were soft and low. They made me feel asleep, as though I was hearing the story in my dreams. Of course, I'd had stories before. But usually told from a book. Grandma had nothing in front of her. No books at all. It meant that we watched her face instead. I wondered if she was making it up as she went along.

'Once upon a time the creator organised a meeting of all the beasts. "I have work for you to do," he said. "You should share it among yourselves."'

I opened my eyes widely. Grandma's voice sounded nothing like her. It sounded like the creator had climbed right into her body and was talking to us. Ezikiel looked at me and raised his eyebrows high.

'The work was shared out afterwards,' continued Grandma, 'in such a way that some would take an hour, some two hours, some a week, some two weeks, some a month, some even two months or more to finish the work.'

I looked around at everyone's faces. All the eyes were on Grandma, even Alhaji's.

'Each of them made his own choice,' she said. 'But there

was a very large portion of work which would take years to finish, and this was taken by the elephant. Back in those days the elephant was the smallest of all animals.'

I closed my eyes. All I could see were tiny elephants.

'It took him many years to finish the work,' continued Grandma. She leant forwards. Everyone leant towards her. 'And that is why,' she whispered, 'the creator made the elephant into the largest of all animals.'

It was silent for a few minutes and then Youseff's children began to clap.

Mama laughed. 'I'm glad you chose an Ijaw story. It is about time you told some Ijaw stories!' She looked at Ezikiel and me. 'Your Grandma may not like Yoruba people,' she said, 'but she uses their stories and proverbs enough.'

Grandma sat back in her chair. The laughing stopped. 'I have no argument with Yoruba people, Timi,' she said to Mama. 'I borrow words from all the peoples. But I do not believe that oil and water can mix.'

SIX

Of course, children were caned at the International School for Future Leaders in Lagos too. The stick was hanging by a piece of cotton on a hook near the blackboard ready to whip any child. But the crimes were serious: stealing, lying, cheating. At the Holy Ghost Secondary School, children were caned for anything. The following day, it was my turn.

A girl my own age passed me a note. It was crumpled into a ball. I kept it on my lap for many minutes until the teacher faced the blackboard and began to write in chalk. Then, I slowly uncurled the note. It was a picture of the teacher, who was big and had a skirt that had clearly been made by sewing two skirts together: the front was a completely different material to the back. The note had the words 'Maths Teacher'. Underneath was a picture of a round woman, and underneath that the words 'Fatty boom boom'.

I did not look up at the girl who had thrown it but I could hear her giggling. And I did not look up when I could hear all the children giggling. I did not look up at all, but I could still see the teacher's big feet coming towards me. I screwed up the paper, and threw it under the desk, but it was too late. She was already swooping down to pick it up.

The seconds that followed I wanted to be somewhere else. Any other place. I would have rather been in the toilet. The teacher did not say a word. She pulled me towards her with her finger. I stood slowly and followed her to the front of the room where the stick was sitting waiting on top of the desk.

I felt the tears straight away. I wanted to run to Ezikiel. I did not dare even look at the door.

'Four helpers,' said the teacher, picking up the stick.

Helpers? Helpers for what? I had never seen a caning that needed helpers. Were they about to whip me, too?

The girl who had thrown the note onto my desk was the first up. Three others joined her. All girls. That left no other girls in the room. I could not believe it. Surely the girls would have stayed still and quiet and not offered to help in any way.

I looked at their shiny faces.

'Pick her up,' said the teacher. 'A limb each.'

The girls picked me at the same time. They lifted me off the ground until my head fell downwards. The classroom was silent. One minute the ground was underneath me and the next I was in the air, my back facing the class, the girls holding an arm or a leg each. I could smell their sweat.

The teacher was behind my back.

I knew the teacher had taken the stick.

I tried not to cry. Holding in tears was similar to holding in urine; it soon became painful.

The whip came down. It was not as bad as it could have been. The teacher was using light strokes, maybe because I was new. The girls did not hold me too tightly. One of them was near to my ear. 'It will be over quick,' she said.

I closed my insides and made my back as soft as possible. I tried to focus on my breathing. I tried to listen closely to the sound of the air going into my nose.

But inside my head all I could hear was Mama's scream.

Mama's scream when she found Father on top of another woman.

Grandma noticed me rubbing my back, and saw the tears that were waiting until I was alone. At the back of the outhouse she lifted my T-shirt. She looked at the marks left by the whip, and tutted. 'It is not too bad,' she said.

She did not ask what I had done to cause a beating, and I did not tell her that I had done nothing wrong.

She went into the house and came out minutes later with a bowl of paste. She leant me forwards over her knees, and rubbed the paste on my back. It was cold and it smelled sour, like the palm wine Father used to keep in plastic bottles underneath the sink. Grandma lifted down my T-shirt and stood me up. 'Better,' she said. 'Now you can help me fetch water. I will show you the first time, then it will be your job to fetch water every day after school.'

My back felt better immediately with the paste. The

stinging stopped. I felt cool and warm at the same time, like someone with a fever in an air-conditioned room. I wondered if Grandma was a nurse. I looked at her and opened my mouth. I wanted to ask but she was pulling me to the back of the house.

First, Grandma showed me where the metal pail and the round bucket were kept. 'This we call bath,' she said. She pointed to a large, round plastic bucket. 'You carry on top of your head. You have been here nearly two weeks now, so no more guest! No more bucket showers or sitting down.'

I had noticed the size of the bath on top of the head of one of Youseff's wives. There was no way I would be able to manage carrying that on my head. I thought of the tap in Lagos, one in the bathroom, one in the kitchen, which I turned hundreds of times without thinking about it. I never even considered that the water must have come from somewhere.

'We are so lucky having the river. It means the only water we need is for drinking and cooking, and Alhaji's bath.'

'Alhaji's bath?' I asked. 'Do we have baths?'

'Of course,' Grandma laughed. 'A man who lives on the bank of a river does not use spittle to wash his hands. I will show you where we wash, in the river. We give you bucket showers as guest. But you are not guests now. Now I will show you where to wash as family. The women downstream, the men upstream. Ezikiel will be upstream. And we can wash our clothes in the river water.'

I thought of Ezikiel upstream with his dirt floating down-stream, towards me. I thought of the bucket of cold water that I had been washing with. I had never before imagined I would miss washing with a bucket of cold water in the morning.

'Does Alhaji have difficulty getting to the river?'

'Ha! That man is strong. He has no difficulty with anything.' Grandma laughed. 'He is head of house so we give him fresh water. It is very important to look after the head. Same way when we have guest they have fresh water for a short time. Then after that, no more guest.'

I looked again at the bath I was to carry full of water from the village tap every day on top of my head, in order that Alhaji had fresher bathwater.

I said nothing.

Grandma led me into the house where a biscuit tin contained some rolled-up naira. She took a few notes. 'Be very careful with the money,' she said. 'They will overcharge if they can.'

'We pay for water, Grandma?'

'Of course! The owner of the borehole is a rich man. He has satellite television!'

We walked to the tap, past the dense bush at the side of the road, where Grandma spat twice on the ground and said, 'Don't look at the evil forest. If you need to collect firewood, take it from the other side.'

I kept my eyes facing the ground towards Grandma's spit, but did lift them to see sparse bush and wasteland between the trees. Sunlight had reached through to the ground of the bush and made everything look warm and bright. It did not look at all evil.

'Do not go into that side of the forest,' repeated Grandma. Suddenly she stopped walking and held my arms close to my body. She held me too tightly. 'Listen, listen, listen. There is no good in that forest. Do not go there.'

I nodded as fast as my neck would let me. I did not look at that side of the forest again.

The village was fifteen quick-walking minutes away. Seven or eight village houses were separated by small fires and women washing clothes in buckets. The women wore old clothes that looked like rags. They reminded me of the women hawkers from Allen Avenue.

'We used to have very good friends here,' said Grandma. 'When we were Christian. Then many people did not agree with Alhaji converting to Islam. It caused many problems. More fighting, more problems.'

I wondered what kind of problems it caused. A queue of people was waiting near a bigger cinder-block house. On the other side of the house I heard the noise of a television. A football match. I could hear the hum of a generator. The people in the queue all had baths and pails, and were talking or laughing. I stood as close to Grandma as possible. In front of the queue, I recognised the dog from Alhaji's, yapping around a boy's feet.

'Boneboy,' said Grandma. 'Let us push our way in.'

Boneboy turned around and smiled. I thought of what Grandma had told me. I looked at his face. He moved backwards to let us in and the people behind us in the queue did not even tut. They all greeted Grandma.

Boneboy had a pail. He looked at the bath I was carrying.

'Let me take the bath. You can carry this.' He pushed the smaller pail towards me.

I shook my head. 'No, thank you. I need to learn.'

Grandma smiled. 'Good girl.'

I smiled, even though my back was beginning to sting once more.

When we reached the front, a man wearing a shirt and suit trousers stood up suddenly from a wooden stool. 'Hey, how are you?' He spoke in English with an American accent that I recognised from our Lagos television.

Grandma passed the man some naira. 'I have brought my granddaughter. It is her first time collecting water.'

'How is that?' asked the man, who stuffed the money quickly into his shirt pocket. But Grandma did not answer. She showed me the three taps lined up and how to turn them hard when the bath was full, so that no water was wasted on the ground. She filled the bath right to the top and took a small piece of wrapper, twisting it around and around until it took the shape of a circle. Then she put it on top of my head. 'Kneel down,' she said.

The man who had collected the money lifted the heavy bucket and put it on my head. Then I tried to stand.

I could not stand up. The bath pressed me down into the ground.

Grandma, and the man, and Boneboy all laughed. Even though it hurt, I found myself trying to stand. I pushed myself upwards and held onto the man's arms. Slowly, slowly,

I got to my feet. The water pressed me into a shorter girl. Every part of my back and neck hurt. I could feel the redness of the skin underneath Grandma's paste, stinging once more. I stood as tall as the water would allow, and waited for everyone to stop laughing.

Then I raised myself even higher and smiled. Grandma smiled with me.

By the evening the tears that had been waiting since the whipping were not so impatient. Ezikiel studied on the veranda, hardly looking up from his homework at all. When I told him about the whipping he put his arm around me and said, 'Try and stay out of trouble, and concentrate on your work. It is different from our old school, but the teaching is good.' He was so busy doing his homework he did not seem to notice me sitting on the edge with my legs swinging over, back and forth. Or watching Boneboy play with Snap the dog, teaching him how to jump in the air for a bone. Boneboy smelled of coconut oil and river water and pepper soup. Every time he walked past me he had exactly the same smell. I wondered how that was possible. He had a way of walking in and out of a room or the garden without anyone noticing him. He slipped everywhere, like a fish. Ezikiel said that Boneboy was the best swimmer in Nigeria, and it was easy to believe. Ezikiel said that Boneboy had to swim through the air only, as he could no longer swim in the river because of the oil spills. I thought of washing my body in an oil spill. Surely, there was no point.

Snap was always attached to Boneboy's feet, weaving through them and looking up at him. I had never seen a dog that smiled before. But Snap did, whenever Boneboy looked back down at him, or threw a bone into the air, or shouted, 'Well done, boy!' It made me smile too.

'You can see how he dances,' said Boneboy, moving his hand up and down as Snap stood on his hind legs. Boneboy started to sing, an Ijaw song I did not recognise. Snap barked, then smiled, then began to dance. It was true.

'Ezikiel, look,' I said.

But Ezikiel was concentrating too much to see the dancing dog.

Grandma, who was removing the string from the corns, began to laugh. 'He is a funny dog,' she said. 'He looks like he is break-dancing.'

Ezikiel looked up. He almost dropped his textbook. Snap the dog was spinning around on his back, his tail and legs in the air, while Boneboy danced around him. 'He is a truly amazing dog,' said Boneboy. 'He could be a champion.'

'Now come,' said Grandma, who was sitting next to a fire she had built dangerously close to the veranda. 'Come, children.'

Youseff's children poured out of the Boys' Quarters, and gathered around Grandma's feet. Ezikiel, Boneboy and I joined them. Grandma gave out a long piece of sugar cane to each of us. I held it in my hands before peeling the outside off with my teeth, and sucking the middle. All of us were sucking so hard that Grandma had to speak loudly at first. But soon, we had enough sugar in our mouths and were spitting the pulp onto the ground. Then Grandma's voice hushed, and made the back of my head feel sleepy.

'Alhaji was a proud man. When I first met him he was just called Sotonye,' said Grandma. When she started speaking in Izon I knew the story had started.

I watched her closely. She seemed bigger in the firelight. I loved to watch her face; every time I looked I noticed something different.

'And he shimmied up palm trees with his legs in a perfect circle. He had no need for the leather belt. I have never seen anyone tap for palm wine quicker. People said that he had the heart of a lion, and he would never marry. But back then my hips were wide and my legs were not cracked. I met him at the village where my uncle lived. I was staying to help the family with all the children my uncle had produced. I used to watch Sotonye's perfect circle legs up and down the tree, from the quiet of the forest, where I was invisible …'

Later, when I went to bed and told the tears to come, they did not. All I could think of, instead of the pain of the whipping, was the face of a smiling dog, and the sound of Grandma's stories.

SEVEN

Ezikiel and I were waiting by the gate when I heard the revving of the car. We had returned from school and finished our homework. Ezikiel helped with mine after he finished his too quickly. 'I wish they gave us more,' he said. 'I need to get top grades for medical school.'

I laughed and rolled my eyes.

When we heard the car we jumped up from the ground. Mama opened the car door and climbed out, walking towards the house. She smiled. I ran beside her. Her legs were long enough that it took two of my steps to match each of hers. That meant that everywhere Mama walked to, I had to run. Ezikiel had longer legs than me. But even though he could easily have walked at the same speed, he always walked slightly slower, holding Mama's legs back. I was careful not to upset the dust with my bare feet. Mama hated me kicking dust on her clothes. She was wearing her very best clothes. She had combed out her hair. Her lips were red with lipstick applied with the tiny paintbrush. I noticed the red bra underneath her white shirt, almost the same shade as her lipstick. Her shirt was crumpled. The top buttons were undone.

'It's like a palace,' she said. 'The Western Oil Company compound. A completely different world. Everything is clean, even the floors. There are seven swimming pools, a golf course.'

Seven swimming pools and a golf course! Oh!

We followed Mama into the house and the bedroom. I looked at the dust on the floor and the peeling paint and the old mattress and the plug hanging over the fan, which was not going to even bother trying for electricity.

'It's amazing,' she said. Mama's voice was lifted higher than usual, and the words were coming quick. She removed her skirt and white shirt, and red underwear. Ezikiel looked away but I looked at Mama's sharp body. There were spaces where there should have been fat. Her skin was smooth. She tied a wrapper underneath her arms before pushing her feet into flip-flops. 'Bars, restaurants. A cinema room, fully air-conditioned.'

She spoke to the air in front of her, as if she could not see us sitting on our mattress. I did not mind. It was the first time Mama had spoken to me in weeks, other than to give an instruction: Sweep the floor for Grandma, Do your homework, Collect water.

'Did you get the job, Mama?'

'Yes, I did,' said Mama, smiling at Ezikiel. 'In a bar. The Highlife Bar. The oil workers go there to watch the wildlife as much as drink. From the table we were sitting at I could see a troop of monkeys travel across the trees. It's like a national park. Honestly, I can't believe that the other side of the wall is another world. One minute you're in an oily swamp, the next, five star luxury. Cool, air-conditioned, five star luxury.'

I felt the hot air around me hold me tighter.

'And they need a waitress,' continued Mama. 'It's not much but it's something. The salary is terrible, but they work for tips.'

'Congratulations, Mama,' said Ezikiel.

Mama smiled so widely I could see the tooth at the back of her mouth, which was a different colour to the other teeth.

'Congratulations, Mama,' I said.

Mama looked at me. She was smiling, but not as widely; I could no longer see the different-coloured tooth.

'They have a cocktail list with twenty-three different cocktails, but most of the patrons drink beer. And they don't call it beer, they ask for sundowners. The manager thinks I'll learn the cocktails quickly. He said they're not complicated. I mean, the money is poor, but better than nothing, and it's a step in the right direction. The tips will be good, I'm sure. Not as good as my hostess job, but at the moment any money is better than none. We're virtually starving.'

I looked at Ezikiel and smiled. Sunflower oil, I thought. Vegetable oil. Imported olive oil.

Mama smiled and looked over my head. 'The security is unbelievable. I was searched four times.'

I wondered what they searched Mama for.

'Can we come and see you there?' asked Ezikiel. His body was stretched up high and I knew that he was thinking about seven swimming pools. And air-conditioning.

'Well, family members are not really allowed. Not for locals anyway.' Mama's voice became quieter. She looked at Ezikiel's face. 'But we'll see. I'm sure they must have a family day for all employees. And at least one of us gets to see civilisation during the day.'

'You will sleep in my room. You have fourteen years. That is too old for a boy to be sharing a room with his mother.' Alhaji waved his hands around as he spoke.

Mama was standing between Ezikiel and me. I looked behind her back to see Ezikiel nodding his head. I could not believe it. Why was he nodding?

'This is a new environment for them. Let him stay with me for a few more weeks, at least.' Mama moved slightly closer to Ezikiel's arm, away from me.

'It is not appropriate, you see?'

'Why not? He is just a boy!'

'He is a young man. He should stay with Alhaji. My word is final.'

I looked behind Mama at Ezikiel, who was still nodding quietly. But his face had changed. His skin had become lighter and patchy as though he was a sky full of clouds.

It was the middle of the night when I heard arguing; the moon was midday-sun high. I was hanging off the side of the mattress, next to Mama; Ezikiel was on his own mattress in Alhaji's room. Even though Ezikiel had nodded in agreement with Alhaji, as though he was not at all upset, I found him in the cornfield afterwards, crying so hard his nose had forced out two snot caterpillars. I put my arms around him and did not let go until he stopped crying.

Mama was still asleep, even more beautiful in the moonlight. Her skin was the colour of golden syrup. She slept with one hand over her head, the other hand resting on her chest. She had not curled up around me. I had not curled up around her. There was an Ezikiel-sized gap between us.

'Do you think I need help?' Grandma shouted in Izon. I crept up from the mattress, and opened the door so quickly it did not have time to squeak. I could feel my heartbeat in my neck. I tiptoed out and stood on a puffy chair, to look through the too-large gap above the door. The children sleeping on the puffy chairs did not wake. They did not even wake to the sound of the call to prayer through the loudspeaker.

Grandma was standing with her hands spread over her face. She had tiny hands; I could see through her fingers that her cheeks were wet. Alhaji was opposite her, hopping from one foot to another like a lizard on hot ground. He looked small next to Grandma, like a child.

'A co-wife!' Grandma spoke through the gap in her teeth. 'A rival!'

'Ah.' Alhaji half-smiled. 'With a co-wife, a *junior* wife,

think of the help that you will get. You see?' His voice was softer than usual, but I could still hear him clearly.

'I want to break your head,' Grandma said, in English.

Alhaji held up his hands in front of him as though he was about to pray. He swallowed hard. It sounded like a hiccup.

'Do you think I need help?'

'All women could use help. And it is my decision. I am your husband.' Alhaji answered Grandma in Izon. It was the first time I had heard him speak Izon in the compound.

'We are not living in past times.'

'The Koran states …' Alhaji did not continue, but moved away slightly as Grandma brought the kerosene lamp into the air, and held it high.

There was a smashing noise, and then it was quiet. Grandma watched the glass by her feet. Small flames danced, then collapsed. She looked at Alhaji through her fingers. Her eyes were wide. I wanted to run over, and put my arms around her. I heard Grandma's stories in my ears.

Alhaji was called Sotonye when I first met him. He used to tap for palm wine. I liked to watch him shimmy up trees with his legs wrapped around them in perfect circles. He never needed the leather belt.

The only light was coming from the moon; still, it was bright enough to see clearly. Grandma lowered her hands from her face. Her cheeks were shining with tears. Alhaji dropped to his knees by Grandma's feet, picking up pieces of glass from the smashed oil lamp.

'Sorry, sorry.' Grandma knelt down to help. Alhaji looked even smaller, as though the world was swallowing him up.

Grandma's fingers picked up the glass so quickly that she cut her hand. Large drops of blood spilt onto the veranda, but she carried on, until all the pieces were together in a pile. Alhaji noticed eventually, and held up Grandma's cut hand to blow on it. His fingers were shaking. Grandma's hands were steady. He took a small pot of Marmite from his medicine bag, and unscrewed the lid. Then he rubbed some Marmite onto Grandma's cut, and wrapped up her hand in a handkerchief. He cradled the pot of Marmite as if it was a baby.

Grandma let him pull her up, leaning on him, but not too much. He looked like he might fall over.

'How old is she?' Grandma started speaking in English once more. It made the words sound less important. 'I will not have any part of it if she is a child. And how will you finance this? These old men marrying children. I will not accept a rival who—'

'She is a college graduate, and almost twenty-two.' Alhaji's words were also English. 'Our finances are not too poor.'

'Well. It does not make any difference. It will still cause problems. We have been on our own for so long now, *abi*? I thought you were happy. Not like those other men. Not like the other men. After all these years you—'

'I need to do this,' Alhaji said. 'I have no choice. They are laughing at me,' he continued. 'Only one wife and no son.' He reached out and stroked Grandma's cheeks, running his fingertips along the lines of her scars. 'And now you have your grandchildren here. You need the extra help. And of course, Allah permits it.'

Grandma slapped Alhaji's hand away. 'Do what you have to.'

I nearly fell from the puffy chair. I had to grab onto the doorframe; a piece of rotten wood came away in my hand. Grandma was looking up, not at Alhaji but at the sky. She shook her fist. Palm fronds cut shadows on her body. The insects were quiet, as if they had flown to the moon when the oil lamp had smashed.

EIGHT

Celestine arrived dragging a suitcase with a wheel that curved to the right. This meant she had to stop every few seconds and move the suitcase slightly to the left. She looked much younger than twenty-two, nearer to my age than Grandma's. She was fatter than Grandma, with a sticking-out bottom and knees that seemed to be glued together. Her feet looked like they wanted to walk in opposite directions. Celestine had thin lips and a wide nose. Her face was patchy from whitening cream, and her hair weave was bleached to the orange colour of the Jesus Loves You sticker on the car window that Alhaji had allowed to remain. He took the opportunity to discuss the prophets whenever he saw it.

'Hello, hello,' she said, and smiled, revealing a lipstick stain on her tooth that I could see from where I was standing on the veranda. I could feel Grandma next to me, watching Celestine. I could imagine her thoughts. I moved closer to her, until our arms were touching.

'Hello,' said Ezikiel. He stopped scratching his mosquito bites long enough to hold out his hand. Celestine walked up the wooden steps. The whole veranda jumped up and down.

'Little prince,' she said, kneeling to Ezikiel as though he was a grown man. His smile became so wide that his lips cracked and disappeared. Then he went back to scratching. There was a bite on his forearm the size of a walnut.

'*Ek'abo*.' Mama said welcome in Yoruba. Nobody noticed or commented, but Ezikiel stopped scratching and looked straight at me. Mama had not spoken Yoruba since we had left Lagos almost three months ago. Since Father had left us. A pain in my shoulder made me breathe in suddenly.

'Little queen,' said Celestine, in Izon. 'Queen. *Alaere*,' and she held my shoulder, where the pain was. Her fingers were fat and sweaty. They felt like the sausages that were No Longer Permitted. I looked through Celestine's wispy ginger hair at Grandma, and forced my lips downwards. Grandma stepped forwards and Celestine removed her hands from my shoulders. Celestine dropped to the ground, and said, '*Doh*,' but she did not lower her head. She looked as though she was reaching to pick something up, instead of kneeling to Grandma. Then she stood up almost instantly to face Grandma, stretching her forehead upwards, making her neck appear less fat.

'Where is my husband?' she asked. When Grandma laughed she looked surprised.

I thought of Alhaji marrying Celestine. We had not been invited to the wedding. I had heard Alhaji telling Grandma that it would be a simple ceremony at Celestine's village. When Alhaji had disappeared for almost a week, nobody spoke about the wedding, but still, I had noticed Grandma crying. It made me never want to hear about the wedding ceremony at all.

'Your husband is in Port Harcourt on business,' said Grandma, in English, still laughing. Celestine looked puzzled; her eyes darted around and her drawn-on eyebrows rose up her forehead. But Ezikiel, Mama and I were just as surprised. I did not know what business Alhaji would have in Port Harcourt. It must have been important; Mama had told me Port Harcourt was a four-hour drive away.

'Come,' said Grandma. 'I will help you to freshen.'

Ezikiel took Celestine's suitcase to the small hut next to the Boys' Quarters where she would stay. As he walked away his long body tilted to the suitcase side and gave him the shape of a question mark. I followed Grandma and Celestine to the area at the side of the outhouse where the rubbish was held until the rains came to wash it down the river. Things were already piling up. Plastic, wire, metal cans, broken bottles. They rustled when we arrived. Grandma had told me they saved it all every year, then God washed it away. I wondered where the rubbish ended up, and who lived at the end of the river.

I walked towards the bushes, expecting to push our way through towards the river, but Grandma stopped me. She had lined up plastic buckets full of river water against the bushes. I did not understand why when the river was so close. Grandma must have known what I was thinking about. 'Don't want any boats going past,' she said. 'Especially those gunboats.' She laughed. 'Don't mind them. Just Area Boys. There is trouble in the creek villages, so we will take baths here today.'

Area Boys? Gunboats? I thought of Boneboy's parents. Grandma had told me that there were still boats full of boys who went up and down the river, but I had never thought they would travel so close. It had not occurred to me to remember that the river was right there, at the back of our compound. Grandma had said that the trouble had stopped. Had the fighting started again?

I looked up at the sky at a black kite hovering above us. At first it did not move at all; if it had been on the ground I would have thought it was dead. But then it swooped very gently and curled back in on itself. I tried to imagine a gunboat.

Celestine stood very still. The only things that moved were her drawn-on eyebrows. I giggled. Celestine's eyebrows were the shape of the kite. They swooped down into a frown. Grandma and Celestine looked at me and sucked their teeth at the same time, I felt my skin get hotter.

Grandma removed Celestine's clothes; the materials sparked, and Celestine twitched like a chicken whose head had been removed. The clothes were thrown in a pile near my feet. I wanted to touch the unfamiliar materials, to hold them in my fingers. To press them on my face. The clothes were soft; they shrank to almost nothing on the ground. The small pile was so bright that it coloured the air around it. I sat on the hot ground watching a patch of air change from pink to purple then green.

Celestine's undergarments were in a camouflage print material, but did not camouflage Celestine's enormous body. Grandma laughed when she saw them, quite loudly, and Celestine folded her arms on top of her massive breasts as if they were cushions.

'You see I am very fat.' As Celestine spoke she sucked her teeth and rolled her eyes. 'It is very desirable to be this fat.'

'Eh!' Grandma chuckled.

'I did not need plenty of *egusi soup*. I went to the maiden-ready-for-marriage room.'

'A fattening room? I thought it was only Efik women who practise that. My friend Mama Akpan runs a fattening room in Calabar. It is an Efik practice. Ijaw people do not use fattening rooms.'

'Yes. My family looks after me well. All men love a round woman, not only Efik men.'

'I am not laughing about your fat.' Grandma scooped up bucket water in a cup. 'It is your undergarments that I find amusing.'

Celestine's thighs were bigger than my entire body. She had a layer of fat folded around her middle, all the way to her back. Her body skin was smoother than her face skin, and her breasts, the size of pawpaw, pointed upwards. Naked, she looked young enough to be Grandma's own daughter. Or even Granddaughter.

I noticed a swelling where Celestine's belly button should

have been. Grandma pushed it in, and it sprung back out immediately.

'*Dodo,*' she said. 'Why did your mother not fix this?'

'It cannot be fixed,' Celestine said. She looked down at the swelling through the large gap between her large breasts.

'Of course it can,' said Grandma, and she tutted. 'We will do it later.'

She suddenly slapped Celestine's bottom. It took many seconds to stop moving. My skin burned.

'Mosquito,' said Grandma, smiling.

Celestine lifted her head in the air and sucked her teeth. Grandma opened her handbag and pulled out a tin, which said 'Boiled Travel Sweets', from which she took a sharp piece of grey soap, then lathered it in the bucket water. Celestine's arms became bubbled and frothy. They reminded me of the dog on the roadside during our long journey from Lagos. The dog was almost dead, foaming at its mouth; its eyes were filled with blood. Its chest was moving up and down quickly, flies moving off and settling again with each breath. I had looked away, but Mama turned my head back towards the window. 'It won't go away just because you can't see it,' she had said.

I opened my eyes wide. Grandma was concentrating; her face was screwed up into a smaller face. She rubbed Celestine down in sweeping circles, cleaning her from top to bottom. She spent a quick time washing between her legs, and I tried not to look, but I could not help noticing the hair that covered her private parts, as thick as the evil forest. Grandma spent a long time washing underneath Celestine's arms. I was pleased. Celestine did smell bad in that area. The smell was like *iru*, the locust bean spice that Father used to use as a punishment. Who needs a flogging, Father had said with the small pot in his large hand, when you can force them to smell *iru*. And then he laughed, too loudly.

Alhaji arrived back before dinner. He got out of the car wearing his best clothes and carrying a briefcase I had never seen before. I wondered if he had worn his best clothes to impress Celestine. As he moved towards the veranda where we were sitting I noticed a red patch on his shoulder. The sun was creating such bright light that I could not see properly until he came to the steps.

From a distance it looked as if he had been shot. My heart thumped in my neck. He came towards us slowly. For many seconds, I could not move. I managed to put my hand over my eyes and realised he was wearing a bright red hibiscus flower in his buttonhole.

The cosmetic case was nowhere in sight. Alhaji walked up the veranda steps, and waited for Celestine to drop to her knees.

Celestine stood up and hugged him, almost lifting him from the ground. 'Husband. I have been waiting for you to return.' She looked at Grandma, who had not even stood as Alhaji approached. Mama opened her mouth as if she was about to speak but then she shut it again, folded her hands on her lap.

'Let me take your bag.' Celestine took the briefcase, which Alhaji did not seem to want to let go of; it hovered between them for a few seconds, like a moth at nightfall between two lamps. Celestine was stronger. The briefcase burst open as she pulled it; Alhaji's cosmetic case fell out, to the ground. It split open. Pots and packets of tablets rolled across the veranda; a large jar of Marmite fell down the steps.

Celestine put her hands to her mouth. 'Sorry, husband, sorry. I am trying to help. I put the bag away, help you to carry.' Her voice was irritating; it sounded like she was pinching her nostrils shut with her fingers as she spoke.

Grandma stood and picked up the Marmite, handing it back to Alhaji, who was frowning with his hands on his hips making his arms into triangles.

'No matter,' said Grandma. 'Sit.'

She ushered Alhaji to her rocking chair; he sat down as Celestine picked up the tablets. Mama joined in. I fetched the briefcase, which was now empty, and handed it back to Alhaji. Ezikiel ran into the house, returning seconds later with Alhaji's can of Guinness. Ezikiel did not look at me as he walked past, but he raised one side of his mouth.

'May Allah reward you well,' said Alhaji. We all looked at him. The words hung in the air long after they were said. I could hear them over the sounds of Alhaji slurping his Guinness, and Celestine saying, 'Sorry, husband, sorry, husband,' in her annoying voice.

Later we ate *banga* soup in silence, until Celestine burped loudly at the end of the meal. It was clearly a burp. There was no way it could have been anything other than a burp. Even so, Alhaji said, '*Al-hamdu lilah*', and when Celestine said, 'Pardon', he continued.

'Praise be to Allah. When a person sneezes, it is good luck. You see?'

'Oh no, husband.' Celestine frowned. 'I was belching. Sorry, sorry.'

I did not look at Ezikiel who would surely be laughing. His half-raised mouth would likely be fully raised. Grandma lifted her eyebrows.

'How is your family?' asked Mama.

'Very good,' said Celestine, in English, 'thank you. I get brother in London, with good computer job. And my sister remain for home.'

Alhaji sat forwards. 'Do not use that pidgin English here,' he said. 'Speak proper English or speak in Izon until you learn. We like to speak in proper English here. Not rotten English.'

Celestine opened her mouth, but no words came out. Not even pidgin English ones.

I was still surprised that Alhaji did not like us speaking Izon. I had thought it would be spoken all the time. But, I was glad we had learnt, that Zafi had taught us.

Grandma had told me that Celestine was from a very poor background and could not speak English well, like Youseff's wives. She said that bush women were backward and she probably could not read or write. I listened without commenting that Grandma could not read or write either.

And when I told Grandma I heard that Celestine had a university degree, Grandma laughed.

'No young woman with good prospects would become the second wife of Alhaji,' she had said. 'He is old, and not that rich.'

Alhaji spent many nights lying with Celestine in his bedroom and in Celestine's Boys' Quarters room. Grandma passed the time on the veranda plaiting my hair into neat cornrows, then complaining they weren't straight and removing them, only to start all over again. It hurt a great deal, but I did not complain. Ezikiel and I sang Itsekiri songs we had learnt at school, as loudly as possible to drown out the sounds of Celestine. The sounds were strange. There was laughter, screaming, grunting, and a high-pitched clucking noise.

'That woman,' whispered Grandma. 'That no good woman is making sex noises like Alhaji is a bush man. Does she not know she is the wife of a respectable chief? Why does she not show her respect?'

I could feel my cheeks get hot.

Ezikiel was fighting laughter next to me; his stomach had become hard and he was holding his breath. Then suddenly his laughter burst out of him. He could not stop laughing.

At first Grandma looked at Ezikiel with her eyes close together. I held my breath. But then she began to laugh. She laughed loudly. Ezikiel laughed and held his stomach. I laughed, too. The laughter was louder than even Celestine's noises.

Then Grandma raised her hand. 'I will teach you a song now.' She laughed again. 'The song from my wedding,' she said. 'All those many years ago.' She had us sing it facing the direction of Celestine's hut. 'Loudly,' she ordered as we sang. Ezikiel mumbled his part – he was still laughing, and his shoulders were shaking – but I sang louder than I ever had before. It was impossible to stay in tune. The notes went from high to low and back again.

'What's going on here?' Mama came out of the house, waving her arms at me, but looking at Grandma. 'I have work in the morning, and all I can hear is this tribal noise.'

She was still waving one hand in the air with another hand on her hip when we heard the shouting from the bushes. Grandma jumped up suddenly as though the ground was on fire. She ran towards the house. Mama did not react, or even drop her hand from her hip, but Ezikiel and I both turned to see where Grandma was going. What the shouting was for. She came out of the house carrying a bag, and did not even say goodbye. She just ran off into the night, and left me full of questions.

NINE

Mama seemed to be working more and more, and leaving earlier and earlier. She did not return until long after the sun had disappeared, and she woke up a long time before dawn to apply her make-up. After the sun came up, she took some off. Even with some make-up taken off, it was thick, like a mask, a different face covering hers.

'Your make-up is too much. It is not modest.' Alhaji was angry. I could hear his raised voice all the way from the back of the garden where Ezikiel and I were looking at an old snakeskin with a twig. We had stopped using our fingers to touch the snakeskin as the scales were melting against the heat of our fingertips.

'Make-up is a necessary part of the job. I have to look my best. The prettiest girls get the best tips.' Mama's voice was also raised enough that we could hear it clearly. 'Oh. And I've left some tips under your breakfast plate. Anyway, we need the money. What else can I do?'

'Ah-ha. The money situation is not so bad that you need to change your face.'

'We have no money for Ezikiel's medication, the school fees, food and water! And even if NEPA gave us electricity, we couldn't pay for it now.'

Ezikiel dropped his twig and looked up. I looked at him.

'Eh! Things are not too bad. I have excellent money-making ideas. There is plenty of business at the Executive Club ...'

'It is fine,' I whispered. 'Mama is exaggerating.'

But every morning, Alhaji pretended to sniff his plantain and eggs, on his way to pray, but I knew that he was checking to see how many dollar bills Mama had left for him. He did not mention the make-up situation again.

'What can he say?' asked Mama. She was standing next to Grandma in the river, washing her arms with soap. They were both wearing wrappers tied underneath their armpits. I did not see the point. None of the boys or men ever came that far downstream. I was about to join them to bathe, but something about Mama's voice made me stop and stand behind the bushes.

'He hasn't even paid Celestine's bride price instalment this month,' Mama continued. 'And that Executive Club! He says he's doing business there, but it's just a drain on finances. All the Big Men do there is drink Remy Martin and tell each other how important they are. Executive Club! Just a club for men to go and show off at. Who has the best car, the youngest girlfriend, the most wives. I know – I've seen it – the old men just go there to watch Sky Sports and sit around in the air-conditioning. It's not exactly money making!'

Grandma giggled. 'All men are foolish! He is a bloody

foolish man. But he has been going to that club for years. And a good name is better than gold. But the bride price for that woman. Paying instalments. For her! Imagine. That woman is no big dowry wife. Anyway, we are not too poor. We have a house and a garden and food. That is not poor!'

But although Grandma's words said one thing, her voice said another. It was higher than usual and she was breathless. Was she worried about money?

'We may have a house and food and a garden, I agree. Of course, there are people worse off than us. But what about Ezikiel's medications? His asthma inhaler and injections. Ezikiel's medicines have to take priority over anything else.'

'Alhaji will not let Ezikiel's health suffer,' said Grandma.

I stood waiting behind the bushes for Mama to say something, but it was quiet after that. All I could hear were the sounds of the river birds and the scrubbing of skin.

Grandma did as she promised with Celestine. At night she tied a large coin around Celestine's middle with green string, and pushed the *dodo* in, placing a ten kobo coin on top of it. The coin did not cover the swelling and Grandma had to borrow Alhaji's English fifty pence coin, which was bigger, and shiny silver. Celestine was happy to have an English coin next to her skin.

'It is probably worth millions,' she said.

The swelling was fixed in no time. Celestine began to wear her T-shirts in a high knot above her waist, showing off her newly normal belly button. Alhaji told her she was too fat for such a display, but Grandma just laughed whenever she saw Celestine carrying water in a bucket balanced on her hair weave, or sweeping the floor with her breasts almost hanging out of her clothes. She wore a bra that was three sizes too tight, which gave her the appearance of having four breasts. She kept her lipstick in the bra, even after it seeped out and stained her right breast a colour called 'Luscious loganberry'. Celestine pointed out the colour to anyone who appeared to be looking at the stain. No matter how often Alhaji told her to be modest, she ignored him, and Grandma laughed even more.

'Each man gets what each man deserves,' said Grandma.

Within a month, Alhaji had stopped visiting Celestine's room at night, and began to say, 'Be quiet, silly woman,' during the evenings when he preferred peace. Celestine walked around the compound sucking her teeth and saying, 'If we had a generator we could have television,' or, 'There is never a party here. I am so bored I could die.'

'I am so lonely,' she said once. Her English was improving.

I was on my way to collect water, with a pail in each hand. I ignored her and carried on walking. Celestine sniffed. I turned around. She was sitting on the ground, her wrapper fanned around her in the dirt. She looked like an overgrown baby. I thought of how lonely I felt when I had first arrived. Of how much I had missed Lagos. 'How can you feel lonely? There are so many people here.'

Celestine smiled at me. 'All the people here hate me,' she said.

I walked towards Celestine and put my hand on her shoulder. 'Nobody hates you,' I said. 'It is just different, that is all.'

Celestine looked up at me and smiled. 'Because of my status as the wife of Alhaji. He paid a big bride price for me! But I am a very nice and educated person. If only they would give me a chance. I would even share my things. I have many items. Even my films. I am buying these films, and you people don't even have a television. Or DVD player, or even electric generator.' She started crying again. 'Kung fu dwarf film,' she said between wails. 'Very funny. And no way of watching it.' She took a box from her bag and showed it to me. I looked at the front cover. A tiny man was in mid-air, legs split, his foot about to kick the head of another tiny man. Celestine beckoned me closer with her hand. I squatted on the ground next to her. She leant towards my ear, covering her mouth with her hand. 'If we had a DVD player,' she whispered, 'I could even show you a dwarf sex film. Very, very, very funny.'

'Please test this.' It was a week later. Celestine waved a piece of meat in front of Alhaji. Grandma had just served cow leg and I was already sucking and chewing, sucking and chewing. The cow leg tasted sweet. My stomach was swollen full but I could not stop eating. Grandma said the meat was too cheap and would need to be fried in groundnut oil, so Ezikiel had to stick to yam dipped in palm oil. He looked at my cow leg. My next mouthful did not taste sweet at all.

Celestine held the white fat, bone and gristle up to the light. 'This could be poisoned.'

'Stupid woman. Eat.' Alhaji looked up at the sky, sighed, and lifted the bowl to his chin.

'That rival could have poisoned me.'

'Eat the food. And stop this stupidness.'

Celestine put the cow leg back in her bowl. She looked from the side of her eye at Grandma, who continued serving the dinner as though Celestine did not even exist.

'Everyone knows she is *amusu*. A witch.'

There was silence. Nobody dared swallow. Cow leg juice dripped down my chin but I did not wipe it away. It felt like an insect crawling down my face.

Suddenly Grandma came at Celestine with a wooden spoon. I had never seen a person move so quickly. 'I will break you, stupid bloody woman!' She hit Celestine over the head and began to shout. 'A fly that accepts to walk in the house of a spider may never live to see another day!' The red wispy hair weave somehow got hooked onto the spoon and was pulled off Celestine's head, then flicked across the veranda where it lay like a dead rat. Celestine's nearly-bald head shone. Grandma smacked it repeatedly. The spoon against Celestine's head made a sound like someone was clapping very loudly. It sounded like the far-away clapping that I sometimes heard at night, but nearer. Mama, Ezikiel and I ran into the house, and stood in the doorway. The two women moved around the veranda, Grandma smacking Celestine and Celestine trying to move away. Grandma was quicker. No matter where Celestine moved to, the spoon stayed near her head.

Ezikiel began to laugh. He pointed to the weave-rat on the ground. I felt laughter in my stomach mix with the cow leg and fear, and become bigger and bigger until I could not help laughing with him. Mama slapped the top of his head and then the top of mine, but we could not stop laughing. Every time I opened my eyes there was something funny to look at: Alhaji covering his face, Celestine's bald head, Grandma with the wooden spoon.

'Stop!' Mama shouted, as Celestine screamed.

'Stop!' Ezikiel shouted, as her screams became so loud it was as if she was dying.

'Stop!' I shouted.

But Grandma continued. Clap, clap, clap, clap, until Alhaji stood up and raised his hand in the air. Celestine was folded up on the ground, her hands trying to cover her head, but the spoon found its way through.

'Stop,' Alhaji said. And she did. Grandma lowered the spoon, leaving a darker area on Celestine's head. Grandma stepped back, and Celestine stood up. She looked as if she would jump on Grandma for a second, with her hands outstretched, as if reaching in order to grab Grandma's neck. Alhaji took Celestine's arm. Her eyes were bulging outwards towards Grandma.

'Never ever accuse my chief wife of witchcraft,' he said. He opened his cosmetic case and took out a pot, from which he took four tablets and swallowed them one after the other with no water. 'You are the *junior* wife, you see? You will listen to the chief wife and do as she says! Never blame my chief wife of such a thing as witchcraft! It is a dangerous accusation. A very dangerous thing to say.' Alhaji pointed to the Boys' Quarters. 'A stupid and dangerous accusation.'

'Please, please,' said Celestine. She was crying. Her eyes were flat against her head again. 'Please, sorry, sorry. I am scared that she will poison me. She is jealous, jealous of me—'

'Get!' said Alhaji. 'I will not tell you again.' He pointed his arm further away from his body towards the Boys' Quarters. His arm was very long. It was the length of one of his legs.

Celestine walked slowly away, rubbing her head and wailing. 'Sorry, sorry …'

I began to watch Grandma even more closely. Was she a witch? Could it really be true? Could she perform *juju*? I knew she believed in witchcraft, and had told me stories of charms and *juju* that had done harm, or good. She had told me of *juju* witches and wizards that needed toenail clippings and human hair and sometimes body parts to perform their spells. She told me that witches and wizards were thrown into the river after they had died – which was another reason not to drink the river water.

I leant forwards to Ezikiel's ear. Grandma was on the other side of the veranda braiding the hair of one of Youseff's daughters. The other daughters all stood in a line behind Grandma's chair, waiting. I did not see the point. It would take Grandma hours.

'Could it be true?' I whispered.

'What?' Ezikiel shouted loudly and moved away from my face.

'Shhh.' I put my finger to my lips and moved it away quickly. I did not want Grandma overhearing and coming at me with a wooden spoon. But I could not stop wondering if it could be true. Grandma was called during the night, and during the day, and sometimes she ran towards the car where Youseff would be sitting with the engine running, or sometimes she would run towards the river, pulling down a thin canoe on the way. Always, she had the bag by her side. Every time I asked someone about Grandma's job they sent me away.

Ezikiel leant his ear back down towards my mouth.

'Could it be true?' I whispered again, this time pointing at Grandma.

'What are you talking about?' Ezikiel hushed his voice.

I looked at Grandma. She was pulling the girl's hair so tightly even her nose had raised upwards and I could see straight into her nostrils.

'Grandma,' I said. 'Could she be a witch?'

Ezikiel laughed immediately. He held his sides and moved his head back and forth. Grandma looked over at us and let the girl's hair go enough that her nostrils flattened down. I turned my head and kicked Ezikiel's foot.

He stopped laughing and started shaking his head. 'You are so funny,' he said.

Later, Ezikiel went with Alhaji to an important meeting about Islam. When I asked him what it was he shrugged and opened his eyes wide, before getting into the back of the car, next to Alhaji. I watched the car pull away. I waved but Ezikiel did not wave back. He kept his eyes facing forward the same as Alhaji's, as though he could not see me standing there at all. He seemed to be following Alhaji more and more. And instead of laughing at him, or making jokes at what Alhaji said, Ezikiel began to ask him questions: What side effects are common with beta-blockers? What medical school is best for me? Do you think I will make a good doctor? I had no idea why Ezikiel was suddenly interested in Alhaji and ignoring me. What had I done?

When all the girls' hair was plaited, Grandma fell asleep on the veranda chair with her head tipped back. I did not realise what I had gone looking for until I was in her bedroom pulling it towards me. The bag was heavy and smelled of rotten meat. I opened the clasp and looked at the doorway. I listened for noises but could only hear the sound of my heart thumping in my neck. Something was shining in the bag. I put my hand in slowly. My fingers were shaking. I could feel something cold and wet, hard objects, something metal. A piece of material. Reaching further inside the bag, my hand hit something. I pulled it back out suddenly. Something sharp had pierced my finger. My skin looked normal for many seconds before a tiny line of blood appeared.

A knife. Would a witch carry a knife? What other job would need a knife? Grandma couldn't be a butcher as we hardly ever had meat. Surely, a butcher would bring home meat every day. And butchers were always men; I had never seen a woman butcher. And a butcher would be paid every week. If Grandma was a butcher, Mama and Grandma and Alhaji would not be so worried about money. But why else would Grandma carry a knife?

I put the knife back into the bag, shut the bag, and crept from the room.

'One day I will open my European Fashion Boutique,' Celestine said, after our dinner of *kpokpo garri*. I thought of the market shop, which had nothing but naked dolls and large canisters full of lace. 'Lycra is the fashion in the US,' she continued. 'It will take off here. Whatever fashion starts in the West, Nigeria follows behind.'

'What is Lycra?' I asked. I had finished my *garri* and was crunching a bag of out-of-date potato chips.

'Very special materials. Contours to a woman's own shape.' Celestine pulled her wrapper up to reveal a petticoat, and tugged it. It stretched and then sprang back when she let go. I darted my eyes to Alhaji, who went on eating his bag of chips. 'All clothes will be Lycra in the future,' she said. 'Very slimming.' I raised my eyebrows enough for Ezikiel to pinch my arm.

'It is a stupid idea for a job,' said Grandma. 'It is not a modest job.'

Celestine shook her head. 'No, sister. Is very good business idea. Lycra holds sweat in close, very good in hot weathers. Keeps the body cooler.'

'It is a stupid idea, bloody stupid woman,' continued Grandma. 'Lycra? For a Muslim wife of a chief? It is not modest. It might be good for Christians but Islam states that Lycra on women is not modest.'

'Where does it say Lycra is no good? It is not in the Koran. You show me where.'

'You cannot read, bloody stupid woman. So I cannot show you.'

Alhaji had his mouth open to speak but there was no gap between the women's words to fit his in, until Grandma asked, 'What do you think?' Alhaji sighed. He looked tired; his loose face skin was even looser, hanging around his neck.

'As an engineer, I know about materials,' he said. 'Grandma is right. Lycra is too hot.' Celestine stuck her bottom jaw out and folded her arms. 'Also it is too tight. Not modest at all. It is not suitable for the wife of Alhaji to be wearing such tight clothes. You see?'

Nobody spoke. For several minutes there was the sound of crunching and far-away shouting. The far-away shouting was happening more and more. It still sounded far away but seemed to creep closer every day. Snap circled the bottom of the veranda area for leftover bones. He was always nearby during mealtimes. Most mealtimes somebody felt sorry enough for him to throw him something.

Grandma sucked the meat off a bone, then picked between her teeth with it, before throwing it to Snap. 'There you are, boy,' she said. Snap danced around the bone and jumped to his hind legs. It was a trick that Boneboy had taught him. We laughed as Snap spun around in a circle chasing the bone already in his mouth. Boneboy laughed the loudest. He had a very infectious laugh. He was sitting in the shade at the side of the house, leaning his back against the wall. I had not noticed him there until he laughed.

'Also,' said Celestine, above the laughter, 'Lycra comes in many colours.' Alhaji stood up, walking towards the house. 'Bright colours, like pinks and purples, beautiful greens.' One by one we walked away, leaving Celestine talking to Snap. 'Blues, bright greens, every shade.' When I looked back, Snap had stopped running in circles and was crunching his bone with his ears flattened down.

It was nearly a full moon when it arrived. We were sitting on the veranda listening to Alhaji talk about the future of petroleum quality testing, when it appeared as if a giant tin barrel was floating towards the compound. I half-closed my eyes. Then I rubbed them. I thought I was seeing things. Everyone looked surprised, even Grandma who believed that objects could float. Celestine jumped to her feet, and then up and down. 'It has arrived!' She ran towards the barrel, and opened the gate. Then a Citroen car crept in. The driver was a small man with a large clipboard. His eyes flitted over me quickly and rested on Celestine.

'Celestine Kentabe residence?' he asked. He got out of the low car and stretched his arms high. He had a lopsided moustache. Celestine jumped excitedly; her breasts followed. I tried not to look at the driver's eyes, looking at Celestine's breasts.

'That's me, that's me, it is for me.'

Alhaji frowned and Grandma shrugged her shoulders. He walked over to the car, everyone following a few steps behind him. I walked slowly. I felt scared about what was coming.

'What is this?' Alhaji spoke to the driver, who was by then staring so hard at Celestine's breasts that he had not noticed Alhaji coming. He jumped and nearly fell over.

'The shipment for Miss Kentabe,' said the man, waving his clipboard and beginning to untie the barrel.

'Mrs Kentabe,' said Alhaji. He stood in the way of the driver's eyes and Celestine's breasts. The barrel rolled off the car and crashed onto the ground. Grandma put her hand on Celestine's shoulders and Celestine stopped bouncing around. I hovered behind Grandma, trying to make myself invisible. Ezikiel stood close next to me. I could feel him holding laughter in his stomach.

'What is it?' Grandma asked.

Celestine smiled widely; her eyes disappeared. She started a bottom-shuffling *owigiri* dance to imaginary music. Her bottom stuck out like a shelf. It could have been used to balance a cup on.

'Lycra!' she shouted. 'Lycra for my European Fashion Boutique!'

TEN

'I am wife, what is husband's is wife's,' Celestine said, after Alhaji asked her where the money came from, before he sent the Citroën driver away, and pushed Celestine towards the house. Her breasts shook when he pushed her, as if they wanted to run in the other direction. There was no arguing, just the sound of Celestine screaming, and then being slapped. Scream, slap, scream, slap, scream, slap. I pressed my hands on my ears; Mama held Ezikiel to her body. She kissed his head. Celestine had been hit so much since arriving, I felt sorry for her. Every time she got beaten for a mistake I wondered when my turn would be. With every slap Celestine received, I winced.

'That is it,' whispered Grandma. 'She has spent all the money we had. That stupid bloody stupid woman.' Grandma's words sounded harder than the screams and slaps coming from the bedroom. She kept tutting and sighing, and sucking her teeth, but eventually Grandma stood up and walked to the house. 'That's enough,' she shouted. Then it was quiet.

The barrel was pushed to the back of the house, and never mentioned again. The only reminders were Celestine and

Youseff's youngest wife, Tare, who wore a different Lycra item every day, and lit up the garden like bright hibiscus flowers, and the money that we no longer had.

We were getting ready for school the following day when Mama came to find us. 'Don't bother,' she said. 'You are suspended.'

Ezikiel dropped his shirt onto the ground. It was almost the same colour as the ground-dust.

'Sorry, Mama?'

'You're suspended. Don't look so shocked; it's temporary. The fees are late. And until they're paid, you can't go to school. You'll have to do your homework here.'

I moved closer to Ezikiel's back. There was no wheeze, but he was hardly breathing at all. Was he holding his breath?

I looked at Mama's face. It was sharp and pinched, and her lips were tight. She was not joking.

For a moment I thought of school, especially of the toilets, and then I thought of the teachers, who never smiled, except when they whipped the children.

I hid my face from Mama, behind Ezikiel's back, and then I smiled. My smile did not last long. Ezikiel was still holding his breath. When his breath did arrive it came out as a sob. I remembered at once his grades, his medical career.

'Mama, I cannot miss school,' he said. 'Not even a day. I will fall behind. Please, Mama, there must be some way of me going. Can I talk to Alhaji?'

'There is no point. He doesn't have a job,' Mama hissed.

'And all my money goes on feeding all these mouths. If we can't even eat then school is out of the question. It's bloody ridiculous, all these mouths to feed. And that stupid woman! I can't believe we're working to feed Youseff's kids, and Celestine's stupidity, but there you are. We have to live here for now, so I can't do anything about it. We need money for food, your medicines ...'

Ezikiel began to cry. I put my hand on the middle of his back.

'Don't start,' she said. 'Don't you start with me. Do you think I want this?' Mama was shouting now. 'Do you think I want to have kids who don't go to school? Do you think I asked for us all to be starving? To have to work every hour just to support these people?' Mama waved her hand around the air.

'If you want someone to blame, you go ahead and blame Alhaji! He is still paying for that stupid woman. Or even better, go right ahead and Blame Your Father!'

Mama worked even longer hours than usual. She took any extra work that she was offered and we hardly saw her at all. We noticed it even more as we were not at school. Our days were spent listening to Alhaji pace the veranda, thinking out loud of money-making schemes, or watching Youseff's wives leave the garden early to look for work washing other people's clothes or selling roasted corn at the roadside.

Grandma and Celestine stayed out of each other's way for some weeks, until one day, when Grandma and I were at the side of the house where Grandma was teaching me how to pound yam, we heard Celestine crying. 'Bloody woman,' said Grandma.

I followed Grandma to Celestine's room at the Boys' Quarters, and waited outside the material door. Celestine was sobbing, and when Grandma entered her room, the sobbing became louder until Grandma had to shout, 'Be quiet!'

'What is the problem?' Grandma's voice was softer, as if it had forgotten that she hated Celestine.

'That man.' Celestine began to sob once more. 'That man, your husband!'

'What has that man done?'

I imagined Alhaji badly beating Celestine. He was half her size, but it was still possible. Mama had told me once that everyday beatings were normal, but bad beatings could kill a woman.

I wondered what the difference was, between everyday beatings and bad beatings. Did the husband use more force? Did he use a belt?

'He is making me pay back the money I spent on my Lycra. But I cannot find a job.' Celestine moved against the material door, opening it wide enough for me to see into her room. She was on her knees clutching Grandma's legs. 'Please, sister, please, please help me. He will throw me out! *Wari fa!* Throw me to the rats!'

'Is that all?' Grandma laughed. 'You are young enough and healthy. Of course you should work. You need to contribute. And the money you spent. All that money wasted!'

'I am sorry for that. I will pay it all back. I wanted to make money with the Lycra.'

'Eh! We cannot eat Lycra!' Grandma peeled Celestine from her leg like a banana skin. 'Get up,' she said. 'I will try to speak with Alhaji to see if I can help you find something. You must work. Now everyone must work. This is not the time for relaxing.'

Celestine hugged Grandma, almost picking her from the ground.

'But I cannot promise. And if you spend our family money again, I can promise. We will put you out!'

Celestine kept her university degree rolled up in a cardboard tube; she got it out to show people so often that the edges had become crisp and curled like a potato chip. It looked authentic. The university stamp was blue-black, the colour of a school toilet fly, with just the right amount of smudge. Celestine's seven names were all there. It was signed in green biro by a Professor Akporovwovwo Mivwodere Efetobo Okoli. I couldn't understand why nobody believed in Celestine's university degree, when it was right there in front of them.

'I will never find that woman a job. Celestine would be good at stamping documents, but the office jobs are taken up. Even Sizzlers, and Mr Biggs, full of fresh young people waiting for work. It is not easy to find employment for that woman. Eh! That woman. The crab may try, but it will never walk straight.'

We travelled to Warri and found the Airport Road television shop, which was freezing with air-conditioning, and I listened as Grandma told a lie. 'She has plenty of sales experience,' Grandma said to the short woman wearing a man's jacket and a beaded necklace. The beads were the size of marbles. I focused on the woman's beads, so that I would not lift my eyes and give the lie away.

'We have no vacancies,' she said. 'And why is this Celestine not here in person?'

'She is very busy. She has just returned from London, where she had an important job in sales.' Grandma smiled. 'Electrical sales.'

'London,' said the woman quietly. 'And you say she has sales experience? Fine. Fine. Send her in for an interview tomorrow at nine.'

We left the shop quickly. I avoided lifting my head until we were home.

Celestine was back the next day, by lunchtime, shaking her head, and sucking her teeth. 'I didn't say anything,' she said. 'Only kindness. Just said I would bring her some garments.'

Grandma groaned.

Celestine continued. 'That woman is wearing man's clothing. She would benefit by Lycra.'

'You are a bloody stupid woman. That job was the only job you would get,' said Grandma. 'You are not qualified to do anything, cannot even read or write.'

Celestine walked away.

I did not say anything.

'There is no university degree,' said Grandma. 'There is only one way she got that certificate.' I waited, but Grandma did not explain. We watched Celestine walk across the compound towards the gate, her bottom squashed into a too-tight wrapper, making a crunching sound as it swayed from side to side, as though the material was about to rip at any moment.

Grandma's Efik friend Mama Akpan ran a business of getting girls fat before their wedding day. Grandma said she owned the last of the fattening rooms, as so many girls were worried about heart disease. She was Grandma's best friend. Mama Akpan was rich, and she was famous for not spending money. She lived in Calabar, in a house with peeling paint, and did not own a car. People had stopped going to her for loans. She had no house-girl, or woman to wash her clothes. The only jewellery she wore was gold-plated, sent by her son, Akpan, in England, who bought all her gifts in the Marks and Spencer sale. Mama Akpan kept them in boxes with the labels still attached, wrapped up in oversized plastic bags. She got them out to show me whenever we visited.

'Look at this beautiful article,' she said, in English.

It was the weekend, and Grandma and I had travelled for almost five hours to arrive at her house. I was glad to be away from Ezikiel. Since being suspended from school he had been in a terrible mood. When we arrived Mama Akpan was waiting at the door with a Marks and Spencer Winter Sale carrier bag. I wondered how long she had been waiting there. She opened the bag and flashed the contents at us before we had even stepped inside. Four or five sets of gold-plated jewellery came out, one by one, like stars on a moonless night.

'It's all beautiful,' I said, although the jewellery was bright. I could imagine Celestine wearing it.

'What can I get you people?'

'Maltina please.'

We followed her towards the kitchen area. Giant bowls were bubbling full of stews and porridges and *egusi* soup. Mama Akpan noticed me looking at the food. 'I have to feed these girls every three hours. *Garri* and rice, beans and fish. *Ekpan koko* and *oto*. Big bowls. Make them nice and fat.'

I opened my eyes wide.

'Lovely and cold,' said Grandma, after Mama Akpan handed her a bottle.

Grandma pressed the bottle of Amstel Malt to her forehead.

'From the new fridge.' Mama Akpan gestured to the large white fridge occupying an entire corner of the kitchen, plugged in next to a generator. It sounded like a giant mosquito.

'You! Spending money!' Grandma teased. 'No, tell me it isn't true.'

'Ha. Well I am old and I like cold Guinness. The other fridge was not reliable.'

Grandma rubbed her chin, and I knew she was thinking about the other fridge. I missed having a fridge.

'You can take the old fridge,' said Mama Akpan, as if she, too, could read Grandma's thoughts.

'Thank you, my friend,' said Grandma.

She flung her arms around Mama Akpan and started performing a dance. Mama Akpan was very fat around the middle, and made Grandma appear much thinner. I wondered if she too had been eating the fattening food. If Celestine had been here, there would have been no room for anything else in the kitchen. The two women jigged around as I laughed and danced on my own; there was no room to join in with them. But they grabbed me anyway and squashed me between their bodies.

After dancing we ate. I had two full bowls but still Mama Akpan poked my middle.

'This one is so thin. What will her husband think?'

'She is skin and bone.'

'Send her to me. For three months before her wedding.'

I looked at Grandma. Grandma laughed. 'Don't mind her,' said Grandma. 'It is only Efik girls who do that.'

I was relieved. I did not want to stay in bed for three months getting fat.

The fridge wasn't the only thing that Grandma received from Mama Akpan. She sent her mattress when she upgraded to a deluxe orthopaedic model, which she told Grandma moulded to her shape.

'You are so blow-up any mattress would mould to your shape,' Grandma said, but she thanked her anyway, accepted the mattress, and laid it in Alhaji's room. Then Mama Akpan sent over some cooking pots and two knives.

'Maybe she just feels it's time she spent some of her money,' I said.

Grandma did not reply.

The fridge arrived just in time. Grandma rented a shop with a brick roof but no door, thirty minutes from Alhaji's on the road towards Warri. She installed the fridge, which was loud and deep. Mama Akpan gave Grandma money for drinks, and rent, and a generator to power the fridge. Grandma filled the fridge with Star Beer, and Harp, Malta, Sprite, Lemon Fanta. She did not advertise. There was no sign. She took the fold-up chairs from the makeshift mosque, sat down and waited until the go-slow arrived. I hovered nearby like a butterfly around the hibiscus, watching the small bamboo and cane houses clinging to the other side of the road, and the women in front of them, washing big-bellied children in plastic bowls. The children cried but still let themselves be scrubbed. Oil and rattan palm trees stood next to the mango trees, near to the houses. When the women had finished scrubbing they lifted the children from the bowls high into the air in order that they could reach up and take a fruit. In Lagos we had taken fruit from the fruit bowl, after asking Mama. I wondered what it would feel like to have Mama lift me to a tree.

We did not have to wait for long.

'One Star Beer and two Lemon Fanta,' a man shouted

from his car window, and sent his small son out onto the road with some naira. The traffic was so slow that the drinks were finished and the bottles returned for their deposit before they had travelled ten feet.

The people in the next car noticed the bottles being returned. 'Are they cold? If they are cold I am taking four beers!'

Soon word-of-mouth had spread down the entire length of the go-slow. Grandma ran out of drinks. She had me write a sign on a piece of cardboard:

Beer Fridge. Sold Out. Open Tomorrow.

Grandma divided the naira into three piles. The medium-sized pile she put into her bag, which was one of Celestine's and had the words 'May the Lord Save Your Soul Samuel Dokubo' printed underneath. The photographer had not done a very good job. Either that or the picture had been taken after the man had died.

Grandma kept the largest pile for Alhaji, and gave the smallest pile to me. I held it tightly. It was the first money of my own that I had held. I waited for Grandma to shout with joy, to sing, or dance, to talk about how much money we had made. How we could return to school. I imagined Ezikiel's face when we told him the news. But Grandma was silent as she folded up the chairs, then unplugged the fridge.

'Tomorrow we will get more drinks,' she said, as we walked along the road, sidestepping the hawkers.

The next day when we returned to the fridge it was gone. Grandma must have seen but she did not walk any quicker or say any words. Her feet moved as steady as always and she hummed. 'The fridge,' I said. 'Grandma, the fridge!'

I ran towards the space where the fridge had been. The empty space. 'But we locked it. It was chained. How could it have been taken?'

Grandma stood in the space for a long time. She looked up and down the road. She looked at the sky. She closed her eyes. But she continued humming the same song.

'The fridge, Grandma,' I said. My voice was shaking. 'Someone has stolen it! Should I run to the police?'

Grandma stopped humming and shook her head. She smiled. 'They will be punished,' she said. 'But not by the police.'

'Who then, Grandma? Why are you humming? It's been stolen. The money we made yesterday.'

'It was a good business,' said Grandma. She sighed again. 'I am sorry it has gone.'

I thought of what I would do. I was not attending school and the fridge had made me feel useful. I could help with money. Now there was no school and no fridge. What would I do all day?

Grandma took my hand and led me away. 'Grandma, are you not going to do anything? Tell anyone?'

'I will tell Alhaji.'

'But the police? They might catch them?'

Grandma shook her head. She began to hum again.

'Grandma, how can you sing? You do not seem to care.'
My voice was high, high, high. My eyes were full of tears.
Why did Grandma not react?

Grandma smiled and squeezed my arm. 'A bird does not
change its feathers because the weather is bad,' she said.

We were hungry. All of us. Not just Ezikiel. After Celestine
spent the food money on Lycra, and the fridge had been
stolen, there was no more money at all. We had not paid
school fees, but there was still no money. Despite Mama's
waitressing there was still not enough money to pay our
school fees. The car was running out of gas, the kerosene
lamps were running out of kerosene, and the food was just
running out. We sat down most evenings in darkness, hungry.
Giant sacks of rice were only an inch deep, the tops bending
and folding down. There were no minerals: no Fanta, Coca-
Cola, or ginger beer. When there was meat, it had to be
fried, as it was turning bad. Grandma again tried frying
some meat in palm oil, but the smoke became so strong she
could not see for many hours. That is why, even though it
was months from Eid, I watched my first death. Alhaji called
Ezikiel who ran to help, pulling the ram towards him. He
held the ram's head, while Youseff held its body. Boneboy
ran to help Ezikiel hold the head, as the ram was strong,
and twisting itself around. Boneboy looked grown up next
to Ezikiel, despite being the same age as him. He had muscles
at the tops of his arms. The ram seemed to know what was
happening. It made a sound like an engine about to start. I

felt like shouting, 'Stop', but I was too hungry to feel sorry for it.

The knife made a clicking sound against the ram's throat. Alhaji sliced and pulled as the ram twisted and turned. Its eyes were open wider than I had ever seen eyes open. I wanted to look away but I could not. The ram's legs skitted and slid on the ground. I wanted it to be over. Eventually the knife broke open the skin, tissue, bone. A hole appeared at the ram's neck. Boneboy held its head tightly in his hands.

Grandma looked at me watching the ram. 'When we kill a goat, we should be strong enough to kill a leopard,' she said.

I smiled. If I did not think about them too hard, Grandma's words were beginning to make more sense.

Ezikiel looked away. Alhaji frowned. The blood overflowed from the ram as though it was too full up of its own blood. The ground changed colour. I moved backwards. The ram's skin bubbled and popped. I looked at its face. Its eyes stayed open.

Preparing the ram for cooking was not easy. I burnt off the skin and hairs with the help of Grandma, who laughed when I turned away from the blood.

'Get used to it,' she said.

Everything was used. Eyes, foot, tail, liver.

Grandma took out the intestines, and gave them to me. They were long and thin and folded over so many times they reminded me of Mama's necklace, which was always getting twisted into knots. I copied Grandma and squeezed them like a tube of toothpaste.

'That's it, push the shit.'

'Disgusting,' I said.

'Only if you don't push it all, and eat the shit, eh?'

When we had finished, the empty intestines were boiled first, then fried in groundnut oil. They sizzled and a delicious smell filled my nose.

'Call everyone!' shouted Grandma. 'Celestine, Celestine.'

The ram was cooking on the fire and Grandma stood behind it, smiling. Alhaji and Mama and I went running to Grandma.

'Where is Celestine? Ezikiel!' Grandma shouted. 'I have found a good job for her,' Grandma told Alhaji. 'Mama Akpan knows someone.'

'Excellent,' he said.

A job for Celestine! That is why the stolen fridge did not worry Grandma too much. I thought of Ezikiel. School fees.

Alhaji seemed surprised. I wondered if the surprise was from Grandma doing as Alhaji had asked, or from Celestine having a job.

'As a mourner,' said Grandma.

Alhaji said nothing for a few more seconds. A mosquito buzzed close to my ear, but I did not flick it away. I wanted to hear all of Alhaji's reaction.

'A town mourner,' continued Grandma. 'Funerals are very big business these days. All this warring and diseases. All these poisons from the oil companies.' She sighed. 'Funerals are good business to work in.'

Warring and Diseases and Funerals!

Alhaji started to nod his head, slowly at first, then faster and faster, flicking his head back and forth until he was making such large nods that his neck must have hurt.

'Yes,' he said. 'A Professional Town Mourner. It is an important job, you see? An executive position! It is a suitable job for the junior wife of Alhaji! Celestine, where are you, Celestine?' Alhaji called. She came running from the Boys' Quarters. 'I have found you a very important position. A very important job. You will be helping people beyond help. Doing good when no more good can be done. It is an extremely important position. You will become a Professional Town Mourner!'

Celestine stood up and held Alhaji's hands. Her eyes shone. She looked at Grandma and smiled enough to show her rotten back teeth. 'Thank you. Thank you, thank you.' Celestine started dancing, wiggling her body in a winding movement. Her body moved easily between Grandma and Alhaji, but they both stepped back anyway. Then she shouted.

At first it was a low cry. Celestine threw her head back, and increased the volume until Alhaji put his hand out to stop her. Grandma and I covered our ears. Celestine stopped the shrieking but continued to dance, and made a noise, a fast clucking, so high-pitched that the rams ran towards the gate. Even Snap flattened his ears and moved behind the outhouse. Ezikiel came running out of the house, carrying a textbook. I had not seen him run that fast since Father came home with tickets for a Stationery Stores game in Lagos. He stopped in front of Celestine. 'What's happening?' he asked, looking at us all. 'Who has died?'

'She has a job,' shouted Alhaji, above the clucking.

Celestine stopped and took a large breath; her breasts inflated like two balloons. She wiped the sweat from her head and smiled.

'I am Official Town Mourner,' she said, and started dancing again. We all laughed. Alhaji brought out his radio and turned on some highlife music, and we danced around the garden until the meat was cooked. Even Alhaji danced. He moved quickly, shaking his head from side to side, and he did not shout at us when we laughed at him. Celestine wailed to the music, her voice getting higher and higher until Grandma said that she should stop before the glasses smashed.

Mama laughed. It was the first time in so long that Mama had laughed. The sound of Mama laughing made us all laugh.

We ate the ram straight from the fire, with no bowls or spoons, and we drank Fanta that Grandma had kept hidden in her bedroom. Ezikiel closed his eyes as he ate. I could not remember the last time he had eaten meat. He made a small humming sound and filled his stomach until his trouser button popped open. We all laughed again.

Ezikiel could not stop smiling. 'School,' he kept saying. 'Back to school!'

Alhaji patted his back and laughed. 'The best student.'

After dinner Grandma was called away by a boy's voice coming from the Christian field. 'Mama Timi! Mama Timi!' Grandma rushed into the house, and came back out carrying the bag. I looked at the bag and felt my cheeks get hot. But

Grandma did not notice. She was picking a piece of meat and wrapping it in paper. She cannot have been a butcher. Who ever heard of a butcher taking meat to work?

I watched Grandma walk quickly to the back of the house, towards the river. Where could she be going?

I looked at Ezikiel but I did not dare ask him about Grandma in case he laughed at me again. And I did not want to spoil his mood. It was the first time in days he had looked happy. Ezikiel and I mixed a paste from the semi-congealed blood and ground-dirt. We wanted to make play-dough models of ourselves and Mama; it held together well enough for us to make two figures holding hands but then it became too gloopy to make any more. I watched the two stick men for a long time until one of them melted to nothing but the hand, which seemed to be reaching up from the earth.

When Grandma returned late in the night we were all still awake sitting around the fire. Grandma sat down on the veranda, next to a lamp. Fireflies were flashing in the air around her head.

'Come,' she shouted.

All of us went to Grandma. It was the time of late night when she told her stories, and Ezikiel, Boneboy and I sat down near her feet. Boneboy wore Snap wrapped around his shoulders like a yellow gold necklace. Youseff's children sat further back, in the shadows. 'No, no,' said Grandma. 'This story is only for Blessing.'

A story only for me. I looked at Grandma's face looking at my face. Why was this story only for me? I wondered if she knew that I had gone looking in her bag. Did I put the knife back in the wrong place? Did I leave the bag open? I looked back at Grandma and tried to keep my face still.

Ezikiel laughed.

'It is true,' said Grandma. 'Everyone else go away. Go to sleep with your full tummies. This story is for Blessing's ears only.'

Ezikiel stopped laughing, but he did not move. Youseff's children went to the Boys' Quarters and Boneboy walked towards the gate, followed by Snap. Snap's fur shone in the moonlight.

Still, Ezikiel remained. 'I can listen,' he said. 'I won't disturb you.'

'No.' Grandma leant forwards. She spoke loudly.

Ezikiel jumped backwards suddenly. 'OK,' he said. 'OK. I don't care, I'm too old for your stories anyway.'

But as he walked to the door I heard him sniffing. And when he reached the door, it did not close properly behind him.

Grandma picked up my hand. She turned it over and studied my fingers in the lamplight. 'My mother taught me how to mix the herbs and river plants that calm the newly born, and the pastes for the breasts to increase milk, and fluids to boost red blood cells.'

I tried to keep my eyes open. I had no idea what Grandma's story was about. Why it was only meant for me. It must be something to do with Grandma's job. The ram meat was making me sleepy, but I did not want to miss a word that she said. I pinched my own arm.

'My mother trained me to be a birth attendant when I was twelve. Your age. And her mother trained her. That is the way it is done. I have delivered thousands of babies.'

My mouth fell open. Babies!

'Some babies lived, and some died,' continued Grandma. 'My mother trained me how to stem the blood from a woman who is bleeding too much, how to pull a baby out by breaking the bone. She taught me about genital cutting. How to cut the girl babies. And how to open up the closed women, ready for childbirth. How to sew them back again, afterwards.'

Grandma was not a witch. Or a butcher!

The bag full of equipment! The knife!

Grandma's voice sounded far away. Then, suddenly, she sat me up.

'It is a good job. There is only money for school for one of you, and Alhaji will send Ezikiel. But you do not need school. I have seen you with the babies. You have a natural gift. You are a special kind of girl. I want to train you now,' she said. 'Like my grandmother trained my mother and my mother trained me. It is time. Alhaji has agreed. When a palm branch reaches its full height it must give way for a fresh one to grow. '

From the doorway I heard a noise. I could see a long thin shadow. The shadow sniffed. Ezikiel.

I looked back at Grandma. My head was bursting with babies. I would follow in the footsteps of Grandma. There would be no more school. No more school toilets, or whip-pings, or mathematics! Grandma would train me. Me! A birth attendant. *A special kind of girl*. I knew very clearly what my life would be. I had never felt surer of anything. When I finally drifted off to sleep that night, I dreamt of a woman opening up like a flower after the rains. For the first time in my life, it did not even occur to me to ask Mama.

I woke up to find Grandma's large flat face shining in the kerosene lamplight. Her eyes flicked from one side to the other. She put a finger to her lips and beckoned me out of the bed where Mama continued to sleep. I followed the light to Grandma on the veranda, where she was waiting with a T-shirt and wrapper that she pulled over my night things. I felt too tired to ask questions, and walked with her to the car where Youseff had the engine running. I sat next to her, and fell asleep.

The car stopped suddenly, waking me with a bang. There was nothing to see in the light from the car headlights but a small row of village huts. Faces appeared from the door-ways, worried female faces, no children, no men. They all knelt to Grandma. Where were the men? Grandma pulled the bag from between her feet and opened the door. The smell of diesel was so thick that I could taste it. A pipeline fire lit up the sky; it was as if the sun had risen at midnight. Tiny bits of black ash settled on my hair, and made me cough. Grandma held my hand, smiled. 'Come,' she said. She led me to the huts and past the rubbish, then through a doorway.

A woman knelt on a hessian floor-mat. Another woman was holding her arms. I could see at once she was giving birth; her eyes were wide and she was panting. Grandma knelt down beside her and pulled things from her bag. Things I had felt with my hand. A knife, scissors, a metal stick, a pot of liquid, some leaves.

When I thought of my worries about Grandma being a witch, I felt my cheeks get hot. And when I thought of looking in her bag, I felt my stomach drop down as though my insides were kept on a shelf that had been suddenly removed.

'Come.' Grandma patted the ground next to her. 'Come. *Bo*.' I knelt down and waited.

'Tonight just watch,' said Grandma. We lowered the woman to the ground, Grandma saying, 'Shh, shh,' and rubbing the woman's swollen belly. The other woman was talking to her in a language I did not even recognise.

Women's faces lined the doorway.

Grandma spilled something onto her hands and rubbed them together, and then she pulled the woman's wrapper up, exposing her.

I gasped. Ezikiel picked up a shell once on Bar Beach in Lagos, and turned it over. 'That's what a woman's private parts are like,' he had said. I studied the inside of the shell, its curves and neatness, all tucked in, and curled over. I put the shell to my ear.

I could hear nothing and everything at the same time.

This woman's private parts were nothing like a shell.

Grandma stuck her hand right in, and pressed the woman's belly. 'How long has she been like this?' she asked, in English.

'Since sun up,' said the woman who was still holding the giving-birth woman's arms.

'The baby is stuck,' said Grandma, and pulled her hand out. She washed the layer of blood from her fingers, hand, wrist, arm. Then she laid a piece of cloth on the floor. Out of the bag came a knife with a smooth edge. She poured some of the liquid she had been using on her hands onto the knife, and made a flipping sound with her hand. The whole area began to smell sour like Father used to, before he had bathed or brushed his teeth. My eyes watered.

'Help me,' Grandma said. We tried to roll the labouring woman onto her right side. We heaved and pushed and pulled but, still, a face at the doorway had to come in and help. Then Grandma gave the two women helping a leg each. 'Hold tightly,' she said. She picked up the knife. With one hand she cut, from the back of the opening towards the ground. The other hand she put in the woman and twisted.

A clunking noise from deep inside the woman sounded like a car going over a large pothole.

I looked at the doorway. The women at the doorway all had their eyes closed. I wanted to close my eyes, too, but it was impossible. They were open wider than they ever had been. The sleepy feeling was gone. I had never felt more awake.

Seconds later the baby slipped out. Grandma's hands worked quickly to wipe the sac away from its head, before she put the baby on the woman's belly, which was already shrinking. Blood fell out of the woman in a shining pool.

The baby cried.

'A daughter,' said Grandma, looking at me and then at the eyes in the doorway. 'God is great.'

ELEVEN

Celestine told me she was the best Professional Town Mourner in the whole state. She wailed with her voice, and her face, and her enormous body, which seemed to increase in size every day. She showed us what she would do at each funeral.

'I can throw myself,' she said. 'Very well.' Suddenly she threw herself around, jumping on the ground and flinging her arms out to the side as she howled. Her whole body shook and wobbled. Big fat tears fell down her cheeks.

We all laughed. Even Mama who was resting in the bedroom. She must have imagined what Celestine looked like.

'For an extra fee,' said Celestine. 'I can throw down a tree.' She raised herself up high and suddenly jumped into the air, landing on a mango tree. It shook and bent over as if it was leaning down to pick something from the ground.

'Stop,' said Alhaji, laughing. 'I can see your demonstration of how good you are but I would like to keep all my trees!'

Celestine was employed by rich families, earning not only

naira, but a meal at the service, takeaway food, and a Tupperware. There was usually a picture of the deceased printed on the side of the Tupperware with words such as 'Rest in Peace Preye', or, 'Peace Be Unto You Etarakpobuno'.

Celestine showed me her increasing Tupperware collection, which balanced on a table in her Boys' Quarters room. There were cups, boxes, vases, and containers with poorly fitting lids, all lined up and balanced on top of each other. The bags with faces printed on them were piled up on the ground. Celestine was never without a bag with a picture of a deceased person printed on the side, staring out. The dead faces looked surprised to end up as a picture on Celestine's bag.

Some days there were no deaths and Celestine would practise mourning. On those days Alhaji took the car to the Executive Club, and Grandma took me and Ezikiel to market, to look at lace or hairpieces. Ezikiel and I loved weaving our way through the blanket stalls, looking for items we had not seen before: locusts, rat poison, multipacks of Y-fronted underpants. We returned as late as possible in order that Celestine's voice would be resting. Other days, Celestine would be called to join the procession of grievers walking through Warri town, wailing and crying. She was by far the loudest. She still wore tight-fitting vest tops underneath wrappers, but she always covered her hair, and instead of a bright green scarf, she used Grandma's black one.

Mama had still not borrowed any oil from the Highlife Bar.

I was beginning to wonder if she had forgotten. With Celestine earning there was money for meat and fish – but still, it had to be fried first. Ezikiel nibbled on corns, and pepper soup containing no meat or fish, cooked only with palm oil. He stuffed his tummy with pounded yam dipped in palm oil and salt, and wished for fried chicken and *jollof* rice. 'I ate starch and *owo* in my dream last night,' he said. 'I'm so bored with eating corn and pounded yam. I need proper food. Why can't Mama steal some vegetable oil from the Highlife Bar? They must have some? Or olive oil. She said the *oyibos* like to dip their bread in olive oil. Could she not steal some for my food?' He stretched his arms up making his already flat tummy dip inwards.

I shook my head. But I did know why Mama did not hurry to bring oil home. Grandma had said that Mama was frightened to lose her job, and the staff watched closely. Mama said she was on trial, and she wanted to keep her job. She seemed to enjoy going to work. Every day when she left she had a smile and when she returned the smile had disappeared. She enjoyed the air-conditioning.

'Maybe you will grow out of the allergy,' I said. 'I heard that nut allergy can be grown out of. Alhaji is convinced.'

'I doubt it. It will be my luck to have to eat nothing but pounded yam for the rest of my life.'

'I will ask Mama, if you like? To steal some olive oil?'

'Don't bother. She doesn't listen to you anyway.'

I turned my head away.

'Or even me any more,' said Ezikiel. His words came out

quickly. 'Why is the palm fruit not growing quicker?' he asked, and despite knowing that he was not really asking anyone in particular, I put my arms around him. He felt fragile. He did not even have the energy to play barefoot football with the village boys in the Christian field. He did not have the energy to walk to the village to sit on the floor and watch a match on the satellite television.

'That is very worrying indeed,' said Alhaji. He walked out of the house towards us and pointed to the patches of colour on the tree trunks, the colour of his toenail. 'If they had someone with experience,' he continued, 'at the petroleum plant. In Charge of Quality.'

He must have been listening from behind the doorway.

He stopped and stood in front of Ezikiel and me. We had no choice but to listen.

'They would produce less polluting gases, and the fruit would grow. You see?' He took a deep breath then coughed loudly. 'This air is full of lesser qualified petroleum engineers.'

I giggled, imagining tiny little men in the air, all with badges on their suit jackets saying 'Petroleum Engineer'.

Alhaji frowned but continued to talk. 'As a petroleum engineer for the last twenty-three years, I would ensure quality and improve standards. It is a very important role. Essential work, you see, and who better than me, a local resident with a Diploma in Petroleum Engineering. I will be able to set in place guidelines and protocols for the maintenance and safety of the oil production. Guidelines, you see?'

He prepared these speeches in detail, like he was practising for an interview. But there was no interview. There was never any interview.

'I would monitor the pollution effects on the environment,' Alhaji continued. He said each part of the word 'environment' as if it were a separate word and made the last part sound like a tut: en-vir-on-menT. He looked around the garden, and half-closed his eyes.

Ezikiel sat up straighter, and when I rolled my eyes and gently squeezed his arm he pushed my hand away. He was listening to Alhaji. Every word.

'I know how to check the emissions of the pipeline, how to maintain quality of the oil, how to make it superior, and therefore more money-making. And I am only taking small salaries.' He turned and smiled, making us both jump slightly. 'When they think of quality they should think of Alhaji.'

Mama was at work when we ate dinner on the veranda. I loved sitting next to Ezikiel, even though Alhaji always tutted as Ezikiel ate his fruits and plain rice. 'A boy needs meat,' he said. 'Fruits are for girls.'

Mama had only been at her job for less than a month. It was probably too soon to save for school fees. It was probably too soon to borrow any oil. But I knew it would not be long. I could wait. Alhaji, though, could not wait any longer. He looked at Ezikiel's bony knees, and reached for his cosmetic case. 'Take this medicine before eating some meat,' said Alhaji. He handed Ezikiel a large purple tablet;

it had to be broken into three pieces before it could be swallowed. 'It will prevent allergy.'

Ezikiel looked at Alhaji, who was nodding frantically – his neck skin was swaying – and then he looked at me. I shrugged.

Grandma said, 'No, no, it is no good. You need to wait for Mama to return from her work.'

Ezikiel looked at Grandma for a few seconds. At first I thought he was probably thinking the same thing that I was. But he popped the pieces of tablet into his mouth, one after the other, and gulped them down. I did not understand why he listened to Alhaji. He listened to every word that Alhaji said as if it was important. Ezikiel took a tiny piece of meat from Alhaji's plate and held it up in front of his nose. It was see-through. Then he put the meat into his mouth and chewed slowly. A piece of dribble formed at the corner of his lips, and he made a moaning sound. It was the first meat he had eaten since the ram.

I tried to imagine the taste, even though I was eating exactly the same thing.

I watched my brother. Everything was calm and quiet. I could hear the chatter of the brightly coloured birds. For a few seconds nothing happened. Ezikiel had said that it was possible to grow up and out of allergies. Or maybe Alhaji's tablets really did work?

Suddenly, Ezikiel's eyes started twitching. Then winking. I watched his face, especially his mouth, for any other signs of allergy. I did not have to wait for long. His face became pale and his cheeks patterned. His lips opened, reddened, cracked, and split. His tongue pushed through his lips, swollen and shiny and red. I could hear his chest bubbling, and hissing, and wheezing. I felt my stomach shelf removed.

Father would know what to do.

I ran. I ran to Mama's room, where she kept a small injection that Dr Adeshina had given to her and told her to carry at all times. That was when she was with Ezikiel at all times.

I felt around the front pocket of the suitcase we had arrived with, but I could not get the zip open. My fingers were not working properly.

I remembered Mama's words when I had given Ezikiel the brown paper pepper bag. *Stupid Girl, Stupid Girl, Stupid Girl.* I rubbed my hands together again and again, and thought of Ezikiel turning blue. I grabbed the suitcase pocket, and ripped. The lining burst open and the injection fell into my palm.

I ran back to the veranda where Ezikiel was now kneeling down and leaning forward to try and breathe. My heart fluttered between beats. Alhaji was smacking Ezikiel hard on the back, and had opened his Marmite. He scooped some out onto his fingers and pushed his hand into Ezikiel's mouth, rubbing the Marmite onto his tongue. Ezikiel screamed. I took the opportunity to stick the needle into his leg and push down the plunger. His leg thrashed around, the needle and syringe still attached. Grandma had her head in her hands. Alhaji smacked Ezikiel's back a final time. I put my ear to Ezikiel's side. I held my breath until I could hear air going into his chest. The blueness faded from his lips like a flame losing heat. His leg stopped moving. His chest rose, and then fell. His breathing became more normal. His nostrils flattened down against his cheeks, and his tongue moved back into his mouth. The area of skin on his throat stopped sucking in. He sat upright. I pulled the needle from his leg. And then I closed my eyes, and thanked God, and Allah. Just in case.

'I don't blame you. You're only a child.' Mama was talking to Ezikiel but looking directly at Alhaji.

'There is no need for anger. The boy has to eat meat.'

Mama had returned from work to find Ezikiel wheezing quietly, on the veranda. I was sitting behind him, stroking his hair.

'My son needs his medication.' She turned away from Ezikiel as though she had forgotten him. 'Can you replace the injection? Can you give me the money for a replacement?'

Alhaji's face swelled full of air. 'There is no need. Look at me! Your old father! How fit I am, you see? My arms, legs, my shoulders. Life can be preserved with the right pharmaceuticals. If Ezikiel follows my regime his allergies and his asthma will disappear. What is the worst that could happen?'

'He could die!' said Mama. 'If he gets an allergy and does not have his medicine he could die!' She was shouting. 'If he hadn't had his adrenaline he would have died! Do you realise how serious this is? Of all the stupid things ...'

Ezikiel started crying. I put my arms around his sharp shoulders.

'Give me some naira and I'll go to Radio Street Clinic for

a replacement,' Mama continued. She too had started crying. Her face was twisted.

Alhaji shook his head. 'There is no need for that. As I said, the boy can follow a simple regime, like Alhaji. Nigerians do not suffer with nut allergies; I am convinced the diagnosis was wrong. The boy is simply lacking in certain things. B vitamins play an essential role—'

'Did you not hear me?' Mama was shouting again, pointing her finger at Alhaji's face. I could not believe it. I hugged Ezikiel so tightly I could feel his shoulder bruising my skin. I would never dare shout anything at Alhaji. I would not even look at him directly. But Mama had no fear of him at all. 'He could die! Die! He nearly died. Now give me the money to replace the medicine. I need to get it immediately. It's not safe for him to be without it even for a day.'

I could feel the tickle of Ezikiel's wheeze through my sleeve, becoming stronger. I could feel myself wheezing, even though I did not have asthma.

'There is no money,' Alhaji whispered. 'And anyway,' he said, in a much louder voice, 'the matter is not in our hands. Only Allah decides when it is time for Ezikiel's death.'

I matched my breathing to Ezikiel's; his breath coming out was much longer than his breath going in. The back of my head began to float. No money? But with Celestine's money there was meat and fish. No money!

'I'll have to spend the school fees. I'll have to take on extra work to make the school fees again,' said Mama. 'Extra work.'

Would that be possible? I tried to calculate how many

hours we had seen her that week. Only three and it was Saturday already. There were no spare hours left.

'Who knows what I'll have to do.' Mama leant closer to Alhaji. She spat the words into the air in front of him. 'Did you think of that? The extra work I'll have to do? Do you understand what extra work involves? Do you?'

Alhaji took a giant step backwards. He nearly fell over. Mama walked away. Alhaji looked as though he was about to cry; he had his mouth wide open and his eyes were dusty. He snapped his head towards me. Ezikiel was shaking and breathing in and ooouuuuttt, his head buried into my shoulder. I thought of the money Celestine brought home being ripped into three: food, school fees, medicine. She had been getting plenty of work as a Professional Town Mourner, but her money was not enough to split into three. And sometimes Grandma was not paid at all, or paid in fish. We could not exchange fish for school fees or medicine. I felt my head spinning.

'You should not have used the medicine,' Alhaji shouted. 'The Boy Was Fine.'

Ezikiel was lying on the ground, curled around the bottom of the palm tree. I was lying on the ground, curled around Ezikiel. I had my arms wrapped around his chest. I could feel his heartbeat on the palm of my hand. Ezikiel's heart stuttered like a boy in my old class.

'It was my fault,' I said.

'Of course it wasn't. It's my allergy.'

'I could have stopped you eating it. I should have stopped you.'

'I knew it was unlikely to be cured. Allergies rarely go away or are grown out of. I knew it. But I wanted to believe Alhaji. And that meat tasted so good. But now Mama will use the school fees. I've missed so much already. And I've got my exams this year.'

'Mama was so mad. The medicine is more important than school. Anyway, Mama said she will make the school fees back. I am so sorry, Ezikiel. It is my fault for not stopping you.'

'It's my own fault. I'm always getting sick.'

'You cannot help getting sick. It's not like you're doing it on purpose. Anyway, sometimes Mama shouts for no reason at all. It is not your fault.'

Ezikiel was silent. His heart stuttered.

'I wish I could have the allergy instead,' I whispered. 'Let me get sick instead.'

TWELVE

I watched Grandma as she drew curved shapes in the dirt
with a long stick. The ground was dry and powdery, and
Grandma did not have to press hard to create patterns. There
were four semicircles, two on each side, the outside shapes
larger than the inside. Grandma shut one eye and finished
the picture with a tiny line on the top and a small round
circle immediately underneath it. We were sitting on the side
of the veranda with our legs swinging over the edge. Alhaji
had left for the Executive Club after morning prayers, carrying
a bottle of Remy Martin. He always seemed to be carrying
Remy Martin. I wondered where Alhaji got the money from
to buy expensive brandy. I wondered why Alhaji did not
spend the money on Ezikiel's medicine, or school fees. It did
not make any sense that Alhaji could have money for brandy
but not for Ezikiel's medicine. Whenever I asked Grandma
about it she said it was important that Alhaji carried on as
normal, even during such difficult times. I wondered why the
times were so difficult, but Grandma's face stopped me asking.

Celestine was at market. Mama was at work, at the Highlife

Bar, and Ezikiel was asleep in Alhaji's room. He had not spoken to me much since Grandma told me about attending births, and when I told Ezikiel that I was to be Grandma's assistant, he shrugged his shoulders, and said, 'So what.' I did not know what was wrong with him. He did not seem interested in birth attending at all. I knew that he was upset at being suspended from school. But I was too excited to worry about it. Me. An assistant birth attendant! My stomach was dancing.

'This is not common,' Grandma said. 'Easy birth, no cutting.'

She drew another shape in the dirt with the long stick. It was similar to the first shape, but with no tiny line at the top.

'This is very mild cutting, the hood just taken,' said Grandma. 'This is becoming popular, like boys. Childbirth is usually not a problem.'

Next to it she drew the same shape as before but with two vertical semicircles instead of four. The inside semicircles were missing. 'This is most normal type, eight of every ten girls in those creek villages. The birth is good most of the time.'

Eight out of ten village girls with missing semicircles!

'Which type did you have, Grandma?'

The words poured out of my mouth like water. We had only been living at Alhaji's for four months, but it was long enough to know that Grandma could be asked anything. My words to Mama were less water and more sand. I rehearsed them in my head so many times that sometimes I was certain I had spoken to Mama and would continue a conversation I had only imagined, and Mama would slap the back of my head and say, 'Stupid child.' Sometimes even my dreams seemed more real than real life. I kept having the same dream, where Mama had her hands covering her face, and when she lowered them her eye was swollen and cut, surrounded by a purple bruise. It must have been a dream, but it seemed so real.

'Fourth type,' said Grandma.

She wiped all the lines away, raised the stick high in the air, and stabbed the ground, leaving a singular, tiny, round hole. There were no lines at all. 'Birth is a problem always. The baby gets stuck, then the mother pushes a hole between urine and womb, and then the husband leaves. Many girls die. One from every ten.'

One from ten girls die! Oh!

I looked at Grandma and tried not to imagine her with a baby stuck, or a hole between her bladder and her womb, or even Alhaji leaving. I looked at the hole. A tiny circle. I did not see how a baby could come out, or even monthly blood, or urine. The hole was impossibly tiny. Grandma's eyes were wet; she was blinking quickly. I tried not to react, to keep my voice steady.

'Why do people want this done, Grandma?' I asked, looking at the drawings in the dirt, focusing on the tiny hole. 'Why would anyone do this to a girl?'

'Women have always done it,' said Grandma.

'People still do it? Even when one from ten girls die? People still do it?'

'Many people. The main reason is tradition, and holding

onto culture, but there are many other reasons. Some say this part …' Grandma drew four semicircles and tiny line on top again. She stabbed the stick at the circle with the line above it. 'This part is dangerous and can send a woman into madness. Or can hurt the husband penis or baby coming out. But those are the same people who used to throw twin babies in the evil forest. Backwards people. It is mainly the village girls having this now, not town girls. The village girls still have the first and second type.'

'I still do not understand, Grandma. Why people would do this.'

'The women of the villages would say that the world may have changed but to ignore traditions and customs would be to live like a reed in a tide.' Grandma raised the stick in the air. 'But this type,' she stabbed the stick at the small hole with nothing else around it, 'is no good.'

My training came slowly. Grandma would tell me tiny pieces of information that sometimes did not make sense until the next piece arrived. Some days she felt like talking. They were the best days. Other days she was quiet, and I waited. There was so much to learn. As well as women's parts, and how different cutting would give different problems, she taught me to recognise the types, and the problems that came with each type. I learnt the meaning of secret women words: fistula, rupture, prolapse. Then Grandma told me about babies. She would lean down during breakfast, or after prayers, or as she gave me a kiss goodnight, and whisper another piece of information: 'If baby is back to back, mother should sleep forward, or painful birth,' or, 'If mother is tired, she needs meat stew and spinach greens,' or, 'If mother dreams of river, there is too much water, the baby is small.'

I memorised Grandma's words by repeating them over and over, like times tables at school. Since we had stopped attending school I had hoped to spend more time with Ezikiel, but he was always with Alhaji at one important meeting or another, or sitting in Alhaji's bedroom studying his medical textbooks. He studied all the time. He told me he did not want to hear anything about birth attending. I missed him. But training to be Grandma's apprentice did not allow me much time to get sad. I did not have time for keeping up my schoolwork like Mama wanted me to. Instead of one times five is five, two times five is ten, I chanted, 'River dream means baby is small, river dream means baby is small,' until I saw Mama looking at me with a frown between her eyebrows.

'Mama, may I ask you something?'

'What is it now? I'm too tired for talking. Is it important?'

I nodded and kept my eyes facing the ground. 'Yes, Mama.' Even though Mama had a frown, I could not wait to ask her. When Mama and Grandma were together, they smiled and hugged to greet each other, but they did not sit close. At dinner they sat close enough for their arms to touch, but they did not; there was always a slice of light cutting a gap between them.

Grandma   Mama

'Well?'

'Why did Grandma not come and see us? I mean when we lived in Lagos?'

Mama sighed. 'I've told you before. She did not want me to marry your father. Ha! She was so right. Anyway, why don't you ask her?'

I closed my ears. I hated Mama talking about Father that way.

'And anyway, it's sorted out now, isn't it? Grandma and I get along fine. We are one big happy family now?'

The way Mama said the word happy changed the meaning of it. The word happy sounded sad. Even angry.

'Is that it? Or are you full of questions today?'

Mama did not look angry at all. She looked directly at my eyes. I had wanted to ask her so many things for so long. It seemed like a good time to ask just one more question. Her face was not twisted. 'Sorry, Mama, but please could you tell me about when I was born? My birth?'

Mama sighed and turned away. Then she looked at me with a deeper frown line than usual. I thought that she would tell me to be quiet. But after a few seconds she started talking again. I opened my ears and eyes wide.

'You were born at the University Hospital of Lagos,' Mama said. 'I had pethadine. An obstetrician strapped my legs into stirrups and out you came. That was it. Nothing spectacular.'

I wanted to know so much more, but Mama did not like personal questions. 'Was it a difficult birth?'

'No. You were number two. Easy. It was Ezikiel who gave

me a fistula, before he nearly died.' Mama laughed. 'You just fell out of me. Then the midwife put you in a tiny cot and wheeled you to a room with all the other babies. She gave you a bottle of Cow and Gate so I could rest. Your father watched you through the glass.'

I imagined a row of fathers, their daughters looking even more impossibly beautiful through the smudged glass, like a camera picture taken in soft focus. I imagined Father thinking I was far superior to all the others, with a prettier face, a softer cry, a smoother skin.

I wondered if too-loud Father was truly quiet for the first time, if he had nothing to say, and no noise to make, and was still like the river at dawn.

'He got so drunk on palm wine,' continued Mama, 'that he fell and smashed the glass screen. He was barred from the hospital until he paid the fifty thousand naira fine.'

It was late in the evening when a boy pounded on the compound gate so hard that one of the hinges came loose.

'Mama Timi, Mama Timi,' he shouted. There was always someone calling for Grandma.

She came out of the kitchen room, carrying her birth bag, and one from Celestine's collection, which had a picture of a couple printed on the front and the words 'Congratulations on the occasion of your marriage Mr and Mrs Adaye from your beloved parents'. The picture of the couple was faint, but you could tell they were happy, with their heads resting against each other. Grandma took my hand.

'You're not going,' said Mama, who had returned from work and was resting on the veranda chair with her feet balanced on Snap.

'Mama,' I said, but then I started coughing. The insects were so thick that every time I opened my mouth to speak another one flew in.

'She will just watch,' said Grandma.

'No way. I know what's been going on. All these question about births and sudden interest in midwifery. She is way too young. There is no way.'

'She needs training.'

'She's not going,' said Mama. She stood up, making Snap squeak then bark. 'I knew this would happen.' Mama looked at Grandma so fiercely I could see the anger in the air in front of her. It was sharp and red.

'I need help. She needs a trade. There is no school. She cannot sit around and learn nothing. It makes sense, *abeg*?'

Alhaji came out of the house scratching his head. Nobody knelt. 'What is going on here?' he asked, looking straight at me as though I was the cause of all problems.

'Grandma intends to train her as a birth attendant,' said Mama, also looking at me as if I was the cause of all problems. She was so angry that her eyes became bloodshot in seconds. 'You must think I'm stupid. I know what's going on. She is twelve years old. She should be studying. Reading books instead of all this nonsense. All these questions. Did you think I wouldn't realise? How will she get to university if she falls behind now? She will be back at school as soon as there is money. It won't take long. It is pay day next week.'

University? It was the first time I had heard that Mama wanted me to go to university.

Nobody spoke. I looked around the garden. A few of Youseff's swollen-bellied children had come out of the Boys' Quarters to watch Mama shouting.

'I don't want her exposed to that life, she's too young to be going to those backward creek villages, and it's not safe.' Mama stood up. 'I heard gunfire again last night.'

Gunfire? I looked at Mama's face. Maybe I had not heard the words properly. Why would there be gunfire? The fighting had stopped.

Alhaji took a large breath and looked at me, then at Grandma. He shook his head. 'No, no. The fighting has stopped now.' His eyes opened slightly as he looked at Mama.

Mama flicked her head towards me. 'Well, maybe. But I don't want her exposed to that life.'

Grandma did nothing, but bowed her head towards the ground.

Alhaji stood taller. He looked at the skinny legs of Youseff's children. He looked at my skinny legs. He looked at Grandma's face. 'She can go with Grandma,' he said. 'But only if her homework does not suffer. She should carry on learning even when there is no school. Even if it is only for one more week. It is good for her to learn a trade.'

'Thank you, sir,' I said, kneeling down. Even though I only said sir, I felt as if I had said the wrong thing. It was always that way with Alhaji. My voice sounded young, and unsure, and shaky.

Alhaji turned his nose up and pressed his lips together before returning to the house.

I did not look at Mama as I rushed to the gate with Grandma. We walked past Ezikiel. He looked at me strangely when I walked out. His head flicked from mine to Mama's then back again. His mouth remained shut.

'There will be money for school soon. There will be money for school,' shouted Mama. Her voice sounded higher than usual. When I did not turn my head Mama's voice lowered. 'You are your father's daughter!' she shouted.

I smiled.

Nimi's room was only big enough to contain me and Grandma, despite an elderly woman who tried to squeeze me out of the way, and follow us in.

'She is my assistant,' said Grandma, to the woman. 'Wait outside.' She waved to the other side of the material door, where the elderly woman stood all evening; a strange, hunched shadow, getting darker and larger as the light changed.

I kept quiet and tried to remember everything that Grandma had told me. I sat by Nimi's feet, and opened the birth bag onto the ground. I pulled out a piece of cloth (wash between women), on which I laid the knife (not used for household purposes, clean on the fire between women), the scissors (keep sharp and completely dry), and the pot of paste that looked like pounded yam and smelled of sweat (we will come to that). I placed the handles and blade towards Grandma, who was pulling Nimi's wrapper up, after washing her hands in bucket water with a small piece of soap. It was a relief to see Nimi's curved lines like the first drawing. Easy birth.

'Fifth child,' said Grandma. 'Quick.'

As I was closing the bag, the woman started moaning and a thick head of curls appeared at her opening. Grandma moved Nimi to a kneeling position. 'Go with gravity,' she said to Nimi, or me, in Izon. She grabbed my hands and washed them quickly with the soap, scrubbing beneath my nails, between my fingers. Then she placed my hands between Nimi's legs. The baby was so warm. A tiny pulse coming from the top of the baby's head fluttered on my finger. The hair was softer than anything I had ever felt. The head pressed against my hand.

'Ready?' asked Grandma.

I nodded while I watched Nimi's face grow, tiny red lines appearing in the whites of her eyes. It looked as if she was going to explode, like her blood would burst out of her body. Everything seemed to be coming out of her, except the baby. I could not tell by Grandma's reaction if it was normal; her face was calm. Around the baby's head Nimi was becoming more and more swollen and spongy, until it was hard to tell where one ended and one began.

'Now, as the baby comes out, feel the neck,' said Grandma. 'Check no cord is wrapped around, then tug and the baby will fall into your hands. Support the baby's head and put it on the mummy tummy.'

I did not have time to protest. I did not have time to say, 'We promised Mama I would just watch,' or ask, 'What is a cord?' I felt a rush of soft weight fall into my hands. A slippery, sticky, impossibly warm baby. I held the baby's head and supported the neck, as if I had been doing it forever. I put the baby onto Nimi's stomach, and watched them see each other for the first time.

The next morning Mama called us into the bedroom. 'I have good news,' she said. She had been at work all night. It must have been at a different bar, as she had told us the Highlife Bar closed at midnight.

I looked at her face. It was shiny. She was looking at Ezikiel.

'There's some money for school fees. And medications. We don't need to wait for pay day next week. We have no money worries right now.'

My hands dropped to my sides. My ears opened wide. No money worries. School fees! What about my training? What about Grandma?

Ezikiel was jumping into the air. 'Thank you, Mama.' He hugged her and lifted her from the ground. She laughed. Ezikiel was taller than Mama.

Mama laughed and laughed. 'It's been a real challenge, but I know how important it is to you.'

'Thank you, Mama. Thank you!' Ezikiel moved to her side and hugged her.

Mama stopped laughing when she noticed me with my

hand over my mouth. I could not move. I tried to drop my hand and smile widely and say, 'Thank you, Mama, thank you, Mama,' but all I could think of was not being able to be Grandma's apprentice any more.

'This is what I have raised?' Mama said. 'This ungrateful daughter? Do you understand how hard I have worked, am working, to get you a good education? Do you realise how lucky you are?'

I thought of the toilets at school. I thought of the teachers. Of no more Grandma teaching me. I tried again to thank Mama, but I could not even drop my hand from my mouth. Ezikiel frowned and flicked his head slightly at Mama. But it was no good. I felt the idea of becoming an assistant birth attendant lift away from my body into the air, and travel out of the room. I felt like I was just a girl once more.

It was Alhaji who saved me. We had all finished eating on the veranda. It was nearly time for Grandma's stories. Ezikiel had smiled all afternoon. Even when we had fried fish, and he had more pounded yam dipped in palm oil, he smiled as though it was the tastiest thing he had ever eaten. Mama too had smiled the whole day. She hummed to herself. I had not heard her hum since Father had left.

'I have catching up to do,' Ezikiel said. 'So I'm afraid I have to miss the story tonight. It is important that I have read as much as possible before returning to school tomorrow.'

Mama smiled over his head. 'You are such a good boy,' she said. 'You make me very proud.' She did not look at me but I could feel her words travel past Ezikiel's ears and into mine, as though she had fired them from a gun.

I looked at Grandma, who was smiling. Why was she smiling? Did she not know that Mama was returning me to school?

Alhaji leant forward in his chair. 'Ezikiel will be a fine doctor. If I had not been a petroleum engineer I would have definitely gone into studying pharmaceuticals. But now I am an expert, and I would not have to study hard at all.' Alhaji laughed.

He stopped laughing and looked at Mama. 'There are some professions,' he said, slowly and loudly, 'that you can teach yourself. Then there is no need for school.'

'I did not like going to school,' said Celestine. 'I had to walk for two hours to get there, and we had to carry our own table and chairs.' She started laughing. 'Some days I stopped on the way to have a rest and woke up at the end of the day. I must have fallen asleep.' Everyone laughed. I imagined Celestine asleep on the roadside sitting at her school desk, with the cars driving past wondering what she was selling.

'Take Grandma,' said Alhaji. 'Never needed school. And she is the best birth attendant in Nigeria.'

Grandma smiled.

Suddenly Mama sat up. She flicked her head from Alhaji to me to Grandma.

'That is why,' continued Alhaji, 'there is no need for Blessing to attend school.'

There was silence. We all turned to Mama's face to watch.

She had her teeth held so tightly that her cheeks had puffed out. 'She's going to school,' said Mama.

'I have decided,' continued Alhaji. 'Blessing is better having a profession like Grandma. Then she will be able to contribute and support herself. School will not help her learn like Grandma can. And Grandma needs an assistant. It would be foolish to offer the job to an outsider.'

Mama did not speak. She bit her lip. 'I gave you the money for fees,' she said. 'I gave you the money to pay their school fees.'

Alhaji sat back in his chair. 'I have paid Ezikiel's fees. He needs school. The boy should go. And the other money,' he smiled at Mama, 'we need for food and essentials. And Blessing can work with Grandma. My word is final.'

I felt my heart lift in my chest and my head dance. Assistant birth attendant! Me! No more school! I looked at Grandma who had sparkling eyes. I made my own eyes sparkle, too. I was about to smile and thank Alhaji but then I looked at Mama.

Mama's face filled with tears. 'But there will be more money. I told you, money won't be a problem now.'

I wondered why money would no longer be a problem. What had suddenly happened to make us rich? Grandma was still being paid in fish, and Celestine had not had a funeral for weeks. Mama said she worked for tips, but surely she was not paid enough tips to cover school fees?

'My word is final,' said Alhaji, cutting the air in front of him.

'I worked so hard for that money,' Mama said. 'I wanted Blessing to have an education.'

Alhaji stood up. 'My word is final,' he said again.

THIRTEEN

The mangrove swamp was full of mosquitoes. Ezikiel and I laughed as we slapped them from each other's arms. Ezikiel laughed the loudest. He had been so happy since returning to school. We were looking at a butterfly, and trying to count how many colours it had, when a loud humming filled the air.

'What is that?' I asked. I looked through the trees at the river. The water swirled. Ezikiel pulled me close to him. He held me tightly.

A boat travelled past us. It was full of boys carrying rifles. A gunboat!

I held my breath. I could feel my heart rising to my neck.

Ezikiel held me even tighter, pressing my arm against his chest until my arm did not feel like mine any more. It was only when I opened my eyes that I realised I had closed them.

The boys in the boat carried the guns away from their bodies, in their bare, thin arms, as though they were afraid of them. I looked at the guns. My fingertips felt cold. I looked at the boys. Their eyes were red. Some of them were wearing nothing on their top half but string vests. They were laughing as they drank from bottles and smoked sticks; the smell was even stronger than the stale smell of the river. They wore necklaces. I could feel something pressing down at the back of my head as I looked at their necklaces. They were not like the necklaces made from yellow gold that the men on Allen Avenue wore.

The necklaces were made from bullets.

I could feel Ezikiel's wheeze on my arm, even though my arm did not feel like mine.

One of the boys was taller than the rest, and skinnier than Ezikiel. He wore large sunglasses. His cheek was scarred in the same way as Grandma's. He smiled widely, showing a golden tooth at the side of his mouth. 'Make this slow boat go faster. We need to complete our mission.'

They all laughed. The boy at the back by the engine pulled a piece of rope, and the boat chugged and then sped up suddenly. The water at the sides of the boat rose and parted and came to the top of the bank where mine and Ezikiel's feet stood still.

I was glad for the thickness of the trees. I felt invisible. Still, I clung to Ezikiel. I wished the butterfly would fly away. It was bright enough to draw attention to us. My skin was so hot that Ezikiel's breath felt cold on my neck. He slowly moved his hand over, pushed his fingers through mine and gripped. Both our hands were sweating. I held on tightly to Ezikiel's fingers until even my own fingers were numb and I couldn't tell which hand was my own. The boat moved away quickly. We watched it disappear. I could hear the voice of the tall skinny boy with the golden tooth, shouting instructions at the other boys in the boat: Pass that palm wine; Give me your mobile phone; Hold your rifle carefully. Ezikiel moved my hand up to his chest and pressed. His heart was trying to escape.

We slipped through the mangroves and palms, underneath the twisted branches and into daylight, and ran towards home, still holding hands. I did not dare look back.

'You were right. It's not safe! Did you see that? They had guns, rifles. Did you see the guns?' My voice was scratchy.

'How could I miss the guns?' Ezikiel was breathless. 'They had so many, how could I miss them? One boy had two guns. Two, and I say guns but really they were rifles, AK-47s, imagine firing one of those, wow!' Ezikiel's words were excited but his hand held my hand so tightly I could feel the bones inside.

I slowed down to let him breathe. 'Where were they going? I thought they would see us. The butterfly ...'

'They were patrolling the water,' said Ezikiel. 'I bet they were on their way to bunker some oil. I told Mama about it but she didn't believe me — well, you've seen it. I told her. What butterfly?'

'How many of them were there? Are they our age? They looked our age.'

'At least ten in that boat.' Ezikiel's breathing became more normal. His hand let go.

'What if they had seen us?' I asked. 'Were they soldiers? They might have taken us. Or shot at us!'

Ezikiel shook his head too quickly. 'No,' he said. 'They wouldn't have taken us. They are Ijaw. They were only boys. Wow! I can't believe we've seen a gunboat.'

We did not discuss who we would tell about the gunboat, but when we arrived home we both fell silent. It was the first time we had not run to Mama to tell her that something happened. Ezikiel moved away from me as soon as we were near the house. But I could still hear his wheeze.

'Do you want your inhaler?' I whispered.

'I'm fine,' he said, but his eyes flew around his face.

I felt my heart move sideways.

Ezikiel became more breathless later that afternoon. His chest sounded bubbly like a pan of boiling water. I could hear him over the sound of my scrubbing the cassava.

'Shall I fetch your inhaler?'

'No.' He shook his head and bent forward, resting his hands on the top of his thighs. 'It's running out. Emergencies only.'

'You can just get another from the clinic. Mama said she has the money now.'

I spoke loudly but I could still hear the rasping sound of his breath. I also felt breathless, as if asthma was contagious. When he stood up I noticed his nostrils flaring every time he took air in. His inhaler was running out. I felt panic rise in my body, right up to my shoulders. I dropped the cassava, moved the bucket of water out of the way.

'No money,' he said, waving his hand at the house. 'We need it for school. I don't want to risk it, in case they spend my school fees.'

'There will be money for medicine, silly. Mama told us we do not need to worry about it. She must have had a pay increase. She must be getting a salary now as well as tips – Alhaji even has money to bribe an electrician to reconnect us. He is going to climb the pole this afternoon. I told you, Mama has money.'

I smiled at the thought of the fan and the radio and cold minerals. Even if NEPA did not provide electricity for days and days, at least if we were reconnected then we had a chance of electricity on some days.

'What if they use my school fees for medicine? What if they use my school fees for the electrician?' Ezikiel's wheezing increased until his chest bubbled and hissed and whistled. As I ran to Alhaji's room to fetch the inhaler I pictured Ezikiel's lungs getting smaller and smaller and smaller. I pushed the thought from my mind. Must not panic. Must not panic, I thought. But I felt so alone. Where was Grandma?

The inhaler was lined up on the bedside table next to a small blood pressure machine and an electric box that measured sugar levels if you pricked a finger and let blood drip onto the end. I shook the inhaler. It felt too light. Ezikiel was silly. He should have told Mama the medicine was running out. She was going to kill him.

When I ran back Ezikiel was slumped forward, and his

ribs were poking through his T-shirt. He took four puffs, shaking the inhaler before each puff. I matched my breathing to his. It took much longer to breathe out than in, the time left after breathing out was so short only a sharp breath of air could go in. I began to feel dizzy, just by trying to copy Ezikiel. Where was everyone? Where was Mama? I looked around the compound for Boneboy, but he was nowhere to be seen. I sat down on the floor next to Ezikiel in case he fell. The breaths became more even. First, in … oooo uuuttt. Then in … oouutt. Then back to regular in … out. Slowly, slowly, his breathing was normal again.

'It's run out now,' he said, when his lips were night once more. He shook the inhaler at my ear.

I wasn't sure what I was listening out for, but Ezikiel should know. He'd had asthma all his life. He was an expert.

We found Grandma and Mama by the table; Mama was drinking water straight from a cup, without letting the cup top touch her lips. Grandma was wearing clip-on diamond-effect earrings. She had her ear facing Mama's mouth, but a large frown crossed her forehead.

'Ezikiel's inhaler has run out.'

Mama stopped talking and looked at Ezikiel. He nodded.

'Why leave it till now?' she snapped. 'You must have known it was running out.'

Ezikiel shrugged. 'I'm sorry, Mama. I used it up playing football. I was running too fast. I was worried we wouldn't have money for school fees …'

'So now you have no injection and no inhaler! This is

ridiculous. Are you stupid?' Mama looked at me when she said stupid. I looked at the ground. 'I really don't need this right now. You're not little children any more! I told you we're fine for money! I told you we don't need to worry now! Nearly adults and can't even tell me when your inhaler is running out. You need to start taking responsibility for your own lives.' She held up her hands in front of her body. 'Look, I have to go to work. Take this.'

She took five American dollars from underneath Alhaji's breakfast plate and gave it to Grandma. 'Take him to the clinic so they can replace it quickly. Get his anaphylaxis injection at the same time.'

I looked at the American dollars. Who had given Mama American dollars?

Mama ran towards the gate, where an *okada* was letting a neighbour down on the other side. She beckoned him to wait and turned her head back to me, Grandma and Ezikiel. Grandma was chanting, 'Ana-phy-lax-is, ana-phy-lax-is,' over and over.

'Don't let it run out again,' Mama said, as she climbed on, her legs sticking out towards us. Where had Mama found the money for an *okada*? 'For God's sake, I really don't need this right now.'

At Radio Street Clinic the staff were quick getting Ezikiel's inhaler and injection. We only had to wait a few minutes in the reception area, which had plastic chairs and magazines set out on small tables. Ezikiel was disappointed when Grandma called us to the door. He had just picked up a copy of *The Lancet*, and was flicking through the pages; he found a page about asthma.

'Come quick, please,' said Grandma. She held up the brown bag full of inhalers that the nurse at the reception had given her. 'I need to get back to prepare dinner.'

As we left he looked back a number of times.

Grandma rubbed his shoulder. 'You will make a good doctor.'

Ezikiel smiled, but then looked away quickly.

We walked home along the dusty road, passing people dressed in ripped-up clothes with their palms stretched out, which Grandma dropped some leftover naira into. Blanket markets lined the other side of the road, selling plantain, oranges, yams, wristwatches, eggs, sunglasses, bush meat, Eva water. Bright flowers grew from burnt-out cars, engines and carriages that littered the roadside. They smelled as though they were still on fire. We walked past a stall which had a sign balanced on the table saying:

Guaranteed Cures and Tonics for:
Haemorrhoids and problems of Anus
Fevers and Chills
Aching Bones
Asthma and Breathing Problems
Herpes and Sexual Infection
Brain Tumour and all Cancers
Barren Women Fertility Expert
Dr Tokoni Torulagha. There is no disease I do
not cure. Except AIDS.

Suddenly we heard gunfire. Real gunfire. It sounded like somebody clapping quickly.

Clapping and clapping and clapping and clapping.

Grandma threw us to the ground as if she had been waiting for it all along. Dust flew into my face and made me cough. All the blanket market sellers vanished, leaving their produce. A market with no people. Some women had left the umbrella they had been huddled underneath. It was yellow and blue striped. I tried to focus on the umbrella, on the stripes.

'Shh,' said Grandma. She put her finger to her lips. 'Be quiet.'

It was silent for a few seconds, before I heard the screech of fast tyres on the ground. A group of boys drove past in an army vehicle, waving rifles in the air. They wore berets at identical slants on their heads. One of them was wearing a football shirt the same colour as Ezikiel's. They fired more shots into the sky. They were not laughing, or drinking, instead they looked all around the roadside, their heads moving in the same direction at the same time. Surely they would see us. I could feel Ezikiel shaking next to me. He took so many puffs on his new inhaler it would be finished by the time we got home. I looked at him. He was blinking very quickly. I put my face in the dirt, and closed my eyes. Ezikiel put his arm around my back. I tried not to shake but I could feel his arm moving up and down and around.

When I opened my eyes, the truck was moving in front of us. The boys looked the same as the boys we had seen in the gunboat, but I knew they must have been different; they wore different colours, and the gunboat boys had been hatless. There were at least ten boys hanging over the edge of the sides. I could smell oil. What were these boys doing with guns? Why did they wear berets?

I looked up as they drove away. My heart had crawled up into my neck. I watched them until they were soldier ants. Their rifles looked like long thin arms pointing up at the sky.

I stood up slowly, brushing the ground-dust from my clothes. I tried to push my heart back down into my chest by swallowing hard.

'Eh!' Grandma dusted herself down. 'These foolish Sibeye Boys.'

'Who are they?' I stood, and helped pull Ezikiel up.

'They look just like boys,' said Ezikiel. 'They are boys. Not even men. Boys with rifles!'

'They are not the same boys we saw on the river,' I said.

Grandma looked at me suddenly. One of her eyes was higher than the other eye on her forehead.

I looked at Ezikiel. He had his head bent to one side. His wheeze was loud at the bottom of his back.

'They are not good boys,' said Grandma. 'Taking hostage and money. All they care about is money. They are stupid boys.'

Ezikiel stopped taking deep breaths with his inhaler. His chest was uneven like Grandma's eyes. 'They don't scare me.'

'They should,' continued Grandma. 'These Sibeye Boys, eh!' She shook her head. 'Many villages have tasted those guns. Using their *juju*.' She watched the road where the truck was disappearing from view. 'Some say they are bullet-proof.'

We watched the vehicle in the distance. Ezikiel had the same expression on his face that he had when Father had left. 'Bullet-proof,' he whispered. 'Wow!'

'Stay away from those boys,' said Grandma, looking straight at Ezikiel.

FOURTEEN

The mangroves were so thick and twisted at the riverside that Grandma could not squeeze through, and Emete's husband had to paddle the boat further along to find a clearer patch underneath the mukusur trees. A few men were trapping fish with cane nets. They nodded to Grandma. We climbed into the dugout canoe that reminded me of Ezikiel's dugout body. When we were ready to leave, the husband pushed the boat hard from the side and I thought it would capsize. Grandma must have had the same thought; she whipped her hair weave off and held it high in the air. When the boat stopped rocking she put it back on and patted her head, to check it had remained dry. I heard the fishing men laugh.

'Will we be too late?' I asked, loudly.

Grandma smiled. 'First birth. We are not too late.'

As we travelled across the water the smell of oil from the river made me cover my mouth and nose with my scarf. Emete's husband stabbed his rod into the riverbed, pushing the boat forward in big jumps as the river became thicker near the village, and swampy, and spread out like the lines at the centre of a leaf. A large toad was sitting at the side puffing its cheeks out, singing a low song. The water was swirling with mudskippers. The day was hot but there was no dust near the river. I opened my eyes as wide as the sun would allow. My head was burning; I wished I had brought my scarf.

I had been Grandma's apprentice for nearly four weeks. I had attended six births. When Ezikiel had returned to school he had been happy, but as the days went past he seemed more and more angry. He studied every evening late into the night until his eyes hurt too much from the lamp light. Whenever I tried to tell him about the births, and my training, and everything I had seen, he told me to go away. He said he was too busy studying to listen to my stories. I did not know why he had to study all the time. And I thought he would be very interested in hearing about the births; it was the closest to medicine that he had ever seen. But he did not seem to want to know about it at all. Mama was always at work, and when she was not she did not look at me. She knew that I did not want to return to school. She probably thought I was pleased that Alhaji had spent my school fees, or that she had taken extra work to raise the money. She would sit down next to Ezikiel and ask him questions about school. She did not look at me at all.

We climbed out of the boat onto a jetty, which was really just a piece of wood stretched out from the river bank; still, it kept my feet from being bitten by anything lurking in that swamp. It would surely be full of snakes and crocodiles, I thought.

The village on the riverbank looked like all the other villages, as if a war had recently happened there. Everything clung to the sides, as though the world was folding in on itself. The huts were burnt out, held together. There were small huts in no particular order and skinny animals tied with ropes to sparse trees, but the area was clear of people, which was unusual. Whenever I had been to these places before, the whole village came out to greet a visitor.

The husband led us to the birth hut, where a young woman lay alone on a hessian mat, next to a bucket of the oily river water.

'Hello, Emete.' Grandma knelt and looked at the river water, then at her hands. She did not wash them, but asked the husband for palm wine as I opened the bag and looked at Emete's tummy. It was small, like Mama's after eating a large meal. Not like it contained a baby.

Grandma felt Emete's tummy, pressing until her knuckles turned white. Emete sat up and tightened her fists. She screamed.

'Has the water come?' Grandma spoke to the husband in English.

He spoke to Emete, who nodded.

'Tell her it's too soon, but the baby is coming,' Grandma said.

Why was the baby coming if it was too soon? Could we not stop it from coming?

The husband spoke quickly and quietly. Emete started to cry. He disappeared as Emete opened her legs. The tiny head was almost there. Grandma tipped palm wine all over her hands and rubbed them onto mine, before she guided my hands inside Emete. The baby's head was no bigger than my palm. Grandma's hands held my own hands gently, pressing when I needed to press, loosening pressure when I needed to let go.

Minutes later a girl was born. She slipped out like a fish, with open eyes and a squirming body the size of a mango. Tiny, formed, warm, open-eyed, breathing. Ten fingers, I counted. Ten toes.

Grandma put her on Emete's chest and shouted, 'Come. *Bo.*' Her words low and full of sadness.

The husband came back in the room and dropped to his knees, picked up his daughter by her foot and stood. Tears fell down his face.

'No!' Emete screamed. 'No!'

He took the baby anyway, carrying her out as she slowly turned grey, each of her breaths quieter than the one before. By the time he got to the door, I could not hear any more of her breaths. I listened carefully, but could only hear the thump of my heart beating in my neck. I wondered what he would do with the baby, where he was going. I focused on breathing, imagining the air going into my body and the air leaving me.

I looked at Emete. She seemed empty. The ground held her down, close to the earth. Blood was still falling, spilling, from between her legs. The room became darker. I looked at Grandma's face as she delivered the afterbirth, which slipped out alive, almost beating; she dropped it into the birth bag. She covered Emete with a blanket. 'Next one is better,' she said, and kissed her head. Emete shook. Her breaths were broken up with pauses.

Emete's body looked not quite alive and not quite dead, as though it was still deciding.

A large fire had been built outside the village. I did not know who had made the fire; I could not see anyone nearby. Grandma and I stopped in front of it. I had not spoken at all. Grandma bent down to the birth bag and pulled out Emete's afterbirth, which was wrapped in a piece of cloth. She opened the cloth. The afterbirth I had seen before did not smell of anything. But this afterbirth smelled rotten. Infected. Grandma threw it onto the fire and watched the flames, which jumped up suddenly and then fell small.

'Bad luck,' said Grandma.

The air smelled of something dead that had not ever been born. The smell stayed in my nostrils for a long time.

A different fisherman took us back. He was skinny and smelled of kerosene.

We got into his boat, and travelled all the way home without looking at the river. I wished I had my headscarf. I wanted to pray.

I wanted Father.

I did not feel sad for long. It was impossible to feel sad when

Mama was smiling at me, and even Alhaji was speaking to me more. He came to find me when I cooked the breakfast, and patted my head. 'Junior Grandma!' he said. As I washed the dishes he walked past and stopped in front of me.

'What do you think of this colour?' he asked, holding up a Western-style shirt. 'I am thinking of wearing it to an interview.'

I looked up. 'It is a nice colour, sir,' I said. I did not ask about the interview. Could Alhaji really find a job? I thought of medicine and school fees and meat and fish and electricity. Mostly, I thought of Mama not being at work so many hours.

He waited and waited. I washed and washed.

'The interview,' Alhaji said, finally, 'is a long time coming. I have been a qualified petroleum engineer for nearly twenty years. I studied at Port Harcourt University. It was very clever of me to realise the effect of petroleum on this area.'

I nodded and nodded.

'But they bring the men from Lagos. Or the white men to do our jobs. They do not want a local man like me. I have never found work in all that time.'

Alhaji looked over the top of my head. I had no idea why he was telling me this. I did not know what to do. He hopped from one leg to the other, the hops getting quicker and quicker. What should I do? What should I do?

I took a sharp breath and knelt in front of Alhaji. 'I am sorry, sir,' I said. Then I squatted near the washing-up and washed and washed.

Alhaji rubbed his chin and nodded. 'You are good girl. And now junior Grandma. Let me call a Youseff wife for this task. You need to rest. There might be a birth any time.'

Alhaji hissed towards the Boys' Quarters and one of Youseff's wives came out. She took over the washing-up without even asking what she had to do.

The next evening Alhaji came back to the kitchen area where I was squatting over a bucket washing rice. 'I have an excellent money-making business that I am setting up,' he said.

I tried not to turn my head around to see if he was standing behind me.

'Alhaji has an executive business brain. Always thinking like an entrepreneur. You see?'

I turned my head and smiled.

He watched me closely. His eyes did not blink at all.

'Very good, sir,' I said.

'Do you want to know what it is? You want to know Alhaji's money-making secret?'

I wanted to take my hands from the water and rice, and run away. 'Yes, sir.'

He pulled me towards him with his finger. I stood slowly until my eyes were level with his, and went towards him. I had never been so close to Alhaji's face. I could see every mark and line on his skin.

His eyes looked past me and around me, before he whispered, 'I'm starting a snail farm.'

'Congratulations, sir,' I said.

Alhaji smiled and let his finger fall back with the others. 'Snails reproduce during the rains, so it is essential to get the right time for picking. They only take thirty to forty-five days, the whole period between incubation and hatching, did you know? Ah, smoke-dried snail meat – that is a treat that Ezikiel will smile about. Did you know that snails can grow a foot long?'

I shook my head.

Alhaji moved away from me and stretched his hands as wide as they would go.

Celestine, Alhaji, Ezikiel, Grandma and I were on the veranda listening to the birds and the river, and watching the heat wave swirly patterns on the ground. Alhaji was telling us all his plans for the snail farm while Snap begged for bones, standing on his hind legs, his tail wagging from side to side like a brush sweeping the floor. I had no idea why Alhaji told me his snail farm plans first. I tried to ask Ezikiel but he sent me away whenever I went near him. 'I don't want to hear about your birth attending. I'm too busy to talk to you,' he always said. He did look busy. He had been reading his book for weeks. 'I'm sorry, Blessing, I just have so much to catch up on!'

'You will be fine. You are the most clever person I know.' I laughed.

But Ezikiel did not laugh. He sighed, opened his book, and went back to reading, his eyes flitting across the pages so quickly I wondered how it was possible that the words went in.

Suddenly there was shouting from outside the compound wall. Snap fell to the ground. I could not understand what was being shouted, something about Itsekiris and Urhobos. Grandma looked at Alhaji, who stood up. Then Ezikiel stood suddenly and then Grandma and then me, as though we were dominos in reverse.

The shouting was so loud and the voices so deep it might have been police, or army, or the mobile police, the Kill and Go police who were paid by the oil companies. The police that Grandma had told me had killed Boneboy's parents. They wore dark sunglasses, making it impossible to see their eyes. I had seen them before on the way to school. But the police, or army, or the government's secret service men, shouted at different times and with different words, and those voices were in unison.

'Kill and Go?' asked Grandma. Her words were shaking.

Kill and Go! My teeth pressed together until I heard a crunching sound.

Alhaji shook his head quickly. 'No. Not the Kill and Go. They do not shout that they are coming. They sneak, when the villages are asleep.'

I thought about policemen sneaking into a sleeping village carrying guns. I thought about their night-eyes still covered with dark sunglasses. My teeth crunched.

I could definitely hear the word 'Urhobo' over and over. We followed Alhaji to the wall at the edge of the compound. Grandma held my hand on the way. Her hand was cool but sweating at the same time. Ezikiel stood so close behind me that I could feel his breath on my neck. I counted how often I felt it, to check that Ezikiel was breathing regularly. I stood up on my tiptoes to look over the compound wall and recognised the boys who were shooting at the sky outside Radio Street Clinic. The Sibeye Boys. The gun boys. I could see their berets. The ground suddenly felt soft. My legs were light. Unsteady. I reached out to hold on to someone, but there was nobody standing next to me. Ezikiel had moved away. The voices became louder. They were almost singing.

Mama rushed over, and gripped my shoulder, digging her nails in, and pushed me back towards the house. Her face was wide open and stretched. I winced and she put her other hand over my mouth. Her fingers smelled of nail polish remover. My eyes watered. Celestine walked slowly behind us, until her arm was pulled by Grandma, who was holding a finger to her lips. Inside the house the air was hotter. I looked at Alhaji who remained outside, rubbing some Marmite onto his forehead. Ezikiel stood behind him.

'These boys are no good. Copy cats! These Sibeye Boys are not the true freedom fighters. Where are their parents? Why do they cause trouble?'

Alhaji spoke loudly enough for us to hear, but the outside voices were becoming more distant. They wouldn't have heard him. They were still chanting, about Itsekiris and something about Urhobos getting out, but I could not understand what they meant. They carried on chanting and shouting until all we could hear was a hum. I wanted to ask Mama what they were shouting about, but her face stopped me. She was biting her bottom lip, breathing quickly. Her eyes were wet.

I had never seen fear on Mama's face. It made my body muscles became tight as though I was about to jump. I held onto her hand as long as possible; until she realised, dried her eyes, and flicked me away.

'Ezikiel.' Mama called him from outside where he stood so still behind Alhaji they shared the same shadow. 'Ezikiel.'

'They've gone, Mama.'

He came into the house and followed us into the bedroom. 'You mustn't watch football at the village any more,' Mama said. 'It's out of bounds. I mean it! Don't go near the village. Get water from the river.' She looked at us both and nodded quickly. 'Listen, this is really important. Really important. I need to know that you understand. Do you understand? Stay away from that village. Do not go near! And Ezikiel, if you have any friends at school who are Urhobo, or Itsekiri, you'd better avoid them at the moment as well. Don't play with the other kids. It's very important. Try and concentrate on schoolwork. This isn't forever, just for now, I'm working on getting us back to civilisation! At least into town. But at the moment we have nowhere else to go, so I need you to listen carefully and stay safe. It is not safe. Do you understand? Understand? And you,' Mama turned her head to face mine, 'you cannot go out attending births with Grandma. It's not safe. No way. Those creek villages are not safe. The government will surely wipe them out.'

I opened my mouth to argue, to explain that I could not

stop my training. That Grandma needed the help and I needed to learn. But Mama looked as if she might smack my head, so I shut my mouth instead. I looked at Ezikiel. He had a half-smile. Why was he smiling? I wondered if Ezikiel would remind us that he told her the Niger Delta was not safe. But he kept quiet.

'Do you understand?'

We both nodded. But really, neither of us understood.

Mama left the room, and went outside to talk in low voices with Grandma and Alhaji and even Celestine. Ezikiel and I sat together on the ground. We held hands for a long time before speaking. I think that both of us were listening for the sounds of fighting or shouting or clapping from outside the compound gates, or the voices of Mama, Grandma or Alhaji.

I had not held Ezikiel's hand for weeks. Our arms touched and pressed against each other. I could hear him crunching the back of his teeth, too. I held his hand more tightly. 'What is happening?' I whispered. 'What is all the shouting for?'

Ezikiel squeezed my hand. 'I don't know. It's exactly what I told Mama. This place is dangerous.'

'Do you think they were fighting?'

'Of course. Those Sibeye Boys don't scare me anyway,' he said. But I could feel his hand get sweaty and his arm stiffen up.

'Do you think there will be trouble here? I mean in the compound?'

'Of course not,' Ezikiel said. 'The trouble won't come

here.' He put his head on my shoulder. 'You should stay near me though,' he said. 'And if you have to go outside tell me and I'll come with you.'

I let Ezikiel's words wrap around me like a pair of arms.

It was the first time in weeks that we had spent together. I was almost happy that the fighting had started.

FIFTEEN

'You look silly,' I said. 'Why are you dressing up?' I had a Youseff baby on my hip and he was making growling sounds like a lion. I had to speak loudly even though Ezikiel was right in front of me.

Ezikiel looked at me and lifted his top lip upwards. 'I have an important meeting to attend,' he shouted. 'That baby is so noisy!' He pinched the baby's cheek. The baby laughed and hid his face in the fold in my arm.

'Alhaji called the elders and chiefs together for a council meeting,' continued Ezikiel, in a quieter voice when the growling had stopped. 'To talk about the warring. To find some solutions.'

'Are you going?'

'Of course.'

Suddenly, Youseff's baby tipped his head back and coughed, then vomited all over the front of my T-shirt. As soon as the vomit was out, the baby smiled and growled. I smiled and held him away from me.

Ezikiel laughed loudly. 'Yuck! That is so disgusting.'

'I need to change,' I said, pulling the baby back towards me.

'What for?' Ezikiel laughed. 'You are not invited! What would you know about politics? You're just a girl.'

I stepped backwards. I had never heard Ezikiel call me just a girl. The words echoed in my head. Just a girl.

'If you are going then I should be allowed to go,' I said. 'I know as much about politics as you do.'

'No, you don't. And anyway, these meetings are a bit of a waste of time. All the old men sitting around, all talk no action. And you need to be careful of these meetings,' said Ezikiel, leaning into me. 'I can't say which chiefs. But I can tell you that some of the chiefs have eaten human flesh.'

I looked at Ezikiel's face. It was not smiling. 'That is not true,' I said.

'That is fact,' said Ezikiel.

'Do not lie. That is so not true. Sometimes you make up silly stories.'

'It is true,' said Ezikiel. Then he picked up my arm and pulled it towards him. 'Yum,' he said. 'Let me take a bite. I bet you taste like chicken.'

I screamed and tried to hit him with my free arm but Ezikiel had become stronger. He opened his mouth and pretended to bite. 'Where's the salt?' he said. 'You have no taste.'

As I helped Grandma prepare for the meeting, I wondered how much money had been spent on all the Remy Martin, where the money came from. 'How did we afford all this?' I asked. I thought of school fees and medicine and Mama working and working and working. It did not make any sense to me that we had money for brandy, but we had let the school fees run out. Nor did it make any sense to me that Alhaji drank brandy anyway, which was against our religion. But I did not dare ask about that.

'The fowl perspires,' said Grandma, 'but the feathers do not allow us to see the perspiration.'

I thought of feathers as I looked at the bottles of Remy Martin and the pots of fried fish soup. It did not make sense to me.

'Your Mama has a pay increase,' said Grandma, when she noticed my face. I wondered if Mama knew that her pay-increase money had been spent on brandy.

When the food and drinks were laid out on a long table on the veranda, I followed Grandma into the house and into my bedroom. I could see and hear everything through the mesh-covered window. Even if I was just a girl.

I sat and waited for all the chiefs to arrive. They greeted each other with handshakes that took several minutes as though none of them wanted to be the first to let go of a hand. When the handshaking and greeting had finally stopped, Grandma pointed to the door. 'Go and serve them,' she said.

I straightened my wrapper and walked to the doorway, slipping on my shoes as I left the house. The chiefs were sitting in a circle. Their backs were upright as if the deckchairs they sat on were office chairs. A bottle of Remy Martin stood on the floor in the middle of the circle. It was already empty. I went to pick it up before spooning fried fish soup into bowls that we had wiped earlier, to make sure they were extra clean. I tried to keep my head down and my eyes lowered. All the chiefs seemed to be speaking at once, so it was difficult to work out who was saying what. They all had shiny faces but feet that looked hundreds of years old.

'It's a collaboration of the politicians and oil companies. You can't lay all the blame at the oil companies' feet when our government is taking bribes from them! Our government would not be in power if not for the oil company. The oil companies are being *allowed* to get away with it. Let us light our pipeline fires, they say, burn our poison gases, destroy the local environment, and here, here is a million dollars for your *convenience*. We will turn our backs while you wipe out democracy.'

'The problem is a *delicate* one.'

'These Sibeye Boys. The gun boys. They are being controlled by the politicians.'

'Eh! The politicians are controlled by the oil companies! This war would not be happening if the oil companies did not pay for the military regime. The oil companies pay direct to the Kill and Go police and the army. They do not even hide it. The blood is on their hands.'

I turned my ears on as much as they would go, but still the chiefs' words sounded too complicated. I understood that the oil companies were paying the government to kill villagers who wanted their oil back. That, I understood. But why would our own government kill our own people? Surely not for money? And if it was for money then who caused the deaths? The oil companies who give money to kill, or the government who take the money and give the guns, or the boys who join the army because they have to? Or the Sibeye Boys who fight the wrong way, for the wrong reasons?

I had so many questions in my head that I was hoping for answers to, but every time a chief spoke another jumped in, and it was difficult to hear each point clearly.

'Area Boys! And those politicians are receiving billions of dollars from the oil companies – it is in their interest to make sure we are all fighting. The Ijaws, Urhobos, Itsekiris, Ogonis. The government are supplying the different groups with weapons. Rocket launchers! I heard some groups are hiring the weapons from the government and police, and paying for day hire! This is genocide.'

I stopped walking around them. Genocide. I had heard that word before at school. What did it mean? Ezikiel would know. I looked at his face. His eyes were wide open.

'Yes. Well, they are not the only group! The Sibeye Boys. They are not the only group making trouble for the rest. Copy cats! They are damaging the reputation of the real FFIN. Us, the real freedom fighters!'

I looked at Alhaji, who was talking about freedom fighters. Was Alhaji a freedom fighter? He was sitting in a deckchair crumpled in half, as if the deckchair had something wrong with it and was trying to fold away. Alhaji's eyes had dirty windows on them and his feet looked the oldest of all. Could he be a freedom fighter?

'I have written to the appropriate authorities, you see?' Alhaji's deckchair squeaked as he spoke. I served the stew, kneeling before each chief and keeping my eyes lowered to the ground. Ezikiel ignored me as I served his pounded yam.

I noticed one of the chiefs had leopard-print skin on his feet like one of Celestine's European-style handbags. I felt the stew I had eaten earlier rise up into my throat.

Ezikiel sat straight. 'Don't worry about us!' he said. The chiefs looked up suddenly as if they had noticed him for the first time. 'Give us respiratory diseases, cancers, make our women suffer miscarriage after miscarriage, and make our children deformed! Some of the stories I hear from my own sister who is an Assistant Birth Attendant, prove that the air is poisoning our women!'

I looked at Ezikiel waving his arms around. Why was he suddenly talking about me? And why was he acting so interested in the arguments? He kept telling me that the chiefs were old men who sat around talking and talking and talking without changing anything.

One chief giggled until Alhaji opened his eyes wider. I felt like laughing, too; Ezikiel had not let me tell him any stories.

'But is it not true, sir,' the chief with the leopard-print skin leant forwards and I tried not to look at his feet, 'that some of our own chiefs, our own community elders, are also paid *convenience* money? To let the Sibeye Boys continue their parade?'

'Ah-ha!'

The group of men all looked at one chief who was so big that when he stood up the deckchair remained attached to him. His bottom must have been even bigger than Celestine's. I wanted to laugh but I did not dare. Ezikiel threw me a smile but then looked away quickly.

'What are you suggesting? How dare you! You know it is our job to act as go-between and negotiator for these boys. For the oil companies and the politicians and the true FFIN and the Area Boys. It is us who have to *negotiate*.'

The chief pulled the deckchair from his bottom. I looked at Ezikiel sitting upright and forwards in his seat. He looked back at me and smiled. Even though his words were strange, it was nice to hear him call me Assistant Birth Attendant. The words that belonged to me sounded important and grown up.

SIXTEEN

'Only get the big ones, the ones covered with slime.' Ezikiel and Boneboy were standing in front of the gate holding a box made from cardboard with holes dotting the top.

'Yes, sir. We will fill the box. There are plenty of snails to pick in the forest; I know the exact place.' Boneboy smiled and puffed his chest outwards. Ezikiel held the box higher in the air. Picking snails. They acted like they were hunting lions.

I watched them walk out of the gate, with Snap following them. Even Snap was jumping and barking excitedly. I carried on cooking the soup, adding Maggi cube after Maggi cube, and stirring as I thought about Ezikiel and Boneboy walking to the forest as though they were going hunting. Boys were a mystery to me. Even Ezikiel, who I had always understood, was becoming stranger. I did not understand what was exciting about picking up slimy snails from the forest floor.

Grandma and I ate together in the garden. The sun had removed the colour from the sky. There was no breeze. Even the dust lay flat on the ground. The rubbish lay still. Sweat waves washed over our bodies. I was glad of the extra pepper I had put into the soup. It took my thoughts away from the other areas of my body that felt too hot. I rolled the pounded yam between my finger and thumb into a small ball, and used it to scoop out some meat and soup. Suddenly there were sounds of screaming and clapping again. I let the pounded yam and meat drop back into the soup. The white yam became bright orange, like a setting sun. Grandma put her bowl onto the ground and stood, beckoning me with her hand. '*Bo,*' she whispered. '*Bo, bo, bo.*' The gunfire sounded close, almost inside the compound. My legs felt unsteady beneath my knees as though the ground was moving again. Were the guns looking for us? Where was Ezikiel? The screaming was happening all the time, but every time it happened I was just as afraid.

A village boy shouted from the compound gates. 'Let me in! Let me in! They are killing!'

Killing! In our village!

Surely he was wrong. People were fighting, and shouting, but not killing!

Words that had been flying around the chiefs' meeting suddenly became objects: real things that I could see.

I stood up, let the bowl fall to the ground. The food spilled out and coloured the ground blood red. I ran to the house, with Grandma in front. I tried to focus on Grandma's cloth. Her wrapper was made of shiny material that looked scratchy and uncomfortable. Youseff's wives were running in all directions, holding children's arms and cooking pots and pieces of material; it was difficult to get past them.

The boy at the gate was younger than me. He had an oddly shaped head, squashed on one side. Even though I could hear guns firing, I immediately thought of an unnatural birth, delivery with forceps by a male doctor. The boy was shaking the gate in his hands and trying to press his head between the bars. 'Let me in! Please!' The bars seemed closer together than usual, and looked thicker.

I coughed but I still felt like I needed to cough even more. The thick dust had begun to move and swirl, and was getting into my lungs. I coughed again, but it did not help. My chest felt like it was being pressed down.

Alhaji ran towards the gate.

I had never seen Alhaji run. It made me want to run, too.

There was the sound of more gunfire. 'We cannot let you in,' said Alhaji. 'How many more will we get? Go away! Go and hide. Do not bring trouble here. Go! Get!'

Grandma and I ran towards Alhaji. He waved us away. 'Go inside,' he shouted, 'it is not safe.' He was standing tall. His vest was stuck to his back with sweat. He moved towards Grandma. 'We cannot let them in,' he whispered. 'You know that! We cannot let them in, you see?'

Grandma moved towards the gate. Her hand reached out through the rusty bars. With her other hand she held mine. 'He is just a boy,' she said, but as she spoke, the boy let go and ran away. I watched him run, the dust rising up behind his bare feet. I coughed again, but my chest did not clear. I looked through the bars at the road outside. The boy was gone.

Suddenly another boy ran past, and another, all shouting for Alhaji to open the gates.

'Go away,' Alhaji shouted. 'Do not bring trouble into my home.'

There were too many. Grandma had moved back from the gate and was pulling me towards the house. My hand slipped from hers and I fell. Grandma pulled me up. Youseff's wives had disappeared. The compound was empty. Where was Ezikiel? My eyes began to cry but no noise came from my mouth.

'Go inside,' Alhaji said. 'Go inside!'

I ran with Grandma into the house where she pushed me in the bedroom and closed the door. Mama was sitting cross-legged on the ground. I sat next to her for a short time, against the door, our arms touching. Then she moved her arm away. I wished Ezikiel was beside me. I stood and walked to the mesh-covered window. Alhaji was outside with the crescent knife he used for cutting corn, and Youseff, who was unarmed but looked fierce, standing next to him. They were near the gate, looking left then right, left then right. I thought of Ezikiel and Boneboy. Picking snails in the forest. Grandma had gone back outside and was in her garden area chanting with her birth bag by her side.

The sky lit up with rifle fire. Bright patches of orange burst into firework shapes. I had only seen fireworks once before, when Chief Ibitoye's son was married. We were not invited but Father had taken us anyway to stand outside the gates. The sky is free, he had said.

Where was Father? When we needed him?

'Come and sit down, Blessing.' Mama's voice was hurried. She was breathless.

'Mama,' I said, and sat down beside her. My stomach-shelf dropped down. My tongue felt swollen, as though I had suffered an allergy. I could not swallow at all.

I thought again about holding Mama's hand, or putting my arm around her shoulder. My hand twitched as if it wanted to, but my brain would not allow it. I did not move, but felt Mama turn away and cross her legs towards the wall.

'Mama. I'm happy you are home from work.' My words sounded faint as though I had a scarf in front of my mouth.

'At work I'd have been on twenty-four-hour lockdown.'

I wondered what twenty-four-hour lockdown was, why we didn't have it. 'Will they come for us?' I asked. 'The guns? Those boys with guns?'

'We'll be fine,' Mama said.

'Ezikiel and Boneboy are in the forest.'

'They will be fine. Fine. The forest is not where the trouble is. Those people start fighting here then take it to Warri town, the opposite direction to the bush where Ezikiel has gone. Don't worry about your brother.'

She reached across and squeezed my hand. I looked at her face; she was biting her bottom lip, turning it white. We held hands for many seconds. Mama's hand felt soft and warm, her thumb rubbed my skin gently in the same place, over and over. I willed my hand not to sweat too much into

Mama's. I wished I had washed after dinner; my hand was sticky with meat juice. I prayed that she would not sniff her hand later and think that I was a dirty child to leave food-stuffs unwashed. If that happened Mama might never hold my hand again.

The rifle fire was louder, closer. I held Mama's hand tightly despite the possibility of meat juice. If the guns came for me, at least I would be next to Mama. Holding her hand.

'Blessing.' Mama started, and let go of my hand. 'Blessing.'

She stood up and walked towards the mesh window. For a moment I wondered if Mama was about to say, 'I love you.' I held my breath. I had never heard those words before, and wanted to hear the exact way she said them. I had not heard anyone in my family say those words to anyone else, except when Father had left. He did not say them to Mama, or to Ezikiel, or even to me. He said them on the telephone to the other woman, the one that Mama found him on top of. He said the words in whispers, his hand covering his mouth and the receiver. I still heard. Even his quiet voice was too-loud.

Mama did not say, 'I love you.' She turned away from the window and looked through me, past me. 'I hate this fucking place,' she said. And a large tear dropped onto her cheek.

The gun fire finished. We all gathered on the veranda. The air smelled smoky. We sat closer together than usual, and closer to the door. We all watched the gate, and there were long pauses between our words where Alhaji lifted his ear to the sky.

'It was those copy cats.' Alhaji held the knife in front of him like a microphone. 'Those Sibeye Boys. They are fighting for money to buy nice car, ticket to US.'

'You can't blame them,' Mama said. 'The boys.'

Alhaji looked around at her. 'Of course we can. I know these boys. These silly boys.'

'The politicians are giving them guns,' Mama said. 'They are being used.'

'The true freedom fighters would never behave like this! Never. You see?'

'Did they all have guns?' I asked.

'This country, this country,' said Grandma. 'All this warring.' She leant forwards and rubbed my leg.

'Ezikiel and Boneboy have been a long time,' I said. My voice shook. It made Grandma and Mama's eyes flick upwards to my face. 'They should have returned by now.'

Nobody spoke. Alhaji sat forwards and patted my head.

Snap returned first. He was barking and howling and yelping. It was a noise that reached deep inside my head, right to the back.

'What's happening? What is this noise?' Grandma, Alhaji, Mama and I rushed to the gate. 'Has somebody hurt that dog?'

I thought that maybe Snap had been kicked by the crazy man who lived in the village. I had seen him kicking dogs before, when I went to collect water.

I walked out of the gate, and looked down the road, covering my eyes from the sun with my hand. The air was hardly moving. The sun was so bright that even with my hand over my eyes I had to half-shut them to see.

It wasn't Snap.

Ezikiel was crumpled against Boneboy.

Ezikiel's eyes were closed, but his mouth was open. The yelps and barks and howls were coming from Ezikiel. My heart lifted into my throat. A bitter taste filled my mouth. I dropped my hand and opened my eyes widely to let in the sunlight. I did not want to see.

Ezikiel was wearing a bright red hibiscus on his shoulder.

SEVENTEEN

Government Hospital was a giant grey stone building with six lifts, but only one working. The other five had notices taped to the front which said 'Engineer called'.

'We'll wait,' said Mama.

'It is taking a long time,' I said. 'Shall we use the stairs?' It was the first time I had been allowed to visit. I had spent two days walking around the compound pressing Ezikiel's stinking Chelsea shirt to my nose.

'I said we will wait. The floor he's on is too high up.'

The lift took fifteen minutes to arrive. It was the longest fifteen minutes of my life. I tried to find the courage to disobey Mama, and run up the stairs, but my legs would not move. I watched the people come to each lift, press each button, read each sign, and tut before moving away. My stomach felt so heavy. Mama had told me that Ezikiel was getting better but I needed to see him for myself. When it did arrive the lift was full. I thought we might not make it.

'Move down, please,' said Mama. Something about her

voice made people move backwards. People always did as she asked. We pushed our way in. A woman's arm was held high above my nose; the smell of her sweat made me retch. By the time the lift door opened I had sick in my mouth.

'What's wrong with you?' asked Mama. She said the words through her teeth. 'I told you, he's fine.'

I swallowed the sick. Everyone kept telling me that Ezikiel was fine but I could not believe their words. The picture that was printed inside my head would not go away. It was Ezikiel with blood pouring from his shoulder. The blood would not stop even when Alhaji pressed down on it with the headscarf he pulled from Grandma's head, or when Grandma laid Ezikiel flat on the ground and stuck her finger straight into the bullet hole.

We walked past rows and rows of skinny men and women who had hollow faces and eyes that came away from their heads. I wanted to run to Ezikiel and see with my own eyes, and check that his face was not hollow, but I walked in time with Mama, two of my steps to one of hers.

Ezikiel's bed was squeezed between other men's beds. The men asleep either side of him looked as old as Alhaji. They wore pyjamas buttoned to the top, and had jugs of water on tiny cabinets next to their heads. As we walked towards Ezikiel, the smell of urine made my eyes fill with water.

Ezikiel was sitting up in bed with closed eyes, supported by a pillow. He looked waxy. A large wet and grey bandage covered his head and shoulder. Naked from the waist up, I noticed that his shape had changed, lost some puffiness, gained muscles. Three tiny hairs stuck out from his chest. I blushed.

'Ezikiel, my baby. Good to see you're better today. Every day there's a small improvement.' Mama's voice sounded happier than usual. It was higher and softer. She must have been so happy to see Ezikiel getting better.

Mama leant across his bed and kissed him on his cheek. So I did the same. We sat on the edge of his bed. Mama opened a book.

'Hello.' Ezikiel opened one eye and lifted one hand and waved. He was smiling. Smiling and talking and sitting up and waving.

It felt better than drinking clean water.

'I got shot.'

'I know.' My voice sounded quiet and strange. I wished Mama would move from the bed so I could sit closer to Ezikiel.

'Picking snails. I got three before I heard the guns. Big ones. With lots of slime. I was in the line of fire. First I heard shouting and then I saw boys, my age, can you believe, running around with guns. Some of them had machine guns.'

I opened my eyes widely.

'I felt the bullet go into me. Actually go inside me. Inside my skin.' He pointed to his shoulder with his chin. I looked closely at the bandage. I could not see any blood at all. There had been a lot of blood. Almost as much as a woman giving birth. I wondered which thing hurt more, giving life or having it taken.

'Did it hurt badly?'

'Oh! At first it was like fire had gone through me, and then it felt like a knife that kept stabbing me again and again in the same place.'

'Ezikiel,' said Mama. 'That's a bit much, thank you.'

I wanted to see what it looked like underneath the bandage. I tried to imagine what the scar would grow like. It was strange to think that Ezikiel's shoulder, which I knew so well, would be different.

'They saw me on the ground,' continued Ezikiel. 'They thought I was dead. I didn't move a single muscle. I couldn't move. Actually, I probably was dying, right then! This boy took a bracelet from his own arm, and put it around my wrist and said sorry.' Ezikiel flashed his arm. A thin piece of red string was tied around his wrist. It was made from plaits of cotton. 'And he had a rifle and a jar of fireflies. A whole jar flashing. At first I thought it was my eyes playing tricks but then this boy opened the jar, and caught one. I don't know why he was carrying the fireflies. He put it in my mouth. A firefly! It tasted disgusting, like *iru*. Anyway, I ate it, I swallowed the whole thing, and the boy said, "You will survive, the magic power of these fireflies will save you," and then he ran.'

'You were very lucky,' I said. 'Praise be to Allah.' I don't know why I said that, but it felt like I should thank someone.

Mama lifted her eyes from her book, gave me a sideways glance, and rolled her eyes back down.

'Lucky!' Ezikiel opened the other eye. He waved his arm. He sat up straighter. 'I am like a superhero.'

Mama snapped her book shut suddenly, and the man in the next bed woke up and cried out. 'These boys are Sibeye Boys,' said Mama. 'And they belong to a cult. You stay away from them, do you hear me? Those boys are trouble. Worshipping deities, performing black magic, *juju*. Poorly educated boys who don't understand anything of life. Those boys are dangerous, Ezikiel. Blessing is right, you were very lucky. I don't want to hear any more silly talk.' She stood up. 'I'm going to get some drinks.'

She patted Ezikiel on the knee. She even patted me on the head. Mama had said that I was right.

'I'll get you both something nice and cold. I won't be long.'

Ezikiel and I looked at Mama as she left, with the same raised eyebrows. 'She must be very happy that you are alive,' I said.

'So am I,' said Ezikiel. 'And there are not many boys my age who have survived a shooting. I'm telling you, Blessing, this bracelet must be magic.'

I looked at the string on Ezikiel's arm again. It did not look magic. I smiled anyway and got up from the bed and went to the curtain at the side. I pulled the curtain around the bed until there was no gap. Then I climbed onto the bed and curled myself around Ezikiel's body. He lay down and pushed his fingers through mine. I put my hand gently onto his shoulder.

'I am happy that you are alive,' I said. 'I am glad the bracelet is magic.' And I let my eyes cry into Ezikiel's bandage.

★

Since Ezikiel had been shot, Alhaji had not slept, and only eaten rice once, when Grandma stood over him with the spoon. His neck skin was getting looser and looser. Even though he knew that Ezikiel was getting better, and would be home soon, he seemed angrier and angrier. He walked around the compound shouting into a telephone that he had borrowed from the owner of the borehole in the village. 'Chief of Police, please, this is Alhaji Amir Sotonye Hassan Arepamone Kentabe. I need to speak urgently with the Chief of Police, about important business matters.' He paced around the house. His voice was high-pitched. 'No, I cannot wait. It is most urgent. My grandson has been shot!' Alhaji stopped pacing and walked towards the gate. 'Hello. Hello. Hello, are you there?' He shook the telephone, and pressed it to his good ear. 'HELLO.'

Later Alhaji dictated an identical letter to the Prime Minister of the United Kingdom and the President of the USA, which he had me write on airmail paper.

I did not change any of the words, even if I knew that they were wrong.

Dear Sir,
I am sorry to write in such circumstance. My only grandson, boy Ezikiel, has been the victim of shooting by gang of Area Boys. He is in hospital. Warri Government Hospital. He is very sick. I need justice to happen and your help to rectify problem of fighting between different Area Boys. The Freedom Fighters of the Izon Nation are getting a bad name from copy cat boys. Violence here is becoming worse. Please

no longer send guns, or let local soldiers bring guns back from peace-keeping in Sierra Leone, to sell to our boys. So boys like my grandson are not shot. Our government too is killing local boys. They are working with the oil companies. Please no longer allow your oil companies to fund a military regime. Please ask them not to pay the Kill and Go police to kill on their behalf. The politicians are giving the copy cat boys guns during elections. Please, no longer send guns to add to these problems. Your help is appreciated.

Alhaji Amir Sotonye Hassan Arepamone Kentabe.
Petroleum Engineer. Kentabe compound next to Village.
Past road to Kopo Village, Outside Warri. Nigeria.

I was using the outhouse when I overheard Alhaji talking to Youseff about the Mercedes. I did not dare come out; I did not want them to think I had been listening. I stood so long near the smell of the soak-away that I could no longer smell anything at all. It is amazing, I thought, what you can get used to.

'That old car is fine for a driver like Zafi, sah, but I am a driver of Mercedes cars.'

'There is nothing to be done.' Alhaji's words came out at the same time as a sigh.

'All drivers who have job with poor family drive the Peugeot, sah, but I have always been with you, sah, a good family. I am a Mercedes driver.'

'The car has to go.' Alhaji's voice was louder now and sharper.

'But the other drivers, sah. I should be moving up in my job, sah, not down. Peugeot is down, sah. And your own status, sah. You cannot go to Executive Club in the Peugeot, sah, they will laugh at us. That old car fine for blind, one-footed driver, sah, but not for man like me with seventeen children.'

I could hear the air come out of Alhaji's nose. 'You dare to talk to me in this way? You dare after all I do for you and your family? How many men would let you keep all those wives and kids? Eh? Only Alhaji! If you dare to speak to me this way again I will put you all out. You see? All. Out.'

The next time I visited Ezikiel he was playing chess by himself. He was back to his usual colour and his bandage had been removed. A tiny circle of red was all that remained of the bullet. He stood as I approached his bed, and hugged me tightly. He smelled of sweat and custard powder. I told him of Alhaji's attempts to write to the President.

I did not tell him that Alhaji had sold the Mercedes.

'Do you think he'll go and wait at the post office for a reply?' Ezikiel asked, laughing.

It was good to hear the sound of his laugh. I had not heard it in a long time.

'He has been so worried,' I said.

'There is no need. Anyway, I'm better now. I can go home next week. The doctors have told me. And return to school the week after that.'

I smiled from my toes to my head.

'They say I'm the fittest patient on the ward.'

I looked around quickly at the other patients. They were all lying flat and had hollow faces. Ezikiel's cheeks were rounder once more. He had been eating a special nut-free diet. I wondered if the hospital had fridges to keep the meat and fish fresh, so that it would not have to be fried, or whether they had vegetable oil. He did not belong there. I could not wait for him to come home.

'I'll make you something good to eat,' I said.

'Like Maggi cube soup,' said Ezikiel. 'I enjoy crunchy food.'

I laughed with him. He was normal. It was as if he had never been shot at all.

The following week, Mama and I travelled to the hospital together. It was unusual to see Mama. She had been working all the time at the Highlife Bar. She looked happy. Her face was smiling; even her eyes were smiling. I thought it was because we were taking Ezikiel home. Ezikiel was sitting on the corner of his bed when we arrived. He was wearing a shirt and trousers that belonged to a much taller and fatter person. A plastic bag was open on his lap, containing a toothbrush, comb and pot of Vaseline.

'There you are,' he said, jumping up and knocking over the bag onto the bed. 'I thought you were never coming.'

Mama smiled. She sat on the bed.

'We don't need to wait for TTOs,' said Ezikiel. 'I don't need meds any longer.'

I wondered what TTOs were and why he said meds instead of medicines. I wondered why Mama was sitting down.

'What do you mean?' asked Mama. Her eyes flicked from left to right.

I looked at her face.

'Home,' said Ezikiel, having the same thought. He sat down slowly on the bed next to her. 'I'm going home today.'

My stomach knew what was coming next. It had worked it out and was churning already.

Mama smiled. 'Not quite yet,' she said.

What was wrong? Was Ezikiel still sick? Had they left some of the bullet in his shoulder?

Mama smiled again. 'There is a slight delay. Nothing for you to worry about.'

Ezikiel picked up his plastic bag and held it tightly in his hand. 'What, Mama? Just tell me.'

'The hospital won't release you quite yet,' she said.

'But I'm fine. I'm much better. All the doctors have said it. I'm the fittest person in here. I need to get back to school. Please, Mama. I've missed too much already. I can't miss any more school. I have exams in two weeks!'

'Don't worry about the exams,' said Mama. 'Just read your books.'

'But I've missed so much school, Mama. Months! What if I don't pass my exams?' Ezikiel's face had swollen up.

'We need to pay the hospital fees,' said Mama. Her voice fell to a whisper. 'Otherwise they won't release you. And the fees are expensive. We're doing our best, Ezikiel. I have borrowed the money but I can't get it today. The friend, er, my colleague, is away for a few days.'

I felt the frown cross my forehead. *Won't release you*. Ezikiel was not coming home, after all. Then why was Mama smiling?

'You just concentrate on resting and getting better.'

'But I am better, Mama.'

'We just need a little bit more money when my colleague returns next week. The treatment's been very expensive.' Mama laughed. 'But worth every penny. Thank God you're OK! Anyway, I think we are going to be fine. Just fine.'

The hospital would not discharge Ezikiel until his bill was paid in full. Everyone helped to raise the money. I had spent all day by the road selling corn. Grandma, as well as attending births, had started selling monkey-tail, the *kai-kai* laced with hashish from the creeks. Mama worked every hour, day and night. Alhaji used some of the Mercedes money to buy equipment, such as copper wire and net, for his snail farm. 'You have to speculate to accumulate,' he said. 'Did you know that a snail will not pass through copper?'

Celestine walked around the hospital looking for people with extra hollow faces. She had business cards printed out which she left by the bedsides:

Professional Town Mourning Services by Celestine.
The voice that reaches God's ears.
Contact Alhaji Kentabe for advance bookings.
Executive Club. 222-3462

The next week when I visited Ezikiel he was standing behind a group of doctors and he was wearing a white coat. He had a serious look on his face but his mouth was smiling widely. He came over to me and sat down on his bed. He did not remove his white coat. I laughed. Ezikiel looked like a grown-up man. I imagined what it would be like to be Ezikiel's patient.

'The doctor in charge has let me follow ward rounds,' he said. 'He knows that I want to study medicine and he's been helping me.' Ezikiel's face was round and well. His eyes were shining like Celestine's English fifty pence coin.

'I'm coming home tomorrow,' he continued. 'They've got the hospital fees! Mama's said she got the rest of the money from her friend. I'm going to miss hospital. I've learnt so much from the doctors!'

'What friend? I did not know Mama had any friends. I thought she was borrowing from a colleague. When are the exams?'

'Next week! I'll be back just in time. But I'm not worried any more. I'm ahead! How many boys in my class have been on real ward rounds learning from real doctors? Imagine, Blessing, when I am a real doctor and we can talk together. You will be able to ask me if you get stuck with your birth attending. And I bet that Father will hear, even from Lagos, when I'm studying medicine.'

I turned my head to Ezikiel. It was the first time he had mentioned anything about Father. The words had come out of his mouth without him meaning them to. He was clenching his teeth to prevent any more. I put my hand onto his arm. 'Tell me,' I said. 'About the different patients.'

Ezikiel smiled at me for a long time before speaking. 'That one,' he said, pointing across the ward, 'in bed five. Bowel cancer, advanced stages. He's had surgery to remove …'

EIGHTEEN

It was so harmattan sandy the next day when Ezikiel was finally released from hospital that his face was the colour of old bone. He held a copy of the payment slip and hugged Alhaji. 'I'll pay you back.'

None of us could stop smiling. Ezikiel was home. We had all been waiting for him to come home since the day he had been shot. Even the house had been waiting. The gap in the air around the compound was filling up again, the shadows around the house becoming smaller until the light filled every corner. I had never seen such a bright day.

Mama smiled at Ezikiel with her mouth and her cheeks and her eyes. She looked at Alhaji quickly before moving her eyes back to Ezikiel's.

Ezikiel began to cry. Even his tears looked happy; they were light blue and shiny. He took deep, even breaths with no wheeze at all. Mama looked happier than ever. We all did.

Alhaji took the receipt and folded it before putting it into his pocket and briefly looking at the empty Mercedes space. 'No need for repayment,' he said. 'When you are a rich doctor then you can pay me back, eh?' He laughed. Then he sat Ezikiel down on the rocking chair and removed his shirt. He looked closely at the tiny mark, which was all that was left of the bullet. Alhaji rubbed Marmite all over Ezikiel's shoulder. He pulled Ezikiel towards him, and did not let go until nightfall.

Grandma was making *jollof* rice and fried chicken with vegetable oil, which was kept in a large pot held together by an elastic band. Mama had borrowed it from the Highlife Bar.

'At last,' said Celestine, when she saw the pot. 'Could she not steal something sooner?' She was wearing one of her own dresses, which she had made from Lycra especially for Ezikiel's homecoming. A large piece of neon pink material was stretched tightly, her breasts squashed outwards and under her armpits. She appeared flat-chested.

Grandma took the pot of oil from Celestine. 'She would have lost her bloody job, stupid woman. Of course she could not take something while she was on trial!' She turned away, before disappearing into the house and banging pots around. Celestine tried to shrug at me but the Lycra prevented shoulder movement; it looked like she was twitching. She walked off towards the Boys' Quarters.

Grandma came back after a few minutes and sat down on my other side. We all sat together on the veranda for dinner, in a perfect circle. Ezikiel's space was no longer empty; everything felt exactly right.

I had not eaten meat for a long time. It was difficult to

chew as my face muscles felt too soft, my cheeks numb. Grandma sucked her bones dry and then piled them on her plate. She threw them to Snap, who ran around in circles excitedly. Boneboy kept his bones and put them into his pocket for later. He kept looking at Ezikiel so often Snap began to whine until Boneboy gave him some attention.

Ezikiel ate his food slowly at first then he increased in speed until his spoon did not pause. It moved continuously from his mouth to his plate to his mouth to his plate. He drank four bottles of Fanta and burped loudly, making Celestine nod and laugh.

'The boy is good,' she said.

'I'm not a boy,' said Ezikiel. He lowered his voice into a growl. 'In the hospital I was treated like a man. I was on the men's ward, and I attended the ward rounds. And I survived a shooting!'

We all laughed except Alhaji. 'The boy is right,' he said. He silenced us all with his hand. 'This Ezikiel, our future doctor. He is growing into a fine man.'

'I learnt so much. My time in hospital has given me a head start.' He looked at Mama and smiled. 'Some real doctors, real-life doctors have told me so. I saw all kinds of diseases, first hand. I even got to make a diagnosis!'

We all leant forwards. Ezikiel's voice was louder and surer. The words sounded confident.

'There was cancer – all kinds. But especially prostate. It is an affliction that only men suffer. Usually men of a certain age. The symptoms include increased need for urination, increased urgency and sometimes, in the latter stages, weight loss.'

Alhaji sat back in his chair and crossed his legs tightly.

'There were road traffic accidents. Traumas. Chest drains, x-rays, echocardiograms. I watched all the tests.'

The word echocardiogram sounded good coming from Ezikiel's mouth. As though the word itself would make a patient feel better. I had no idea what it meant but I let it repeat in my head, *echocardiogram*.

'Malaria was everywhere. The doctors don't even test for it. If you arrive in the emergency room with a fever, you're given quinine immediately. Front-line treatment. They told me the statistics. The morbidity and mortality figures. I won't scare you all ...' Ezikiel leant forwards. In the lamplight he looked even younger. His face and words did not match together. 'But we should all be sleeping under nets.'

We stayed together until the moon was in the centre of the sky, listening to Ezikiel's stories about leg ulcers, and impacted faeces, and the best way to remove a gangrenous limb. The air smelled of kerosene and Marmite. Fireflies danced between us.

Mama returned to work in the middle of the night. 'Night shift,' she said, and walked away suddenly. She smiled as she climbed into the old Peugeot where Youseff was waiting with his hands on the steering wheel. As the car pulled away, I watched Grandma's face. She was spitting into the air towards the gate. I had no idea why she was doing it, but I did not have time to ask her. Ezikiel was pulling me into the house. We sat down on the mattress in Mama's room, an oil lamp next to us.

'Tell me, Blessing. About the births. Tell me all about what you've seen.'

Since trying on the white coat Ezikiel had changed. He no longer ignored me when I talked about birth attending, or turned his head away when I left the compound with Grandma and the birth bag.

I smiled. At last! Ezikiel was ready to hear my stories. His ears were open wide.

I talked of the way it felt to be the first person to hold a new baby. The softness of their heads. I told him of the women giving birth who lived between worlds, not quite alive, not quite dead. I talked about Grandma. How everyone bowed as she went to the villages, men and women, and how she refused payment from the poorest families. The words spilled out and out and out until we were so tired from all the talking and listening we could only lie down and begin to fall asleep, our hands pressed together again.

'I have missed you so much,' I said.

NINETEEN

'I have a present for you. Not me, I mean, well, actually, my *friend* has bought you both a gift.'

The way Mama said the word 'friend' made me stop eating and put down my spoon. Was she talking about the colleague who had lent her Ezikiel's hospital fees? We were sitting at the inside table, as the harmattan wind was making our skin turn dry and white and chapped despite Vaseline. Ezikiel carried on, as if he had not heard the tone in her voice, or did not think it was odd that Mama, who said she did not like having friends, had suddenly found one. When he told me that she had a friend I had thought he was mistaken. But Grandma, sitting next to Ezikiel, had not only put down her spoon, but had pushed her plate away. The food was her favourite *gbe*, the larvae of the raffia palm beetle pickled in palm oil; it was only half-eaten.

'He's coming later today to visit.'

Ezikiel smiled. He had enjoyed being back at school and sitting his school exams. I told him he was a lunatic.

'He?' said Grandma. 'You have found an Ijaw man?'

Without waiting for Mama to answer, Grandma stood up and hugged Mama's back. Ezikiel dropped his spoon into his bowl. The bowl rattled on the table. Mama did not move. She still had a spoon in her hand.

'Where did you meet him? At work? Is he bar staff with you?' Grandma was talking quickly.

'What is happening?' Celestine entered the kitchen wearing what she had told me was called a cocktail dress.

'Mama has a manfriend.'

'Oh?' Celestine shrugged.

'Ijaw.'

'Oh.' She shrugged again.

'Actually,' Mama said, finally putting down her spoon, 'he's not Ijaw. Not that it matters, but well, he's just not, that's all. I've all kinds of friends. I wouldn't stop being friends with anyone just because they don't happen to be Ijaw. We happen to have many things in common and it's not easy to find friends, at least not around here. And anyway, he's just a friend. Like I said.'

I moved closer to Ezikiel, who was sliding his bowl slowly away without looking up. I held onto his other hand underneath the table. His fingers were clammy. He did not push me away, but he did not squeeze my hand either. It felt like I was holding the hand of a sleeping person.

Grandma did not speak for many seconds. She lowered her head. She was breathing slowly; her nostrils were flaring. I wanted to run but I did not dare move. I thought of hiding underneath the table, but she might have picked the table up and thrown it across the room. Eventually she opened her mouth. She spoke softly but her voice sounded hard. It came out in bursts. 'Do you not learn, silly girl?'

It took me some time to work out that Grandma was talking to Mama.

'Well. It's nothing,' Mama said. 'Just a friend. I told you. Just a friend. We're just friends. Nothing more. Can't women have friends?' She paused and took a deep breath as though she was about to dive under water. 'It doesn't matter that he happens to be white.'

There was silence around the table.

Ezikiel squeezed my hand. Even though he was holding me tightly, I could tell that my hand was shaking. It had turned clammy, too.

I looked up to try and meet Mama's eyes, and check if I had heard correctly or if Mama was pretending, turning crazy. Ezikiel dropped my hand and folded his arms.

Eventually Celestine spoke. 'A Westerner? You are the luckiest. We will be rich!'

She started dancing around the kitchen. I turned my head away from Mama's face and watched Celestine closely. I did not know what else to do. Celestine moved her bottom from side to side and clapped her hands. Her head circled and her hips swayed. '*Oyibo, oyibo, oyibo,*' she sang, '*Oyibo* pepper, *oyibo* pepper. If you lick you go yellow more more.'

I suddenly realised why Mama had money. Could Celestine be right? Was Mama's rich friend sponsoring us? Is that why we could suddenly afford school fees for Ezikiel, and meat and fish and electricity? Why would Mama's friend give her so much money?

Celestine turned away from us. The back of her Lycra dress stretched, becoming see-through. Celestine bent forwards and stuck out her bottom. Suddenly the Lycra came apart and split open. We could see her camouflage-print underwear.

Later that day, Ezikiel went to school to collect his report card. I waited for him to arrive back. I had all my fingers crossed and my arms crossed and my legs crossed when the car pulled into the gate. But Ezikiel did not laugh. He looked straight through me as though I was not standing there. And when the car stopped travelling, Ezikiel slipped out, and ran towards the outhouse without even shutting the car door. I looked at Youseff, but he just shrugged. I felt my heart run across my chest. Please, please, let Ezikiel have good exam grades, I thought. I waited near the outhouse for a long time, but Ezikiel did not come out.

TWENTY

Mama paced the veranda for an hour while she waited for Dan, and turned white from the breeze. Still, she was not as white as Dan. I had never seen such pale skin.

Of course I had seen white men before, in Lagos, wearing business suits, rushing from their office to their driver, or from their driver to their office, but Dan was surely the whitest man in the world. I could see through the skin on his arms. His veins were the colour of the hottest part of a flame. They branched down his hands and forearms, which were poking out from his short-sleeved shirt. The shirt, its top buttons open, was stuck to him with sweat despite the cool of the breeze. I noticed he had no hair on his chest. Even Ezikiel had three chest hairs. I wanted Ezikiel with me, standing next to me. But he would not come out of his bedroom. He had put a chair against the door to prevent me from getting in.

Dan had red hair, the colour of a cockroach wing. His lips were pale. At first it looked as if he did not have any. He smiled. His teeth were see-through at the edges. Had he brushed them too hard?

'How are you?' He stepped forward and stretched out his hand towards me. In his other hand he was carrying a red and white basketball and a striped hula-hoop.

I stumbled backwards and nearly fell off the veranda. He laughed. His laugh was very quiet and tinkly. It sounded like he was pretending to laugh at a joke that was not funny. He handed me the hula-hoop. His eyes moved up and down and around me.

'Thank you, sir.' I forced a smile at Dan and held the hula-hoop tightly. I was wearing a clean wrapper and a T-shirt that said 'Nike' on the front. They were my very best clothes but they were still old enough that tiny holes had appeared from too much washing. I did not own a bra, and there was a tiny hole on the front of my chest. It was only the size of a Lagos mosquito, but it was all I could think about. I crossed my arms, hugged myself.

'Ooh ooh, *oyibo*, *oyibo*.' Celestine ran towards the veranda. She had changed from her dress into a Lycra top and wrapper. Her high-heeled shoe stuck in the ground. She had to stop running towards Dan, take her foot out of the shoe, and bend down to pull it free. While she was pulling her shoe, Dan looked at Mama and raised his eyebrows high. She smirked. I did not like the look that passed between them.

'Hi. You must be Celestine.' Dan reached out as she ran towards him.

Celestine threw his hand aside and knelt at his feet, her head bowed so low she appeared to be kissing his sandals.

'Get up, get up. Please, please,' said Dan.

He offered her his hand. Celestine laughed as she stood. Soon they were both laughing. I'm not sure why they were laughing, but at that moment Grandma walked past. She said nothing but sucked her teeth. It sounded like a bird calling. Then she walked into the house without greeting Dan at all.

'Dan,' Mama said.

Her voice was louder than usual. It made Dan stop laughing. He walked to Mama's side and coughed, with laughter occasionally still bursting out of him as though he was an engine running out of petrol.

It was late afternoon when Alhaji returned from the Executive Club. He climbed out of the Peugeot to find Dan sitting on his veranda chair, reading an old copy of *The Pointer*. When Dan lowered the newspaper and revealed his white face, Alhaji's jaw dropped open.

'Welcome, welcome,' he said, after closing his jaw.

As he walked towards the veranda, Alhaji made no other sign that he was not expecting to see a white man sitting on his chair.

'Hello. Pleased to meet you, sir,' Dan said, shaking Alhaji's hand instead of kneeling or even saying '*Doh*'.

Alhaji kept his eyes on Dan the whole time, but I could feel the questions leaking from his skin:

Who is this *oyibo*?

Has he been sent from the Western Oil Company to interview me?

Do they have a crisis in quality management that requires my urgent attention?

Do they want my help in a diplomatic matter involving the fighting between Ijaw and Itsekiri and Urhobo tribes?

Has the President sent this man to deliver his personal reply to my letter (which I wrote some weeks ago)?

I giggled, causing the eye contact between Alhaji and Dan to disappear. Mama stepped forward and opened her mouth to speak just as Celestine said, 'This na Timi boyfriend. Dam.'

Mama's boyfriend? Celestine had it wrong; Mama had said that they were friends.

'Actually it's Dan,' said Dan, but nobody was listening.

Alhaji took the Marmite out from his medicine bag and unscrewed the lid. He sat in the chair, and applied some to both of his temples, rubbing slowly, closing his eyes. It was not a good sign.

We all sat down. Celestine served tea from a chipped china tea set that I had not seen before. My cup and saucer clanked together as though they did not fit.

I could feel Dan watching me. I moved my arm to cover the tiny hole in my T-shirt.

'How's school, Blessing?'

I looked up at Mama. She nodded very slightly, and flicked her eyes towards Dan.

'I do not attend school, sir.'

Mama sat back into her chair.

Dan looked at Mama with a thick line between his eyebrows.

I saw the shadow of Grandma in the doorway and felt brave at once. 'I am training to be a birth attendant,' I said.

Mama groaned and put her hand over her eyes, and Celestine sucked her teeth. The shadow of Grandma became taller and bigger, and filled the doorway.

Dan did not say much. Every few minutes he took two bottles from his bag: sun cream and mosquito repellent. He sprayed himself all over, and then offered the bottles to us. We shook our heads. Then he put the bottles back in his bag. He listened to Celestine's stories about European Fashions and Professional Town Mourning, and he listened to Alhaji, who had stopped rubbing his temples, and started hushing Celestine to bring the conversation back to Petroleum Engineering. Nobody mentioned politics. Or religion. Or Grandma's shadow in the doorway. Or Ezikiel hiding in the bedroom.

'What are your interests, Dam?' Alhaji eventually asked. He had put the Marmite away in his cosmetic case and taken out a pot of tablets. He shook the pot.

Dan jumped slightly and looked at the gate.

'What team do you support?' Alhaji's voice sounded squeaky and high as if it was being pushed out too quickly.

Dan looked at the sky and I thought religion would come up, after all.

'Oh, I'm not a football fan,' he said.

Alhaji looked puzzled. 'You prefer NBA?'

'No, no,' Dan laughed. 'Of course I'm interested in culture and art, music, that kind of thing,' he flashed a look at Mama, 'but my main interest is ornithology,' he said. 'Birds.'

I looked at the ground, concentrating on the strap of my sandal.

'Dan's a keen birdwatcher.' Mama laughed, throwing her head back. I felt my cheeks get hot.

Alhaji scratched his chin. 'What do you watch them for?' he asked.

Dan's smile increased until his see-through teeth were on view and his lips almost disappeared. 'I've always been fascinated with birds, since I had my first binoculars when I was four. You know, I watch their habits, record the unusual species. It's really a fascinating hobby. Really fascinating. Really. But of course, I don't get much time at home. Never enough hours in the day.' He laughed and looked around at us all. We had our mouths wide open. Except Mama. She was smiling and nodding, smiling and nodding.

'It sounds funny when you try and explain it,' said Dan, still laughing.

Nobody spoke. Alhaji had stopped rubbing his chin. A large frown between his eyebrows was splitting his head into two. Eventually a bird flew over us.

Alhaji jumped up. 'Look! There's one!' He pointed to the sky, stabbing the air with his outstretched finger. 'Do you need a pen and paper to record it?'

Dan smiled. 'Oh no. Thanks.'

A few seconds later and another bird flew over us. Then another. 'There! Two birds! You see? Get a pen for him. Quick!'

'Please, no, no, thank you. No, honestly. No, no, thank you, really,' said Dan. 'I only record the unusual species.'

Alhaji sat down, and folded his arms. 'Well, why say something when you mean something else? You said you like to record the birds. Most species here are unusual. No grey birds in our country! You are in Nigeria. You see?' Alhaji said Nigeria in three parts: Ni-ge-ria.

Celestine refilled our cups, and we all slurped our tea. All except Dan, who was a silent tea-drinker. But I did notice his cup and saucer were also clanking together.

Celestine tutted loudly then smiled at Dan, before walking away slowly, with such hip movement that she reminded me of a riverboat during a storm. Grandma walked past with a bucket and went back to her garden area where she poured water on her herbs and cacti. She started talking, loudly. 'A wise fish knows that a beautiful worm that looks so easy to swallow has a sharp hook attached to it.' Then she whistled. I had never heard Grandma whistle before.

Snap came running towards us, and saw Dan. He growled for the first time in his life and ran at Dan's leg, which was uncovered by his very short trousers.

Snap opened his mouth and bit.

Dan was collected by a Mercedes containing a driver and a security guard who was carrying a rifle. The guard was wearing mirrored sunglasses, making it impossible to know where his eyes were looking, or even if he was asleep behind them. I wondered if the glasses were given in school when he learned how to be a security guard. Did such a school exist? Or was he given a rifle and a pair of sunglasses by the Western Oil

Company? Why did Ezikiel not come out of his room? Why did Mama lie and say that Dan was only a friend?

These questions filled my head as Dan was saying goodbye to Mama. They were kissing underneath the almond trees. Dan did not notice the black kite hovering high above them. He did not hear Grandma muttering. 'Big trouble,' she said repeatedly. '*Wahala, wahala, wahala.*'

Ezikiel came out much later. 'I don't want to hear about the *oyibo*,' he said. He had been acting strangely since he arrived back from school, but he would still not tell me what had happened. Maybe he got a B instead of the A he was hoping for? He cannot have failed. That was not possible. But as I watched him closely I felt bubbles in my stomach. He did not look at Mama. He did not even look at me. I thought he might go to Alhaji's room and read, but he remained nearby, playing with the basketball, weaving it in and out of his long legs as he listened while Celestine talked about Dan. Even the ball sounded sad as it bounced slowly, with a dull thump on the ground. I kept my hula-hoop on my lap. I did not want to upset Grandma further, but I could not wait to put it around my middle.

Snap was lying pining and wailing under the veranda. Boneboy was stroking him and singing to him. Alhaji had had to kick Snap to get him off Dan's leg. Snap was not a dog used to being kicked. His ears had flattened and he had cried a new baby cry.

'He bit him hard,' Celestine said.

We all shook our heads. 'Poor man,' we muttered. 'Terrible thing to happen.'

Grandma leant forwards. 'I bet he thought it was a bone.'

'What?' asked Alhaji.

'Well. That *oyibo*'s leg,' continued Grandma. 'All white and thin. I bet poor Snap thought he was lucky to find such a bone.'

A few seconds passed while we looked at one another. Celestine let out a laugh. Then Grandma. Then Alhaji. Then me. The laughter built up so much that tears were running down our faces. We laughed so hard we had to hold our bellies. We could not stop. Then Ezikiel looked at Mama and said, 'I wish Snap had bitten him harder, and broken his leg.'

Everyone fell silent.

I picked up the broom and pretended to concentrate on sweeping the floor. My ears were wide open.

'This white friend. This white man. This *oil worker*.' He spat the words out of his mouth as if they tasted disgusting. He looked straight at Mama, and raised his body high, puffed his skinny chest out. 'You say he's a friend?'

'That's right. I told you. He's a friend. You should really have come out to greet him. It was a bit disrespectful, Ezikiel.'

'You know the reason he is your friend?'

'Ezikiel, I don't have time for this. I'm tired. Anyway what are you talking about?'

'This white man. This *friend*.' Ezikiel paused. I opened my mouth to speak, to say something before Ezikiel said something worse. Maybe he really had failed his exams? He was going to say something bad. I needed to stop him. But the words got stuck, and did not come out. Ezikiel was about to say something worse, and I could not speak to stop him.

'I don't want money from your *friend*. I don't want school fees from him. I refuse to go to school with his money! He's after one thing,' Ezikiel said. 'One Thing Only. You are prostituting yourself!'

The bottom of my stomach sank. I did not even pretend to sweep. I was still but the broom was shaking. Maybe I misheard. Surely, Ezikiel would never speak to Mama in that way. Alhaji's mouth dropped open. Celestine screamed. Grandma said nothing but raised one eyebrow and spat into the air, quietly.

Mama moved quickly; she slapped Ezikiel across the cheek. The words were suddenly out of my mouth. 'Stop,' I said. 'Please stop, please!' But my voice was lost to the sound of the slap, which took many seconds to leave my ears. Ezikiel turned his back towards Mama. He walked at first but his feet became quicker and quicker and quicker until he was running. We could hear him crying as he ran towards the river. Mama gave me a look so fierce the broom jumped from my hands and fell to the ground.

It was evening when the electricity suddenly returned. We jumped up into the air. I ran after Ezikiel into Alhaji's bedroom. I unhooked the plug for the fan, pushed the plug into the wall, and stood right in front of it, letting the cool air cover my face and neck. The radio flashed to life with the electric: 12:00, 12:00, 12:00. It reminded me of the sign above the doorway of the Evangelical Church of the Christ Almighty on the road towards Warri. Except Alhaji's clock radio flashed 12.00, and the sign above the doorway of the Evangelical Church of the Christ Almighty flashed words such as, 'Redeem your soul before it is too late', or, 'Wash your sins away this Sunday', or, 'Only the righteous will be saved'. We usually found JFM station and listened to music, dancing around Alhaji's room, but that day, Ezikiel turned the dial to a talk station. I sat down next to him on the mattress. His face was swollen and his eyes were red. What had happened to him?

'Is it your exam results?' I asked. 'Did you get lower grades?'

Ezikiel looked at me through his red eyes. He took his report card from his pocket and passed it to me. I held it in my hands for many seconds before turning it over.

Fail! Fail! Ezikiel had never failed exams!

'The Sibeye Boys are looking for new youth members. We are not a terrorist group. I repeat we are not a terrorist group.'

Ezikiel picked up the radio and looked at it. The sound was not clear. He turned the dial slightly to the left, and there was no sound. He turned it to the right, slowly.

I looked again at the report in my hands. I had to read the word 'fail' over and over but still it did not look real.

'Is there no truth, sir, that the group is involved with the illegal arms trade, bunkering oil, and even the abduction of hostages?'

'There is no truth whatsoever that our group is involved with these activities. But we do have sympathies for such groups. We believe that our oil riches belong to our people.'

The static returned. Ezikiel turned the dial further to the right, and then tried holding the radio in the air above his head.

'… criminals are the politicians, with their billions of dollar bank accounts. The government task forces and the oil company security forces have wiped out whole Delta villages. The Sibeye Boys stand for the Ijaw people. We will fight for the people and take back what is rightfully ours—'

The electric stopped working before we could hear the rest of the argument. But even though the radio was no longer switched on, Ezikiel did not move. I waved my arm in front of his face, but got no reaction.

'Bloody NEPA plc,' he said.

'Never ever power always please light candle,' I sang. But Ezikiel did not laugh. He did not move at all.

'Ezikiel,' I said. He did not move. He just stared straight ahead as though he was still listening.

'I'm so sorry,' I said. 'It must have been all the time in hospital. All the time off.'

Ezikiel leant forwards. 'I don't care about school,' he said. 'I won't take money from that *oyibo* for school fees. And I don't care about being a doctor.'

I let my mouth drop open. Why was Ezikiel lying?

I looked again at the card. Something turned in my head. Underneath the word fail were even worse words:

'Advised to Leave School.'

I put my hand to my mouth. Advised to leave school! That was the real reason that Ezikiel had to leave! I had only ever known one boy to be advised to leave and he had something wrong with him. It cannot be the right card. I checked it again. Advised to Leave School!

Mama was going to kill Ezikiel.

Ezikiel snatched the card from my hands and pushed it back into his pocket. 'I don't care,' he said. 'I don't even care.'

'I do not understand! How can they do this? You are such a good pupil!'

'I'm not surprised,' said Ezikiel. 'Think how long I've left an empty seat in the classroom. All that time off.'

'But that is not your fault. Not your fault.'

'Yes, but not doing the work they set is my fault. Failing my exams is my fault. And anyway, I don't even care.'

I looked at Ezikiel for a long time.

I imagined a white coat lift from his back and fly off towards the moon.

'Blessing, Blessing.' Ezikiel called me from the other side of the gate. Why did he not come into the compound? I walked over from where I had been cooking on the fire. The compound was empty. Why was Ezikiel hiding outside? I wondered if he was avoiding Dan. I wondered if he was avoiding Mama, who he still had not told about his report card.

'What are you doing out here?'

'Come,' said Ezikiel, holding out his hand. In his other hand he held something wrapped in a piece of material.

My heart began to race. 'What is that? What's going on?'

'Come,' he whispered. 'Shh.'

Did he have a present for me? Where did he get the money for a present? Fear fell into my stomach. Ezikiel was wild-eyed, all limbs, clumsy and twitchy. He pulled me away from the compound and towards the river. By the time we got there sweat was dripping down the back of my knees and sand flies were biting at my arms. 'Where are we going?'

Ezikiel stopped at the riverbank. He was out of breath. He bent forwards and rested his elbows on his knees. His spine curled through his skin and T-shirt like a chain. The river was dark and shiny with a layer of oil. The trees had lost their reflections. I could see the men trapping fish further along the river, through the mangroves' thick claws. 'Ezikiel,' I said, 'will you tell me what is going on?'

Ezikiel's breathing was normal again. From his hand he put the material-covered object on the ground and unwrapped it. I squatted next to him. As the material opened, something bright flashed from inside. Fireflies.

The fireflies flashed even though it was daylight. There must have been twenty in the jar. 'I caught them all,' said Ezikiel. I picked up the jar and looked at them closely. They seemed to flash in unison. Between flashes they looked like regular bugs, but flashing, they were beautiful. They glowed like Celestine's clothes. The air around them became slightly green.

Ezikiel stood. 'I have brought you here to be my witness.'

'How did you catch them?' I asked, looking into the jar. 'What are you talking about?'

From his trouser pocket he took his asthma inhaler and adrenaline injection.

'Do you need them?' I asked. 'I don't hear a wheeze.'

Ezikiel laughed. 'I no longer need them,' he said. 'I no longer need any medicine at all.'

He turned and faced the river.

'What do you mean?' I asked, but I knew. Even before he raised his arm. Even before he pulled it backwards. Even before the inhaler and injection went flying through the air, and landed on top of the oily water.

The injection sank immediately. The inhaler bobbed for a few seconds. I thought about getting in to get it. I was scared of the oily water. The river was deep and I couldn't swim. There were crocodiles. But Mama would surely kill Ezikiel for that foolishness. I watched as the inhaler floated downstream, a pale blue piece of plastic that had saved Ezikiel's life many times. We watched it disappear.

'Oh, you are going to be in so much trouble.'

'I don't need them. I told you. I'm invincible.'

'Ezikiel, Mama is going to kill you! Are you crazy? She will kill both of us! She has not even seen your report and now this? Oh, we are in so much trouble.'

'Mama cannot kill me. Even bullets cannot kill me.'

He bent down to pick up the firefly jar. From the material he showed me a photograph. A boy the same age and height as Ezikiel was leant against a Mercedes. He was holding a rifle. His eyes were wild; he was smiling and held the rifle in such a way to make me think it had just shot someone. My breath was coming fast.

'Who is it?' I asked. 'What is that?'

'This,' said Ezikiel, waving the picture in front of my eyes, 'is our President's son. It is time for young men like me. It is our time.'

I could barely hear Ezikiel's words. I kept glancing at the area of water where the medicine had disappeared. Ezikiel had turned the firefly-lid slowly, putting his fingers at the top of the inside, until a firefly was near to him. Then he suddenly grasped, and took his hand out before screwing the lid tightly back on.

'What are you doing?'

'I am protected from harm,' he said. He waved his red string bracelet at me. 'My asthma is cured.'

I looked at Ezikiel carefully, but I did not recognise him at all.

Ezikiel put the firefly in his mouth and swallowed.

The firefly flashed in his throat.

TWENTY-ONE

The moon was falling when Grandma woke me. Next to me the bed was empty, and, as I climbed out, I could not help looking at the space. Mama had not been home for days. She had not seen Ezikiel since they argued. She had no idea that he was walking around without his inhaler or his injection and with a jar full of fireflies and a picture of a boy holding a rifle. She had no idea that he had failed his exams and had been 'Advised to Leave'. She did not know that Grandma intended to continue my training, when she had banned me from leaving the compound.

'Don't mind her,' said Grandma. 'It's nothing.'

My stomach felt full of something that did not belong there. Sickness rose to my throat. 'Is it safe, Grandma? For me to come with you? Does Mama know I'm going out?'

'It is safe,' she said. 'Anyway, Mama is not here. So we can start your training again. It is important not to miss too much.' We walked to the car and I waited for Grandma to say something else. But she was silent. Her head turned away. For the first time, I noticed a patch of grey hair at the top of her neck. Worries ran across my head with tiny feet. What would Mama say when she knew I had been out of the compound? Was the fighting really finished? Was it safe? But I wanted to be Grandma's apprentice once more. I did not tell Grandma the worries.

As we travelled the road became bumpier. I could not stop thinking. Ezikiel did not have his inhaler. What would happen if he had an asthma attack? I needed to tell Mama but she had been at work all the time. When I told Grandma she said that since Ezikiel had had an allergy, Alhaji kept spare inhalers and injections, and I should not worry, but I could not help it. Ezikiel needed his medicine. And he needed Mama.

The villages at the roadside relaxed into morning; fires were lit, kerosene lamps glowed in doorways, children pushing tyres, running alongside the car. The light changed from dull grey to bright yellow. I had to blink repeatedly in order to see. By the time my vision had returned to normal, I could see the policemen at the roadside. Youseff slowed the car.

'Stop! Stop!' The rifles we were used to seeing on the backs of men were in their arms. My heart slowed with the car. 'Papers.' A policeman looked in the window at me sitting next to Grandma. Even though the bright daylight had arrived, he shone a torch onto my face. I half-closed my eyes. 'Papers,' he repeated. Youseff handed his papers out of the window.

Grandma opened her bag. She took out some naira and passed it to the policeman. Her eyes faced the floor.

The policeman did not stop the torchlight shining on my face. I could not see properly to know if he was looking at the money. 'I need a little more than this,' he said in English. 'For my troubles.'

The air became thicker. It was difficult to breathe normally. I wondered what Mama would say when she found out we had disobeyed her and gone birth attending. Or when she found out that Ezikiel had thrown his medication into the river.

'Oga sir! Wey de money? We no get money! We be village people.' Grandma spoke but did not move her eyes. I had never heard her speak pidgin English.

The policeman laughed and spoke back to Grandma in Izon. 'There are other ways of payment. Plenty of other ways. Plenty, plenty, plenty.'

The torchlight moved slowly away from my face. I kept my eyes facing forward. I could barely stop the sick from coming up into my throat. The light moved. It moved so slowly that I could not be sure until one part of my body shone, and another part was left in darkness.

Areas of my throat lit up. My mouth filled with spit that I did not dare swallow. The light rested on my breasts. I breathed out, and held my breath away from me. My chest flattened even further into a younger child's chest. The torch moved down my chest and over my belly. It finally rested on my lap. Youseff did not turn his head at all. He looked straight out at the empty road ahead. The policeman grinned. His front teeth were sharp, like tiny knives. He flicked the torch on and off and on and off again, and laughed. My skin burned. It felt as though I was being touched. Surely it was impossible to feel a beam of light on my skin. But I could feel it, heavy, pressing my skin, my body. I could not move. I wanted to cry, and feel Grandma's hands on my face, wiping the tears away, but Grandma was shaking. Everything is different, I thought. It is not safe. Mama had been right.

'Wait.' Grandma's voice rushed out, sounding like a cough. 'Wait,' she repeated. 'Please, sir.' She opened her bag wide, and took out more money. She passed it to the policeman. He pushed his head through the window and licked his lips, running his tongue over his top lip then the bottom. He held his hands in the air. Then he pulled his head out of the car. We watched him walk away.

The village was empty except for half-burnt huts with charred doorways. My stomach moved forwards inside me. A large pile of animals lay dead and rotting next to the road. They had been chopped, and piled in a way that reminded me of a book I had read, where you could put a chicken's head on a goat, and a sheep's legs on a pig, and so on. I had never seen so many dead things. It made me feel sadness all the way down to my feet. The air smelled of condensed milk that had been left in the sun. A pipeline fire blazed in the distance, causing tiny particles of black ash to blanket the ground. Some of the ash found its way into my sandals, and melted against my sad feet. I covered my mouth with my hand. I had never seen a village that looked burnt and dead, but still all I could think of was the policeman's creeping torchlight, what might have happened to me, if Grandma had not paid him money. Grandma noticed my thoughts. 'They were trying to scare, that is all.'

Screaming exploded from a hut. An elderly woman was sitting outside on the ground, rocking and wailing. The husband hovered by the doorway. In one of his hands he held a clear plastic bottle and I could tell from the colour of his eyes and the smell of his breath that the bottle held palm wine. Father had a bottle just like it.

'Come on.' Grandma pushed me into the hut.

Inside, the girl was on her knees, leaning over an upside-down box. The room was so hot it felt cold; everything slowed down again, including my heartbeat.

As I opened the birth bag I watched the girl, who was barely older than me. She was tiny, all over, except her belly, which looked as though it contained a large watermelon. She tried to place her head onto the floor but her belly and the pain were preventing her from moving her head low.

Grandma moved behind her. She opened the girl's legs and kneeled down to see what was between them. She already had the knife in her hand.

'Help me.'

We rolled the girl onto her side. She allowed herself to be turned, and although her body was stiff, she did not cry out.

The husband, who had stained brown teeth and moon-yellow eyes, came into the room, shouting. 'Carry her go church!' His words were slurred and bubbly. 'Na the devil wey don do am!' He gestured to his young wife with one hand, but his other hand scratched his genital area. 'We no need you people here. You be the Kentabe. I know who you be! Na Muslim wey you be!'

He spat phlegm as he said the word 'Muslim'. It stopped the bubbling sound to his voice.

I had never heard anyone disrespect Grandma in such a way. I kept my eyes facing the floor. I pressed my teeth together until my ears hurt.

'Please leave, sir,' said Grandma. 'Your mama has called me here, and I need to help your wife.'

The husband laughed. 'I don send for Reverend Mother,' he said. Then he left.

Grandma was sweating. I waited to see what she would say to the husband, but she was concentrating on the girl. Lines of water ran down the middle of Grandma's breasts and caused a wet patch to grow above her belly. The girl, who was praying, had not cried at all. The girl was so closed between her legs that I couldn't even see a urine hole. The hole that Grandma eventually found was the thickness of one of Alhaji's Cooks' Matches.

'She has been cut and closed,' said Grandma, 'then opened a tiny bit for her wedding night. Look. You can see the thick scar tissue.'

I held my own face. My head became light. I thought of Grandma. White dots appeared in front of my eyes. I focused on taking deep breaths. What would happen if I fell to the ground? Grandma would never want to train me again. I tried very hard not to imagine Grandma having the severest form of cutting, and suffering like this girl, but the thought kept crawling into my head like a fly returning to land in the same spot after swatting.

Grandma cut her upwards along the scar tissue, sawing in places with a tiny knife, as the scarring was so thick. When the flesh came apart again she looked more normal at once, as if her parts had been hiding all along. The girl did not make a single sound. She remained quiet, even when Grandma pushed her hand inside and turned, forcing her to open completely. The sound of her flesh ripping, tearing, the burning she must have felt, and yet she remained quiet. I could not imagine the pain.

She was silent when Grandma delivered her baby, round and big and shiny and dead. It had wide-open eyes. The girl did not even cry. But after the baby was out something followed it that belonged deep inside her. At that time I did not know what it was. I just watched as something purple fell out of her, and was pushed back in by Grandma who was by then shouting for the husband. *Something purple that belonged inside her*. I could not move. The devil was inside her and coming out. It was the devil. The husband had been right.

'Wetin? Na wetin?' The husband's voice was shaky and quick. He entered the hut, to see his dead baby. His face turned grey.

The girl finally screamed.

'Call the driver,' said Grandma. 'Get someone now!' Her voice was high, full of fear.

'My pickin! Oh Jesus! Jesus, my pickin! Oh, pickin, pickin, oh!' He fell to his knees, but he did not make any attempt to pick the baby up. 'My pickin! Satan! Na devil handwork, na devil handwork. Na devil wey don do am!' He looked between his wife's bloody legs.

'You never cut am well! Devil handwork! Devil handwork!' He pointed to the girl. He was crying so hard by then that his voice sounded bubbly again. 'Her thing don touch my pickin head. Oh my pickin! The devil don come. Him dey here. Him dey for this room. Una be winch! Oh my pickin. You never cut am well!'

He pointed at her girl parts that Grandma had opened. She was so covered with blood it was impossible to see them clearly. His voice was no longer slurred. He threw himself onto the ground wailing and beating his fists, causing the ground to shake. 'The devil dey here. Oh Jesus! Jesus. My pickin don die oh.'

'Are you surprised?' I heard a voice shouting. 'There was no hole to push the baby through! The baby was stuck and you did not open her. She was closed. You did not open her!'

The voice flew at the husband and smacked him hard across his face. All the eyes in the room looked at me. Even the dead baby's fish eyes.

I realised that the voice was mine.

*

Youseff refused to put the woman in the car. 'Let her go,' he said, 'she is already dead.' Grandma lifted her head high and looked straight at his eyes without blinking. Youseff looked away, opened the car door, and helped them in. It was cramped in the back; the door kept opening and Youseff had to stop the car, get out, and push the door shut. The husband sat in the front next to Youseff, and did not once turn his head around to check that his young wife was still alive. At one point he closed his eyes, and began to snore. Grandma kept her hand inside the girl for the hours it took to drive to the hospital. The girl had turned as white as Dan. Blood seeped out of her around Grandma's arm. I was in the boot praying the entire journey. I prayed that the girl would survive. I prayed that the purple would go back inside her, where it belonged. I prayed that I would forget what I had seen. But I never did.

We finally reached the Women and Children Specialist Hospital and parked outside the main entrance. I climbed out of the boot and over the girl and ran towards the glass doors. It was very dark and smelled of Robb, the vapour rub Alhaji had used on wounds before he discovered Marmite.

'Please help! Emergency!'

My loud voice was not loud enough; I had to shout three times before a nurse came towards me, and by then the husband was running through the doors. It sounded as though I was speaking through my scarf.

'Wicked women don winch my wife!' He shouted more

quietly than I had, but he was heard more easily. 'That thing! Make una come oh. Come quick oh! Nah these wicked Muslims wey don kill my pickin. Na the devil wey don use them!'

'Cool down, sir.' The nurse waved at two men with a stretcher as she spoke. 'Where is your wife?'

'That moto wey that Muslim dey! Aha, if to say she born inside Christian church, my pickin go dey alive. This thing touch my penis! The pickin done die! Him get no chance. I for fit ...'

He continued but by that time the nurse, porter and doctor had seen Grandma and started running towards the car. The men carrying the stretcher ran behind them.

It was difficult getting the girl and Grandma out, but somehow we managed. Grandma still had her hand inside the girl and was pushing against the purple the entire time. The people we walked past looked away. This is all a dream, I thought. We walked through swing doors, which seemed to push us back outwards. The corridor was lined with patients, nurses running between them. The husband pushed everyone out of the way.

The anaesthetic room smelled stale. It was full of shadows. A large cockroach scuttled up the side of a machine. The doctor waiting there was wearing a mask but I could tell by the way he raised his eyebrows that he was shocked to see Grandma with her hand inside the girl.

The husband hovered by his wife's head. He was pale grey; I thought he might collapse. I did not know where to stand. Hands fluttered around me and I kept bumping into equipment or nurses. I moved next to the husband and pressed my arms to my side. The girl had her eyes shut and was still praying. A Bible was given to the husband, who held it to his chest. His hands were shaking. Suddenly he turned to the doctor. The doctor nodded but did not lift his head. He was busy putting a needle into the girl's arm.

'Oga, sir! We no get money for this operation oh! We no fit pay. We be ordinary people! Fisher people!'

'It's an emergency,' said the doctor. 'We treat emergency cases without payment.'

I felt the husband's shoulders relax against my arm.

'Yes. That is true, true.' The nurse behind us spoke as she flicked a syringe filled with clear fluid. A bubble rose to the top. 'But this lady here, she is going to need aftercare. You understand?' She attached the syringe to a tube on the girl's arm. 'Aftercare.'

The husband made an excuse about a drink of water, and when he was given one by the nurse he made another excuse about using a public telephone, and when the nurse said it was not working he made the excuse that he needed the bathroom. And then he left. We heard his heavy footsteps in the corridor get faster and faster, until there could be no doubt from the sound of his flip-flops on the shiny floor that he was running.

TWENTY-TWO

I found Ezikiel by the river. He was sitting on the riverbank digging into the mud with a stick. 'Ezikiel!' I ran towards him. 'I have been looking everywhere for you. Did you come to try and get back the inhaler? Grandma said Alhaji has a spare so there is no need to worry.' My voice sounded high and strange. Ezikiel did not look up from his digging. 'I am so happy to find you. Have you told Mama about the report yet? I need to tell you what happened! I have so much to tell you.'

'I was there, remember,' said Ezikiel.

'What?' I sat down next to him.

'I was there when she brought that white man home.' He stopped digging and looked up at me. His eyes were red.

'Oh,' I said. 'Mama's friend. No, not that. But I still cannot believe what you said to Mama! What were you thinking? I know that you are angry about school but I thought you had turned to a crazy! Has Mama said anything? She is going to kill you. Anyway, that is not what I meant. I mean the birth I have attended last night with Grandma. And the police at the roadside! Oh, Ezikiel, it was awful.' I felt tears crawl across my eyes. 'It was so awful. They stopped the car and threatened us, well, me really. And this purple thing came from …'

I had wanted to ask Grandma so many things about the woman who had been cut so severely, about the purple that fell out of her, but the cutting, like childbirth, was a secret. Every time I tried to talk to her she told me that watching and doing were the best learning, not talking. The information that Grandma did give me was still in pieces, as though women were jigsaw puzzles. I moved closer to Ezikiel but my arm was frightened to touch him.

Ezikiel shrugged. 'Can't be as awful as Mama's new *friend*. I wish he was purple. I've never seen anybody that white. He looks like a ghost. Of all the men Mama could have,' he paused, 'she chose a white man to be her boyfriend.'

I looked at Ezikiel's face. It was folded up small like a private letter. 'What? It is not serious. Mama is lonely—'

'Are you stupid?' Ezikiel leant towards me.

I felt my eyes open wide. The air became cold.

'What? What do you mean? I only wanted to talk to you about the birth and tell you about the spare inhaler, I do not know why you are being mean …' My words ran away from my mouth. 'And I do not know why you disrespected Mama like that. Shouting and calling her names? She will not forgive that. Wait till she finds out about your report.' I stopped, thinking of the worst words I could. 'What would Father say?'

'Ha! Father isn't here,' said Ezikiel quietly. 'Just the white oil worker boyfriend. And imagine what Father would say about that!'

I tried to close my imagination but it stayed open like a book that had been read too often.

'I do not know what is wrong with you,' I said. 'What kind of doctor speaks to his mother that way? What kind of doctor believes that he is suddenly cured of asthma? What kind of doctor throws medication into the river?'

Ezikiel stood up. 'No kind of doctor!' He was shouting. 'No kind of doctor, because I'm not going to be a doctor.' He stabbed the air in front of him with the muddy stick. 'It's a stupid job anyway. And I don't want to hear about the stupid births you attend or about Mama's stupid boyfriend.'

'But you have always wanted to be a doctor. You just need to resit. It is not the end of the world!'

'Not now. I don't want to be a doctor. I don't want anything. I wish you'd just leave me alone!'

Ezikiel ran off towards the compound. I looked for signs of my brother in the curve of his back. I recognised the way his bad shoulder sloped at a slight angle. The way his head nodded in time with his step, as if it had little legs of its own. His sticking-out ears. Ezikiel. Ezikiel. Ezikiel.

When Dan visited later that day Ezikiel had already left. He slipped out of the gate as soon as he heard Alhaji ask Grandma to make *jollof* rice. Mama did not mention it. It was as though she did not care. She had not come out of her room to see Ezikiel at all in days.

Dan greeted Alhaji with another handshake, but he did bow slightly, revealing thin, patchy hair at the top of his head. He would soon, surely, be bald, I thought.

He gave Grandma a candy bar, and she handed it to me. The chocolate had melted and I had to suck it straight from the foil. Dan watched me. I shuddered.

We all waited on the veranda, while Mama finished dressing. Alhaji tried to make conversation with Dan about the Quality of Petroleum, but Dan seemed distracted. I went to the bedroom, to check that Mama was coming out. She was applying lipstick with her tiny paintbrush. I sat next to her on the floor mattress and watched. It was the first time we had been alone for days. 'Mama,' I said. 'I am sorry to disturb you.'

Mama made careful brushstrokes from the centre of her bottom lip outwards, and when the whole area was covered she applied another layer, just in the middle. Then she took a handkerchief from underneath her pillow, pressed it between her lips, and pushed them together. And then she said, 'What is it, Blessing? I'm trying to get ready.'

I took a long breath and focused on Mama's bottom lip. 'I have started my training again with Grandma. I hope that I have not upset you.'

'Why would it?' Mama turned back to the mirror. 'Do what you want.'

I focused on her back. Her breathing was even. 'And Ezikiel

threw his medication into the river.' The words rushed out as though they were joined up into one long word. Mama's back stopped breathing. Please do not be angry, I thought. But her back started breathing again. She turned and faced me. She took some powder out of a purse, and a small sponge, and rubbed the powder over her face. Then she opened a pot of perfume, dabbed some behind her ears, then down her neck, and between her breasts, leaving a snail trail line. 'Ezikiel is old enough to be responsible for himself,' she said. 'Anyway, I'm too busy at the moment to be dealing with all this.' She rubbed her hands together quickly. 'I wash my hands of it.'

Ezikiel? Responsible for himself?

'Mama, there is something else. But I think Ezikiel needs to tell you.'

'What is it? Look, just tell me. I don't have time for this!'

'Please, Mama. Ezikiel needs to tell you.'

Mama looked at me, and reached forwards, dabbing some perfume onto my wrist. She slipped on her Sunday sandals, and walked out of the room, smiling. My fingertips rested on the point where Mama had dabbed perfume. I brought my wrist to my nose, and inhaled as deeply as possible. The smell was too sweet. It made me feel sick.

When I returned to the veranda, Alhaji was still talking.

'The thing about refining petroleum,' he stood, waving his arms around in circles as he spoke, 'is that it should be done here, where the source is.'

Dan nodded and raised his eyebrows at the same time.

'What a waste,' continued Alhaji. 'They have qualified petroleum engineers here, already, who could be dealing with quality issues of refining.'

'I agree,' said Dan. 'It would eliminate some of the problems of these local gangs sabotaging the pipelines, although it's been relatively quiet on that front recently, but I don't want to talk too soon. Disaster. And I agree, I really do, really. And it really is wasteful.'

Mama was sitting beside him but they were not touching. She had her ear raised up to one side as if it would help her to hear every word Dan said. She looked younger, happier, but although she was no longer frowning, the lines from her frowns remained.

'It does seem wasteful.' Dan paused between each sentence; he was thinking carefully about which words to use. He kept repeating the exact same words in a different order. I wondered if he always thought about which words to use and if he always said them twice. 'The current system is flawed, I agree.'

'How long is your contract?' Grandma asked. She had not spoken directly to Dan before. Mama glared at her so hard the chair started rocking. Alhaji looked baffled.

'Oh yes oh,' said Celestine. 'When you land for London, you go fit send fashion come for me.'

Dan laughed, but Alhaji did not. He was busy frowning at Celestine's pidgin English. She closed her mouth quickly, before any more came out.

'My contract finishes at the end of this year,' said Dan.

Mama's frown thickened.

'Then I guess I'm back to the Big Smoke, back to grey skies.' Dan looked at Mama's frown. 'Of course, they do renew contracts now and then.'

He looked at his watch. 'I'm afraid it's a very short visit today, and I really must be going,' he said. 'I've been put in touch with a bird pal by my ornithology club.'

'A bird pal?' Alhaji leant forwards. 'What is that for?'

'It's a local man in Warri town who's also interested in birds. Probably knows the best lookouts, spots for bird-watching.'

'How much money are you giving him?' Alhaji asked, laughing. 'He will show you any bird hanging out for the right price. You see?'

Dan laughed. 'Well, actually, I only pay his travel expenses. It's really a way for the international community of bird-watchers to help each other. The Nigerian Conservation Society has been helpful to a point, but the local knowledge is essential if I'm to make headway with the list.'

Everyone was silent. Even the birds, who must have been hiding.

'Meeting this bird pal,' said Alhaji. 'This is not the time for birdwatching in Nigeria. The political situation is too delicate.' He threw his hands in the air in front of him. 'Bloody birds. You see? You will get yourself killed. And what list?'

Dan laughed again as if Alhaji was making a joke. 'This spreadsheet was specifically designed for Nigeria. Here.' Dan handed Alhaji a document from his bag. 'Birdwatching is becoming popular here. I mean – the national parks are super. I'd love to visit Okomu, if I can. It's meant to be phenomenal.'

'I understand that you record the birds,' said Alhaji, without really looking up, or at the document at all. 'But it is a waste to write them down. What a waste of your time.'

'Well, it's a hobby. It probably does seem strange, but the excitement you feel if you have a few sightings of a rare bird. It could really attract the tourism industry to Nigeria. The birds you can glimpse here are world class. Really. The thrill of finding a rare bird. Well, it's indescribable. Really emotional. Really.'

Alhaji looked down at the document and showed me. It listed hundreds of birds with beautiful names and a row of columns next to each name. The Latin names were beside each. Ezikiel would have loved looking at them, if they had not belonged to Dan. My eyes flicked over the page. Bee-eater, Blue-breasted, *Merops variegatus loringi*; Courser, Bronze-winged or Violet-tipped, *Rhinoptilus chalcopterus*; Malimbe, Red-headed, *Malimbus rubricollis*.

'The boxes are for ticks?' Alhaji asked.

'Yes – for additional sightings. Ten boxes for each bird. Of course, occasionally you exceed that, but for the rarer birds I'll be lucky to get a single sighting. But that's why a local birdwatcher's input is essential. The bird pal will help me, particularly with the rarer ones.'

'Well, how do you know that you are not ticking the same bird twice?' Alhaji shook the list. 'Birds like to come back to the same spot. They are creatures of habit, you see? You are writing the same bird again and again.'

Dan laughed. 'I guess you're right,' he said. 'It's a possibility.'

Mama tutted. Grandma sucked her teeth. Celestine smiled. Alhaji looked at my face and nodded. 'You see?'

I nodded and looked down at the list, focusing on the birds' names. Alhaji handed it to me to look at properly. Dan began to thank Grandma and Celestine, and shake Alhaji's hand. He started arranging another visit. I could hear his voice repeating the same information over and over. Their voices became distant and fuzzy and far away. My eyes lit up with the names of Dan's birds:

Fire-crested Alethe, Naked-faced Barbet, Cinnamon-breasted Bunting, Whistling Cisticola, Purple-throated Cuckoo-shrike, Lemon Dove, Laughing Dove, Velvet-mantled Drongo, Short-toed Snake Eagle, Cut-throat Finch, Freckled Nightjar, Black-bellied Seedcracker, Beautiful Sunbird. Tiny Sunbirds.

My eyes skimmed over the letters quickly until the letters became birds on the sky-page. Tiny sunbirds far away.

TWENTY-THREE

When Mama found out that Ezikiel had been 'Advised to Leave', she was so angry her hair shrank. I watched her weave get closer and closer to her head until it looked like a much shorter weave. Alhaji could not speak. We were on the veranda and Ezikiel had shown his report card, first to Alhaji then to Mama. He then folded it back up and pushed it into his pocket. 'I don't even care,' he said.

'You stupid boy!' Mama was shouting and going towards him with her arms, hitting the back of his head over and over again.

Ezikiel stayed perfectly still, and did not even cover his eyes. 'I don't care,' he repeated.

Alhaji finally closed his mouth. He moved towards Mama and raised his hand in the air. I thought he might hit Ezikiel on the other side of his head, but he stopped Mama. 'That's enough,' he said. His voice sounded very old and very tired.

Ezikiel did not move. His eyes were facing forwards and his head was still. He had shut himself down. He could not hear her any more, I knew.

'You stupid boy! Now you'll have to resit. You might even have to repeat the year! Oh God, I told you to do the work in the hospital! How did you get that far behind? How?'

Ezikiel did not move. Mama hit the back of his head again. 'What a disappointment! What a joke! A son who is asked to leave school because he's so stupid?'

I felt tears scratching my eyes. I could not believe that Mama had said those words to Ezikiel. I wanted to go over and put my arms around him, but Mama's hair had shrunk so short that I did not dare move.

'Stupid, stupid idiot son!' Mama hit and hit.

'That is enough!' Alhaji pushed Mama backwards. 'It is not his fault.'

Ezikiel opened his insides up and looked at Alhaji.

'It is not the boy's fault. He has been shot! Shot! He had to spend so much time in hospital. I will speak to the head-master, and get Ezikiel's place back.'

Ezikiel turned his head back to the front. 'I don't want my place,' he said. 'I'm not going. I'm not going to school. There's no point!'

He ran into the house leaving Mama and Alhaji shaking so much the veranda shook. It felt like the whole world was shaking.

The call for prayer came bursting into my room like Ezikiel used to. It was still dark; the sky buzzed with insects and the air was sticky. I rolled over, unable to move from the mattress. My eyes were heavy. I had not finished my dream of Father carrying Ezikiel and me on his shoulders. I loved seeing Father in my dreams. It was the only place I could remember his face clearly any more.

Suddenly the Christian singing and clapping started up. It was louder than the loudspeaker. Our neighbours must have been having an early morning revival. I swung my legs off the mattress and stood up. There was no point trying to sleep. It could go on for days. I changed and wrapped my scarf around my head, tucking my hair under, checking for loose bits. Alhaji hated seeing hair at the mosque. As I walked to the makeshift mosque the light changed. Sweat landed on me as if it had been dumped there.

The morning got hotter and hotter and hotter. It was so hot by the time Ezikiel and I went to market later that day that the plantain sellers were huddled under umbrellas, and nobody bothered to shout when we accidentally stepped on their produce. The usual market smells of nutmeg, cinnamon, pepper, camphor, and body odour, were gone. All I could smell was meat turning bad. The men selling the meat were shouting, 'Very Cheap Price'. Ezikiel said it would have to be fried first and cooked slowly for many hours. His stomach grumbled as he spoke. We had run out of vegetable oil, and I did not imagine that Mama would remember to bring some more home.

The area in front of the Shining Light of Christ our Saviour Church was usually noisy with women wearing white robes, praying and dancing. That day they stood still, with no energy to move or pray, flicking the Bibles in front of their faces.

Their white robes were see-through with sweat. I thought of Dan's teeth. I noticed the men across the road under the mango trees, drinking from plastic bottles as they watched the women. The men's shirts were covered with rainbows of citrus-coloured stains; maybe the bowls their wives had washed them in were melting. They did not take their eyes from the see-through areas of the women's dresses. I wondered what my body would look like in a see-through dress. Would the men stand and watch me? Would I still look like a child?

I looked down at the ground and tried to concentrate on Ezikiel. At first when he said that he no longer wanted to be a doctor, I had not believed him. But he said it all the time. And when he told me he was to sell his *Encyclopaedia of Tropical Medicine* I began to worry. 'It is your favourite book,' I said. 'What about the river-dwelling parasites?'

'I don't need it any more,' he said. 'I'd rather have the money.'

'What for?' I asked. It was my birthday coming soon. I would be thirteen. Maybe Ezikiel was planning to buy me a present? He had been acting strangely since showing his report to Mama and Alhaji. And no matter how often Alhaji told Ezikiel he could win his place at school back, Ezikiel refused to let him. And Mama said she washed her hands of him, and he should do whatever he wanted. Even sell his books. She was still too angry to help.

'None of your business,' Ezikiel said. But I thought I noticed him smile.

As we walked further into the market, I wondered if Ezikiel

would want to play the game we liked of finding the strangest produce, but his face did not look like it wanted to play games. He walked as quickly as Mama, and I had to run to keep up with him.

'Why do you follow me?' he asked on a number of occasions, but he did not send me away.

'You know why. Alhaji told me to accompany you,' I said. 'And I do not understand. If you sell your book how will you be able to study?'

'How many times? I told you, I do not want to study. I do not want to be a doctor. It's too many years wasted in a classroom.'

The words reached my ears but they were the wrong shape and bounced straight back out again. 'You have always wanted to be a doctor. I know you are angry but—'

'I'm not angry about that, stupid.'

I was running quickly but rubbish kept slipping into my flip-flops. 'What, then?'

'Is it not obvious? Aren't you just a little bit angry? Or do you think it's OK for Mama to have a white *boyfriend*?'

I wondered what I thought about it. Did I think it was OK?

'Anyway, I have to go. I'm meeting some friends.'

Friends? Ezikiel had friends? First Mama and now Ezikiel. Where were they finding friends? 'What friends? I thought Boneboy was your only friend here.'

'Just some boys my own age.'

'Why aren't they at school?'

'You are so full of questions.' Ezikiel pulled one of my plaits gently. He handed me the textbook wrapped in newspaper. 'Take this to the bookseller and get a good price.'

'Can I come to meet your friends?'

Ezikiel laughed. 'No way.'

'Well, who are they? Where did you meet them? Does Mama know you are meeting friends? Is Boneboy going with you?'

Ezikiel suddenly pulled my plait harder. 'Ouch!'

'Listen,' he said. His voice was clear even through all the market noise. 'It is none of your business. And if you tell Mama you are in deep trouble.' He looked straight into my eyes. 'Deep trouble.'

I touched my plait. Ezikiel had never pulled my hair before.

He ran towards the alleyway. I watched him until he became nothing but a long, thin boy-shadow.

I found Boneboy lying underneath Snap. They were both asleep, and curled in the same position. I shook Boneboy gently. Snap continued to sleep. He made snoring noises like an old man. Boneboy's eyes opened suddenly and he smiled. 'Hey, I was dreaming,' he said, in English.

'Sorry,' I said. 'But I wondered if you are going with Ezikiel? To meet his new friends?'

Boneboy lifted Snap onto the ground. Still, Snap remained asleep. 'I am not going.' Boneboy sat up and stretched his arms into the air. His T-shirt lifted up, showing his sticking-out belly button.

I looked away at Snap.

'Anyway, those boys are no good.'

'What boys? Ezikiel's friends? Who are they?'

Boneboy laughed and held his hands up. 'You are asking more questions than a detective!'

'Sorry,' I said, smiling.

'I don't know them. But I know they are no good boys. Ezikiel should stay away from them – I've told him, but he doesn't listen.' Boneboy looked up at the sky and lifted his shoulders. 'So, what can I do?'

He must have noticed a frown on my face, because he put his hand on my arm. 'Don't worry,' he said. 'I'm sure Ezikiel's old enough to make his own friends. He'll soon get bored with them. And I should not judge him,' he looked at Snap, 'when my own best friend is a dog!'

We laughed, and Snap finally opened one eye, looked at us for a few seconds, then shut it and continued snoring.

'Tonight I will just watch. You are in charge.' Grandma and I walked quickly through the village. The fighting seemed to have stopped and we did not see any more policemen by the roadside with rifles in their hands. A group of boys were sitting around a television watching football on Sky Sports, eating cashew nuts from old plastic bottles. The village had a mixture of brick houses and mud and thatch huts. A satellite dish covered the roof of one of the brick houses. It was so large that it provided shade, which the women sat underneath, with daughters between their legs having their hair plaited. Alhaji would have loved a satellite dish, and a tele-vision, and a generator, and money to fuel a generator.

Tombra was surrounded by women. It was difficult to get through. Grandma clapped her hands and said, 'Out,' and they moved to the sides of the house. I could see at once Tombra was ready to push; her arms and legs were shaking. She vomited. A bowl of soapy water and a rag appeared. Grandma stood at the back of the room with another woman. 'She is training,' she said, in Izon. 'I am just here to watch.'

I picked up the rag and mopped up the vomit. 'Hello, Tombra.' My voice sounded so young. Surely Tombra could see that I was only twelve years old. Surely she could see my child's body. How could she accept me as a midwife?

'I need to push.'

'That is good. Let me examine you.' I looked over at Grandma who nodded her head, and smiled. I washed my hands in the bowl and picked out a clean cloth. I washed Tombra. She had shaved off her hair; all that remained were tiny scratchy hairs that reminded me of Father's chin. I pushed my fingers inside her. The baby's head pressed on my hand straight away. I could feel the baby's thick curls. 'He or she has lots of hair,' I said. Tombra smiled. Then as quickly as she smiled she screamed. 'Now, get ready,' I said. 'Get ready to push.' I gently held the baby's head. 'Now push.'

Tombra screamed again and moved her head down onto her chest. She gritted her teeth. As the baby's head came towards the world I swept my hands around the neck. 'No cord, good.' Grandma was watching me and smiling. Her eyes lay on my head like a scarf. 'Now pant, stop pushing. Now gently give a small push.'

Tombra pushed. The veins in her neck swelled into shapes. A fish, a circle, a knife.

She screamed the noise that I only heard at that time; when a woman was pushing a baby's head out. It was a noise from another, older world.

The head arrived. The baby was deep blue. Its lips were white. It had a tiny nose and puffy cheeks. Beautiful. I could hardly stop myself from crying. I looked over at Grandma.

She had stopped smiling. She nodded. 'Good, Blessing. Now quickly.'

'I need you to do a last big push,' I said. Tombra balanced on her elbows. She took a large breath. She pushed so hard her private parts swelled up and out, spilling over my hands. Shit fell out of her. I cleaned it up quickly. The baby did not come. I put my hand around the baby's neck and head. 'Another,' I said. She pushed again. Still, the baby's body did not come. Sweat or tears fell down my face. I looked at Grandma. She was standing still watching. 'I need help,' I whispered.

'I am here to watch,' she said.

'Push again. Push as hard as you can.'

Tombra pushed and pushed. Everything fell out of her but the baby. The baby's face was changing. The blue was getting paler and paler. I pushed my fingers inside Tombra, as far as they would reach. 'The shoulder is behind her pelvis,' I said. 'Grandma, I need help.' The heat of the room was making my head light. 'Please, Grandma.'

'I am just here to watch,' said Grandma. 'This is how it is done. How will you learn?'

I squeezed my hand around the baby's back. 'Now push. Push as hard as possible!'

I pulled and pulled. Tombra pushed and pushed. Still the baby remained.

'I can't go on,' said Tombra. She vomited again. The sick fell between her breasts, which were oozing. The smell of the sick and milk and the heat of the room made me want to run. I felt tears drip from my eyes onto my arms. Grandma was beside me.

'Stop.' She wiped my face of tears. 'Now I am here. I am just watching. Not helping. You know what to do.'

'The baby's shoulder is stuck,' I said. 'I remember. But I cannot do it.' I had sick in my mouth.

'Look at the baby's colour. This baby needs to come out.'

Tombra moaned. Her head moved backwards. Her eyes rolled upwards until they looked completely white.

'Let me try cutting her,' I said.

'It is not the opening where the problem is,' said Grandma. 'It is inside. The baby's shoulder.'

'I cannot do it.'

'You have to. This is the job.'

'Is there nothing else?' I looked at Grandma. She was moving backwards towards the wall.

'You can cut the mother's pelvis or the baby's shoulder. But quickly choose.'

I looked at Tombra. The baby's head between her legs was

turning paler and paler. I looked at Tombra's pelvis. I could not cut through a woman. I looked at the baby. I could not cut through a baby. 'I cannot choose.'

'I am not choosing for you. You are attending this birth. You are in charge. This is the job. These choices are the job. Can you do the job, Blessing? Are you strong enough?'

I pushed my fear deep into my belly. I held it there, clenching my muscles. I can do it, I told myself. I can do this. 'Tombra, I need to break the baby's collarbone. If I don't do this then the baby will die.'

Tombra screamed. 'No! No! Cut me open! Cut me open instead! Cut me!'

I looked at Grandma. 'Quickly,' said Grandma.

I lay Tombra flat on the ground. I pushed her knees to her chest one last time. I pulled and pulled, but still the baby did not move. I put Tombra's knees back down.

'I will break the baby's bone,' I said. 'And you will both be fine. I promise.' My voice sounded calm but my blood was so hot in my veins that I felt like exploding. Grandma had taught me what to do if the shoulder was stuck. She told me how a pair of small sharp scissors was enough to cut through a baby's bone. I knew what to do but it did not stop the feeling of sickness in my stomach and the pain in my head behind my eyes. I pushed all the feelings away and picked up the scissors.

I carefully moved them inside Tombra, holding the ends. I felt for the baby's bone. The baby was turning paler and paler. I placed the scissors over the baby's collarbone and pressed the flesh around it away with my fingers. I closed my eyes, and took large breaths. Then I closed the scissors hard and as quickly as possible.

The bone snapped in my hand.

I pulled my hand out and put the scissors on the floor. 'Push!'

Tombra pushed. I pulled. The baby fell into my arms. Blood covered its body. Its arms and body were twisted around.

My lungs opened and I could breathe again. 'A girl,' I said. 'She is alive.'

I looked at the alive girl, and the alive mother. I looked at my own hands. I felt something grow in my stomach that had never been there before. Something warm.

Grandma stood up, a smile completely covering her face. I stood by Grandma's side, and slipped my bloodied hand into hers.

TWENTY-FOUR

The next time Dan visited, Alhaji was ready for him. A pile of textbooks balanced near his feet, and as the car pulled up to the gate, he picked up *Quality Issues in Modern Petroleum Engineering* and opened it. The edges of the book were curled like Celestine's university certificate. 'Alhaji, sir.' Dan walked towards us carrying a rucksack, and wearing a baseball cap, which he did not remove, even when he bowed slightly.

Alhaji jumped up. He held the textbook firmly; his hands did not shake.

Dan turned to us. 'Hello, Blessing, and Grandma. How are you?'

Mama was in the bedroom applying more make-up in a natural way that she had said made her look as though she was not wearing any. When she heard Dan's voice she suddenly appeared, and was wearing red lipstick after all. Some of it had escaped from her lips and coated her teeth. I made a small movement pointing to my own teeth and pretended to rub. But Mama scowled at me until I stopped. She had not been working that day, but still wore her pencil skirt and blouse, with the front buttons loosened enough to show the strap of red underwear inching out that matched her lipstick. She kissed Dan on each cheek, leaving a large stain of red that made him look embarrassed. He smiled widely, showing his neat, white, slightly see-through teeth.

Dan put the rucksack down onto the floor, and opened the front compartment. He took a small box from the inside and handed it to Mama. Their fingers touched for longer than they needed to. The box was wrapped up with flowery paper, and so much tape that it took Mama several minutes before she could open it. She looked more excited than I had seen her for a long time. Finally she managed and lifted the top of the box for me to see two small diamond earrings. Mama had always loved diamonds. But she had never owned any before. Not real ones. I knew, just by looking at her face, that the diamonds were real. Her face lit up until it also sparkled. She turned the box slowly from one side to the other until more light from the earrings danced on her face.

She laughed. 'Oh, Dan, you've spent too much,' she said, but took them straight out, removed the large gold-plated hoops from her ears, and put the diamond studs in instead. She gave me the hoops, big enough to put my hands through, like bracelets. Then she touched the diamond earrings one at a time.

Dan reached into his rucksack and pulled out a chocolate bar for me, a make-up set for Celestine and Grandma, and a small book for Alhaji.

'*New Practices in the Petroleum Industry.*' Alhaji smiled. 'Thank you. It will prove very useful.' He put the other textbook down.

'Where's Ezikiel?' asked Dan, looking towards the house. 'I'm beginning to think he's avoiding me.'

Mama touched her earrings. She laughed too loudly, and for too long.

Ezikiel returned by lunchtime. 'I'm hungry,' he said. His voice was quiet. My stomach relaxed. Then Dan gave Ezikiel his chocolate bar.

'What's this?' Ezikiel asked, looking at the chocolate bar, which was clearly a chocolate bar. He turned it over and over in his hand.

'Just a small gift,' said Dan, smiling. 'It's nothing really, just thought you might fancy a bit of chocolate. And I hope you don't mind but your mother told me about the problems with school. I think I might be able to help. You know, get you in another school.'

Ezikiel turned the bar around again in his hands and slapped it on the table. Grandma was holding a pan of stew. She carefully put the pan onto the ground.

'How dare you act that way?' Mama said. 'Did I raise you to be ungrateful?'

Ezikiel looked at her for a long time. 'You give me a chocolate bar? A chocolate bar? Offer to help me find a school. Well, instead of that, I'd prefer my country back, please.'

The words hung in the air long after they were said, like

the smell of fish long after it was eaten. They moved back and forth in our ears.

Mama stood from her chair and leant close to Ezikiel's face. 'How dare you,' she said. Her neck swelled as she spoke.

Dan pulled her back to sit in the chair, and smiled, but with his mouth closed, his lips stretching over his teeth, making them look even paler than usual. 'Don't worry,' he said. He raised his hands in front of him, stepped back. 'I understand.'

Ezikiel laughed, from deep inside his belly. I watched him to guess what he would do next, but I did not know. I could not read him any more. There were no little clues. No scratching his cheek when he was about to ask something stupid, no leaning back in his chair when he was going to laugh, or hanging his head down when he was about to cry. There was no twitching of his right eye when he was lying, or sighing when he was thinking about Mama. There was no grinding his back teeth when he was worried, or swaying his shoulders when he was happy. He was perfectly still. I did not know my brother at all.

'What do you understand?' he asked, and before Mama could raise her hand to hit him, he stood.

Alhaji also stood, and moved from leg to leg. He laughed, quietly.

'You people come here,' Ezikiel slammed his fist down onto the table top, making us all jump, 'and take our women,' he looked at Mama, 'and our money. And our jobs.' He looked at Alhaji. Nobody moved. 'You pay people to kill us, and you rape our land, then our women! And you give me a chocolate bar?'

I held my breath until the back of my head fell. I had never heard Ezikiel speak that way to an adult. Mama would surely kill him. The words did not sound like Ezikiel's. Where had they come from?

He stared at Dan's face for what seemed like a long time until Dan's skin became red and patchy and criss-crossed, then Ezikiel walked out, banging his arm on the doorframe.

It was quiet for a long time. The kind of quiet where everyone was hoping for some noise.

'Well,' said Dan, still smiling. His skin was patterned. 'He's angry.'

Mama could not speak, but looked like she would explode at any time. She was holding her mouth closed tightly; her lips also appeared thin and colourless.

Alhaji burst into apology. 'Sorry, sir. Ah! Speaking to you like this! I am most sorry, sir. Teenager, you see? Teenager.'

Celestine was wide-mouthed but with nothing to say. The quiet filled the air. Boneboy slipped away, into the house. Eventually Grandma picked up the pot of stew, we all sat down, one by one, and she spooned equal measures into our bowls. As she walked around us she had her eyebrows raised, and she said, 'Hmm,' repeatedly until Mama stood up and left the veranda.

During the next days, I prayed five times a day for electricity to work the fan, but Allah did not hear me. Or he thought it was a stupid thing to pray for. Either way, it was too hot. Now Dan was giving Mama money, we had plenty enough to buy electricity, if only NEPA was reliable. When the electricity did come on, I could never enjoy it, as I did not know how long it would last. Mama complained all the time. 'This place is so backward,' she said. 'It's ridiculous to live for days without electricity – it's like going back in time a hundred years.' She seemed very angry about the electricity. I thought she must have been used to it by then. I wondered if Dan would buy us a generator and fuel. Maybe then Mama would smile again. I knew he must have given Mama money as we had meat and fish almost every day, and not just the gristle bits. But Dan had not visited the compound since Ezikiel's outburst, and Mama had not spoken to Ezikiel at all, even after Alhaji whipped him with the buckle end of his belt and he called out to her. Even after he said he was sorry.

I spent most of my time rubbing Celestine's shoulders as she made whimpering noises. She suffered the most. Her ankles puffed up, making her appear barefoot despite her flip-flops, her face and neck became one, and her back ached, which was caused by the size of her breasts. They had grown so impossibly large that the rest of her seemed smaller. She was clearly pregnant, by at least six months, but nobody had mentioned it to me. Not even Grandma.

'Let me take a mineral,' she said, between moans.

I ran to fetch a Fanta. The area under the table where

Grandma kept the minerals was bare. I looked around but there were no drinks except the barrel of water.

'It has run out,' I said, as I returned to Celestine and handed her a cup of water.

'There are no more minerals. I do not have any left. Only beer. I need to go to market.' Grandma was frying unripe and ripe plantain, on a small kerosene stove. The smoke made my eyes water. Mama did not say anything. She twirled her diamond earrings around and around.

Celestine looked at the water, and sucked her teeth. 'I can't drink this.' She tipped the water onto the ground. It left a multicoloured pattern. 'This water will kill us,' she said, putting her hand over her enormous belly, 'quicker than thirst.'

She turned her head and noticed Mama twirling her earrings. 'In London,' she said in English, 'them get restaurant McDonald's for every street.' She rubbed her belly, making it wobble. 'Better meat and French fries. Yum.'

Mama ignored Celestine. She looked down at her plantain and started to eat.

'When you go there, you go chop plenty hamburger. Then you can get better shape. No more skinny branch! No more *lenge lenge!*'

'Who is going there?' asked Grandma, rushing over, the plantain pan still in her hand.

'Not me,' said Mama. 'I've no plans to go to London.' She continued to eat, but smiled at Celestine, even though Celestine had called her a skinny branch.

'No be now,' said Celestine, jumping up and down, and

stretching her arms in the air, 'but if you marry Dam, you go do am.'

I switched my head to the side. Marry Dan! Surely Mama was only his girlfriend?

'Eh!' said Grandma. She looked at Celestine with wide-open eyes. 'Who is marrying Dam?'

'That woman is crazy,' said Mama. She stood up and walked out of the kitchen with her plate of egg and plantain balanced on her arm. 'Who'd want to leave here?'

After we had finished eating, Dan's shining silver car arrived. It did not make much noise but Mama heard it; she smiled suddenly and ran to the gate and opened his car door. He jumped out. He was wearing khaki shorts like a schoolboy. He waved at me. My hand lifted up and waved back at him, before I could stop it.

'Hello, Blessing.'

As they walked towards the veranda, I watched Mama let go of one of her earrings. She took Dan's hand in hers. They held each other's hands all the way to the veranda steps where I was sitting. I did not know what to do with my own hands. I folded them on my lap.

'Where is Alhaji? And the others?' Dan asked.

'They are in the house.' Mama pointed to the door with her face.

'Let me go and say hi.' Dan kissed Mama's hand, then let go and walked into the house.

I sat on the veranda next to Mama and looked at the car. I wondered if Dan would feel how hot and dark it was, and realise that we needed a generator. I wondered if Mama had told Dan that the generator for Grandma's fridge was only hired, and had to go back soon as the fridge had been stolen. I wondered if Mama had mentioned Grandma's fridge at all. Mama did not move away as I sat next to her and I was thinking about resting my head on her shoulder when the gate swung open again and Ezikiel walked towards us. Mama was smiling until he walked closer. 'What's wrong with you?' She looked at Ezikiel as he approached the veranda, twirling, spinning, laughing.

'Mama, my Mama,' he said. He reached his arms out and rushed towards her. As he neared the veranda, he tripped and fell, banging his jaw. Instead of screaming in pain, and complaining that his jaw might be broken, and getting an asthma attack, he laughed. I looked at him. I felt Mama's arm next to me become thinner and tighter. Her hair shrank again.

'You've been drinking.' Mama's voice was quiet. 'You've been drinking palm wine.'

If there had been a breeze it would have got lost. But the harmattan was a long way off, and the air was so still that even laughing, Ezikiel heard her.

He stopped laughing, but continued to smile, and looked at Mama through his red-edged eyes. 'I am a palm wine drinkard.'

I winced. It was Father's favourite book.

Mama stood and walked towards Ezikiel. She looked as

if she would step on his head, but she jumped down off the veranda and sat beside him.

'What's the matter with you, Ezikiel?' She reached out and touched his hair.

He breathed out loudly enough for me to hear. Tears made his red eyes pink. My heart rested between beats. Seeing Mama touching Ezikiel's hair felt like going home. She had forgiven him. Maybe he would go back to school now after all, and repeat his exams. I prayed for time to stop.

Dan came back out of the house, rubbing his eyes, blinking in the angry light. His eyes searched for Mama. They found her and Ezikiel at the same time.

Ezikiel lifted himself up. He sneered at Dan. 'What are you doing here?'

Dan smiled as usual, but his eyes darted to Mama's and asked a question. He tried to answer Ezikiel, but started to cough.

'I said,' repeated Ezikiel as he walked towards Dan, causing Dan to step back towards the house, 'I said what are you doing here?' Ezikiel's silhouette looked bigger than Ezikiel, like a shadow when the sun was setting. Dan's shadow was bigger than Ezikiel's. As it grew and grew, Ezikiel's shrank, until all that remained was a long thin line.

I watched Dan for signs of fear, or anger, but all I saw was the smile fixed on his lips. It looked as if Mama had painted it there with her tiny paintbrush. His eyes smiled. I had no idea what Dan was thinking, even though I could see inside his body through his thin skin. 'I came to visit your mother,' said Dan, 'and you.'

He stepped forwards; I thought he might give Ezikiel a chocolate bar. My legs shook. My heart fluttered again between beats.

It was worse than the chocolate bar. Dan tried to hug Ezikiel.

Ezikiel pushed Dan so far backwards that he nearly fell into the doorway. He walked back out, hands up, and smiled again.

'It's OK,' Dan said to Mama, who was rushing towards him.

'It's not OK,' said Mama, grabbing Ezikiel's arm and looking around the ground. Her eyes rested on a large piece of wood. I moved Grandma's bag, containing the birth knife, out of sight under the veranda. Mama slapped the back of Ezikiel's head. The sound brought Alhaji running from the house, an old copy of the *Nigerian Guardian* wedged under his arm. His head moved from Ezikiel to Mama, back to Ezikiel. 'What is happening here?'

Ezikiel and Dan stepped forwards. Ezikiel opened his mouth to speak, but Dan interrupted him and moved towards Alhaji.

Alhaji stepped away and looked at the others. His stare settled on me. I looked quickly at the oatmeal colour of the veranda, focusing on the splashes of dirt in the wood. Ezikiel moved behind Dan, and pushed him again.

'What?' asked Alhaji. 'What are you doing, boy?' Alhaji was already removing his belt. I looked at the buckle.

'I pushed Dan, sir.'

'Why? Why did you do that? What do you think you are doing?'

'Because he deserves it.' Ezikiel pushed Dan again, harder, and Dan slid across the floor, almost losing his balance. 'Do you know what kind of man he is?' Ezikiel was screaming then. Mama walked over to Ezikiel and raised her hand to slap his face, but he caught her arm before it could come down and twisted it behind her back.

'Please, let go of your mother.' Dan regained his balance, and tried to remove Ezikiel's arm from Mama, who was so shocked by Ezikiel's behaviour she could not speak. Alhaji was standing still with his hands on his hips. Eventually Mama regained her senses, reached across Ezikiel with her free arm and slapped him. Hard.

Ezikiel let go of her twisted arm. He pulled Mama towards him, and smacked her across the cheek and ear, leaving an instant red line across her face. One of Mama's diamond earrings fell onto the ground.

Ezikiel pulled Mama's face even further towards his.

Ezikiel kissed Mama on the mouth.

Like Father used to.

For a few seconds the world stopped turning and everything seemed to move away from the ground. I felt dizziness like I had never felt before, the kind that cannot be cured by falling over.

There was silence for some time, the type you get after someone had just told some terrible news: Father is leaving, Ezikiel is shot, Dan is arriving.

'Ezikiel,' I said. 'Ezikiel. What is happening to you?'

My heart lifted into my mouth. I ran at Ezikiel, turned my back to Mama, and Dan and Alhaji. I fell into Ezikiel, clutched him, held his face between my hands, kissed his tears. He tasted of kerosene.

TWENTY-FIVE

One evening, after Mama had left for work, I heard more shouting. My heart became frightened. Alhaji had wanted to throw Ezikiel out onto the street after what happened with Mama and Dan. But Dan had said that Ezikiel was only a boy, who was missing his father, and was confused. Dan said that Ezikiel needed Alhaji more than ever. Alhaji had agreed that Ezikiel could stay but still, he had joined Mama in not speaking to him. When I heard the shouting I thought that maybe Alhaji had changed his mind. But I could not hear Ezikiel's voice. Maybe it was fighting, or maybe killing. Since Ezikiel had been shot we had only heard far-away shouting and clapping gunfire. But as my ears listened, they heard a voice that I knew. Celestine. She was shouting at Alhaji. Her voice was far louder than the gangs of boys. She was in Alhaji's room at the back of the house but Celestine was shouting so loudly that every word could soon be heard from the veranda where I was sitting with Grandma and Ezikiel. Her voice was slipping in and out of Izon and in and out of the pidgin English that Alhaji did not like her to speak.

'Na you suppose provide for your family. Where is the money? Only *oyibo* support this family! Wey de money? Petroleum Engineer! Ha! Where is your job? Wey de job? You say you fit handle two wives! Ha! You cannot even support me! Do you think I am happy mourning, going to someone's death, shouting till my lung is empty and I cannot speak? Or to dey waka through the town, sometimes for many hours until my leg go dey start to bleed? And that nonsense driver, him be idiot, bloody fool man keep having children like that all over the place and no money to feed them. If my parents knew what man they sent me to!

'Me and Grandma get to work morning till night so you fit carry our money go throwaway for *ashewo* and brandy for that Executive Club! You have no job! You think we don't know? *Ashewo!* You think we are stupid women who will be your slaves? Be your bloody slaves? Well I am not stupid bloody woman! And the money you give to the imam for what? So that other people can come to use the mosque and not pay a single bloody penny. And that man is wearing gold. Gold! And we have nothing to drink not even safe water. What would my family say to come and live with such a man? I get university degree and for go far with am. I could have gone to any place. I for even go America! Here I am no water no food no generator. University degree!'

My heart was thumping loud enough to be heard on the outside. Grandma bent her head downwards as if she was praying. She did not attempt to speak, but slumped her shoulders. I had never seen her slouch. Why did she not say anything? Ezikiel had his mouth open and his eyes closed. Still, Celestine continued. I imagined the sound that would surely come any minute, of Alhaji's belt cracking down on Celestine's back.

We ran towards the shouting. When Alhaji stepped aside to let me and Grandma in, I felt his body shaking. I had never before imagined Alhaji scared. Grandma knelt next to Celestine and whispered in her ear. Her face was concentrating on Celestine. It was as though she could not see or hear Alhaji at all.

'This is witchcraft,' said Alhaji, looking at the back of Grandma's head.

Celestine screamed. 'Yes,' she shouted. 'Oh God!' She panted and rolled onto her side.

'She is having the babies,' Grandma said.

'But it is too early,' Alhaji said. He stepped backwards. Nobody answered him. 'It is too early, you see?' He looked at Grandma. His face crumpled, folded.

I ran straight to the kitchen and fetched the birth bag and some palm wine, my heart beating loudly in my ears; I could not hear my own footsteps. When I returned, Alhaji and Ezikiel had already left. Grandma worked quickly. I looked at her for signs of fear, but there were none; she opened the bag and set out the contents on the floor.

Celestine's parts were all there, even the button, and she was covered in hair, which had grown since I had seen it when she had first arrived, and now ran down her legs like creeping bougainvillea. Grandma washed her with water and soap, before shaving some of her hair away with Alhaji's razor. She then stuck one hand on top of Celestine and one inside. Celestine screamed. It was as though, after all the months of acting as Professional Town Mourner, she had been waiting for this moment.

'I am dying! I dey die oh!' Celestine thrashed around as if she was on fire and trying to put herself out. She fell against the wall so suddenly that a part fell open, and bright outside light came into the darkness of the room, cutting patterns across her body.

Alhaji and Ezikiel stayed away, but every few minutes I saw Alhaji's shadow at the other side of the window. The shadow rocked back and forth.

A foot first. A tiny foot first. I recognised the colour of the dead baby, like the inside of a boiled egg when the yellow was turning grey. I felt vomit in my mouth. I looked at Grandma, but Grandma was busy concentrating on trying to free the other leg. I could not control the tears from falling down my face. Please don't die, I prayed. Please don't die. Please don't die.

'Silly little one,' Grandma said, under her breath.

Celestine had stopped screaming and was panting with her tongue hanging out; she was still throwing herself around, making it difficult for Grandma to get hold of the baby's other leg. 'Keep still,' Grandma said, repeatedly, but Celestine looked far away, she could not have heard. She was not enclosed by her body. She had spilled out and filled the room, the air, and my head. She was everywhere. Between worlds. The spirit world was definitely calling her that day.

I didn't even ask if I could help, I just held Celestine as tightly as possible, closing my body around hers, trying to keep her from spilling out any more. I passed Grandma the knife. I wanted Celestine to start screaming again, loudly, leaving no doubt which world she was in.

The other leg finally came. Twin One was born blue and floppy. Grandma gave him to me while she tried to stem the blood that followed. The blood did not look real. It over-flowed from Celestine as though she had too much.

'It's a boy,' I said to Celestine, but even then, she did not smile. Her face did not change at all.

He was warm and sticky, and small enough to fit in one of my hands. I could feel his heart beating on my finger. My own heart was pounding. I checked it wasn't a pulse from my fingertip by putting my ear against his little chest. His heart was beating but his chest was completely still. I rubbed him hard with the small kitchen blanket and smacked his tiny back. I blew in his face, and rubbed him again. He was not breathing. He was going to die and it would be my fault. I was useless. I could not even save my own uncle. He would die. I had wasted my prayers on electricity.

I looked at the baby, but my hand had stopped working. The world around me swirled and blurred. It felt as though the room was melting.

'Keep going. Smack him,' Grandma said. 'You can do it, Blessing.'

I snapped back to life. I rubbed and smacked and rubbed and smacked. I prayed. I concentrated on pushing life through my fingertips into his tiny little body. I pushed from deep inside my stomach, and held my teeth together. My head was empty of bad thoughts. I would not let my uncle die. I held my breath in. Then, from silence, he gasped, and opened his little mouth. He let out a noise like a hiccup, followed by a high-pitched scream so loud that even Celestine stopped screaming. I looked at my tiny uncle, life rushing through his body, his mouth open. And I thought, *I did that*. I felt myself breathe again, and the air tasted better.

I picked him up, and put his head near my mouth. And then I whispered the call to prayer into his little ear. Grandma watched me and said, 'I am proud of you,' without using any words at all.

Celestine rolled her eyes into the back of her head and began to shake all over. The shaking became violent; I thought it might be the devil himself.

Grandma slapped her hard across the face.

'What?' Celestine was back in the room and began to shout again. 'Is it over?' She spoke with a voice that sounded years older than hers.

'Nearly,' said Grandma, 'just one more.'

Minutes later another head appeared. Even smaller and covered with matted black hair. Grandma touched the soft spot of the baby's head. She leant forwards to Celestine and spoke in a clear voice, pausing between each word. 'Listen to me, my sister. This baby needs to come out now. Push. Now.'

'I can't do no more pushing. I can't do it.'

'Yes, you can. I am your sister, and I am with you. I am telling you what to do. I will keep you safe. Listen to my voice. Only my voice. Now push. Push!'

I could not believe that Grandma had called Celestine her sister.

Celestine grasped Grandma's hand. She pushed until tiny red veins crawled over her face. She pushed until the veins became a spider's web on her cheek. She screamed, making Twin One in my arms jump and open his eyes wide and let out an even bigger scream.

Twin Two came into the world with his eyes open. He was even tinier, but alive. He cried even before his whole head was out, put his thumb in his mouth, and sucked. The blood must have been running out. It still flowed but became watery. The placenta came quickly, and Celestine passed out before looking at her sons.

Alhaji was pacing up and down the veranda. I had been sent to tell him the news. Ezikiel was sitting on the veranda chair. Alhaji paced up and down in front of Ezikiel as though he was not sitting there.

'Congratulations, sir,' I said, kneeling down. 'You have two sons.' My voice sounded young and shaky and unsure. The words did not sound real.

Ezikiel jumped in the air and punched the sky. He held

out his hand to Alhaji. He smiled and opened his mouth to speak. But Alhaji just pushed him aside and bounded towards the house.

'I have cancelled the prayers today,' said Alhaji. He waved his arms; his eyes were sparkling. 'I declare today, my twin sons' birthday, a Day of Rest.' He looked around the garden. 'A Celebration Day.'

Everyone clapped hard and for a long time.

I held the twins in my arms. An arm each. Everyone looked at them and then at me.

'Look at this junior Grandma who helped to bring my sons into the world!' Alhaji pointed at my face.

I smiled. I looked at my little uncles. They felt so light in my arms. They looked back up at me with wide eyes.

Remember this forever, I told myself.

'Youseff, take this money, my Emergency Money, and buy plenty of minerals, while I take care of my junior wife, who has given me twin sons!' I wondered where Alhaji's emergency money had come from. Did he have it when Ezikiel needed school fees? If Ezikiel had not missed so much school, maybe he would have passed his exams.

Alhaji could not stop smiling. He carried a twin in each arm, and started to sing.

'You were lucky not to die,' Grandma said. We had gone to wash and turn Celestine in Alhaji's room where she had stayed since the birth. 'Allah must have been watching over you.'

'Ha! I would be better dead. Better to die than go through that!' Celestine began to cry. 'It was not worth it!'

Grandma flicked her eyes at me, before placing the twins on each of Celestine's breasts.

Celestine looked at the boys. 'It was not worth it,' she said again.

I imagined Mama looking at me, after I had been born, the words she must have said.

'Don't speak like that,' said Grandma. 'Even small ears can hear you. These sons are pieces of your own soul that have broken off. You are split into three now, Celestine. If you are hurting them then you will hurt yourself.' Grandma spoke the words so quickly, I was not sure I had heard them correctly. 'Your soul is divided,' she continued. 'That is why childbirth hurts so much.'

Sometimes I wonder if Grandma knew everything.

Nobody mentioned the words which fell out of Celestine's mouth before the twins were born. Nobody except Grandma mentioned Celestine's lack of interest in them. And nobody mentioned that twins were bad luck and used to be thrown away in the evil forest. Bad luck was not discussed at all. I tried not to think about Grandma seeing Celestine's parts, the button and hood all there. I tried not to think about the noises Celestine made during the nights when Alhaji visited her room. I pushed the thoughts as far down as I could. I felt like pulling a headscarf tightly onto my head.

Day seven was naming day. Grandma put a weave on

Celestine, and powdered her face, before helping her to get in a wrapper, and tying it loosely, pulling a T-shirt over her head. A puffed-out picture was printed on the front of the T-shirt of a woman smiling and wearing a large scarf wrapped high around her head. She looked like Twin Two when he arrived, all squashed upwards in the shape of a cone. Underneath the picture, large black writing said: 'God Bless You, For Celebrating My Wife's 40th Birthday. Folashade Abiodun Congratulations and Many Happy Returns. 40 Years. Produced By Ade Abiodun'. Grandma stood looking at the T-shirt for a few seconds, rubbing her chin. Then she smiled, and brushed the ground-dust from Celestine's hair weave. Celestine dropped on her knees to Grandma, and collected more ground-dust, and the whole process had to be repeated.

Mama picked up the twins for the first time. She had been smiling widely since Dan had sponsored the celebrations with what Mama called a 'stack of naira'. She held her arms straight out and curled her hands around the twins' legs. They rested on the muscles at the tops of her arms, which must have been uncomfortable on the twins' heads. She looked at both of them before her smile fell away and a frown between her eyebrows cut her face in two.

'Hello,' she said, 'how are you?' She paused. They both started to cry. Mama held them at some distance from her body, making a gap between her and them. The gap became wider and wider.

'Mama, let me take them for you,' I said.

'OK, Blessing, good girl.' Mama passed them to me quickly. 'That was a nice cuddle, wasn't it?'

Two rams were cooking; the area smelled of roasting meat and pepper, burnt onions, cinnamon. My stomach growled loudly enough for Alhaji standing next to me to open his eyes wide and pat me on the back.

He leant down towards my stomach and spoke to it directly: 'The food is travelling to visit you soon,' he said. 'You see?' He had to speak in a loud voice; Dan had bought us a generator and some fuel! The humming and chugging was a happy sound.

I laughed. Alhaji laughed with me. He patted my back.

Alhaji seemed calm. He stood straighter since the twins had been born. His spine shot straight up towards the sky. The twins made everyone happy. Even Ezikiel smiled whenever he looked at them. I loved to watch Ezikiel smile again.

Saliva dripped down my chin as if my mouth was raining. I could not wait for the food. The large white table on the veranda was *covered* with plastic buckets full of rice, fried fish, pounded yam and sauce. Dan must have given a lot of money! A ghetto blaster played a tape of *Now That's What I Call Music*. The ghetto blaster was so old, and the tape had been used so often, that the ribbon regularly got caught and the sound became strange, and Alhaji rushed over and removed the tape, winding the ribbon back carefully before it broke for good. People stopped dancing, and waited and laughed. Then the music was returned and bodies began to move, their bottoms shaking and shuffling as if they were trying to get away from their bodies. My bottom stayed still. I waited for the sound of King Robert Ebizimor who remained my favourite, even though he was older than Alhaji, and Ezikiel said I should listen to R 'n' B or hip hop or Afrobeat like everybody else my age.

Grandma served the food. The amount she put on plates was so big that the plates would have broken if people had not kept one hand underneath the whole time. There was *jollof* rice, fried fish, fresh fish, pepper soup, smoked fish, spicy stewed snails, barbecued plantain, *banga* soup, *efo-riro*, roasted bush meat, cow tail, *egusi* and *ogbono* with *eba*. I had eaten two bowls already, of all the food piled on together, and I had returned for a third. Alhaji laughed when he noticed me back for more again. 'Where are you hiding that food?'

'The food is very good, Celestine,' I said, the smoky smell filling the air. It amazed me how all the different flavours could be put together and mixed well in the bowl and in my mouth.

'Oohh, my favourite!' Celestine's voice sounded normal at last. She ran towards me and held me tightly, lifting my feet from the ground.

Grandma laughed and shook her head. 'You saved the life of her son,' she said, smiling. 'You need to get used to her lifting you. She will be doing it all the time.'

Then Celestine ran towards the food table. Grandma raised the spoon between the table and Celestine.

'Designer rice,' Celestine shouted, picking up a large tub of *ofada*. 'And the reason it is named designer? It is exclusive. Perfect for me on my special day. The designer rice will go well in my stomach.'

I laughed. 'It is the twins' special day.'

'Yes, them, too. But imagine. They cannot put designer rice in their little tummies. And whatever goes into me comes out through my breast into their mouth. So it is very important for me to have exclusive food.'

I giggled again and looked at Grandma. She lowered the spoon and smiled back at me. Since Celestine had given birth I had been worried about her. It happened sometimes that women's heads did not recover in the way that their bodies did, and I worried that Celestine might be one of those women. Grandma had been worried, too. She had told me. Seeing Celestine hold up the rice and lick her lips, swinging her hips in excitement, I knew she would recover.

The guests drank Maltina, or Star Beer, or Stout, and the smell of Father was everywhere. Somewhere in the back of my mind I saw Father drinking beer, empty bottles on the carpet. Mama shouting, pointing to the mess. I must have been very young; I was holding my teddy bear. Father standing up, and picking a glass bottle, and rushing towards Mama. I shook my head slightly, until I could only see real life.

Mama and Dan stayed near the house, occasionally going inside and returning a few minutes later with swollen mouths.

Alhaji and the imam named the twins. Both twins were silent as the razor moved over their heads, and they remained perfectly still as if they knew danger. It was suddenly quiet enough to hear the scratch of the razor.

'This one Mostafa Ware Ebike Abdul-Salaam. The chosen one. Servant of the peace.' Alhaji held up Twin One. He screamed, making the visitors jump and step backwards, causing those behind them to nearly fall. Nobody dared laugh but I could tell by the way people held their breath and squeezed their lips that they were laughing inside their heads.

'This one Amir Ware Arepamone Abdul-Haq. Prosperous. Same as Alhaji.' The squeezed-together lips became even smaller.

Alhaji picked up Twin Two who was sucking his thumb. The way Alhaji looked at his son reminded me of fat melting in a pan. His face smoothed out. First he looked younger, then his neck skin tightened. Then his skin began to glow as though he had swallowed hundreds of fireflies.

The imam began to read from the Koran, but Twin One was screaming loudly and he had to get the loudspeaker. Still, it was difficult to hear him. We all laughed and looked at Celestine who smiled proudly. 'He is my son,' she said. 'That is definite.'

TWENTY-SIX

On the night before my thirteenth birthday Ezikiel wrapped a scarf around my eyes and tied it behind my head. He took my hand and pulled me. I could hear the sounds of night: the fire hissing and spitting, and the cleaning of pots, and things buzzing and scuttling. We walked for a short time before Ezikiel let go of my hand. I reached for the scarf and pulled it upwards. I did not know what I would find. Boneboy and Ezikiel were sitting at a fire. They had a plastic bottle between them. Palm wine!

'Come, come and sit with us. You need to sip your first palm wine. You are a teenager.'

I looked at the bottle. I looked at Boneboy and Ezikiel. They both had red edges around their eyes. They must have drunk some already. 'I cannot drink that,' I whispered. I looked around where we were. Ezikiel had led me to the neighbour's Christian field. It was empty of Christians. There was a platform in the centre of the field where they held the revivals, and the ground was covered in rubbish.

'I cannot drink alcohol,' I said. 'You are going to be in so much trouble.'

'Just sip it,' said Ezikiel. 'You are a teenager.'

I looked at them both and felt something strange. 'I cannot drink that. You should both come home.'

Boneboy looked at me. He started singing a song.

Ezikiel joined in.

I looked around the darkness of the Christian field and I looked at the fire for a long time. Then I leant down and picked up the palm wine. Ezikiel and Boneboy both clapped and laughed and rolled around the ground. I opened the bottle. The smell was enough to fill my mouth with sick.

I put the bottle to my mouth, and took the smallest sip possible. It still made my stomach twist.

Ezikiel and Boneboy cheered.

Then I tipped the bottle upside down and watched the ground become wet and smelled the air become sour. 'You should not drink this,' I said. 'It is forbidden.'

Boneboy stopped cheering. He looked at my eyes for a long time. I did not look away.

The next morning I could still taste the sip of palm wine on my breath. I opened my eyes slowly to see if the world looked different now I had thirteen years. Mama was already awake and sitting on the mattress with a gift wrapped in ribbon. 'Thank you, Mama.'

I pulled the ribbon apart and opened the box inside. A

necklace. My first necklace. I put it straight around my neck and held it in my fingers. 'Thank you, Mama,' I repeated. She smiled.

Then she leant forwards and kissed my cheek. 'Happy birthday, Blessing. You are growing up into a young woman.'

I let go of the necklace and touched the place where Mama had kissed me.

Grandma was waiting on the veranda. Celestine was frying me a celebration breakfast and singing loudly. Boneboy was at the bottom of the veranda playing with Snap. 'Happy birthday, teenager, Happy birthday, teenager.'

I laughed. Boneboy walked up the veranda steps and handed me a present, wrapped in silver shiny paper. Where had he got the paper? I looked at him to see if he had red eyes from the palm wine the night before but he was already running down the steps and towards the gate, Snap close behind his feet. I held the gift and looked at Grandma. She had her eyebrows raised high in her forehead. I opened the parcel carefully to save the paper. Inside was a tape: King Robert Ebizimor!

'Look!' I showed Grandma and Celestine. 'He found this for me even though he teases me that I have no taste in music.'

I tried to stop my words from coming out so quickly but they were in a rush. Grandma laughed. Then she handed me a large packet wrapped in newspaper. 'Thank you, Grandma.' I looked at the packet. It was a strange shape and size. I wondered what she would have given me. She did not believe in presents. I looked at her face. It was waiting.

Slowly, slowly, I opened the present. A bag. A bag. I opened the bag. A tiny pot of paste, a knife, a small pair of scissors. Equipment!

'Every birth attendant needs her own equipment. And her own birth bag,' said Grandma. 'Happy birthday.'

I looked at the bag and I looked at Grandma and I smiled. My own birth bag! Me! A birth attendant with my own equipment! It was the best present I had ever had. I looked at Grandma and Celestine, and around the garden. I thought of how I had felt when I had first arrived from Lagos. For the first time, I realised how happy I was to be living at Alhaji's. I felt like I was home. I carried the birth bag with me all day, even when I went to use the outhouse. Grandma laughed.

It was July and the rains had come. The area around the village was waterlogged, and Youseff had to stop the car and let us walk; our flip-flopped feet were covered in golden mud. The mud had driven all the insects into the hut, and the ground was moving. A large, winged cockroach scuttled over the bottom half of the woman's leg. Its wings were the colour of Dan's hair. Grandma caught it and slapped it to death with a flip-flop.

'Cut her now,' said the woman.

Grandma had taken the baby girl and wrapped her in a large blanket, and was wiping the white sticky layer from her face. I was gently tugging the placenta from the woman as Grandma had shown me.

'We would not want it to crawl somewhere it should not go, *abi*?' Grandma said.

The woman laughed; it was her seventh baby.

Even so, the birth was long and painful. She needed cutting twice, and Grandma had to stitch her up. But she did not complain at all. I wondered how it was possible to have so much pain and not complain. She only screamed once, during the second cut, and even took some sips of tea between pushes. Her daughter came out blue and floppy but quickly turned deep pink. Her fingertips were already the colour of a walnut. Grandma showed the woman.

'She will be a beautiful tone,' she said, holding up her tiny hands, which were still see-through, not quite real yet.

'Cut her now,' the woman repeated.

Grandma unwrapped the baby, who jumped and jerked in surprise, and began to check her.

'Now,' said the woman. 'Do it now.'

Grandma smiled and looked at me. The baby lay still in the unwrapped blanket. Her legs fell open to the side. Surely, the woman did not mean for Grandma to cut off the baby's girl parts?

I concentrated on what I was doing. I tugged and tugged and finally the placenta came from the woman. I held it up and looked closely at it. 'It is all there,' I told Grandma.

'Good girl. Now wait outside,' she said.

I looked at Grandma. I looked at the woman who was sitting forwards and breathing deeply. I looked at the baby with her wide-open frog-legs and wide-open newborn eyes.

'I want to stay,' I whispered. 'Please, Grandma.'

I did not know what Grandma would do. How she would talk to the woman. Grandma had taught me all about cutting, and the different types that women had, and how it made childbirth difficult and caused problems. I had seen the purple coming from a woman, which Grandma had told me was caused by her pushing so hard for so long against something closed. I had seen that baby die and the purple come from her. And she had been cut. Grandma had stabbed the ground and told me that she herself had been cut and closed and opened again. Grandma taught me that cutting was illegal, and people's thoughts about it were changing. She said that only backward people still cut their girls. Times had changed, she had said.

Cutting girls caused infection and complications in child-birth and death for one out of every ten girls that had it done. Grandma had told me.

She was surely going to talk to the woman, and explain that it was wrong. And tell her what she had told me.

Why did the woman ask Grandma to cut?

Why did she think that Grandma would do such a thing? Grandma? Cutting girls? Causing problems for childbirth? Causing death? The woman was wrong even to ask Grandma. She must have got it wrong. Grandma wanted me to stay outside so that she could talk to the woman and tell her it was wrong. That it was dangerous and could cause pain for the whole of her daughter's life.

Grandma must have known what I was thinking. Her face

fell. 'I will talk later,' she said. She nodded towards the material door.

I walked out as Grandma went into her bag. I thought about standing by the material door, and listening, but I knew that Grandma would have told me to stay if she had wanted me to listen. So I walked further away to the edge of the village. It was a noisy day. Some of the village children were jumping in and out of giant puddles. The rain sounded like a tap open in my ears. But still, through all the noise, I heard the baby scream.

My skin turned cold.

That night it seemed as though I had only been asleep a short time when I woke up to voices carried through the window. Mama was asleep beside me. It was hard to fall asleep. I could not stop hearing the sound of the baby screaming. I could not help wondering what had happened. I did not believe that Grandma could have cut the baby. I could not believe it. There was no chance of that. But the sound of the scream kept returning to my head until I had no room for the voice that told me Grandma would never do that. And she had not wanted to speak at all on the way home. But Grandma cut? It was impossible. She did not agree that girls should be cut. She saw the problems it caused every day. Surely, she would not want to cause those problems?

The moon was setting; it was almost dawn. I climbed off the mattress and pushed my flip-flops through my toes, opening the door quickly to prevent the squeak. It was still dark in the house. I heard cicadas, and the beginning of bird-song. A mouse or rat was shuffling in the corner and a cock-roach scuttled around the chair legs. The Boys' Quarters' children were asleep on the puffy chairs. Youseff's daughters. Fatima and Yasmina. I looked at their shadows. Had they been cut?

I crept outside and watched the moon for a few minutes, sharp and yellow, like a bad tooth disappearing behind grey clouds. There were no stars. I heard voices from the back of the outhouse. Dan's voice. Alhaji had insisted he sleep on the puffy chairs. At one point during the night, I had heard a tap on the door, but Mama was asleep, and did not wake easily. I ignored the tapping and it went away.

'Come, come! Take what you want.' It was Celestine's voice. She was speaking in a mixture of pidgin and proper English. 'You can take it.'

I walked towards the outhouse and stood behind the wall.

'Celestine, stop.' Dan voice sounded high.

'I will give you anything. Look this. Take wetin you want. Take it.'

'No, Celestine, really.' Dan was laughing then. 'Please, don't be silly.'

I crept down low, peering around the corner to look. I almost knew what I would find. I could hear trouble in Celestine's voice.

Celestine had removed her T-shirt and her giant breasts were swinging in the moonlight. Dan was standing in front of her, fully dressed, with his hands raised and his palms open in front of Celestine's breasts.

Dan and Celestine! I turned my head away and then turned it back quickly. Celestine's breasts were still there. I wanted to sneak away and pretend I had never seen them, but I was too frightened to move. The skin on my neck pricked up. I could not turn my eyes away again.

'Put your clothes back on, come on. Don't be so silly. Come on now. Let's forget this ever happened. Really, honestly now, let's not be silly.'

'You should feel me,' she continued, walking towards Dan, with her breasts swinging towards his stomach. 'I be real woman. Let me thank you for paying for naming day celebration. I know you paid plenty naira for me.' Her belly was wrinkled like Grandma's face, and oddly shaped, with an extra fold of flesh like a very short skirt. Her voice was full of tears. Her nose was running. 'You need a woman like me. No more *lenge lenge*! Skinny branch! Please. Take me. Take me. Please.'

Dan stepped away until his back was against the wall where I hid. I moved slightly away, and tried not to make any sound. Suddenly, a voice made me jump up. Dan saw my face, and moved around from behind the outhouse wall. Mama was standing with a tissue in her hand, wearing her night things. Her eyes were still asleep.

'What's going on?' Her eyes slowly opened. They looked from Dan to me and back to Dan again. She looked at my nightdress, which was too big and gaping at the front of my chest. A look fell on Mama's face of something that I did not know. That I had never seen before. It made me feel disgusting. Her usually closed-tight jaw dropped wide open. I could see the yellow tooth at the very back of her mouth. Celestine made a shuffling sound from the back of the outhouse. Mama's face changed shape. She walked quickly to where Celestine was pulling her T-shirt over her head. Celestine's breasts shone like gold in an armed robber's bag.

'Bitch,' said Mama.

Dan covered his mouth with his hand. 'Timi, it's a misunderstanding,' he said, through his fingers. 'My fault entirely. Celestine was simply using the outhouse and I walked in.'

A few seconds passed and Mama was quiet. Her lips were pressed closed tightly; she scratched her head.

'You be no good wife,' Celestine said. 'This one,' she pointed to Dan, her breasts still naked, swinging in the same direction as her arm, 'needs a good woman. A real woman! He needs one like me. Not a skinny branch.'

I held my own face. Dan walked towards Mama; Mama screamed and ran at Celestine with her fist. She ripped Celestine's weave straight out of her hair.

'Bitch!' Mama shouted. 'This fucking family!'

Alhaji came running out of the house with a kerosene lamp. He handed me the lamp and pulled the women apart. He was shaking so much that I thought he might fall. He pushed Dan out of the way. 'Get out of my house!' he shouted. 'Get! Get!'

Dan took a long breath. He did not speak, but he looked at Mama, nodded and turned to walk away.

Alhaji started shouting even louder. 'And just you remember this! I will be claiming a fine from you both! A fine from you both! You see?' He looked at Celestine. 'Claiming back some of the bridewealth that I have spent! Wasted! All that money! That bridewealth! On a betrayer! I will claim it all back. Every penny …'

Mama dropped Celestine's weave on the floor, and followed Dan to the gate. I stood in the shadows. My legs wanted to run but Alhaji was looking straight at me.

We stood in silence while Celestine arranged her clothing. It took her a long time to put her night things back on. Alhaji then pointed to the house and she walked in. As he bent to take the kerosene lamp from my hand I saw tears on his cheek. His body stayed bent forward as he followed Celestine.

Grandma pretended to be asleep, but when I went into her bedroom later in the morning she opened her arms and held me without speaking. Whenever I opened my mouth to ask her about the baby girl or tell her about Celestine, she put a finger in front of her face and said, 'Shh.' When we came out later for food, Alhaji was in the mosque, and Celestine was in the Boys' Quarters. We sat outside eating fried plantain and watching Alhaji pray. Ezikiel was lying under the palm tree listening to a radio station from a small transistor radio that he told me he had found. I wondered if one of his friends had given it to him. He always seemed to be going out with his friends. He lifted his head.

'What's happened?' he asked, flicking his arm towards Alhaji, who had been praying continuously for hours. 'What's going on? It's something to do with *him*, isn't it? The *oyibo*?'

'Nothing,' said Grandma. 'Mind your business.'

Ezikiel switched the radio off and got up. He walked to the veranda and sat on the edge swinging his long legs back and forth. I sat next to him. His eyes were red. He smelled like *garri* a day too old.

'Ezikiel,' I said. He turned to me and smiled. Like my brother. Like Ezikiel. I wanted to tell him about so many things. I leant my head on his shoulder. 'Ezikiel,' I said. 'I have so much to talk to you about. Will you be home today?'

'I'm going out in a minute,' he said.

'Where?'

He moved away slightly, letting my head drop down suddenly. 'None of your business,' he said.

'But I need to talk to you,' I said. The words sounded wobbly.

'I'm busy. I have important business to attend to.'

Business? Ezikiel? I had never heard of Ezikiel attending to important business. I wanted to ask him if he knew about cutting. About who did it. I wanted to hear him say that any worries I had that Grandma might have done such a thing were stupid.

'The FFIN are not getting the attention of the world press, more action is needed. They have the right cause but peaceful talks are not getting them anywhere. More direct action is required.' He threw his arms out to the side, nearly hitting Grandma who was walking past. 'Ha! Some groups are kidnapping the white oil workers. They call the oil black gold, so the groups call the oil workers White Gold!' He paused, took a long breath. 'Sometimes when I hear about the Sibeye Boys—'

Ezikiel noticed Grandma and stopped talking. Grandma jumped up and bent over Ezikiel. She spat at the air in front of his face, her hands waving up and down in front of his eyes. 'Stay away from those boys and stay away from that evil forest.' Grandma slapped the back of his head. 'The devil is in you,' she said. 'I can see him.'

TWENTY–SEVEN

Dan bowed his head before Alhaji and did not look at Celestine. If he had looked he would have seen her black eyes. Grandma held me while the sound of Celestine's screaming filled the air.

'It is necessary,' Grandma said, when I began to cry. 'She is lucky, bloody stupid woman. Lucky not to be thrown onto the street.'

'Alhaji, sir.' Dan said. 'If I've in any way caused you any offence I am truly very, very sorry.'

'Yes,' said Alhaji, and looked at Celestine whose black eyes made it appear if she was wearing sunglasses. Mama had her arms folded. She looked straight at Celestine's eyes.

'I am sorry for the mistake,' Celestine said in perfect English. She did not get up, but remained seated, and spoke with a shaking voice. She was wearing a loose blouse, and the buttons were done up right to the top.

'That's OK,' said Dan. 'Let's not speak of it again.' His voice was warm and sticky like Fanta left in the sun.

I watched Ezikiel watching Dan. He did not say anything

at all, but kept twirling his red string bracelet over and over and over.

'I want you to find me a job,' said Alhaji, eventually. 'As a Quality Petroleum Engineer. A management position.'

'Oh, I really have nothing to do with recruitment, sir,' said Dan. 'That's another department entirely, and I rarely have cause to see them.'

Alhaji turned his head slowly to Celestine, then Mama, then back to Dan.

'But of course I'll ask around,' Dan said.

Ezikiel did not want to visit Dan's house. Mama had made him wear a shirt and tuck it into his trousers. A piece was hanging over the back but I did not dare tell him. His cheeks were pushed closer together from holding his teeth tightly.

'Hurry up,' said Mama. She pulled oil between my plaits.

'I don't feel well,' said Ezikiel, through his closed-together teeth.

Mama did not even look up. 'You are coming. You are coming and you will behave yourself.'

'But I don't feel well, my asthma ...' Ezikiel leant towards her and tried to wheeze. But no wheeze would come.

'I'm not discussing it with you. You're coming.'

It was only when Mama let go of my last plait that I realised she was pulling me too hard; my head fell backwards.

We followed Mama to the shining silver car and driver that Dan had sent to collect us. Youseff sucked his teeth at

Mama as we walked past, but Mama did not hear him. Ezikiel raised one eyebrow.

The car was cool inside with air-conditioning and piano music played through tiny speakers. The cream-coloured leather seats looked completely new, as though we were the first people to sit on them. The driver nodded at us through the rear-view mirror. His eyes moved over our faces until they found the low-cut top of Mama's dress, and then they stayed there for most of the journey.

As we left the compound, nobody came out to wave us goodbye. Not even Celestine. I wondered where they all were. Did Grandma know I was going out for the day?

I looked out as we drove past the village. Everything was different through Dan's car window. People stopped and stood back from the car as we passed them. They did not wave even though I waved at them. Maybe they could not see my face through the shining glass. We drove past the evil forest, past the queue for the village tap, and past the next few villages and past more forest so thick it felt like we were going through a tunnel. We drove all the way to Warri, and all the way through to the other side. And all that time we did not speak.

Dan's compound was surrounded with palm trees and men with guns. A metal gate hid behind the trees, all the way around the compound. At the gate the driver stopped the car and got out, and two men with guns came out to greet him. They looked underneath the car with a mirror attached to a long metal stick.

'What is that for?' I whispered to Mama.

'They're checking to see if we've got a car bomb,' said Ezikiel.

I closed my eyes and prayed that they would not find a car bomb with the tiny mirror. Why would there be a bomb underneath the car?

Mama sighed and smoothed down her hair.

The men with guns looked at us in the car. They looked closely at Mama. Mama did not move her eyes once. She looked straight ahead and crossed her legs. The men made a tutting sound. They spoke to the driver for many minutes, before opening the gate and waving us in.

On the other side of the gate the air changed. It was impossible, I knew, but it really felt like we were breathing different air. Everything was cooler and quieter. I looked at the top of the gate. The air must have been travelling back and forth. But as the car stopped and we climbed out I breathed deeply, and felt certain the air tasted cleaner. Was it possible to filter air in the same way you could filter water? Maybe the air was pure air and arrived in giant pouches with the pure water.

Dan's place was an apartment but nothing like our Better Life Executive Homes apartment on Allen Avenue. He answered the door wearing school shorts and a T-shirt and sandals made from fabric. I looked down at the wrapper Mama had made me borrow from her suitcase, and wished for my old T-shirt with holes in it. I looked at Ezikiel's hanging down shirt and wished that none of it was tucked into his trousers at all.

'Welcome,' said Dan. He opened his arm slowly into the room. The cold air-conditioning made it feel like walking into another world. Tiny bumps crept up my arms. We walked in one by one, still wearing our shoes. I hovered by the door. 'You can leave your shoes on,' said Dan.

I thought of all the outside dirt that must have been trodden into Dan's apartment. The hallway led to a parlour, which had no furniture inside except a long sofa made from black leather, and a glass table in front of it. A television was hanging on the wall with no shelf. How did it stay there? Had Dan glued it directly to the wall? I wanted to walk towards the television but I did not dare move across the white carpet in my shoes. How did Dan keep the carpet so white when he allowed shoes inside?

'What can I get you to drink? We have everything. Anything you want.'

Ezikiel moved his top lip upwards. We followed Dan to the kitchen. I nearly gasped. There was a television in the kitchen! It came out on a stand, and turned itself on as we walked in. Even Ezikiel stopped walking suddenly and put his hand to his mouth. The kitchen looked brand new. The worktops were so clean it was as if no cooking had ever been done there. Where were the pots and pans? Where did Dan keep the food? Our apartment in Allen Avenue was so full of things that you could not see the worktops. The living room was so full of furniture that you could not walk in a straight line through it; you had to zig-zag. Maybe Dan did not own too many things? Did they not pay him enough money? Did he give all his money to Mama? To us?

We sat on high-up chairs and leant our elbows on the shining worktop. Dan opened a cupboard and inside was a fridge! A fridge in a cupboard!

'Here,' said Dan, handing a bottle of Coca-Cola to Ezikiel, then one to me. He opened a drawer and pulled out a metal bottle opener, flicking the tops off our drinks. He poured two glasses of beer and pushed one towards Mama. I did not say a single word even though I had never seen Mama drink beer before.

'This is nice,' said Mama. Then it was quiet. There was no noise at all. I counted to one hundred and sixteen.

'So, Blessing,' said Dan. He drank his beer in sips as though it was tea. 'So, your mother tells me you like music.'

I looked at Mama. She nodded. 'Yes, sir. I like King Robert Ebizimor. Highlife music.'

Dan smiled. 'Excellent. I like jazz myself. As well as opera. The arias. Marvellous to listen to but not the same as watching opera live, of course.'

Dan had a far-away look in his eyes. 'And Ezikiel,' he continued, 'do you like highlife music?'

Ezikiel raised his top lip as far as it would go and gulped down some Coca-Cola.

'I like rap, hip hop,' he said. 'Like everyone else our age.' He looked at me and shook his head. 'Tupac.'

Dan raised both of his eyebrows at the same time. 'Tupac? Is he American?'

Then Ezikiel started throwing his body from side to side. His voice was talking but it sounded like singing; the words came in two sudden parts like a heartbeat. I was so busy listening to the rhythm of the words that at first I did not hear what they said. Something about the Lord saving him, helping him, but suddenly the heartbeat stopped and a word burst out of Ezikiel's mouth. Motherfucker. My hand flew over my mouth. I could hear my heart beating Ezikiel's word over and over in my neck.

Dan's mouth fell open. I could not see what happened to Mama's mouth because she moved so quickly across the kitchen. She slapped the back of Ezikiel's head and knocked him off the high-up chair.

'Sorry, sorry,' said Ezikiel as he climbed back up. He was holding his hands over his head, blocking Mama's arm, which had stretched right back ready to knock him down again.

'How dare you use that language? What kind of child did I raise?'

It was quiet for a long time. I counted again but kept losing the number I'd thought of and having to start again. Still, I got to eighty-four before Dan spoke.

'Maybe you'd like to watch a movie? I've got a great selection – all the latest DVDs. Do you like movies?'

I nodded my head. It had been so long since we had watched a film. Father used to like *Rambo*.

'Have you ever seen *The Karate Kid*? It's old, but I expect you'd like it.'

Ezikiel did not move but he did lower his hands from his face.

'Well, let's all sit down and watch a film. I'll see if there's popcorn.'

We all watched Dan opening cupboards and drawers. He whistled as though Ezikiel had never used bad language at all. He had forgiven Ezikiel's language and the matter was finished.

But Mama had not finished. Her arm was stretched out behind her. As soon as Dan went into the other room to set the film, she let it fly back towards Ezikiel's cheek.

The rest of July Alhaji became increasingly impatient and bad-tempered. Even Youseff kept out of his way and offered to run any errand for Grandma. Celestine prayed every day, and was not allowed to mourn. Her prayers became louder, and slower, as though she was practising anyway. Alhaji had burned her Lycra collection in the barrel that it had arrived in. She had wept for four days and then followed Alhaji around everywhere. She fetched his dinner, rubbed his feet, served his drinks. Mama stayed out at work all of the time, and Dan visited at least once a week. He told Alhaji that he had asked his colleagues if there was a vacancy for him. Ezikiel left as soon as Dan arrived. Mama said that suited her fine.

It seemed as if Alhaji had forgotten who he was. He walked around shouting orders as usual, but at strange times. During dinner, he would suddenly shout, 'It's time for prayers,' and we would have to wake the imam from where he slept at the back of the makeshift mosque. Alhaji would forget to dress in the morning and come out wearing his large Marks and Spencer Y-fronts and vest, and Grandma would have to speak quietly in his good ear, making him turn and run back to his bedroom. I got used to seeing his back. He usually ignored me but he started ordering me to do things, such as sweep the already swept floor, or cook the already cooked plantain. I did whatever he asked.

'Stupid girl,' he said one day, when he found a torn newspaper.

'Sorry, sir,' I said, even though it was not my fault. I avoided Alhaji and spent most of my time in Grandma's bedroom, which Alhaji never entered. Her room was the hottest room in the house, and had no window. The walls were bare. There was a hessian mat rolled up and balanced against the wall. The mattress on the floor was too soft for Grandma's back. I lay down on the soft mattress and closed my eyes for hours, trying not to think.

'Blessing.' Grandma entered the room, and sat on the mattress next to me.

'What is wrong with Alhaji, Grandma?'

'He is a proud man,' said Grandma, 'and pride for men is like love for women. Very strong. The most important thing for men is pride. So don't mind him.'

'Grandma, I need to ask you some things,' I said. 'I wanted to talk to you—'

'Don't mind him, he will be fine,' she said. 'He knows what a bloody stupid woman she is …'

'No, Grandma, not Alhaji. I was hoping to talk to you about the birth. And the woman who asked you to cut the baby girl. About cutting.'

Grandma stopped talking and lay down next to me on the mattress. She turned her face to mine and turned my face to her. 'I have told you plenty about cutting,' she said. 'That part of your training is finished.'

'I know, Grandma.' I lifted my stomach as high as it would go and pressed hard. 'But I wanted to ask if you did cut her. The baby, I mean.'

Surely Grandma would say no and I could start letting myself think again. My head would stop spinning around and around.

Grandma kept her face perfectly still. Even her eyebrows stayed level. 'I cannot lie to you,' she said. 'It is the old way. All the girls used to have it but now it is only a few. And I am an old traditional birth attendant. These choices are hard to understand, why women make these choices. Why we must also make choices as birth attendants. But I make my own choices, and I have my own reasons. It is not done much now. But, yes, I did perform cutting.'

My hand flew to my mouth so quickly it caused a smacking sound. 'But you told me it is most of the village girls, Grandma. You said eight girls out of ten would still have it done.' I paused and tried to keep my face as still as Grandma's. I could feel my eyebrows moving all over the place. 'Why would you do that? Cutting girls?'

'I did perform cutting,' said Grandma. 'And now only

sometimes mild cutting. And some of my friends do it, other birth attendants. Only the type one or mainly type two. Just a scratch to show it has been done. Many years ago it was normal. Everyone did it. Anyway type three is the real problem and nobody does that here.'

'What about the infections and the problems they have? The problems we see, that you have shown me? The girls with type one and type two cutting still had problems.'

'People still do it. And they know the problems. Sometimes problems can seem so terrible until you hear about other problems. And type one is like boys.'

'What do you mean, Grandma? You told me that cutting is not like boys!' I could feel my cheeks getting hotter and hotter and hotter. 'You said cutting girls was not like taking the spare skin from the end of a penis. You said it was more like cutting the penis off itself!'

Grandma sighed. I had never heard her sigh that loudly before. 'I understand why you feel angry. But it is compli-cated. If the problem is risk of death and trouble with child-birth, that is bad. But sometimes problems for those people will be worse if the girls are left. The girls and their fami-lies can be thrown from a village. I have seen it. They will not marry. They will starve to death.'

'Why do they throw the girls out?'

'It is complicated,' she said again. 'And you will have to make decisions of your own, for your own reasons. This is the job.' Her eyebrows stayed exactly still.

I did not understand Grandma's words. I watched her face

closely. There was no decision waiting to be made in my head. I would never cut a girl.

'I will never cut a girl,' I said.

One of Grandma's eyebrows moved all the way up her forehead. 'Sometimes even if you think something is wrong it must be done. A scratch from me is better than a butcher from another attendant. Some things you cannot stop happening.'

I heard Grandma's words but I still did not understand. Some things you cannot stop happening? The words did not make sense. Of course you can stop your own hands.

I looked at Grandma's tiny hands.

Then I looked at Grandma's face, closely. She looked different. Her face had changed.

'Grandma—'

'No more questions,' she said. 'An owl is the wisest of all birds because the more it sees the less it talks.'

That evening Grandma called us around the fire. Youseff's children sat in the dark on the outside of the circle. 'Why do they always sit there?' I asked Grandma, who was on a stool.

'They always sit on the outside,' she said.

I sat next to Celestine, who had started coming to listen to Grandma's stories with the twins on her lap. The twins did not listen at all, but Celestine was listening to every word. I had stopped saving a space next to me for Ezikiel. He never came to listen to Grandma's stories any more.

Grandma passed around a piece of sugar cane to each of

us. We began to tear and chew and suck. When the noises from each mouth became quieter, Grandma began speaking in Izon. I had heard Grandma tell Alhaji she did not mind speaking in English, but only Izon would do for her stories.

'Grasshopper and Toad appeared to be good friends. People always saw them together.'

Grandma looked at me. Celestine flicked her head from me to Grandma back to me.

'But they had never eaten a meal together,' continued Grandma. 'One day Toad said to Grasshopper, "Dear friend, tomorrow come and dine at my house. My wife will cook and we will eat together." The next day Grasshopper arrived at Toad's house. Before sitting down to eat, Toad washed his forelegs and asked Grasshopper to wash his. Grasshopper made a very loud noise.'

Grandma also made a very loud noise. We all jumped. I nearly fell into the lap of one of Youseff's daughters.

'"Friend Grasshopper, can you leave your chirping behind? I cannot eat with such a noise," said Toad. Grasshopper tried to eat without rubbing his forelegs together, but it was impossible. Every time he chirped Toad complained and told him to be quiet. Grasshopper was so angry he could not eat. Finally he said to Toad, "I'll invite you to my house to eat tomorrow."'

Celestine leant forwards. She smiled at me. 'This better than a DVD,' she said.

'The next day Toad arrived at Grasshopper's house. As soon as the meal was ready Grasshopper washed his forelegs and invited Toad to do the same. Toad washed his forelegs and hopped over to the food.

'"You need to wash again," said Grasshopper. "All the hopping in the dirt has made you dirty again." Toad hopped back to the jar and washed again. But the same thing happened. When Toad reached for the food, Grasshopper stopped him. "Don't put your dirty hands in the food."'

We all started laughing. Grandma had the funniest grasshopper voice. When we stopped laughing she continued. The moon had sunk low down and was behind Grandma's head, lighting her up like a lamp. 'Toad was furious. "You don't want me to eat with you. You know I use my forelegs for hopping around. I cannot help it if they get dirty."

'Grasshopper also shouted. "You started it. You know I cannot rub my forelegs together without making any noise."' Grandma lifted her face as high as the moon. 'From that day on they could no longer be friends.'

Everyone began to talk, but I could see from Grandma's face that she had not finished yet. We all fell silent again.

'But they missed each other too much,' she continued. 'So they accepted each other and lived side by side. Grasshopper never tried to make Toad understand why his legs made noise. And Toad never tried to make Grasshopper know why he hopped. Sometimes things were the way they were. They lived happily ever after.'

Everyone was surprised to hear the end of Grandma's story. Her stories hardly ever had a happy ending.

Everyone was surprised except me. I smiled to myself.

Sometimes Grandma explained things so that I really understood. I knew that I would never cut a girl. And I knew that Grandma knew it, too.

The day Alhaji started his new job he could not eat his breakfast. Every time the spoon of egg went towards his mouth it was pushed away with his words.

'This management position at the Western Oil Company, it is an essential role, you see?' He was wearing a grey suit and a blue and purple striped tie. His buttons were done up tightly and his loose neck skin was hanging over the top.

'Yes, sir,' I said. Alhaji looked different. Shiny.

'I might be home late. Very late. And you will have to be a good girl and wait for me. You see?'

'Yes, sir.'

'And even though you will miss Alhaji, just remember when payday comes, Alhaji will buy you some sweeties from the market, and even a jewellery. Maybe a watch. Imagine that, a watch of your own.'

'Thank you, sir.' I looked at my wrist and tried to imagine it covered by a watch. I wondered what it would feel like to know the time again.

Alhaji paused long enough to put the spoon near his mouth but swallowed the egg in one gulp. 'And there will be more fuel for the generator. So that we can have light. And with the second pay cheque I will buy a television.' He paused. I thought of the generator Dan had left us. I wondered if he would bring us more fuel to power it. Alhaji straightened his back, and straightened his tie. 'But money is not the most important thing, you see?'

I nodded.

'I will be preserving the environment by teaching my less polluting methods of oil refining. No more gases burnt into our air. The crops will grow. And the black bark of the avocado pear tree, which is very worrying indeed, will disappear!'

Alhaji swelled in size like a ball of pounded yam in sauce. He made a tiny clicking noise at the back of his throat. He touched my hand.

A week later it was all over. Dan paced the veranda. Alhaji had shrunk back to his usual size and was sitting in the rocker with his head in his hands. I was cooking on the fire outside, stirring the stew pot with a long ladle, adding palm oil and salt and Maggi cube, tasting, then adding palm oil and salt and Maggi cube.

'I didn't know, sir, I'm so sorry!'

'It is an outrage, you see? A bloody outrage!' Alhaji stood from the rocker, knocking it over until it lay on the floor with its legs sticking up.

'Honestly, I'm as disgusted as you, sir. I can't believe that this kind of thing actually goes on.'

'Ghost worker! Alhaji! What do they think, that they can put me on a desk and give me bloody biscuits! Say you are free to play the computer games, surf the internet, like I am a boy. I am nearly sixty years old and a Petroleum Engineer. A specialist ...'

'I really can't believe it goes on, sir.' Dan was walking up and down quickly. It was difficult to see his face. He did not slow his walk at all, even when Mama came out of the house wearing only a wrapper tied underneath her armpits.

'It's disgusting,' said Mama. 'This country. Treating local men as children, patronising them with imaginary jobs. What an insult.'

Alhaji looked at Mama. 'What are you wearing? You think you can wear this thing in my house, behave like town prostitute?' He stood and walked towards her. His hand was high in the air. I dropped the ladle into the stew quickly, causing splashes of sauce to jump out and burn my arm.

'Don't raise your hand to me!' Mama moved backwards. 'I didn't cause this problem. I'm on your side, in case you'd forgotten.'

Alhaji lowered his hand. He turned around and looked at Dan. 'You found me the position,' he said. 'You had a good laugh at Alhaji. Get him a false job, let them pay him off. Ha! I imagine what you say to your friends. Sleep with his daughter then take his pride. Even try and sleep with his junior wife. All that bridewealth wasted and now no employment!'

'I'm sorry, sir, I really had no idea, I can assure you.'

'Assure me. Assure me. You could not afford to assure me. I am worth more than your money!'

Dan stopped pacing. 'Um, sir, I really don't think—'

'You do not think. You even admit it yourself, you do not think. Well, Alhaji is not a ghost worker. Alhaji is alive! A living worker. They can keep their ghost-worker job.'

Alhaji sat down on the rocker, and put his head back into his hands. 'You see?'

Grandma called me over to where she was sitting on the veranda. Mama Akpan had given Grandma her old gold-plated Marks and Spencer jewellery, which Grandma wore all at the same time in case anyone decided to steal it. She sparkled and shone and lit up as I walked nearer, as if she herself was gold-plated.

'There are two births,' said Grandma, breaking my thoughts. 'You do one, I do one.'

'What do you mean?' My heart was running fast on hot ground.

'There are two different village births.' Grandma opened her birth bag and separated the contents into another bag. 'Only one Grandma.' She laughed. 'You have to go on your own.'

I felt my own skin shine.

I found Mama frying plantain on the outside fire. She had a pile of plantains by her feet. They were almost completely black, which is when Mama always said they tasted the sweetest. 'Mama, can I ask you something?'

Mama did not look up from the frying pan. 'Yes, Blessing. What is it?'

'I wanted to ask your permission.' I paused, listening to the sounds of bubbling oil. 'To attend a birth.'

Mama looked up suddenly. Her eyes looked at mine,

flicking from one to the other. The frown between her eyebrows became deeper. 'Uh, um, I …'

Mama could not speak. She did not know how to answer me. I felt something, a taste in my mouth that had never been there before. Mama did not know what to say, and I did.

'I want to train, Mama. More than anything. And I will not go without your permission.'

'Um, I … maybe, but um, you should be careful, I, uh …'

'Thank you, Mama.' I stood up, and walked near to her, and suddenly found a courage that I never realised I had. I reached my arm and touched her shoulder. It was sharp. 'Thank you, Mama.' As I walked away I felt Mama watching *my* back. It felt good.

The village was far into the mangrove creeks. I climbed into the waiting dugout canoe and closed my eyes. I did not want to see any boats full of boys carrying rifles and wearing necklaces of bullets.

The tiny village had only four huts but dozens of small children were playing football outside them. 'Sweet pen,' they shouted as I arrived, 'sweet pen,' as if I was a white girl, or they somehow knew about Dan.

I entered a mud and thatch hut, dark and smoky inside. The girl, Nyengiebi, was alone and on her knees, leaning forward to rest her elbows on the ground. She smiled at me, but still, fear entered my belly. What if the baby's shoulder got stuck?

'Sister,' she said. I was relieved. I was shaking as I opened the bag and tried to hide it from the eyes of Nyengiebi by turning my back to her. When the instruments, the knife, scalpel, clamp, herbs and pastes were out of the bag, and set out on the newly-washed blanket, I stopped shaking, and began an examination. First I rubbed my hands with the alcohol gel, which the hospital had given to Grandma. I pulled Nyengiebi's wrapper up and pushed my fingers inside, as Grandma had shown me many times. I tried to imagine that Grandma was in the room, hear her voice. *Do not be gentle. This woman is giving birth.*

'You are nearly ten centimetres,' I said, and tried to make my hand still in case I shook inside her. 'Nearly time to push.' Nyengiebi nodded. Her other children were in the doorway, three, all girls. I thanked God and Allah and the Ancestors that the woman had given birth before and her body knew what to do.

The next contraction came suddenly with no build-up. Nyengiebi grabbed me and dug her nails into my flesh.

'Push now,' I said, and held her tightly. I felt the baby's head crowning, pushing against my hand. 'The head is there. Now stop pushing and pant. Like this.' The words came easily from my mouth. I knew exactly what to say. I knew exactly what to do. I showed her, by breathing quickly until my head felt light. I slipped my fingers around the baby's neck and pressed softly. No cord. 'Good, the baby is nearly ready to come. On the next contraction I want you to push hard, and hold the push as long as you can.' Nyengiebi nodded and took some long breaths. The contraction came quickly, her stomach turned as hard as bone. She pushed, gritting her teeth. The veins in her neck bulged and her eyes popped outwards. A scraping noise came from her mouth. I prayed. *Don't let the shoulder get stuck, don't let the shoulder get stuck.* The baby came out quickly, and I had to catch it like a football. I put the baby straight onto Nyengiebi's chest, and wiped the white stickiness from his face.

'A boy,' I said. The children at the doorway jumped into the air and ran out. Nyengiebi lifted her head to look at her son, as I cut the cord and started the next stage, of tugging the placenta. It took a long time, but eventually fell out. I examined it carefully for tears, to check none had been left inside. I put it in a small bag, and left it at the side of the room for Nyengiebi. Then I took the baby and wrapped him in a piece of cloth, before attaching him to Nyengiebi's breast. I stayed with her for many hours, until we had all stopped shaking. She had lost the front of one of her teeth. It had chipped off when she pushed him out.

'It always happens,' she said, opening her mouth. Four of her teeth were chipped in a similar way.

She looked at her son closely, examining his toes and fingers. 'Did you ever see such a beautiful boy?' she asked.

'No,' I lied. The boy's head was a strange shape and his eyes were close together. But I could see how beautiful he was to his mother, who kept smiling and making tiny sounds in the back of her nose. I stayed for longer than I had to. Eventually I stood, and smiled at Nyengiebi before leaving. The husband was waiting outside with a bag full of river fish and a bottle of freshly tapped palm wine. I took my gifts and stood a little bit taller. It was almost as if I had grown a few inches in a few hours. But that was impossible. I looked at my hands for a long time. My own hands. I smiled.

TWENTY-EIGHT

'Ezikiel, Grandma, Alhaji, Celestine, Blessing! Are you there? Gather up everyone! There's some news. Quick!' Mama shouted as she came out of the house with Dan, pulling his hand and making it appear as though she was dragging him by the arm like a small child. It was the afternoon and we were full of river fish, relaxing with swollen bellies in the heat. We all looked up except Ezikiel who looked towards the gate. 'We have some great news.' Tiny crinkles had appeared at the corner of Mama's eyes. 'Ezikiel,' she said. He looked at her, and tutted. Dan came out from behind Mama and stood next to her, pushing his arm into hers. He was smiling but he smiled all the time, so I could not tell whether he was happy or not. They stood smiling for some time, while I held my breath. A bitter taste settled on my tongue. I tried to swallow but the spit in my mouth did not want to travel.

'We're engaged!' Mama stepped forward and threw her hand in the air, flashing a large ring on her marriage finger. It covered the line which was still left from Father's ring, which he used to claim was solid gold, even after Mama had told him that when Dr Adeshina had seen it he told her that it was cheap jewellery and that she needed to take the ring off. 'That is solid gold. Twenty-five carats. The highest quality. Who do you believe?'

She had removed the ring, and did not speak to Father for two weeks, a punishment at which Father laughed and said was no punishment at all.

Dan's ring was silver with three diamonds. I wondered if the diamonds represented Mama, me and Ezikiel. I felt sick.

Dan picked up Mama's hand. 'A diamond for our past, our present and our future,' he said. 'Set in white gold.'

Ezikiel snorted. 'White gold,' he muttered. 'White gold? That is what you are! That is what they call the *oyibos* around here! You people take our black gold and they take you. What do you know of our past?' Ezikiel stood up. 'Of our present?' He was shouting then, with a man's voice. 'And what the fuck do you know of our future?' He ran towards the gate. We could hear him crying as he ran away, even though he coughed to try and cover the noise. I could not believe Ezikiel. Since leaving school his brain was melting. My brother, who was planning on medical school and could speak Latin, was behaving like an Area Boy.

When he had gone, there was silence until Mama's smile dropped, and even Dan's became shaky. He looked as if he was trying to say something to someone without making any noise.

'Excellent.' Alhaji eventually stepped forwards and shook Dan's hand furiously. The smiles returned. 'Congratulations, congratulations.' He slapped Dan on the back. 'Ha! My son.'

Dan looked at him suddenly, but then he laughed. Celestine jumped up and down, jiggling her breasts, shouting, 'Hey hey, *oyibo*,' and then kissing Dan, on the mouth. Alhaji looked at her and Mama clenched her fist. The white gold ring seemed to cover all her knuckles.

'Well, I hope we won't cause any problems,' said Dan, looking at the gate Ezikiel had disappeared from. 'But we're really, really, frightfully happy.'

I tried to force a smile on my face.

'Are you crazy?' Grandma raised her voice. 'This cannot happen.'

'Don't you start with me,' Mama screamed. Her face became wrinkled and old. Dan looked surprised. His smile remained but his mouth opened. 'You want me to be like you,' continued Mama. 'Well, I'm not like you. You want me to be happy here? This fighting? Living in poverty? The best you can hope for is to make a few dollars giving out drinks ...'

Dan frowned and dropped Mama's hand, stepping back.

'This is not about you. Not all about you.' Grandma pushed Celestine and even me out of the way. She faced Mama with her hands on her hips, drawing in a giant breath. 'What do you think will happen, that you can live here? In this country? With this madness around? Oil and water do not mix! You are made of water, you are a part of the Delta, and the river runs through you. That man,' Grandma pointed to Dan, 'is made of oil!'

Mama laughed. 'You are a crazy old woman living in the last century. The world is changing and if there's anyone who won't accept us it's only you! Maybe we'll move to London to get away from that. Old-fashioned attitudes.'

'Eh? You think London will accept oil and water?'

I gasped. Mama was leaving. *What will happen to Ezikiel if Mama leaves him?*

'What will happen to that boy if you leave him?' said Grandma, lowering her hands.

'Who?' asked Mama. We all looked at her. Even Dan. The white gold ring threw off light that danced over Grandma's gold-plated jewellery, which bounced back and forth. Even their jewellery was fighting. 'Oh,' said Mama, 'Ezikiel will be fine. Now, Blessing, come here.'

I went to Mama. I did not know what to do. I went to kiss Mama's cheek, but Mama turned her head away, and I kissed her ear instead. It was shaped like a shell.

'Congratulations, Mama,' I said. I shook Dan's hand. 'Congratulations, sir.' Dan grabbed my arm. His fingers became a loose circle around me. His skin was wet.

'No need for formality, little miss,' he said.

He tried to tickle me.

Mama laughed. 'You can't call him sir when he is your daddy, when we move to London. Imagine – the restaurants, art galleries, the shops! – I'll be able to do so much when I don't have to work. When Dan keeps me in a manner befitting a lady.' Mama squeezed the side of Dan's stomach. It looked at first as if she had pinched him. He laughed.

I thought of all the things Mama had told me. 'Be proud

of who you are,' she had said. 'Of where you come from.'
Did she really want to leave?

'I can see I'm going to have my work cut out with you,'
Dan said, squeezing Mama's side back. 'You'll be mooching
around all day, and there'll be no dinner on the table.' They
laughed. Could they not see us standing in a circle around
them, all looking at the ground? Grandma had tears covering
her face and they had not even noticed.

I moved away with my mouth open. Mama had never looked
happier. Her skin glowed. She looked brighter than all of us,
even Grandma who was shining with gold-plated jewellery.

Grandma stepped forwards and put her arm around my
shoulders, moving me towards the door. 'Are you both crazy?'
she asked, as we walked into the house.

The arguments began the next morning. 'He is not going to
convert – I don't even know what you are thinking.' Mama
and Alhaji were at the other end of the compound but we
could hear every word where Grandma and I sat underneath
the palm tree taking off the stringy ends of a bucketful of
okra. 'It will be a Christian wedding.'

Alhaji clutched his chest. 'Not in my house,' he said. 'You
are Muslim! You see? That means he will convert! Or there
is no wedding. I will forbid the marriage!'

'Forbid all you want,' screamed Mama. 'You're as bad as
she is – living in the last century. Don't you understand that
you can't forbid anything? Anyway, you call yourself Muslim
but ...'

Grandma dropped the okra she was holding into the bucket. It made a tiny splashing sound.

'Not in my house! What are you talking? You will not have a Christian wedding in my house!'

Grandma picked up more okra, and continued cutting and pulling, cutting and pulling. Her hands did not change speed and her face did not change shape. She did not look up.

'Grandma,' I whispered. 'Shall we go inside?' There was something wrong about listening to an argument between Mama and Alhaji. My stomach felt like it knew what was coming next. I remembered how arguments ended with Mama.

'That's fine,' said Mama. 'We'll do it at Dan's work. I wanted to have the wedding there anyway.'

Alhaji shrank. The world closed around his body. He did not raise his hand, or push Mama against the ground, or put his hand around her throat. He shrank.

Alhaji was not like Father at all.

Mama's words made Grandma put the bucket down, and fold in half. She sighed and looked sadder than I had ever seen her. I wanted to comfort her, to put my arms around her, but a hundred cuddles from me would not remove Mama's words from Grandma's ears. A daughter should never speak to a father in that way. Mama had lost her mind. I felt angry with her then, and sorry for Alhaji, who always seemed to be doing his best.

TWENTY-NINE

I looked at the dress that Mama wanted me to wear. It was puffy and pink satin with ribbons of lace criss-crossing all over it. Around the neckline was a layer of pink lace. I touched the sleeve. It scratched my fingers.

'It's imported,' Mama said.

'Thank you, Mama.'

'Now, it's very important that Ezikiel wears his suit. I told him to come early and get ready. Where is he? If he's late today I'll kill him.'

Ezikiel had been hiding since the day that Dan and Mama became engaged. There was no way he would wear the suit. I knew it. But Mama had still not realised. She held up a waistcoat in front of her face. 'He will look so nice in a suit,' she said. I wondered if the waistcoat was imported, too. Dan must have paid for everything.

'Mama, I think Ezikiel is hiding.'

Mama dropped the waistcoat onto the floor mattress. It looked as if it was holding my dress. 'What? What are you saying now?'

I looked at her face. I looked at the door. Everywhere was quiet. I could not hear any shouting, or music, or birdsong, or banging of pots. I opened my mouth and told the words to come out. 'Mama, Ezikiel is, he, well, Ezikiel he is finding things difficult.'

Mama threw her head and her arms upwards. 'Difficult? Of course he is. Blessing, I really don't need this now.'

'I am sorry, Mama.'

Mama let her head drop back down to its normal position.

'Ezikiel is very angry, Mama.'

'Angry? I'll show Ezikiel angry! The way he's been behaving – disrespecting Dan. If it wasn't for Dan he'd be on the street. He should be thanking Dan, for God's sake. Honestly, I don't know what's going on with your brother.'

'He is angry.' My words sounded small but they were the only ones I could think of.

Mama leant close to my face. She looked straight at me. 'I don't want to hear any more,' she said. 'This is my wedding day, and I'm not going to let anything spoil it.'

The wedding was supposed to be small, Mama had called it intimate, and I had looked up the word in the dictionary that was the last of Ezikiel's books. Intimate meant small and meaningful. But I had never heard of a small wedding. Weddings were about showing off. Food, money, dress, band, cake, Tupperware. The dress had to be big, and white and scratchy, even though Mama had been married to Father before.

Even though Mama and Father had never divorced, I thought.

Had they? Surely if Mama had divorced Father we would have known. There would have been paperwork. But rules did not seem to apply to Mama. When I had asked Ezikiel about it, he told me that Mama and Father had only had a ceremonial wedding. They had never made it to register the paperwork. So maybe Mama had never really been married to Father before at all?

I thought about it while we waited in the garden, for what seemed like hours, for Mama to come out of the house. Mama had been up before the loudspeaker, making herself look extra specially beautiful. Alhaji kept looking at his watch. Grandma sat down next to Celestine. Both of them wore traditional clothes that they had had made for the wedding. When the tailor asked for the same-sized piece of cloth for each woman, Grandma had almost fallen over. 'Surely,' she had said, 'you need a lot more material for that woman. I would fit twice into one of her costumes!'

The sun had lowered and given the sky wedding jewellery, the river birds had begun their afternoon song. Dust blew upwards; everyone had half-closed eyes.

'This wind,' said Alhaji, 'this wind is early.' He was pacing up and down, wearing a traditional outfit made from the same colourful lace fabric as Grandma's, and a hat. He had changed many times, from Western-style suit to traditional costume, back to Western suit, then traditional costume and so on.

Eventually Grandma had said, 'You will wear the same material as your family, so everyone can identify you as the head,' and Alhaji had nodded in agreement, raising his face towards the sky.

'This harmattan wind gives us meningitis and sends animals crazy. But Allah gives and he takes. By blowing the harmattan he gives meningitis but he takes the mosquitoes, so he reduces malaria. You see?'

I wondered what Allah would give to me now he was taking Mama. When he took Father, he had given me Grandma, so maybe Alhaji was right. Suddenly, Alhaji turned his head towards the veranda, and when I followed it, there was Mama. She looked beautiful and strange at the same time. Her face was not shiny but covered with powder. Even her nose did not shine, and seemed smaller, more pinched, like Grandma's. Mama's eyes appeared more almond-shaped, like mine, as she had drawn a line upwards and outwards with a black make-up crayon. The most impressive things on Mama's face were her lips. They were even fuller than usual, and had an outline of dark red against the middle of brighter red – the amazing colour of fresh blood. I tried not to imagine Dan kissing Mama's lips. Mama's face looked like a mixture of all our faces. The dress was the whitest white I had ever seen, and shaped like a cake. It had a round layer at the bottom made from lace, and a plain white middle closing tight on Mama's waist. The top of the dress was covered in diamonds. Tiny, brilliant, shining diamonds.

'Millions,' said Celestine. 'Those diamonds are worth millions!'

'Don't be silly, bloody stupid woman,' said Grandma. 'They are sequins, worth only a few naira. I bought them at market last week.'

I did not look up at Celestine. I was worried that my eyes would tell her that I had thought the same, and Grandma might think that I too was bloody stupid.

'My daughter,' said Alhaji. He held his arms towards her.

It must have been difficult for Mama to move in the dress, as she did not run towards Alhaji. She moved slowly across the veranda. I looked at Grandma's face. It looked the same as normal. Her cheek scars were as still as the river. She had seen the dress before, but still I found it strange that Grandma did not cry. I think that even Mama, if she was to see me one day, her only daughter, in a giant white scratchy dress, would surely lose some tears.

'You are beautiful,' said Alhaji, moving towards Mama. 'What a dress! You see? Only the best for my daughter. My lovely daughter.'

I had no idea how Alhaji managed to forgive Mama, when she had been so disrespectful towards him, but he did. Without any anger in his voice he walked forwards and held out his arms. Grandma leant towards me and whispered, 'An oil lamp feels proud to give its light even though it wears itself away.'

I helped prepare the food tables, smoothing over a table-cloth, carrying plates, and cutlery, serviettes, glasses. There was lots of shouting, people hurrying from one side of the compound to the other carrying pots of food, crates of Supermalt. Youseff's wives rushed around everywhere with their hair half-done, in curlers, or a half-dressed baby hanging from their breast. Alhaji had organised a large tent to be put up over the food table, and even though the wedding was due to start, the men were still trying to work out which pole went where. They whistled whenever Mama walked past in her wedding dress. 'Lucky husband tonight,' they said. I felt sick all through my body, right down to my feet. Even my toes felt sick.

Dan arrived too early, before everything was ready. The food was being cooked and the smell of barbecued meat had brought the local guests early, too; they were forming a queue at the gate. The crowd parted for Dan, who ran in like a girl, almost skipping. He smiled at the men putting up the tent, he smiled at Youseff's half-done wives, and he smiled the widest when he saw Mama rush into the house, even though he only saw her back, and even though it was bad luck to see her in the wedding dress before the ceremony. 'Blessing and Ezikiel. Come here, please.' Ezikiel's arm stiffened into a tent pole. We went towards him, and he tried to hug us. Then he gave us both a flower for our buttonholes, even though we did not have any buttonholes. Dan looked at my dress. I wanted to climb into a T-shirt and wrap a wrapper around myself until I felt safe and normal. Ezikiel had worn his football shirt underneath the white shirt Mama forced him into. I knew he would not wear a suit. The football shirt made his white shirt look pale blue and you could still see the writing at the back: 'Essien'.

Dan stood holding us awkwardly. 'Let's try and make this a good day,' he said, looking straight at Ezikiel, who was scowling. My face ached from holding a smiling position for so long. Dan's face must have permanently ached.

'This is going to be such a good day, really, I'll bet you're as excited as me. I can't wait to see your mother – is she nervous? No, don't answer that, of course she probably has the jitters, every woman would. I mean it's not every day you get married! I've been awake all night – I hope my eyes stay open, just excitement really, couldn't sleep. Well, I'm sure you kids will have a great day, lots of food, dancing. It'll be really fantastic. Really great!'

I looked at Ezikiel's eyes. They had changed colour.

The white people from Dan's workplace turned up early in large cars and vans, surrounded by MoPol security men carrying guns. We heard the screeching sirens carry them through the next village and down our bumpy road. 'Is that really necessary?' Dan asked aloud. They had an armoured vehicle and a security guard for each guest. I did not know if it was necessary. It was what always happened. The sirens blaring, armoured vehicles carried the white people through our villages, and we watched them, blurring and blaring past us. I had not questioned if it was necessary before. The security men waited by the gate; I could see the tips of their rifles over the top. I wondered if they could smell the *suya*. I wondered if the white men would save them some food. I wondered what they thought about us.

Local people had travelled from as far as Port Harcourt. It felt like Lagos, having such a mixture of people together. I counted five different tribes, and seven different languages. 'Where is the white man?' they said, ignoring Mama in her wedding dress. They pointed at Dan, the whitest of all the white men. His face was shiny from the sun cream, which he kept spraying on throughout the day; tiny beads of sweat were white from the cream. From a distance it looked as though he had very bad acne.

The local guests wore colours so bright it hurt my eyes to look at them. The men carried briefcases, and their wives and girlfriends held small handbags that matched their shoes perfectly. The women had beautiful jewellery sets, the earrings matching the bracelets, matching the necklace. And each family matched each other. The women had styled the materials on their heads in different, difficult patterns. The tops of their heads looked like jagged mountains against the blue sky. They all arrived with gifts, and gave Alhaji bottles of Remy Martin and expensive aftershave, as if it was his day, instead of Dan's. They patted Alhaji on the back so hard, and so often, that he stood with his back against the house wall for much of the day. When his back was not against the wall, Alhaji walked around waving his arms in the air and greeting his friends, making sure they had a drink immediately by sending Ezikiel to the bar area with their orders. 'Get them a fresh glass,' he said. Or, 'Fill their glass. I do not want to see people with empty glasses.'

'We are gathered here today ...' The minister that Dan had brought with him from the Western Oil Company compound was wearing a robe that dragged on the floor and picked up ground-dirt until it became a similar pattern to Mama's wedding dress. He was a white man with a red nose. Around his neck was a large silver cross. He wore an earring. He looked nothing like the pastors I was used to seeing at our old church in Lagos. The pastors I had known were good-looking, with smart tailored clothes and neat, well-oiled hair. Even Pastor King Junior, who was seventy years old, wore a three-piece suit lined with purple silk. It surprised me to see Dan's minister wearing women's sandals. Surely, a man of God should be wearing polished shoes that clicked on the ground and tapped in time to the choir. I worried about what Alhaji would say when he noticed the minister's earring, but Alhaji was at the back with the imam, who was reciting the Koran loudly. He did not have the loudspeaker, he was shouting.

The minister shouted in English, and the imam in Arabic, mixed with a bit of Izon. Alhaji had expected that most of the guests would attend his section, his Muslim section, but the guests all stood watching the minister, and Mama and Dan, who were like two teenagers, giggling and holding hands. Ezikiel took my hand during the ceremony. We went and sat down by Alhaji's feet, with Grandma and Celestine and the twins, listening to the imam. Alhaji looked at us as we sat, and smiled. His head turned to each of us in turn and we all looked up. A look passed between all of us. The imam's voice made perfect sense to my ears. Mama did not even notice.

Mama and Dan said their vows quickly and quietly. I focused on the chanting of the imam and let my mind travel upwards and away from the wedding. Then, as the Christian minister clapped the Bible shut, our imam stopped suddenly. I stretched my ear towards Mama when she read a poem. She read quietly; it was probably just for Dan's ears. 'I do,' she said eventually, and Ezikiel sucked his teeth next to me. His arm was shaking. I put my hand over his and held his fingers tightly. When Dan said, 'I do,' I could hardly hear him, but he must have said it; Mama jumped on her tiptoes and threw her arms around his neck giving him a full kiss that made Dan's friends whistle, even though the ceremony was not yet finished. The bottom of my stomach felt like it had been removed. Everything dropped down. The shaking stopped. My body gave up. I felt as though I was in a dream. I was hoping that Father would burst through the gate and pick me up, and tell Dan to get out, too-loudly.

The compound had been swept clean of dust. Two long tables were set up next to the veranda. It was meant to be one for Western food and one for our food, but our food spilled over onto the Western table, there was so much of it. Alhaji had ordered it all from the Warri-based catering company that his friend's son owned. They specialised in

Chinese food, which was Celestine's favourite, but Alhaji had insisted on our food for Mama's wedding. On one end of the tables were the soups: *banga* soup made from palm kernels, white soup containing seafood and meat; rice and pepper soup, *isi-ewu*, the spiced goat head soup from Akwa Ibom that Alhaji loved, fresh fish pepper soup, goat-meat pepper soup, *kpomo*, the cow skin in pepper soup. Next to the soups were the stews: palm-oil-prepared stew, stewed snails, *efo-riro*, the spicy sauce containing spinach, fish and meat, *nkwobi*, the cow tail that Grandma loved, *egusi* and *ogbono* with *eba*, *jollof* spaghetti and rice, *amala*, pounded yam, fried rice, designer rice, smoked fish, fried fish *polofiyai*, *keke-fiyai*, *gbe*, *sea harvest fulo* … the table was bursting with food. A hundred different smells entered my nostrils. They danced together in my nose, one on top of the other as though all the foods should be eaten together on the same plate. At the far end of the long table, away from the house, was the barbecue. Plantain, bush meat, goat and mutton took turns on the fire, giving the whole area a smoky, spicy smell of tender meat. A large stack of paper plates balanced at the edge of one of the tables, with a serviette folded on every plate.

At the other end of one of the tables sat the Western food, what Dan described as a buffet. 'Can't have a wedding without a good wedding buffet,' he said. It consisted of cold meat, wrapped in dry pastries, and dried pieces of bready pizza, small round balls made from egg and sausage, and no sauce anywhere. A large tray of cheese underneath a see-through plastic lid made the area smell like urine. One of the cheeses was covered with blue cracks like the bottoms of Grandma's legs. Tiny sandwiches cut into neat triangles were shaped on a plate to look like a fan.

'Bloody waste of time,' said Grandma. She put a sandwich in her mouth, chewed a few times, then swallowed. 'The effect is ruined now.'

There were giant bowls full of potato chips, shaped like pieces of bacon, which Alhaji said was fine to eat, as it was only flavouring from chemicals. He did not mention the sausage rolls at all, which Boneboy kept eating until his belly swelled out like a coconut. It was more food than we had seen in a long time, but the Western food looked plain next to our wedding food – I was amazed when people ate it. The white men stood around crunching, dropping crumbs of pastry so large that the rats would think they had died and arrived in Paradise. I wondered where all the white women were, what they were like, if they would have eaten the pastry like the men, or if they might have tried our food.

Ezikiel hid in the house shadows. I took him a plate of our food, including his favourite spicy stewed snails. 'I can't eat,' he said. 'I feel sick.'

I touched his arm. He looked sick – his face had turned grey and hollow. 'Try some,' I said. 'It is your favourite.'

'The only thing I'll eat now,' said Ezikiel, 'is fireflies. To make me strong.'

'Disgusting! Are you still eating those?'

'Of course. They protect me from harm. Have you heard my asthma?'

It was true. I had not heard Ezikiel's asthma in a long time. I wondered if he had grown out of it. I did not believe that fireflies cured asthma. If that was the case many people in the world would be eating fireflies, and as far as I knew, Ezikiel and his new friends were the only ones.

'I hate him,' Ezikiel said. He was spitting on the ground. 'I hate him.'

I did not say any words in case I made Ezikiel angrier. I put the plate of snails onto the ground next to Ezikiel's spit.

I walked back to the wedding party. The white men wore ties over their shirts, and had the same smile. Their eyes flitted up and down and around me. I kept scratching my arms and legs. It felt like having a torch-light shone up and down my body all day. They raised their eyebrows all the time, and ate the Western buffet. Even the cheese with the blood running through it.

'Have you tried this Stilton?'

'Shame there's no port. Or Jacob's Crackers. Can't get a good cracker in Nigeria, that's for sure.'

They laughed, loudly. Their stomachs were soft, like women's stomachs, hanging over their trousers. Since working with Grandma, I had grown used to being able to tell, just by looking at the softness of a woman's stomach, how many children they had borne. Some of the men were up to five births – full term. I continued folding serviettes, pretending not to listen. One of the men kept looking at my hands as though they were food.

'Or a decent brew. I can live without cheese and biscuits but I'd kill for a decent brew. The Nigerians make it far too weak, and the teabags, God, the tiny little teacups – it's like going back a century.'

'Of course, that's exactly what it's like. A hundred years ago in England.'

I put the remaining serviettes down on the plate, and walked away.

The band arrived late and began setting up quickly by the gate to greet any other guests with highlife music. Soon, every local guest was dancing and singing, joining in with the well-known songs, all except the white men, who stood as still as rocks and clutched tightly to glasses of beer. They did not move from the shadow of the food tent.

When Alhaji stood on an upside-down box and coughed loudly, the band stopped playing. Everyone gathered around. Alhaji was smiling and looking straight at Mama.

'I want to thank you all for attending this special occasion. These two love birds ...' Alhaji paused until Dan laughed. 'These birds have fallen in love. And today we celebrate gaining our new son, Dan. He is now one of the Kentabe family.'

Everyone clapped and cheered. Even Dan.

'We are very happy to have Dan, you see? We are happy for both my beautiful daughter and her new husband. Please raise your glass to the happy couple.'

Everyone said 'Cheers' and took a drink. Everyone except Ezikiel.

'Now I can introduce the happy couple, Timi and Dan. Please, take your first dance, you see?'

Mama and Dan moved towards the middle of the crowd. The band began to play Mama's favourite song by Stevie Wonder. Dan looked so happy dancing next to Mama's face. The crowd looked happy. Even Alhaji looked happy. Everyone watched them spin around very slowly and stand very close. People tried to sing the words but missed some out or got them wrong. It was only me and Ezikiel who knew that song. Father had played it all the time.

Underneath the food tables there was the big pile of gifts. It was obvious which gifts came from the white guests and which from the locals, because the local people's gifts were wrapped in newspaper, and the white people's gifts were wrapped in shiny paper with bows and ribbons. Mama did not open any, but looked at them many times, and moved her body from side to side in excitement.

I was hiding underneath the gift table when Boneboy found me. I must have been sure that Father was coming. I watched the gate area, fully expecting to see his feet. Boneboy suddenly reached out and touched my face. His fingers were cool. I let my head fall into his hand. His hand smelled like home. Like river water, and pepper soup, and coconut oil. 'I cannot believe it,' I whispered. 'I did not think it would really happen.' I closed my eyes.

When I opened them Boneboy was kissing my lips.

He held his mouth to mine for many seconds without moving. I did not dare move at all. His lips opened and I felt his tongue, a soft piece of fish melting into my mouth.

Eventually Boneboy let my face go. His mouth remained open, his pink tongue through his teeth. My lips felt strange without his against them, like half of something. It was as if part of me had stuck to Boneboy and peeled off. I wanted that part back. My head moved towards his. My lips pulled so hard in his lips' direction. Then something snapped in my head. I blinked. I smacked my own cheeks. He crawled out from the table and ran into the house.

'I hate you!' Ezikiel screamed. The dancing had finished and the food had finished and the speeches had finished and then suddenly Ezikiel had appeared. The drummer was moving so quickly it looked as though he had four arms. Still, Ezikiel could be heard.

'I fucking hate you! I will never accept you as my father! You are not my father! You will never be my father!'

Dan was standing in front of Ezikiel. His smile had dropped. He stretched his arms towards Ezikiel. He tried to touch him. Could he not see that Ezikiel did not want to be touched? Ezikiel did not want Dan to touch him. Not ever.

'Of course I do not want a white father. We don't want a white father. What was she thinking?' Ezikiel began to cry. 'We want our father back. Our own father who made us.'

I couldn't believe the words Ezikiel had said. He never

spoke of Father any more. Before, he had said that he did not miss him at all. He had said that he did not care at all when Father left us. It was a lie. He felt exactly the same as I did.

'Do you know what your father is?' shouted Mama. 'He hurt me!' She stopped and moved toward Ezikiel, lowering her voice. 'He hurt me.'

Pictures turned in my head. Mama with a purple bruise, Father coming at her with his fist, Father banging Mama's head down onto the ground as though he was trying to break a nut.

Ezikiel's eyes changed. His eyelids became tighter, reducing the amount of world that he could see. 'A white man? A fucking oil worker! He's going to get what he deserves.' He flicked his head at Mama, then back at Dan.

'I'll show you, White Gold. Me and the Sibeye Boys!'

THIRTY

Ezikiel ran and ran and ran. Boneboy tried to chase him but Ezikiel's legs were not holding back. Mama's wedding day carried on as though it had not heard Ezikiel's words:

'Me and the Sibeye Boys!'

Could Ezikiel be a Sibeye Boy? A gunboy? My brother? I did not want to believe it. I told my ears they had it wrong. But my heart was crashing, crashing. And Alhaji was drinking the Remy Martin as though it was water, and Mama was not smiling and had stopped holding Dan's hand, and Grandma was in the house shadows, chanting, or praying.

I tried to carry on as though I had not heard Ezikiel's words. But people were talking. A boy who disrespected his mother on her wedding day! What kind of boy behaved like that?

A Sibeye Boy, I thought. But it could not be true.

As I went through the wedding, opening bottles of Supermalt and smiling and smiling and smiling, my thoughts were running on burning ground: Ezikiel's friends, Ezikiel's friends that he did not introduce us to, Ezikiel saying he did not want to be a doctor.

But a Sibeye Boy? The kind of boy who killed? For the wrong reasons? And who gave the true freedom fighters no chance. Who gave Alhaji no chance? Ezikiel?

It cannot be true, I thought, making the words in my head scream loudly.

It cannot be true.

But I felt the world outside the compound come in. Ezikiel had opened the gates.

Suddenly, screaming came from outside my head. Cars! Fast tyres on the dusty road. Shouting. A high-pitched screaming. A flash of white.

Mama!

I had gone inside for more Supermalt. Fast-moving shadows ran past the window, people rushing and crying and screaming. I ran to the door and out to the garden. Men had filled the garden. Tall skinny men. Boys. They were wearing masks over their faces. They were shouting, laughing. Guns crossed their bodies. Necklaces of bullets.

The Sibeye Boys!

They sent the wedding party outside the gate, pointing their rifles to where they wanted people to go. The rifles had more power than words. They did not need to explain anything, they just pointed and people went. The men guarding outside the gate were gone. The guests walked quickly and did not look up at all. None of them looked back at us.

I wanted to run back into the house but Mama was alone on the veranda on her knees, her arms behind her head.

One of the boys had a rifle pointed straight at her face. A rifle. Like a long, thin arm. It looked straight at Mama's face.

I ran at Mama and dropped to the ground next to her. She screamed and leant her body into mine. I felt the scratch of her wedding dress on my skin.

We are going to die.

The boy pointing the gun moved backwards. He laughed. 'Like mother, like daughter. I should take you, too,' he said in English, pointing the tip of the gun at my head. I wondered what it would feel like, being shot. Dying. Would I go to Heaven or Paradise? Had I been good enough?

'We could have fun with you.' I recognised his voice. I was sure. Where did I know his voice from? I wanted to look at him, but I did not dare lift my eyes. 'But we will get more for pure White Gold. They take our black gold and we take their White Gold.'

I had heard those words before. Ezikiel's words. They were Ezikiel's words.

'We are soldiers. And we will fight to the death.' He lifted the rifle and shot into the night. The sound made me jump towards Mama and made Mama jump towards me. I prayed then, harder than I had ever prayed. I prayed for Mama and for me. I could not believe it was happening, the thing everyone had told us about.

The thing Ezikiel had told us about.

Armed robbery, gunmen, kidnappers, Area Boys, these are things that happened to other people.

Where was Grandma? Please, please let Grandma be hiding. A few men ran past us, carrying something. Pulling something between them. Legs, a pair of legs. Dan's legs.

I lifted my eyes. Dan was being dragged between the men. His face had been covered with a bag. All I could see was his neck, wet with tears.

Dan! Oh!

The men, the local boys, were dragging him between them like a doll. His legs looked crooked, wrong, hurt. They were twisted the wrong way. I thought of a ram being killed. I pulled Mama to me. I could feel her squeezing her stomach tightly. I put my hand over her arm. 'Do not move,' I whispered. My words sounded too quiet.

The man in front of us lowered his rifle. He moved backwards, allowing me to see Alhaji and Celestine and Grandma huddled together wrapping their arms tightly around each other, as though they were one person. I looked at Grandma and Grandma looked at me. I could hear the twins screaming from the Boys' Quarters. I could imagine Youseff's wives offering their breast, trying to keep them quiet. I tried to focus on that: Youseff's wives feeding the twins. I tried to focus and not to think but the question came into my thoughts anyway.

Where is Ezikiel?

I heard Ezikiel's words over and over and over:

'I'll show you, White Gold. Me and the Sibeye Boys.'

My head was twisting and turning but the words remained until they sounded like a prayer:

I'llshowyouWhiteGoldmeandtheSibeyeBoysI'llshowyouWhiteGold
meandtheSibeyeBoysI'llshowyouWhiteGoldmeandtheSibeyeBoys
I'llshowyouWhiteGoldmeandtheSibeyeBoysI'llshowyouWhiteGold
meandtheSibeyeBoysI'llshowyouWhiteGoldmeandtheSibeyeBoys

The men began moving backwards, towards the gate. I could hear the sound of cars revving their engines. Of shouting from outside. The men pulled Dan between them. I watched his feet and thought it was good that he was wearing wedding shoes. He usually wore sandals and his feet would have torn on the ground.

It is lucky to be wearing wedding shoes, I thought.

Then my eyes began to cry.

There was laughing, and shouting, and screeching of tyres. Then there was silence for too long. The twins were quiet and Youseff's wives were quiet and Dan's birds were quiet. Finally, finally, Mama took a breath.

'They've taken him,' she said. Even though the words were hard they sounded soft, soft, soft. 'I told him it's not safe! This fucking place, this fucking place! I told him, let's do the wedding at the oil company! But he said no. With the family. With the fucking family! And now look. They've taken him!' She held her hands in the air; her fingers looked broken.

Mama shook and shook. 'Dan!' she shouted. 'Dan!' But he was not there. All we could see was nothing.

'They never kill the *oyibos*,' said Celestine. Grandma looked at her with raised eyebrows. 'Most times they are not even hurt.'

We all nodded even though we knew it was not true. It was hours later but we had still not moved from the veranda. Grandma had lit all the oil lamps one by one until we could see each other's faces clearly. Until we could see much more of the compound than usual. Until the nothing that we had seen was something.

'Things are out of control,' said Alhaji. 'The control was gone when these boys started taking children. One child was three years old, snatched from her mother's arms. They will take anyone. Calling the MoPol vans ice-cream vans. Making jokes about people's lives, you see? And these boys are calling themselves Ijaw!'

Mama was sobbing. She was still wearing her white puffy wedding dress, red with ground-dust. She had a gap around her. The gap looked more real than she did.

I did not know what to do. Every time I went near Mama to put my arms around her or to sit beside her, she flicked me away. I sat as close to her feet as she would allow, and looked around the compound shadows.

Where was Ezikiel's shadow?

'Come. You need to change clothes.' Grandma lifted Mama from the ground, and Mama let her. They walked inside the house leaning on each other.

Ezikiel did not come home. No one mentioned him. It was like they had not linked the dots. Ezikiel had said he was a

Sibeye Boy. He had said, 'I'll show you, White Gold.' Then Dan had been kidnapped.

White Gold! He had said 'White Gold'!

Nobody mentioned it. Nobody mentioned Ezikiel. But still, I could hear the questions that nobody asked.

People began to arrive at the gate and offer their advice:

'I know someone who knows the Sibeye Boys …'

'These Sibeye Boys mean no harm …'

'The Western Oil Company will pay and he will be returned unharmed …'

'They will be keeping him in the forest camp …'

'Do not worry, Dam is one of us now …'

'Dam is our husband; they will not hurt him …'

'These stupid boys, what does this say to the world?'

'Let us call a chiefs' meeting. The chiefs will negotiate a release …'

'Let me call Chief Buloebi …'

'They are just boys …'

'My brother will contact the FFIN leader, Apostle Inemo. Dam will be returned. The FFIN will stop the Sibeye Boys …'

'He is probably drinking a cold beer and surfing the internet …'

'He will be using Facebook!'

'That boy, Ezikiel, he has caused problems …'

'What kind of boy invites trouble to his own home?'

Later, after Mama had changed and the last of the guests

hiding outside had gone home and the tables were cleared, many cars arrived, one after the other. Shiny cars and vans containing journalists, who looked at us quickly before looking into mirrors, and asked us questions while a woman went between them with a hairbrush. Then larger vans arrived, containing security forces. Men with long rifles that looked exactly the same as the rifles the boys had pointed at us. They moved the journalists away from the gate and stood in a line. The security forces wore bigger sunglasses than the police, and thick jackets, even though the heat could be seen in the darkness, making everything low to the ground wavy, dreamy, not real. They spoke on large walkie-talkie radios, standing a short distance from each other, listening to instructions through tiny earpieces, like headphones. I watched their faces carefully. I prayed that Ezikiel would not come home until they had left. Would they take Ezikiel to prison?

'Why does this happen,' said Celestine. 'It's terrible, *abi*?'

We were eating boiled eggs, except Mama who was holding her boiled egg as though it was a tiny baby, close to her chest, in her arms.

'These stupid boys,' said Alhaji, 'causing trouble. Giving us Ijaw a bad name.' He put the whole egg in his mouth at once and had to stop talking while he chewed as small pieces of egg were escaping from the side.

I could not swallow my egg. I could only think about Ezikiel. Where he had gone.

What would happen if Ezikiel had an asthma attack and he was too far from Alhaji's emergency supply of inhalers?

'They are not stupid,' said Grandma, who had given her egg to Celestine saying she was not hungry. 'They are young.'

'What, what?' Alhaji spat a layer of egg onto Mama's legs. She did not even move to wipe it off.

'It's not their fault.' Everyone looked at Grandma. Even Mama who was still holding the egg so close. 'It is not even our fault. But we are foolish for bringing Dan here. It is not safe. You should have never been married here.' There was silence for a few minutes. 'It is not their fault. It is not the boy's fault. If we take every smoking wood from a fire and condemn it as bad, we would be killing the fire itself. It is the fault of the oil companies. All this warring. Fighting, fighting ...'

'What do you mean? Oil company. Ha! They are not kidnapping us!' Alhaji laughed at his own joke. His laughter sounded hungry and young, a baby bird waiting for food.

'The oil companies,' said Grandma, looking at the wide backs of the security men by the gate, 'pay ransom.'

'Of course they pay ransom!' Alhaji had swallowed the rest of the egg.

'What government do you know who lets kidnappings happen all the time, then pays ransom?' said Grandma. At first I did not understand what she was talking about. I watched Alhaji think. His left eye twitched. He turned his good ear towards Grandma.

'The oil company are taking billions of dollars from our land. They know it's not theirs to take.' We all listened carefully to Grandma speaking normal words. 'So they let us busy ourselves killing each other. And they let us think we have a way of taking back what is ours by kidnapping those *oyibos*.' She sat back in the rocking chair as Alhaji leaned forward.

'Well, why don't they just give the money to FFIN? The true fighters of the Ijaw people.' He smiled. 'Ha!'

'That would be like admitting the land isn't theirs,' Mama said, suddenly. 'But that's not Dan's fault. I mean, for fuck's sake, he doesn't know anything – he's trying to do a job. None of that is Dan's fault. He's a good man! A good man!'

The air around us was thick, making everything look slightly blurred, as if the world was becoming too old.

'I feel so helpless,' said Mama. 'I feel so helpless, Mum.' She moved towards Grandma. I opened my ears. It was the first time I had ever heard Mama call Grandma 'Mum'.

I knew then it was real. Mama loved Dan. She really loved him.

'Ezikiel said those things,' said Mama. 'Ezikiel. A Sibeye Boy? My son? He did it, didn't he? Contacted the Sibeye Boys. How else would they have known about the wedding, about Dan being here at that time? Ezikiel did it, didn't he? Ezikiel did it.'

Mama lifted her face from Grandma's shoulder. She did not look at anyone else. We all had our faces lowered. We did not want the question to come to us.

'If one imitates the upright, one becomes upright. If one imitates the crooked, one becomes crooked,' said Grandma.

THIRTY-ONE

Two security forces men sat us down in a row on the veranda to give what they called an 'Update on the hostage situation'. It felt as though we were in the middle of one of the Rambo films that Father used to watch on Sundays, after church. The sun was angrier than I had ever known it. There was no electricity for a fan, and no money to power the generator Dan had bought for us. Dan had begun to bring us fuel, and I knew that he was still giving Mama money. Plenty of money. But it had run out already. And he was not here to give any more. Despite that, the security men still did not remove their jackets. I could smell their sweat from where I was sitting.

'The situation', said the security man, who was still staring at Mama's nearly-flat chest, 'is delicate.' He said the word 'delicate' loudly and I jumped, almost falling off the edge of the veranda. Mama reached out and held my arm, and I nearly fell off again. But she gripped me tightly, and when she sat back upright, she did not let go. I looked sideways at Mama's face. Her jaw was pushed forwards, but she was not frowning. She looked very young, a girl. For the first time in my life, I could see the inside of Mama, unsure and frightened, like Ezikiel.

'Is Dan safe?' asked Mama. Her voice was loud and clear again, and made me shift slightly, in order to sit up straighter.

'He is safe. No harm has come to your husband.' The security man walked towards Mama, and leaned towards her face. 'We will protect you,' he said. He smiled with his mouth open, and his tongue hanging out of the side.

'What are they asking?' Alhaji was swinging his legs back and forth. He had not wanted to sit on the veranda, and said this was his house and he would not be treated like a child, until the security man came over and said, 'Sit,' and then he had sat down with the rest of us. He looked more crumpled than ever, and older than anyone.

'That is for us to know,' the security man continued. 'The company will pay it. There is no need for worry.'

Ezikiel returned that night, with red eyes and dry lips, singing, twirling, dancing across the compound until he reached the palm tree that Mama and I were sitting under. Mama stood. 'Where have you been?' she asked. Her voice was cold and flat.

Ezikiel laughed. 'Where is White Gold?' he asked.

I felt my insides curl in on themselves and twist.

'What have you done?' asked Mama. A midnight look crossed her face; her skin became icy blue. 'Where is he?'

Ezikiel shook his head. He was beginning to realise what would happen. I listened for a wheeze. He raised his head.

'I just mentioned him to some people. That's all,' he said. 'Just some friends I met in the forest.'

The evil forest?

Mama stepped backwards from us. It reminded me of a game where you had to guess the answer from asking questions about what the other person was thinking. Every time you misread their thoughts you took a step backwards. But instead of losing a playground game, we were losing Mama.

'You are not my son,' she said.

What have you done, Ezikiel, what have you done?

I ran towards Mama, but stopped before my arms reached out in front of her. I wanted to put my hand over her mouth. 'Stop, Mama, no! No! Please ...'

Ezikiel was pale; his breathing was coming quicker. I could hear the wheeze that I had not heard in a long time. His asthma was not cured, after all. 'I was protecting you,' he said. Mama took another step backwards. 'I was protecting you.'

Mama's legs kept moving away from us. She did not wait for the answers, but took a step back, then another, then another. Her legs were long and the steps back big.

'You are not my son,' she shouted. 'I don't know who you are but you are not my son.'

I watched Ezikiel's face. His half-closed eyes became wide. My stomach felt as if it was on fire. The burning travelled through me from my throat to my feet.

There is no going back now, I thought.

Ezikiel was feeling the same burning. Tears fell and fell and fell. He could drink palm wine, and smoke sticks, and disrespect adults. But he could not have Dan kidnapped. Not on Mama's wedding day. He could not be a Sibeye Boy. There was no return from that. Ezikiel could not be a Sibeye Boy. A Gunboy. It was against everything that Alhaji believed in.

'You are not my son!' Mama shouted. 'You are not my son! You are not my son! You are not my son! You are not my son!' She shouted over and over until Ezikiel screamed again.

He looked at me and held his mouth closed, pressing his lips together. He looked at my eyes for a long time. Then he turned and ran towards the gate and away from us. He ran and ran and ran. I watched his back. Ezikiel, I thought. Ezikiel.

Mama put her head in her hands and made a gulping noise, then lifted her head. Her face was dry.

I held my breath for as long as possible, waiting for Mama to disown me too by saying, 'You are not my daughter.'

I waited and waited and waited. She did not say it out loud, but I heard it anyway.

I could not fill the Dan-gap around Mama. I was too small, too female, and I looked just like Father. I rubbed Mama's shoulders and stroked her matted hair. When she cried, I wiped the tears from her cheeks with my thumbs. I said, 'Don't cry, don't cry, don't cry,' until Grandma gave me a look and said, 'Cry, cry, cry.'

Mama stopped eating and became so thin that within two days her collarbone stuck out. She could have carried things in the space between her bone and her skin. She drank sips of bucket-water, her hand shaking as she held the cup, leaving water splashes on the table. The Western Oil Company sent trays of food – fried chicken, *moi-moi*, fried rice – but nothing tempted her. She did not look directly at me but I did not mind. I could not look at Mama's eyes either.

The mesh on the windows rattled and crashed. I jumped from sleep and out of bed in one step. An explosion! Boneboy was running past outside my room. 'Quickly!' he shouted. He pulled my hand. We ran outside to the veranda where Mama had been pacing up and down, up and down. She had stopped still and was looking at the sky, holding her hand to her chest. Grandma, Alhaji and Celestine came running from the house. Alhaji pushed me out of the way. Youseff's wives and children ran from the Boys' Quarters. The veranda creaked and lowered as everyone climbed on it, pushing and rushing towards Alhaji. Some small children fell backwards off the side and started to cry. A boy's head cracked on the ground, and made a noise like the breaking of a kola nut. Still nobody moved. We stood in a line and looked into the distance as a cloud of black smoke rose upwards. Eventually the boy stood and ran towards his mother. He stopped crying and looked at what we were watching: the smoke-cloud changing shape and becoming a twisted mangrove.

'Pipeline fire,' said Alhaji, and he put his arm around Mama's shoulder. She let him.

It had happened before. We were getting so used to

explosion noise waking us from sleep that it should not have made me feel so sick. I looked at the smoke rising in the darkness like a cloud. I looked at Grandma. She had her eyes shut and was spitting into the night air.

We all returned to bed for the last hour of night, but I did not close my eyes.

It was dawn, and the imam was shouting the call to prayer through the loudspeaker. At first it was difficult to hear the boy who was running towards the gate.

'Quick, Grandma,' he said. He was not older than ten, but had a voice which sounded so strong it broke through the prayer-calling and brought us all out of the makeshift mosque. I was standing at the back, and had not even fully rolled out my prayer mat, but I was already praying for Ezikiel to come home and Dan to be returned.

The boy had been running fast and had to take some deep breaths before he could get a sentence out. All the time he was pointing behind him. I floated above myself, looking down. Everything seemed to be happening slowly.

'Ezikiel!' The boy gulped air in, and held his stomach, bent forward like an old man. 'Ezikiel has been burnt.'

As we ran towards the gate, a group of boys came around the corner shouting. They were carrying Ezikiel high above their heads. He was screaming, like Twin One, maybe louder, and his voice sounded bubbly as if he was gargling water at the same time. A pressing at the back of my neck was so severe that my eyes could not see anything except a blurred picture.

As they approached, Grandma held the gate open and waved them quickly in. I wanted to help but I could not move. My feet froze to the ground. I could not see Ezikiel as he was held high in the air, but I could smell his burning. Burnt skin, like *suya* that had been barbecued for too long and was beginning to turn black.

I remembered the explosion during the night. It went off in my head a second time.

EZIKIEL!

I closed my eyes and saw the mangrove smoke twisting in the air. I felt a mangrove twist around my head, its claws pushing into me.

The boys lowered Ezikiel under the palm tree. As his body touched the ground he screamed loudly and they stepped back, and almost fell into a heap on top of each other. When they stood they ran backwards towards the gate. They did not speak or look at our faces. Then they were gone. I watched them run past the gap in the fence.

At first, I closed my eyes. Then I re-opened them. I could not recognise anything of my brother, except his tiny shoulder bullet wound that had turned black and burnt against the rest of his skin, which had peeled away revealing pink and white underneath. He looked like an over-stewed chicken. My heart continued to beat, just.

Ezikiel's T-shirt was removed, but his trousers were stuck to his legs, and were like an extra layer of skin. His face was swollen bigger than any allergy swelling I had ever seen. His skin stretched shiny. The beret was stuck to his head. A loud scream broke through the thick air. It was the loudest scream of all. It came from the sky, the trees, the earth.

Grandma spoke first. 'Go and call his mother,' she said to the imam who was hovering by the gate. 'Get a message to his father!'

Oh God! Oh Allah!

'Get the birth bag.'

I ran. I wanted to run and run, and never ever see my brother that way again. But I found the birth bag quickly and ran back to him. When I returned with the bag Alhaji was also crying then screaming, and kneeling next to Ezikiel. He had opened his Marmite and was scooping out large handfuls, trying to rub it onto Ezikiel's head.

'The pot is not big enough,' shouted Alhaji. 'The pot is not big enough.'

Grandma pulled out all of the birth pastes and ashes. She handed some to me, and we covered Ezikiel as quickly as possible, making skin where there was none. I told my hands to work. It is not Ezikiel, I told them. It is a woman giving birth. Do the job.

Every time our hands touched the areas of his body with blisters, he screamed, and Celestine screamed. And every time we touched the blackened areas, Ezikiel made no sound at all.

Why did he not scream? Why did it not hurt him when we touched the worst parts?

Alhaji touched a large blister on Ezikiel's chest. He screamed again.

'No, baby Ezikiel, no!' Celestine's screams became louder until Ezikiel could no longer be heard.

'The pot is not big enough!' Alhaji scooped Marmite from the pot, and rubbed it onto Ezikiel's screaming body. The Marmite stayed on Alhaji's fingers and did not stick to Ezikiel's burnt skin. Pieces of skin peeled away and stuck to Alhaji's fingers instead.

Grandma pushed Alhaji out of the way, and picked Ezikiel up in her arms. She was strong, but Ezikiel looked much too easy to pick, like bad fruit. 'Start the car!' She ran towards the car, and nodded at Youseff, who had already started the engine and opened the back door. They pushed Ezikiel screaming onto the back seat.

After the car drove quickly away, I dropped to my knees against the tree. Celestine wailed. And Alhaji just sat in the same spot, holding the empty jar of Marmite in his hands.

THIRTY-TWO

Ezikiel did not come home that night, or the next, or the next. I prayed to everyone I could think of.

Alhaji patted my head as though I was Snap. He was holding his cosmetic case close to his chest, every now and then taking out a pot or packet and swallowing another tablet with no water. 'A Sibeye Boy?' he kept asking. 'A Sibeye Boy?'

I sat under the palm tree, picking up the red ground-dirt in clumps and rubbing it in my hands, until they were raw and pink, like Ezikiel's body. I closed my eyes for most of the day, and counted, because I did not know how else to measure time. I thought of Dan with a hood over his face, his legs twisted and dragging underneath him. I thought of Ezikiel with his skin peeling off. I was not allowed to visit Ezikiel. He was only allowed one visitor and that was always Mama. I took a breath every five seconds. One two three four breathe. One two three four breathe.

On the third day Mama returned from the hospital. Her hair was even more matted in clumps, her face make-up-less.

She smelled stale, like a wrapper left out during the rains. Her lips were cracked and blistered, and she had crescent moons of darkness underneath her eyes.

'Blessing,' she said, and sat down next to me. Our shoulders touched. 'My Ezikiel,' said Mama, and her shoulder shook so much that I could not help but put my arm around it. Then Mama started crying. She looked at me. One of her teardrops was so large that I felt certain I could see my own reflection in it. How much pain could a person suffer?

'I'm sorry, Mama,' I said. 'I'm sorry.' Mama nodded, and fell towards me. It felt strange holding Mama like she was the child and I was the adult. We stayed for many hours, until the insects began to sting. Darkness covered the garden like a blanket.

Grandma's story that evening brought us all together. All except Ezikiel. We held the sugar cane in our hands. None of us could be bothered to chew or suck. Only one oil lamp was lit, but I could see Alhaji's shadow at the other end of the veranda, and Celestine's outside the Boys' Quarters, and even Mama's under the palm tree. Maybe they thought Grandma's story would make them feel better.

'This garden is magic,' said Grandma, looking around the darkness. 'When I was born with a hole where my nose and mouth should have been, my mother left me out to die. But the sun hid that day, and when night came the palm tree dripped water into my mouth.'

I looked at the palm tree and Mama's shadow underneath it. I did not imagine it would drip water. But could the garden be magic? I listened to Grandma's words carefully.

'And the water spirits came dancing around my head, and gave me a cry loud enough to break my mother's heart. I survived the night and in the morning my mother could not take it any more. She came out and picked me up and fought the rest of the compound who told her she was a lunatic. She thought she had saved me but it was the garden. The garden brought the water spirits. Some things are more than we can understand.'

I looked around the garden, and the shadows, and the darkness, and I realised something was missing. Something other than Ezikiel. There were no fireflies. I suddenly knew what I had to do. What I could do.

Grandma opened her eyes and looked at me. One of the shadows moaned. I rocked back and forth. I looked around the garden. 'Bring him home,' I whispered.

Grandma looked inside me through my eyes.

'Bring him home,' I said, in a voice that was not mine.

Grandma nodded and looked at the night sky. The rains were coming.

Ezikiel being gone made the house feel as though the roof was missing, or one of the walls had disappeared. Alhaji was sitting at the table, pretending to read the paper, and Grandma pretended to cook. Celestine pretended to read a magazine that Ezikiel had given her. Mama did not pretend. Her face was puffed up and her skin white and dry. She looked older than Grandma. She went from whispering 'Dan' to whispering 'Ezikiel', until they were almost the same person: Dan-Ezikiel.

I sat next to Alhaji, and took a deep breath. He was taking so many tablets by then that his words no longer made sense. Nobody mentioned it. It was quiet in the house; the broken clock, which only ticked every few seconds and had no hands, sounded as loud as a gunshot. It came at the end of every question. Could a person survive allergies, a shooting and a fire? Bang! Could Ezikiel have had Dan kidnapped? Bang! Was it Mama's fault that Ezikiel ran off with the Sibeye Boys? Bang! Was it my fault?

'What exactly happened?' I asked. 'Tell me. What exactly happened?' My questions sounded like they came from another person. I had never asked questions to everyone before. But there was no fear in my voice. I was not afraid.

Boneboy lowered his head. He could not look at me.

'It was a pipeline thing,' Alhaji said, quietly. The clock sounded even louder.

He opened his case and took out another painkiller, turned the page of the newspaper, and coughed.

'What caused it?' I asked.

Grandma stopped stirring the soup, Celestine looked up from the magazine, and Alhaji lifted the paper over his face; I could not even see the top of his head. I waited.

'It was Ezikiel,' said Grandma, eventually. 'Joining that

gang of Sibeye Boys. Over twenty boys in hospital now. Breaking a pipeline. An explosion like that. Imagine.'

'If he had joined the proper FFIN this would not have happened. He could still fight the oil companies and the politicians. We need to stand together as a nation—'

'What happened?' I repeated. 'What exactly caused the fire?'

Everyone bowed their heads.

'What happened?' I repeated. 'Please. I need to know the truth. Why did Ezikiel join those boys? Did he really cause the fire? Ezikiel?'

Nobody spoke. I looked at Alhaji.

'Izon means truth,' I said.

'Ezikiel caused the fire,' said Mama. 'But it was an accident. He split the pipeline on purpose but he didn't expect it would cause the explosion! Really, it is my fault.' Mama was crying. 'I disowned him. I disowned him for telling the Sibeye Boys that Dan was here. All he did was give some information and I disowned him. He went off because of me. It's my fault! But I was so angry. What they do. What they could do to Dan. Is he safe? They will hurt him.' Mama shook. 'They will hurt Dan, and Ezikiel is in hospital, and it's all my fault.'

'It is not your fault, Mama.' I went over to her and knelt down. She was shaking and crying.

'My own son! I disowned him. And now he's, he's …'

'It was not your fault,' said Alhaji. 'We are all to blame.' Alhaji's words were not slurred. He was sitting upright and looking at Mama. 'If I had returned him to school more quickly,' he said.

'No!' said Mama. 'I was so wrapped up in Dan that I didn't see it coming.' She paused and I could see Dan's face written on hers. My stomach twisted. Was Dan alive? Was he safe?

'He'd been acting strangely since the shooting,' said Mama. 'It's all my fault! Dan would be safe if not for me. What have I done? I have been a terrible wife, and I have been a terrible mother. A terrible mother!'

Grandma stood up suddenly. 'A child who has no mother will have no scars on his back,' she said. And she walked over to Mama and pulled her into her arms.

Mama was on the veranda with Grandma and Alhaji. She had been at the hospital all day and returned to speak in lowered voices to the family. None of them had spoken to me. Not even Grandma.

'Bring the boy home,' said Grandma.

'What?' asked Mama, her voice shaky but loud.

'Bring the boy home.'

'You can't do that,' said Alhaji, laughing slightly. 'He's in the best hospital, he needs the treatment.'

'Bring him home!' Grandma shouted above the rifle fire and the background shouting, which was happening every day. I did not have the energy to care about the fighting. Let them kill each other. Let them kill us.

'He cannot come home,' Alhaji repeated. 'The hospital and doctors are what the boy needs. He will get better. He needs medicine. Medicines will cure anything. Prevention is better, but cure is possible. You see?'

'Listen to me,' said Grandma, in a clear and loud voice. 'I have looked after you my whole life. Cooked, cleaned, given you a daughter and nearly died. I have raised your second wife and even her children as my own. I have given you my life at your feet.' I imagined Grandma standing in front of Alhaji, her hands on her hips. 'I am asking you this. Bring the boy home.'

There was quiet for a few minutes. I had prayed to God and Allah. I had prayed to the water spirits. I had spoken to our Ancestors, Yoruba and Ijaw. Someone must have heard me. Please, please let Ezikiel come home.

'He cannot come home. Imagine what will happen,' said Alhaji. 'It is not safe to move him.'

'Bring the boy home,' shouted Grandma. The rifle fire coming closer to the compound sounded like laughter. The shouting was nearer and nearer.

'Eh! Is that our neighbour?' Grandma's voice was louder than the rifle fire. It stopped briefly but then started again. 'Put your guns down,' Grandma shouted. 'Our husband is kidnapped! Our son is dying!'

My heart lifted into my mouth. The words were out. The truth was hanging in the air and I wanted the lie back. The rifle fire was quiet. I could only hear the words that Grandma had spoken.

'Grandma is right,' Mama said. I sat up. 'Ezikiel should come home. And Dan needs to come home,' she sobbed.

'Bring Ezikiel back. For Blessing. Blessing needs him to come home. She needs to be with him when ...'

I closed my ears and my eyes. Mama did love me, after all.

THIRTY-THREE

I was waiting under the palm tree when Ezikiel was carried home. I had made a comfortable bed from a mattress and two large blankets covered with a sheet to prevent the blankets from scratching Ezikiel's body, where his skin used to be. Alhaji had bought back Ezikiel's *Encyclopaedia of Tropical Medicine* from the market bookseller. I thought about bringing it out and reading to him, but there was a danger of him asking about burns or scars or infection. I need not have worried. When Ezikiel was carried over on a stretcher, lowered to the ground under the shade, I could see at once that he was beyond speaking.

He was in the place that women go to, when they are giving birth.

He was stretched, and shiny, and pale pink. Pieces of skin were hanging off his face. He smelled of Robb and antiseptic, mixed with something foul. He had a urine bag hanging down the side of his skinny leg, empty of anything but a tiny layer of bloody urine. His eyes were swollen shut. His chest rattled every time he took a breath, which was only once every five seconds or so. He was too weak to cough but I tapped his chest anyway. I wanted to scream. I wanted to cry, to cut myself so the pain outside would numb my pain inside. I felt again like I was above us, looking down. That it was unreal. I was hovering in the sky with Ezikiel. We were holding hands. I prayed only to the garden. Please, garden, if you are magic, let him live. I looked at Grandma on the veranda. She looked back at me.

'It's me,' I whispered into Ezikiel's ear. It had yellow pus dripping out of it like tree sap. 'It's me, Blessing.' He did not move, or breathe any less slowly, or try to open his stuck-shut eyes. I knew he could hear me. I lay under the palm tree looking up at the sky. I thought of Grandma as a baby lying underneath the same palm tree and being given life. I thought of Ezikiel fighting for his life. I thought of Allah, who gave, and who took.

Sometimes the sky is too blue, I thought.

Grandma ran to and from the herb garden, fetching muddy-coloured pastes that she rubbed gently onto his body and face with a T-shirt that had been washed regularly for many years; it was soft. Alhaji crushed all his precious tablets into one bowl and mixed the powder with water. Every so often he came over and put a drop into Ezikiel's mouth. I stayed sitting by Ezikiel's head the entire time, cleaning his mouth when the blood-stained spit leaked down his chin, and then rinsing the cloth in a bucket of river water. I did not drink a sip all day for fear that I would need to leave Ezikiel's side to relieve myself. He might have been waiting for me to leave to save me some pain. He always tried to protect me from pain.

Mama rocked on the veranda, whispering, 'Why me, why me, why me?' She could not look at Ezikiel. Her head moved in all directions. Celestine kept the twins away. Alhaji came out of the house and paced the veranda saying, 'The President will hear of this,' over and over again. His hands shook.

In the afternoon, after hours of hearing Ezikiel take his rattling five-second breaths, Mama came to us. She put her hand on my shoulder. Her hand was so cool against my hot skin that I jumped. Then she knelt by Ezikiel's body, and lay down next to him, curling around him like she used to every night before he was moved to Alhaji's room. Before he became a Sibeye Boy.

I was about to move away and leave Mama to spend time with Ezikiel, before she had to tell me to go, but she just pulled my arm, and patted the floor the other side of him. I was still unsure that I might have misread her thoughts until she pulled me down with her. We surrounded Ezikiel. For a short time, there were no holes around any of us. There was nothing missing. Not even Father. Mama held my hand on top of Ezikiel's chest, and squeezed tightly as his chest rose for the last time. She stopped shaking her head and looked straight at me. We counted to five. Then ten, then fifteen and twenty.

He was gone.

THIRTY-FOUR

That night we took it in turns to say goodbye. Grandma sobbed as she held Ezikiel first, kissing his bloody mouth. I could not look at her. She had been wrong. She was wrong about Ezikiel. The garden was not magic. It did not save him.

Celestine kissed the top of Ezikiel's head. She did not make a single sound. Alhaji sat next to Ezikiel, and rubbed some Marmite onto his chest, where his heart lay still and silent. 'If you had just stayed away from those boys ...' he started, but then he closed his mouth and put his ear to Ezikiel's chest to check that his heart had not re-started. Alhaji cried and cried and cried, and instead of wiping his tears or hiding his face, he let the water drip onto Ezikiel, and he pressed his own chest.

Mama sobbed, holding Ezikiel to her as she shouted, 'You are my son! You are my son! You are my son!'

Finally, one by one, everyone went into the house, leaving me sitting next to my brother. All my memories were mixed up with Ezikiel. There were none when I was alone. He had always protected me, taught me and loved me. He was gone, and I was suddenly alone.

I stayed for a long time. Even though night had fallen, the moon did not rise. The stars had finally appeared and were brighter than any I had ever seen. Even so, I could not find Ezikiel among them. The garden was still. There was no song from insects, no breeze, and no longer any smell. I looked at Ezikiel, already less swollen, more like his old face. His stuck-together eyes were beginning to open. They looked at me in surprise.

'Goodbye, my brother,' I said. There was nothing else I could say. I did not have long. The water spirits were already dancing around his head, flashing like fireflies, and the ground was holding him down.

The funeral happened the very next morning. Celestine wailed hard and loud, and the entire area knew within minutes and started organising food and Tupperware. We walked behind her in a long line, with Alhaji and Youseff carrying Ezikiel's body, covered in a sheet. We had dressed him in his Chelsea football shirt that said 'Essien' on the back. He had a newer shirt but Father had given him the Essien shirt, and Ezikiel said it was the best gift he ever had. Mama and I walked behind them. Grandma walked at the back, wailing as loudly as Celestine and stopping every few minutes to throw her body to the ground.

People gathered. They also wailed and lowered their heads, following the procession, asking, 'Who was it killed him?'

loud enough for Mama to hear and bend over, clutching her empty stomach.

I could not wail. I could not do anything except hold Mama up. She let herself be held up by me. Her arms and shoulders were cool and clammy; she slipped too often. I wished Dan was there to help hold her up. I had been wishing for Dan more and more. Since the explosion I had wanted Dan to be with Mama. I knew she would not survive losing Ezikiel. She would not survive. The only person she would continue to live for would be Dan. If Dan was killed, Mama would find a way to die. I could not lose Mama. I had lost Father and Ezikiel, and now Mama was the only person left who knew everything about me. If I lost Mama I would lose myself, and I knew that the only person that could save her was Dan. I realised how much I needed her, loved her. I needed Dan to help her live.

I wished for someone to hold me up. Suddenly someone was there. Boneboy had seen Mama slipping on my arm, and had moved himself between us. We leant on him. I let myself fall into him. He carried me. He carried us both.

By the time we returned to the compound we had collected dozens of people, all of them quiet, as Celestine asked questions of Ezikiel.

'Why did you die?' she shouted. 'Why did you leave us behind?'

We listened, each hearing our own answer. I had always believed that interrogating the dead seemed silly. Surely the dead could not answer any questions. But I found myself listening for Ezikiel's voice. I listened harder than I had ever listened for anything.

'What was the cause of your death?' She shouted so close to Ezikiel's face, and so loudly that I was sure that he must have heard her.

I closed my eyes. 'Who killed you?' shouted Celestine. I opened my eyes and found that I was looking directly at Ezikiel's hand. It looked shiny, like it was covered with oil.

Ezikiel was lowered into the ground next to Grandma's herb garden. Where Ezikiel and I had found the old snakeskin so delicate we had to use twigs to touch it, or the heat from our fingertips would melt it to nothing.

Alhaji got into the grave and turned Ezikiel's head to the right to face Makkah. He lay on top of Ezikiel's body. We waited a long time before he climbed out. We covered Ezikiel with ground-dirt, and recited the Koran. I felt glad. Ezikiel liked the chanting, said it took him away from this world. And he looked happier in Alhaji's makeshift mosque than he ever had in church. Before Ezikiel was covered in dirt I leant over the side of the grave, and put his *Encyclopaedia of Tropical Medicine* underneath his hands. I leant my body as far as I could to Ezikiel's head, and I whispered something only he would be able to hear.

Then it was quiet. The only noise I could hear came from inside my own body. My heart that beat and beat and beat.

I looked at the ground, and the dust next to Ezikiel. I

did not want to see my brother inside the ground. I did not want the ground to hold him. My eyes ran. They ran across the compound to the gate. And suddenly, just like that, as if my eyes knew before I did, Father's feet were there. Father's feet.

Father!

The moment I had waited so long for had arrived. His shining office shoes. I did not dare lift my eyes up in case they had it wrong. But Father's were the only shoes I had ever seen that stayed black and shiny and clean of dust. The shoes were clean. Father's shoes! My eyes moved upwards. Father's legs were walking in all directions. His shirt was hanging over his trousers.

My eyes found Father's face unshaven. His own eyes were red and moving quickly around the compound. I looked at the ground, which held Ezikiel. Oh!

'Father!' My voice jumped through the air. 'Father!'

I ran. I ran away from Mama, from Ezikiel inside the ground. My heart moved upwards, into my neck, and crashed in my ears. I ran towards Father so quickly the dust rose up even before my feet.

But as I ran, I could hear a voice. It sounded like Ezikiel's voice. 'Stop! Blessing, stop!'

Father was not running towards me. His legs were wobbling underneath him. His back was bent low. Father was curled, like Snap.

'Father,' I said, standing before him.

It did not take me long to really see. In the time it took

for the dust to settle back to the ground, I had seen that Father was so drunk that he could barely stand. I had seen the way his face was twisted and his mouth was curled and his fist was clenched.

I had seen the woman at the gate. The other woman, who Mama found Father lying on top of.

She was holding her hands near her face, which was more beautiful than Mama's, and ugly at the same time. The other woman had a round and soft body, with a long neck and smooth skin. But her face was sharp, and her small mouth looked like it had been held tightly shut for too long. Maybe she had just eaten *agbalumo,* Father's favourite fruit. Ezikiel and I played stations with the seeds that Father saved for us.

There will be no more Father saving seeds for us, I thought. Or playing stations.

There will be no more Ezikiel and me.

I prayed that Mama would notice the woman's ugliness, too.

'My son! What have you done!'

I let the ground come up and meet my knees. Father did not look at me at all. 'Father,' I said. 'Daddy. Baba.'

He walked away from me and then lurched forwards like he was reaching for a banknote on the ground. His hand found my face. Then my throat.

Father's skin remained cool even during the road-melting afternoon heat. I kept thinking of his skin, which was still cool, even as he squeezed and squeezed and squeezed and I felt air being pushed from my mouth until there was no more air. Until I could no longer feel Father's cool skin.

'Where is my son?' Father's breath was full of palm wine. His eyes were looking but not seeing.

He does not see me here, I thought; he thinks I am somebody else.

'Blessing,' he spat.

And all at once I remembered. Everything. Father was a loud man. When Father drank, Father hit Mama. Father hit Mama so hard he broke her nose, making her less beautiful than his other woman. He cut her skin with a broken bottle giving her a train-track scar across her back. He held her by the throat.

And now he held me by the throat.

'Get off her!' Mama was screaming. 'Get off her! Our son is in the ground! Our son is dead.' Mama fell to her knees and leant towards Father's shoes. 'Please, please, leave her, let her go.' Mama's voice was far away. Or underwater. 'You want to kill our daughter?' Mama's voice was quieter and soft. I felt my eyes close. I was sinking.

'Move away!' That voice was not soft. Grandma? No. It was a deep voice. A roar. A Big Man's voice.

'Move away and get out! You are not welcome here! Move away from our daughter!' The voice was louder than the loudspeaker and clear and sure. It made me open my eyes. Alhaji. Grandfather!

Father's hand loosened around me and the air went in. But I did not want to breathe it. I wished for his hand to

CHRISTIE WATSON · 414

remain and kill me. Kill me, I thought, and let me go with Ezikiel. I leant my throat towards Father's hand.

Father snapped his hand away. I fell to the ground and tried to be held by it. But the ground did not have arms for me. My eyes were open.

Alhaji stepped forwards and pulled me back in a single move. His hands felt hot. He held my chin and moved my eyes upwards to his, before moving my bottom lip downwards with his thumb. Grandma and Celestine sat down beside me, and held me and rocked me as though they were one person. I could not tell whose arm was whose.

'Our son is being buried. Our son. Our son. Your son!' Mama was screaming. She was pulling Father's legs, grabbing him and the earth and the air. 'I hate you!' Mama was shouting. 'I hate you!'

'Let's go.' A voice came from the gate. A small-mouth voice. I could not look. I turned my head back to Ezikiel in the ground. 'Let's go home.'

'What? You, what? My son is dead and you bring her?' Mama knelt up then, took a breath and screamed. She beat Father's chest with her fists. It sounded like somebody running. Alhaji put his hand on Mama's shoulder, moved her backwards.

Father fell. His legs could no longer stay up.

He began to laugh. His clothes smelled sour and I could see the stains on his trousers. My eyes were finally open. I looked again at Father's shoes.

Father's shoes were not clean at all.

I stayed underneath the palm tree for three days after the funeral, picking up clumps of ground-dirt again, rubbing my hands together. Grandma and Celestine watched me from the veranda. Celestine was worried. I could hear her. But I could not respond. My head was full of oil. I felt like I was underwater. Like Father had his hand wrapped around my neck. I had to force my body to breathe.

'If she does not improve we need to send her to the head doctor.'

'She will be fine,' said Grandma.

Celestine opened her mouth to say something, but then she shut it again.

'The garden is magic,' said Grandma. 'It will save her.'

I suddenly looked up and dropped the ground-dirt. I looked at Grandma looking at me.

The garden is magic, I thought.

Grandma had not been talking about Ezikiel at all.

On the fourth day Grandma picked me up from where I was sitting. My legs were numb from staying in the same position for so long. Grandma walked me over to the outhouse fence next to the herb garden, where Ezikiel was buried. She held me underneath my arms; I was a baby learning to walk.

'Look,' she said, and pointed to the ground.

A dozen plants were standing, green and tall, with tiny buds of petals at the tops.

'Roses,' I said. It was the first thing I said since Ezikiel had gone. My voice sounded shaky and unsure. 'Roses.'

The roses were growing exactly where Ezikiel's head would have been. They were not there at all a week ago. They had grown red and tall and proud and delicate all at the same time.

I looked at them for a very long time. I held Grandma's hand, leant my head on her arm, and let my eyes cry.

THIRTY-FIVE

'Sometimes, things fall apart,' said Grandma, 'so we can put them together in a new way. It is time to make things right.' It was light and the police, security forces and press were arriving again, this time in cars with blacked-out, bullet-proof windows. They had agreed to stay away for Ezikiel's funeral, and the days afterwards, but then, as they returned, there seemed to be more of them. I wanted to hide in the bedroom but it was much too hot. Dan had been gone for nearly two weeks. At first I had not cared. But after Ezikiel died, after Father had arrived at the funeral, Mama became less and less every day until she was like a shadow, or a gap where Mama had once been. And I knew that Dan would save Mama. After Father had left, someone had to save her. And I knew that Dan could. Somehow, I just knew. Dan was my last hope.

Later, the whole compound was full of tall men wearing sunglasses that covered most of their faces. They drank tea made by Celestine, who wound her way in and out of the men, and reminded me of a brightly coloured bird that Dan had once pointed to. I had never noticed a bird so bright before.

The men asked questions over and over and over to the gap where Mama had been:

'Did Dan give any indication that he was concerned?'

'Did he mention seeing or meeting anyone acting strangely?'

'Did he mention being followed?'

'How many guests attended?'

'Is there involvement with the Sibeye Boys from anyone who attended the wedding?'

Mama had no words any more. She looked far away, like the crazy women Ezikiel and I used to watch gathering on Bar Beach and praying to the sea.

I kept thinking of Father's shoes.

Grandma watched Mama and held me close. 'Hide your face,' she said. 'I do not want them asking you anything.' I pushed my face into Grandma's arm. I could have stayed there forever. I felt nothing. Empty.

Ezikiel, I thought. Ezikiel.

'Those militia scum, behaving like barbarians!' Grandma ran over to Alhaji and whispered something into his ear that caused his face to turn pale. 'I did not mean our son, Ezikiel. He was just a boy. A lost boy! He may have told those Sibeye Boys, but that is hardly kidnap, you see?'

He was, I thought. *Was*.

The press camped outside in large vans with satellite dishes attached to the roofs. The British and American vans were shiny and new. The Nigerian press van looked old. Even the equipment was different. Large fluffy grey microphones were held by the Nigerian journalists. The British journalists had tiny earpieces and small microphones attached to their clothing.

We watched the vans and the equipment and security and police forces in the compound, which we knew so well. I wanted them all to leave. I wanted to see the empty field and wide-open spaces, and Youseff's wives back and forth from the village tap, and Dan looking at the sky, and Snap jumping up for a bone.

I wanted to see Ezikiel, sitting underneath the palm tree, reading a textbook. I wanted that most of all.

But the area under the palm tree was where the journalists filmed their reports. They wanted the shade. I could hear them speak the same words in different ways.

'WearefromDeltaRainbowTelevisionCompany,' the local journalist said. After asking his questions they sped off in their van, which made a terrible screeching sound as it left. Like the sirens of the white men's vans. The television questions stayed in the compound long after they were asked, more direct than the security men's questions. They filled the air. We breathed them into our ears.

'Was your son Ezikiel involved with the kidnap?'

'Was Ezikiel part of the Sibeye Boys?'

'No news.' Grandma was no longer asking a question. 'How can we even mourn Ezikiel when there is no news?'

'They need to grieve.' Alhaji pointed to Mama and me. 'Quickly, before the grieving period is over. It is not good to keep the tears in.' He put a tablet into my mouth. My mouth was dry; I could not swallow it so I let it melt slowly. A bitter taste spread over my tongue.

'How can they cry for one when another is missing?' Grandma did not bother to lower her voice. They spoke as if Mama and I were not even there. As if I was a gap like Mama, a Blessing gap.

'We must use up all our attention for Dan. Your Mama needs Dan.'

I looked at Grandma. She did not hate Dan. Maybe she had never hated Dan. She hated Father. It was Father that Grandma hated. Not the fact that he was Yoruba. The truth had been there all along, right in front of me. Sometimes we see only what we want to show ourselves.

'I cannot even mourn. Imagine not being able to mourn our son. Those boys better return Dan healthy and well,' Celestine joined in, 'or I will break them!'

I only half-listened. I was unable to eat. I felt as if I was falling with no ground at the bottom, and no one to catch me. With Ezikiel gone, who would I share the memories with? What if I forgot everything? What if any good memories of Father disappeared from my mind altogether? All I could remember was Father's shoes, which were not clean at all. My head was spinning around until I could not see properly. The world looked different.

The next morning the security and police numbers were

reduced. There were no phone calls, no press vans, and the height of the security guards was decreasing; all we were left with were three men as short as Alhaji, and at least sixty years old. Mama rocked silently. With every rock, I pictured Father. I began to watch the gate. Would he return? Would his hand squeeze the air from me again? How could I have been wrong about Father for so many years?

The house was quiet. I could not speak. Celestine did not wail. Alhaji did not borrow the village telephone to complain to government officials. Even the twins were quiet. Worry was preventing our sadness. We were numb. Grandma came to where I was sitting under the palm tree now that the journalists were not taking the shade. She sat down beside me.

'An anthill that is destined to become a giant anthill will become one no matter how many times it is destroyed by elephants,' said Grandma.

I did not look up. Not even for Grandma. I did not have the energy to move my head. I concentrated on the spinning feeling.

'You will be a giant anthill,' she said. 'No matter how many elephants.'

Then she pulled me up and brought her hand back into the air behind her. I wondered what she was doing. Could she be stretching?

Grandma suddenly let her hand come flying towards my face. She slapped me. Hard.

'What?' I jumped to my feet. 'Why? What are you doing?'

I held my cheek, which was stinging. Grandma hit me? Grandma slapped my face!

Grandma sat upright. 'Now it is time for you to get up. I need your help.'

I looked at Grandma and waited, but no explanation came. No apology. Nothing. She just sat still as if nothing had happened. I held my own cheek.

'Grandma, you just hit me!'

She looked up. 'Of course.'

'But why?' The stinging had spread right across my face.

'Do you feel sadness?'

I shook my head. The spinning had stopped. 'No, Grandma. I feel pain! I feel angry! Why did you hit me? What have I done?'

Grandma laughed. 'Good,' she said. 'It is time now, for anger. Time for action.'

I stood still for a long time looking at the compound. The sting and shock of Grandma's slap had made me stand up for the first time that day. I did feel pain. I touched my face.

Pain. I felt pain.

I touched my face again. It hurt.

I was alive. Not half-alive. Not sinking. I was living. I would live. I would survive and be a girl once more. I would feel pain and sadness and anger. I would *feel*.

I looked at Grandma. I touched my face again. Then I smiled.

The walk had taken us nearly two hours, and my flip-flop broke halfway there. I had to go barefoot, and burnt the bottom of my feet on the hot ground. A large blister bubbled on my heel, but I did not complain. Feeling pain was much better than feeling nothing. It was better than spinning. Grandma was right. I thought of Dan, hungry and alone in a room with no toilet. I tried to imagine him with a gun against his head, a hood over his face, a man smacking his cheek with the butt of his rifle. His skin was too thin; it would split open easily.

We walked away from the river, and past the forest, until the smell of the water was not in the air, and the river birds' noise sounded quiet, quiet. Women waved at us on the way, from their roadside huts, where they could see the Western Oil Company buildings in the distance. It was still inside my head. I wanted to ask the women about how it felt, to watch the glass buildings from where they lived in shacks and were hungry. I was so angry. It felt good to be angry. I let it grow inside me. The anger burned my throat. I was angry with the Western Oil Company, who gave our government the money with full knowledge that on the other side of the gate, children were hungry, and had no school, no electricity, no future. The Western Oil Company who paid the Kill and Go police to wipe out any village on the other side of the gate who caused problems. The same Kill and Go police who had killed Boneboy's parents. The Western Oil Company who put the guns into young boys' hands.

Burnt-out engines lined up, with flowers growing from inside them. Beauty found a way to grow in the ugliest of places. The dusty road rose and fell like Ezikiel's chest. People hawking wares ignored us as we walked along the roadside, and concentrated on waving at cars. We walked past trays and trays of oranges, and a man with a hook in place of his arm selling brightly coloured sweets wrapped in plastic. Animals bleated, horns blasted, shouting and laughing, music coming from a large speaker, a man with dreadlocks sitting on top, nodding with every beat. It was impossible to talk, or to hear myself think, and for that, I was glad. The man sitting on the speaker nodded at me when we walked past, and I was aware of him watching me as we walked away. My bottom was growing outwards and upwards. I could feel his eyes on it. I hoped Grandma would not notice.

I will get to grow up, I thought.

As we neared the Western Oil Company compound, the road became smooth and easier to walk on. The rubbish lining the roadside disappeared, and even the air smelled fresher, the smell of burning stopped suddenly. The buildings sparkled and shone above the high walls, reflecting the bright blue of the day. Mango trees and palms shaded the road, and bursts of bougainvillea and bright red hibiscus attracted butterflies so large they glided instead of fluttering, from one plant to the next. The way they moved made me think of Dan's birds.

The chatter of the women when we arrived at the Western Oil Company gates was so loud that I wanted to cover my ears. I looked over at them. I had never seen so many women in one place, not even market. There must have been a hundred standing together at the gates, and dozens more approaching from all directions. Even covered in reddish ground-dirt and fall-out dust from the pipeline fires they had picked up on their way, the women looked like flowers in full bloom, fat and bright. Hopeful.

The security men stood with their rifles raised high, shouting for the women to back away. They raised their rifles with their voices until both things were very loud. I focused on the moons of sweat that had formed underneath their armpits, and turned their uniforms a different colour.

'We are not doing anything wrong,' shouted Grandma, in Izon, and a hush fell onto the group. 'This is a peaceful protest.'

One of the security men laughed. 'What can a group of women do?' he said. 'Foolish women. Go home to your husbands.'

'Dozie,' said Grandma. The man looked across the crowd at her. 'Little Dozie. I pulled you from your mother's womb. Even then you were difficult.'

He was silent after that.

'We want justice! We want justice!'

We chanted at the Western Oil Company building; the mirrored glass showed our reflections multiplied as though we were millions. This gave us courage and we shouted louder, even when the men with guns also multiplied. Then we started singing. I copied the women around me as closely as possible. Grandma had taught me many songs but I did not know that one. We sang in unison, like a choir that had been practising all year for that one song. Grandma started it. It was an Ijaw song called *Wo Ekilemo*. Praise him. Her voice was low and quiet, but one by one we joined in. The sound of us women singing was so powerful that the glass moved on the expensive windows, and people inside the building started shutting the windows, even the high-up ones. The slams made us sing even louder. I imagined the white men on the other side of the windows, watching us as they drank their tea. I wondered if they understood why we were protesting. I wondered if they even cared. The security men waving their guns started swaying, as if their bodies were disobeying their commands. They were Ijaw, too, you see. They removed their hats, and rocked from side to side. I sang loudly until the part that said 'I have overcome death, poverty and sickness'. I could not sing that part. My mind kept flashing to Ezikiel's face. But then I joined in again, and our voices rose so high I thought they might reach Allah's ears.

Then we all took off our clothes.

'There is nothing more powerful than a naked woman,' Grandma said. 'Nothing in the world.' The press arrived shortly afterwards to find hundreds of naked women. One press van nearly crashed into the security office. The cameras started flashing; it became impossible to see. The sun burned my naked skin. At first I held my arms over my chest and my private parts. There were young men in front of us. But soon, I removed my hands. I was swimming in a sea of women.

The cameras flashed at Grandma. 'Look at us!' she shouted.

'Your sisters and daughters and mothers! Look at our disgrace. You feel shame. Now you all feel shame!' She stood in front of us all, waving her fists and her breasts at the Western Oil Company windows. She looked older naked. And even wiser. The security men surrounding the Western Oil Company had turned their backs away one by one. Their shoulders were shaking. It was the biggest protest we could make. Those men would never recover. Dozie bent down first. He placed his rifle on the ground. Then he stood, slowly. The others followed. One by one the rifles were placed on the ground. The men walked away in a line, their heads hanging low between their shoulder blades.

Shouting and screaming came from the other side of the gate. No more men with rifles appeared. For the first time, the Western Oil Company was unguarded.

The press did not ask questions until the song was finished, and the windows of the building started opening again. White faces looked out, and shouted. I tried to hide behind Grandma's arm, but Grandma pulled me out and said that every woman had a duty to speak sooner or later; it was my duty to speak on behalf of Ezikiel, and on behalf of Dan.

'We want Dan freed!'

'We are singing for the deaths that will continue to happen unless we are listened to.'

My eyes opened wide. Grandma spoke as if she had a university degree.

'We want a hospital. A clinic. A school. A future for our sons. Like we are promised.'

Another woman with a scarf wrapped so high up she looked as tall as Youseff, shouted, 'We no want dangerous gas burnt in all this pipeline fire, give us cancer, coughing, asthma, like our lungs are less important than any other place. We want our fruits to grow, our animals to be able to eat grass and not drop dead. We want to drink water that has no oil in it. We want you to stop paying people to kill us. To stop funding the military regime. To admit to the blood on your hands!'

'Is it true that your white son-in-law has been kidnapped by a group calling themselves the Sibeye Boys?'

'Yes, it is true.'

'Do you support the group then, by leading this protest?'

Grandma paused. She did not know how to answer; her hands were shaking. I did not know what to do or what to say. I thought as quickly as possible. Then Celestine stood next to Grandma and took her hand and held it in the air. Naked, they looked like mother and daughter. Or grandmother and granddaughter.

'Of course we don't support them. We are against those boys! They are not the true freedom fighters! But they are our sons!' Grandma shouted. Her voice was loud. I imagine it would have been heard back at the compound it was so loud. It would have been heard on the river in the mangrove swamps where Dan would be laughing at the soldiers on hearing it. Ezikiel would have heard it, all the way from the spirit world.

'They feel they have no choice! No future! And that is the fault of the Western Oil Company. But we are angry with them. Those boys have blood on their hands! We are sick of the failed promises. Sick of sickness. Sick of our environment filled with pollution, and our rivers filled with oil spills. Sick of guns. Sick of no electricity. Sick of our government putting billions of pounds in their own pockets. We are sick of the oil companies giving these men money, knowing it will not go to the people. We are sick of no jobs. We are sick of white men shipped in to do jobs the local men could do if they had the chance. If the government and the oil companies gave local people what is theirs by birth then this kidnap would not have happened. No kidnaps would happen. Give us back our sons. We are sick of the fighting between Itsekiri, Ijaw, Urhobo, all tribes. The land belongs to all of us! All of us! Not the oil companies! Not the government! Not the bloody Sibeye Boys! When we stop fighting each other we can take back what is ours! Stop raping our land! Stop raping us! Give us back our sons!'

All the women started chanting in English. 'Give us back our sons! Give us back our sons! Give us back our sons!' Eventually the chant died down.

The journalist moved his microphone closer to Grandma. 'We want those local boys to feel our shame. Look at us, your sisters. Look at us and see how we feel. We are full of shame. Kidnapping. Violence. We are sick of their behaviour. We need them to feel shame. Stop the violence. Stop the kidnapping. We want better healthcare. We want the world to know what is happening in our country. We are living with nothing, nothing. War, fighting. Those people using our oil to make their cars drive fast, do they know we are dying? We are being murdered and our sons are turning into murderers! No chance of future for our sons. Their only choice is kidnapping a white man, using violence. We are ashamed of our sons' behaviour. We want better future for them. Give us our sons. Give them chances at jobs. Health, school. Let our fish live in the river and our trees grow. Give us back our sons!' Grandma closed her mouth. She was breathing quickly and her eyes were shut. When she opened them she looked straight at Celestine and smiled.

Then Celestine started to dance.

I had never seen Celestine dance like that. Her body was water. She looked small and moved easily. It was a complete surprise. I could hear music despite there being none. I could see, from her movements, the pain of losing Ezikiel, of losing Dan, of becoming the second wife of Alhaji. Her body spoke to everyone that day. She danced so well that I wanted to be her, and it was impossible not to join in. Her dance was infectious. We were all dancing within minutes. It felt good to move freely. I danced out the pain of Ezikiel's death. I danced out my own pain. I danced away Father. I danced for Dan. Dan, who was see-through and loved birds. Mama would never find Dan on top of another woman, of that I was sure. She needed him, and I needed her. I danced for Dan, and danced and danced and danced. It felt like praying, like flying.

Eventually men with guns came out from the Western

Oil Compound, and surrounded and rounded up us women as though we were sheep or cattle. Grandma was forced to shout, 'Home, back home,' and everyone put on their clothes, and started walking off in different directions. I did not feel at all scared. The very worst things had happened. What could they do?

'We have to go,' Grandma said. 'That last peaceful protest ended up with the oil companies paying the government men to kill seven women.' We walked away, past the men who had laid down their guns and were lining the roadside with their heads and eyes lowered to the ground.

'Sometimes words are more powerful than guns. And sometimes silence is more powerful than words. It is the things that are not said that are important.'

Celestine danced on the way home. Something changed in her forever that day, and it wasn't until years later that I realised she had become a woman. Before that she had been just a girl. A young girl. Celestine had been a silly girl. But she became a powerful woman.

Celestine stood taller. She took Grandma's hand in hers.

'We danced those guns to silence,' she said.

THIRTY-SIX

The very next day we heard his voice. 'Hey, hey, I'm here, I'm safe, I'm safe.' Dan's voice. It was Dan's voice.

Mama lifted her head for the first time in weeks. She stood suddenly, and ran towards the gate, flicking her sandals off until she was barefoot; a layer of ground-dust rose up behind her. When the dust settled I saw Dan walking through the gate with his arms stretched out as if he knew Mama would be running towards him at that moment. Two oil company security men stood each side of him with rifles crossing their bodies.

Dan's body swallowed Mama until they were tightly wrapped into one person. It was not until they separated into themselves that I could see how thin Dan looked, and burnt as red as his hair. Swollen mosquito bites covered his face.

'Blessing,' he said, and held his arms out again, as if he expected me to run into them, too. I stood still in my mind, but my body ran to him. I had no control over my legs. They were running. Dan hugged me tightly; it felt as though he might not ever let me go. It was a good feeling. I breathed in the awful stale smell of him and felt glad; he smelled of survival. Mama hugged both of us. The three of us stood there for a very long time, right in front of the roses in the herb garden. In the area where Ezikiel was buried.

Eventually we separated. Mama held Dan's hands tightly, kissing them and holding them to her face. She kept saying, 'Thank God, Thank God,' over and over.

'I was so frightened,' said Dan. 'I was so frightened I'd never see you again. Thank God! Thank God!'

I did not thank anyone. I just felt my heart rise from my stomach to my chest. My lungs opened and I could breathe again. I looked at Dan. He stood straight upwards. His hands were open.

'Where's Ezikiel?' Dan looked around the garden and then he looked at Mama's face. He held her face in his hands and leant forwards. 'No,' he whispered. 'No! What happened? What happened?' I could see from the tears filling his eyes that he knew. He knew from looking at Mama.

'He joined that gang of boys, the Sibeye Boys; they split open a pipeline. There was a fire,' I said. 'An explosion. He could not recover.'

My words sounded clear and strong. I couldn't believe them, even though I said them out loud. Dan looked at me, and held me, and kissed my head. He said nothing. Which was exactly the right thing to say.

'It was my fault,' said Mama. She began sobbing into Dan's T-shirt. 'I disowned him. He had you kidnapped and I disowned him! It was my fault!' Mama sobbed and sobbed and sobbed. Dan held her tightly and did not let go. 'It's all my fault! My son!' The first words she had said in so long sounded full of shame.

'I'm so sorry,' he said. 'I'm so sorry for you both.' Then Dan pulled me into his arms and held me together with Mama. 'I'm so sorry,' he whispered. 'I'm so sorry.'

I looked at Mama's face, pressed close to mine. 'It was not your fault,' I whispered.

Dan did not leave Mama's side for days. His skin peeled off in blisters. It constantly reminded me of Ezikiel. I could barely look at him.

Dan had changed. He watched his birds while he ate large bowls of fresh fish pepper soup, as if it was his favourite dish. He knelt to Alhaji. He knelt even lower to Grandma.

'I'm so very sorry,' he kept saying. 'I feel responsible. I just can't believe he's gone.'

'It is not your fault,' said Mama. 'It is not your fault.' She refused to eat, and spent hours sitting in the area where Ezikiel was buried. Her skin hung from her body like a coat that was too big. But she had started to speak. And tears fell from her face. The world started to turn again, more slowly than before, but still, it turned.

Grandma stopped ignoring Dan, and served him first. She sat near to him at dinner, and sang a celebration song. Celestine could not hug Dan, she was still too ashamed of her behaviour before, but she did give him her favourite cup to drink from, and she demonstrated the loud mourning she would have done, if he had died. Dan laughed, and we all laughed, and the same feelings spread through us as if we were tied by blood, not just marriage. It felt good to laugh, as if it was waiting there all along, as if Ezikiel was laughing with us. We looked at Dan as one of us. He had earned his Nigerian—ness by surviving. Ijaw people are survivors. He would never be my father. It did not matter. I was beginning to understand things that had been obvious. That I had kept blocked from my mind. That people could keep secrets from themselves. I had kept Father a secret. Made him something he was not. I had made him into a good man. I did not understand why I had done that. But he was not the father I had thought that he was. And Dan was more than I had thought.

Of course, Dan was very frightened. He kept looking at the gate to check it was free of kidnappers. He sat down on the veranda one day and started talking; the words fell from his mouth like the rains. Some of what he said did not make sense, but it was honest. He spoke honestly about every-thing. We did not question him; we listened. It was painful. The words cut my ears. Every time we heard another part of the story I cried a little more. Dan cried.

'It was the happiest day of my life,' Dan said. 'My own family. When I asked Timi if she'd rather write her own vows, less traditional than the obey me sort, she was, well, sort of *perplexed*. Why would I? she asked. Oh, the joy I felt. A simple thing, a marriage between a man and a woman. So simple really. So beautiful. And then they took me. A hand pushed me into the boot of a car, and I couldn't breathe.

And I remember thinking, I will die today. Of that, I'm sure. Honestly, I could think of nothing else but myself. And all the time Ezikiel had been hurt ...' Dan cried again. He looked at the gap where Ezikiel should have been sitting. We waited for his crying to lessen before he continued. Dan was not afraid to cry. Loud. Sobs, like a woman. He cried much louder than Mama. It made Mama cry a little louder than before. She kept looking at Dan as if she was checking that he did not mind her crying so loudly. Mama was not strong like I had thought. I had been wrong about so many things.

'I counted eight minutes,' Dan continued, 'as they told us to. I remembered the hostage advice the oil company had given us during a "hostage training day"; I mean that says it all, doesn't it?

Do whatever they ask.

Eat and drink whatever they give you.

Don't panic. That's easy for them to write down but in that situation, if it's really happening, God, it's, um, I'm sorry. They also said to:

Try and make friends.

Avoid conversation about political beliefs.

Avoid giving information about family members, and particularly co-workers.

Discuss football.

'When I thought of that I wished for Ezikiel. I thought ...' Dan stopped talking. My stomach twisted and turned until Boneboy picked up my hand. His hand was hot.

Dan sobbed and blew his nose onto a handkerchief. He pulled Mama towards him.

'I told the men it was my wedding day, and they laughed. They laughed and said things to me, terrible things, dragging me into that boat. I needed to use the bathroom. To relieve myself. I'm very ashamed to say that I couldn't control myself ...'

Alhaji crossed his legs, looked away, and made a small sucking sound at the back of his throat.

'The mangroves were so thick they had to push the boat through them. I saw a kingfisher. It became dark then. They smacked my jaw with their rifles; I was in and out of consciousness. I remember closing my eyes and finding a picture of your face.' Dan pulled Mama even closer towards him. 'She is my life, your mother.' Dan looked at me, and Ezikiel's gap.

I thought of love. The love that had happened between Dan and Mama, I had not seen before. It did not happen in every lifetime. I felt glad for Mama, that she had a love strong enough to survive this. Strong enough, I hoped, to make her survive. I wanted that kind of love one day.

Boneboy held my hand.

'They pretended they were going to shoot me,' Dan continued. He held Mama's hand so tightly I heard it click. She did not move. 'They told me I was being executed.' He did not need to say any more. His voice became a voice in my head, amongst the other voices. I knew exactly what he was thinking, his insides. I imagined the rest of what had happened to him.

'And as suddenly as it all began, it ended,' Dan continued. 'The gunmen were quiet that day. So quiet, I felt sure they would execute me. The boy who seemed to be in charge took off his mask. His face was younger than I expected. Probably no more than fifteen, sixteen at the most. He untied me and gave me some water. And then they put me on a boat, which was met in the creeks by another boat, full of security men, police. Well, they just handed me over. The Western Oil Company must have paid the full ransom, otherwise I would never have got out alive.'

It was quiet for a few minutes and I wondered who would be the first to tell Dan. To tell him that those boys who kidnapped him were local, that Alhaji knew them, that the Western Oil Company had not paid a single kobo towards Dan's release.

It was Grandma who had shamed those boys into releasing Dan. They had heard about the women's protest outside the Western Oil Company. They had felt the shame and anger of their sisters, wives, mothers at their violence. Grandma had been right. There is nothing in the world more powerful than a naked woman.

'I need, I mean, we need ... we need to leave. We're leaving,' said Mama. She was leaning against the side of the house. We were all sitting on the veranda eating dinner. Since Ezikiel had died, Mama had found it difficult to sit still, or stay upright. She touched the wall as if it was a person. As if it was Ezikiel. 'We're leaving for London. The Western Oil

Company has issued a visa for me and Blessing. We can't stay here.' Mama leant forwards and nearly fell. She sobbed and her breath broke into tiny pieces. 'My heart is broken,' she said. 'I can't risk losing Dan again.' Mama looked across the compound to where Ezikiel was buried. She touched the wall again.

We all stopped eating. It was the first thing we had eaten all day and we were on second bowls. All except Mama, who had not eaten for many weeks. Her skin looked as if it belonged to someone else. Not eating was making her look ugly. And she did not seem to care. Grandma made a choking sound as if some of the fish was stuck in her throat. Alhaji sat upright in his chair. I felt my brain swell up and press against my skull. I was spinning again. I knew that news would one day arrive, but still, I thought I might fall and let the ground hold me. I could not look at Boneboy, at Ezikiel's grave. It was quiet except for the hum of Dan's generator. I wondered where the money for fuel would come from if Dan left. Where any money would come from when Dan was gone. Then I looked at Mama, and felt my brain move again inside my head. She might die, I thought. If she carries on staying here, not eating and touching walls, she might die.

'Eh! You can send European Fashions!' Celestine jumped up and started dancing. The twins looked at her with their mouths open, as if even they could not believe how silly she was.

'Blessing,' said Mama. 'Blessing.' Her voice sounded far away already.

I looked at Grandma. I looked at Alhaji, and Celestine and the twins. I turned my head to where Ezikiel was buried. I looked at the house, the gate, the perimeter fence, the outhouse, the generator. I looked at the palm tree, the herb garden, the walnut trees. I looked at the rosette flowers, the snail farm, the makeshift mosque. I imagined the sound of the call to prayer through the loudspeaker, the river birds, the sound of the river water during the heavy rains, the harmattan wind. I smelled the roasting corn, the *suya*, Mama's perfume, Celestine's sweat. I remembered the feeling of the softness on top of a baby's head when it was entering the world. I closed my fingers around the memories.

Finally, I looked at Boneboy. 'I cannot leave,' I said. I had never sounded more certain.

It was late afternoon the next day, the stickiness of midday was relaxing, the heat was no longer visible, and the ground was hardening again. Grandma found me behind the outhouse where I was sitting with my head in my hands.

Grandma removed my hands from where they covered my face.

'I do not want to go,' I said. 'Dan should stay here. He is Nigerian now. When you marry one you become one. He is our brother. Our uncle. He is our father!'

I couldn't believe it. The words had left my mouth and with them a rush of thoughts entered my brain. I remembered again Father drinking palm wine and shouting at Mama, slapping her hard across one cheek. Father drinking Star Beer and throwing a plate across the room, Mama picking up pieces of china from the floor. Mama's scream as she found him on top of another woman. His cool-skin hand around my neck. Thoughts of Dan, watching his birds, choking on fishbones, being bitten by Snap, and being jumped on by Celestine. Being kidnapped. And loving Mama like I had never seen love.

I started crying. Grandma nodded. 'I know,' she said. 'You do not have to go.' She put her arms around me, swallowing me up with a cuddle, and kissed my head. 'But it is the best thing,' she said, over the top of my head, 'if you go.'

I moved away from Grandma and looked at her face. I could not believe what I was hearing. Did she not love me as I loved her? 'Eh!' I said. 'You think I should go?'

I wanted to explain. I wanted to be an Ijaw girl and stay forever near Warri. I needed Mama to understand I was as much a part of the Delta as the mango and almond trees, the mangrove swamps, the river, and the red earth.

'I cannot leave you,' I shouted. 'I cannot leave here, my home. This is my home! I do not understand.'

'I do,' said Grandma.

'Why?' My mouth was wide open. I was shocked. I could not believe that Grandma felt any differently than me. After all that time she was my world. I thought I was hers. I felt so much shock my skin became cold.

Grandma thought for many seconds. Her face ruffled up into a thousand wrinkles. Finally, she smiled. 'Some people carry the world inside them,' she said. 'You are one of those people. I am old and Alhaji is old and Ezikiel is gone. We will not be here forever. A fish that can see its water is getting shallower cannot be stranded. You need to be with your Mama. She has suffered enough. And your Mama needs to be with Dan. He is a foolish man, but a good man, and all men are foolish anyway. He is a good man.'

'I do not understand. Nothing makes sense. I will never leave here! This is my home. I just do not understand ...'

'Yes, you do,' said Grandma, and then she stood up, pulling me up with her, as if that was enough. Then she pointed to the area where Ezikiel was buried. Mama was lying on top of the ground with her face pressed down in the dirt. She was so thin that she looked like a pile of clothes. I watched her back rise slowly upwards and flatten back down into the ground. I looked at Grandma.

I spent the whole day walking around the compound looking for answers. Alhaji told me I should go to London to make a better life, study, make money, explore the world. But I could not leave my life in the Delta. I was home. I was never alone. Even when I was alone, Ezikiel was still with me. And Grandma. I could not leave Grandma. I would rather die. Mama did not say anything; she just lay down on top of the ground where Ezikiel lay underneath her.

Dan called me over in the evening. 'I hope you'll come with us,' he said. 'I know how difficult this must be for you. It won't be easy – things will take time but I think we have a real chance to build a life together. As a family. And we don't have that chance here. Not at the moment, anyway – not here. Your mother needs professional help, at least counselling. I think she needs proper help, what she's been through ...' Dan closed his eyes but I could still see behind his eyelids. Mama was there, Father's hand wrapped around her throat.

'I hope you'll come. But I understand if you don't.' And then he held my hand. I looked closely into his eyes for the first time. I smiled and held Dan's hand back. 'I love your Mama, and I want to take care of her,' he said. 'Help her to get well again. And I love you, too.'

'I know,' I said. It was enough to make him smile the biggest smile I had ever seen. I played it again and again in my head. *I love you, too. I love you, too. I love you, too.*

It was the first time I had heard the words. I stretched my brain into my memories as far as they would reach, but I could not hear Father saying those words to me. Just to the other woman.

Celestine followed me around the garden, singing.

'Papa don't preach,' she sang. 'Imagine. London. All that Lycra. Hamburgers.' But later she pulled me close and whispered. 'You go and study and never forget where you came from. You could change things for people in the Delta. Make use of your time, study hard. You could change the world. Because you will always be one of us, *abi*?' I looked at Celestine closely. 'Go, but make sure you come back to us. Make sure you return home. Warri no dey carry last!' By then she was winding her way around the garden and talking about fast food but I could see there was more to her. Much more than Alhaji had bargained for.

THIRTY-SEVEN

There was another wedding. A small affair, unheard of in Nigeria. The only guests were me, Grandma, Celestine, the twins, Boneboy, Alhaji. And, of course, Ezikiel. He filled the air around us. Flying and dancing and singing. Ezikiel was everywhere, making long, thin shadows. I watched the day turn to night, the sun turn orange, filling the sky with jewellery. Everything seemed possible. The flowers packing the garden with the smell of happiness. Life and death smelled the same, but happiness and sadness smelled very different. Sadness had numbed my senses until it was impossible to remember what the river sounded like at dawn, or what the early evening sun did to my skin, or how it felt to hear Ezikiel call my name. Happiness lifted the blanket from me and I could feel once more, with my whole self.

Mama looked more beautiful than I had ever seen her, even though her skin was hanging off. She glittered and shone in the sunlight, and her frown line added spice to her face. She hummed a song I recognised but could not remember. She could not smile, but to hear Mama hum a song; it was better than holding a new baby.

Mama and Dan stood at the front of the mosque like two young people – she in her simple wrapper, he in grey trousers and shirt, the imam before them, no loudspeaker. She, leaning against him. Him, holding her up.

Dan held the Koran softly, as though it was Mama's hand, stroking the outside with his fingers. He spoke words in Arabic, badly, but Alhaji nodded his head anyway, and shook ever so slightly. Dan bowed his head to Allah. I noticed how strong his shoulders looked. How straight his spine was. Mama covered her hair completely with a scarf, pulling it over her forehead. Even so, I could see all of her, inside her body, right to her bones. I could feel Ezikiel right beside me, holding my hand.

The imam chanted the Koran and spoke in Arabic. Dan did not smile with his mouth. The smile vanished from his lips and travelled to his eyes, where it stayed. Dan's eyes lit up the garden, moon-blue, icy and sharp.

There was no music, only the birds singing in the garden trees, and the sound of distant laughter from the street outside. Dan did not notice. He did not look up at any bird, even the brilliant yellow bird darting above us and over us, showing off his beautiful feathers. Dan could only look at Mama.

The smell of kerosene, and roasting corn, and decomposing spinach leaves from the snail farm, and bright, bursting flowers changed as the light fell, became stronger, sweeter, honey. The wedding took hours, as though the imam realised it was the only chance to have Dan hold the Koran. But the time seemed to pass slowly; even the sun dropped down centimetre by centimetre, which was unusual. Usually it fell into the ground causing darkness to shock us every evening. But that evening there were no shocks, no surprises. It was perfect, as it should have been.

After a long time of peaceful chanting and happy air, Alhaji put his hand out, and the imam stopped. 'Now,' said Alhaji stepping forwards, 'now you are our husband.'

Dan laughed and pulled Mama towards him to kiss her mouth. Nobody looked away. I felt no hotness creeping over my cheeks.

They kissed with their eyes wide open.

Afterwards there was wedding cake. It had been baked by Mama Akpan who by then had an inside kitchen with a range cooker and eight hobs. The cake was chocolate inside, covered with white icing. I could not wait to try it. Grandma cut it into pieces and handed a small piece to Mama and nodded. Mama knelt down slowly onto the ground, in front of Dan. She reached up to his mouth with her arm and put the cake to his lips. It was the traditional thing to do. I felt amazed that Mama had performed something traditional. Grandma laughed and smiled. She reached for Alhaji's arm.

Dan laughed, opened his mouth, and bit. He chewed slowly. Then he pulled Mama up towards him, away from the ground. The ground did not want to hold Mama for long. Nobody clapped, but Grandma pushed her hands together in front of her chest and squeezed.

Dan turned to Alhaji. He reached out and patted his shoulders. Alhaji nodded and smiled. Then Dan dropped down to his knees before Alhaji and lowered his head. He knelt and looked up at Alhaji. He bent his head again and reached up to take Alhaji's hands. Alhaji pulled Dan up to standing and put his arms around him. They held each other. Both of them. Oil and water.

'Thank you, sir,' said Dan. 'I promise to take good care of her. Really, I will, I can promise you.'

Alhaji laughed. 'Now you are family. That means that we all take care of each other. You see?'

Mama held me close to her body. I could feel every bone on her arm, but I could also feel her breath going in, coming out, and then going in again. Grandma slipped her hand into mine. The other side of her, Celestine held onto Grandma's arm.

Alhaji became as big as the moon and shone just as brightly. Dan's moon-eyes widened, as if Alhaji was becoming part of Dan.

Youseff's youngest daughters whispered to each other all day but rarely said anything to anyone else except 'biscuit' or 'ball'. They played with the basketball that Dan had originally bought for Ezikiel, rolling it towards each other for hours.

'Blessing,' they said at the same time, as they rolled the ball to and fro. 'Blessing.'

I walked towards them.

'Where is London?' they asked. Their bellies had shrunk flat with all the dried snail-meat protein from Alhaji's snail farm. They no longer caused round shadows on the ground.

'Oh, very far,' I said, laughing.

'Is it outside the garden?'

I realised that Youseff's children had only left the garden for a few occasions in their lives. 'Yes, it's far. Outside the village. Far from here, outside Nigeria.'

They stopped rolling the ball, stood up and put their hands over their mouths. 'Are you going?'

I looked around before I gave my answer. I could see myself lying under the palm tree with Ezikiel like two spoons. Snap jumping for a bone. Celestine arriving and being washed by Grandma. I saw my brother being buried. Most of all, I saw Grandma. Grandma was everywhere. I looked over at the wall that Mama was leaning against. She looked straight at the garden without blinking. Her eyes were open but she was asleep. I wanted her to wake up. 'Yes.' I patted the girls on the head. 'Yes, I am going.'

I did not notice Boneboy staring at me from behind the almond trees. I had not noticed Boneboy at all.

The journey to the airport did not take long, but it was uncomfortable. In the car Alhaji was sitting next to Youseff, who was driving, Dan was next to Mama, who was next to Grandma, who was next to me. There was no room for Boneboy. I waved goodbye to him and turned around. I could not look at him getting smaller and smaller and smaller until he disappeared. I would not look back. I would not.

Dan was wearing a T-shirt given to him by Celestine, which said 'I was kidnapped by militants and all I got was this lousy T-shirt'. Alhaji told Celestine it was a ridiculous gift and there was no way Dan could ever wear it. Dan wore it anyway. The luggage, which consisted of mainly foodstuffs that Grandma had said were essential and unavailable in London, was piled up on our laps. Celestine and the twins were in the boot. The car drooped down so low with the weight of us that I was sure we would never make it.

'A 737 should be able to reach 6,000 kilometres an hour, but at a certain altitude, the air pressure drops down to …' Alhaji spoke but none of us were listening.

'Don't forget to send a Big Mac!' Celestine said.

'Meat goes bad quickly in the West. Not enough salt,' Grandma said. 'Also Blessing will be too busy studying to be sending gifts.'

I knew that I would send gifts every month, but I also knew that they would probably not receive any of them. A parcel from London was too much temptation for a postal worker, if it even made it past the aircraft staff. I focused on the gifts I would send anyway: a brand-new knife for Grandma, a radio for Alhaji, a properly fitting outfit for Celestine.

When we arrived at the airport I was unable to get out of the car for several minutes; my muscles had stopped working from being squashed in the same position for some time. Alhaji pulled us out one by one, laughing. He did not stop patting Dan on the back.

We walked through to the chaos at the terminal. I tried to take in as many of the scenes as possible. Round-bellied, scabby-legged children in rags, begging, hand-poking passers-by, men with fast shifting eyes hanging around pillars, religious men walking in groups, Big Men in shiny suits waved through without checks. I opened my eyes as wide as they would go, until my teeth hurt.

Remember, remember, remember.

Everyone we spoke to asked for dash.

'Give a little something for making your passage easier, sir. Have you paid leavers' tax? Where is your Certificate of Departure?'

Most of it was directed at Dan, who had lived in Nigeria long enough to know that bribery was a necessary part of travel. Alhaji was outraged. He took it as a personal slight that his countrymen were demanding a bribe from his son-in-law, and he nearly got arrested at passport control.

'Get away from my face!' he shouted at the man stamping the passports who was refusing to stamp Dan's passport without seeing proof that he was carrying less than five hundred US dollars.

'Please take out your wallet, sir.'

'You are a shame for your mother and for your country,' Alhaji shouted. The police were called over, and our bags checked. The foodstuff spilled out onto the floor. Plantains (underripe, will be ready Tuesday unless you want to make

him strong then they are ready now! Eh!), *garri*, packets of
pounded yam, dried fish, river plants, chin-chin, peppers,
cashew nuts, even a bag of tripe. And smoke-dried snails.
Dozens of snails.

'Ha!' said the official, and Dan had to bribe him after all.

The goodbyes were quick. Dan did not want to miss the
place in the queue, which now stretched all the way to the
car parking area at the side of the airport. He wanted to go
home as much as I wanted to stay.

I hugged the twins and Celestine together.

'You go fit send lipsticks,' Celestine said, between sobs.
'And European Fashions.'

Alhaji shook Dan's hand for longer than necessary. He
patted me and Mama on the head, and said, 'Be good.'
Grandma held Dan, then Mama. 'The boy is good,' she whispered in Mama's ear loud enough for us all to hear anyway.
She turned to me. Her face was wrinkleless it had swollen
so much from crying. She held my cheek in her hand, her
fingers that smelled of antiseptic and pepper sauce. Then she
fell to the ground with me, and kissed my face, wiping tears
away from my cheeks. 'I'm sorry,' she said. I split in two.
Half of me would go with Mama. Half would always remain
with Grandma.

'Remember who you are,' she said. And then she whispered something to me that only I could hear.

We walked through the gate in single file. Something
was missing. Dan and Mama did not look back. I allowed

myself one last sight of Grandma. She was holding Celestine's hand and leaning against Alhaji. Alhaji put his arm around them both.

I felt as if I had forgotten something really important.

'I cannot go!' I stopped walking. My feet refused to move in front of one another.

Mama stopped walking, and sobbed. She brought her hand to her mouth. Her eyes could not look at me.

People shuffled past us, the airline staff waved their hands, trying to move us forward using only air. 'I cannot go.'

Dan lifted my face upwards with his hand. 'Are you sure?' he asked. 'Really sure?'

He had tears in his eyelids, waiting to fall.

I nodded. 'I am sure. It would not be right for me,' I said. 'I am not angry; I am not trying to be difficult. I am not even sad. I am home.'

Mama dropped her day bag and sniffed loudly. 'I have lost one child,' she whispered. 'Don't make me lose another.' Her eyes found mine and it was as though everything else was outside of us. There was Mama and me, and then everyone else. We had a world of our own, I realised. A whole world that only contained us.

'You will never lose me,' I said. My words sounded confident. The words of an adult. I smiled. I held Mama's eyes and looked so far into them that it was difficult coming out. 'No mother and daughter ever live apart, no matter how big the distance between them.'

Mama looked straight back into my eyes. I could feel

Dan dancing around us, and the airport sounds and people rushing past, shouting, but nothing else was real. The link between me and Mama felt like the most important thing in the world. Important things are always difficult, I thought.

Are you sure, Mama asked my eyes. *Yes,* they said.

It was the first question she had ever really asked me.

Dan held me close. He kissed the top of my head. 'I will look after your mother. And you had better come to visit regularly. I mean it.'

Mama held me at arm's length. Then her arms folded. She kissed my cheek. 'I have to go, you understand? I'm not coping well. I can't stay.'

I nodded. I did understand. Dan was Mama's home.

'My Blessing,' she said. 'I gave you that name. Did you know that?'

I shook my head.

'Alhaji wanted to give you a Muslim name, and Father wanted a Christian name. But I said it did not matter. You were a Blessing in any faith. My Blessing.'

Tears fell from my face. My eyes were not feeling as confident as my voice.

Then Mama said the thing I had waited to hear my whole life.

'I am so happy to be your Mama.'

She did not say 'I love you' out loud. But I heard it anyway.

The aircraft was a distance from the airport. I watched

their backs. I walked slowly towards the airport building. One foot in front of the other. I looked back at the plane, and the sky, and the ground. I looked at the airport windows, but they were too dirty to see through. I picked up some ground-dust and kept it in my hand. I took in as many hot breaths as I could. At the top of the stairs I turned around and looked directly at the yellow Nigerian sun, blinking until I could no longer see the aircraft, or Mama's back.

I ran, shouting. Grandma was standing at the large window, clutching her chest. Celestine was holding her up. Alhaji saw me first. He jumped into the air. He ran towards me.

'I knew it, you see?' His voice was loud enough to make the planes sound quiet.

Celestine whistled. 'Blessing!'

Alhaji hugged me and lifted me and spun me. 'You will stay home with us, for always?' he laughed.

'Yes, sir.'

'No more sir!' he shouted. 'You are a true Ijaw Muslim girl. You will call Alhaji Grandpa!'

Grandma fell to the ground. She cried and cried and cried. I put my arms around her shoulders and kissed her cheek scars, full of tears. 'I will never leave you,' I said. 'I could never leave you. I belong to you. I belong here. I am home.'

'I thought you would go,' said Grandma. 'I thought it was the best thing.'

'The frog is not tied to the pond by a rope,' I said.

And Grandma laughed and laughed and laughed.

We stood and watched the plane gathering speed on the runway. The men with brightly coloured jackets jumped out of the way, and fired gunshots into the sky to move any birds. The sound exploded in my head, but I no longer jumped. The fear had gone. My heart was beating steady and strong. The plane got faster, and faster, the windows blurred until they became one window, one face. They took off seconds later and glided upwards into the sky. Their backs to the Nigerian sun. They climbed higher, leaving a fluffy trail that resembled a water spirit. It swirled and danced and twisted. Lost its shape and found it again. It was light and dark at the same time. It stretched upwards, grew to the size of a football field, spread out across the ground, darkening and lighting everything all at once. It became thin and long. And then it was gone.

EPILOGUE

'You didn't go, Mummy?'

'Leave my home? My beloved home? Where else will I get such beautiful fried fish?'

'I know, I know,' she says. 'There is no place like home.'

I laugh as Eniye jumps off my lap. 'Anyway, cheeky,' I continue, 'there are two possible endings to every story.'

She runs around the arrivals area, her legs weaving in and out of the crowds of families waiting dressed in their church clothes, looking at the gate where the arrivals pour into, unable to take their eyes away in case they miss their family member walking through that gate. I do not look. I know that they are coming.

Eniye stops at a carpet market, women selling cashews, pawpaw, bananas, sugar cane, maize, to the people waiting. There is always the opportunity for a little business. Women know this most. They ignore my daughter who watches everything hungrily, swallowing all the airport sights. She runs right past a boy, about sixteen, who looks like Ezikiel. A man, maybe his father, puts his arm on the boy's back.

Eniye is skinny and tall and angular, and moves around like a gazelle, gracefully, unable to sit still unless I am telling her a story. Eniye is physical, like her father. Strong. She likes to swim. Run. Dance. Or play with the hula-hoop that has survived all these years. It makes me angry whenever I see it, the hula-hoop that outlived my brother. I never let it show on the outside. When Eniye puts it around her middle she has a connection to her grandparents that is too important to spoil. She runs back.

'Mummy, when are they landing?'

'The flight is delayed. You have to be patient.'

'I've been patient for hours,' she laughs.

'Who is this cheeky daughter? Did I raise you to be cheeky?'

And then I hear a voice. 'Did someone mention a cheeky daughter?'

'Daddy!' She runs towards him and he scoops her up to the ceiling. He holds her up high with his strong arm.

'Where is she?' He shields his eyes with his other hand, and walks towards me looking around the airport. 'I see her mother.' He leans towards me and kisses my cheek. His lips are butterfly wings. Our daughter laughs and screams from the air, still held above his head by his hand as if she is a baby. He looks up. 'Oh, there you are!' He drops her down in a laughing heap onto my lap. 'I didn't see you up there.'

He smells of river water and coconut oil and pepper soup. Whenever he kisses me, my lips buzz as if his are electric. 'How was your day?' I ask.

'Good. Plenty of fish in the river today!' he laughs. His laugh is too-loud, making people jump. It makes me smile, think of Father's good pieces. 'How about you?'

'Plenty of people being born in Nigeria. A midwife will never be unemployed.' I laugh, too.

'Or a snail farmer,' says Eniye. I think of our twins, who are now nearly grown, still calling themselves Twin One and Twin Two, who are as fat as Eniye is thin, and in the snail-farming business; a surprising success. Eniye worships them. They take orders from grandfather Alhaji who sits next to the farm in a deckchair. He is so frail. Yet he insists on tending Grandma's herb garden himself. Will not let anyone else touch it.

Grandma is gone. Before she left she pulled Eniye from my body.

'A daughter,' were her last words. 'God is great.'

'And you've been busy telling me stories, *sha*.' Our daughter's voice is muffled. Her face is pressed against my shoulder. When looking at her I imagine myself at her age and I live it all over again. Having children is getting to live two lives.

'They should be here!' My husband looks at his watch. 'The plane should be landing now.'

I feel twelve years old again. I look at my own daughter and wonder how it is all possible. At first I had not understood Mama. But as I grew older, maybe not wiser, certainly more realistic, I realised she did the best she could. She loved me, in her own way. Not everyone is born to be a mother.

It does not come naturally to some women. They are the ones that Allah should have made into men.

'Do you forgive Mama?' Eniye asks questions we only think about. She is our hearts exposed and beating in front of our faces. I look into her eyes and see Grandma staring straight back at me. 'What about Grandma? I still can't believe she cut girls.'

I look at my daughter and try not to even imagine her with parts missing. Even Grandma had some things very wrong.

'There is nothing to forgive. We are all a mixture of right and wrong.'

'Except me.' My husband laughs. Too-loudly. 'I am always right!'

My daughter moves laps, jumping on her daddy so suddenly he groans. We offer so much physical affection I worry that we suffocate her. I always want her to know she is loved. But I will make my own mistakes, I know. I can only hope that she will forgive me for those; that forgiveness is all a parent can hope for. I notice the boy again, the one who reminds me of Ezikiel. He is watching us laughing and holding each other, and the expression on his face reminds me how lucky we are.

'Mummy. Can you tell me the story again?'

'Not again. You've heard it a thousand times at least.'

'I know. But I love to hear it. Except the part when you and Daddy kissed for the first time underneath the present table at the wedding!'

I look at my husband, who looks back. Something passes

between us, even now, after so many years. I am still surprised. Now with my husband, I am no longer half of anything. He was always there, right in front of my face. So close I could not see it. There from the start of my life. And my life really started when we moved to my grandfather's house. Until then I didn't know what family was. I thought Father was family. I knew nothing. I think of my family now: grandfather Alhaji, the twins, Mama and Dan, who speak with me every week. Celestine, who is like my sister.

'Which story do you want?' I say. 'We haven't got long. They will be here any minute. And this is the last time. So remember it well.'

I make myself comfortable, leaning into Are's arm. I laugh. It still sounds strange thinking of him as anything but Boneboy.

I love telling the stories. It is what us Ijaw women have always done. More and more is being written down. But the best stories are told. And the very best stories are told to a daughter. Saying them out loud keeps people alive. Ezikiel lives on. He dances in our ears.

'Tell the one about Uncle joining the Sibeye Boys. Oh no, wait! Actually, start at the beginning. The very beginning. Tell me about leaving Lagos. About your father. About Uncle worrying about River-Dwelling Parasites. About Celestine arriving. Tell me about Grandma. Oh wait, no. Tell me about Daddy watching you leave for the airport. When he watched the car disappearing away. Please. Tell me again. Tell me again. Start at the beginning.'

And so I settle back into the plastic chair and let the sights and noise of the airport fade to nothing. I hold my daughter, and put my mouth to her little ear. And I begin again:

'Father was a loud man ...'

AFTERWORD

The Niger Delta, known as 'The Big Heart', is home to proud people, with good reason. It is a beautiful land, with extraordinary wildlife, an amazing landscape, bustling cosmopolitan towns and peaceful villages. Port Harcourt and Warri are fast becoming centres of cultural importance, with thriving arts and literature scenes, an abundance of restaurants, and independent theatre groups. The Niger Delta is a place of laughter, music and diversity.

But the majority of people who live in the Niger Delta survive on less than one dollar a day. They enjoy none of the enormous wealth generated by the oil-rich land. Many people of the Niger Delta have no access to schools, healthcare or clean water. They live with the effects of the environmental devastation caused by the continued gas flaring and frequent ecological accidents, which have amounted to over one and a half million tons of spilled oil: starvation, asthma, chest infections, cancers, and birth deformities. They live with the threat of violence, rape and death. The mobile police are simply known locally as 'Kill and Go'. Meanwhile groups of militants are bunkering oil, sabotaging pipelines and kidnapping oil workers, distracting from the voice of the majority of true freedom fighters protesting peacefully.

There is strength and beauty in the Delta, in the resilience, humour and hope of its people. Real freedom fighters are working hard to ensure basic human rights for all people of the Delta, and are becoming a force that the oil companies and government can no longer ignore. Different ethnic and religious groups are coming together. Their united voice is becoming louder, stronger than the guns of the militants. They were there a long time before oil companies, government or militia groups. And they will remain.

To find out more about the political situation in the Niger Delta, I recommend the following books:

A Swamp Full of Dollars: Pipelines and Paramilitaries at Nigeria's Oil Frontier by Michael Peel (2009, I.B. Tauris)

Where Vultures Feast: Shell, Human Rights and Oil in the Niger Delta by Ike Okonta and Oronto Douglas (Second Edition, 2003, Verso)

The Next Gulf: London, Washington and Oil Conflict in Nigeria by Andy Rowell, James Marriott and Lorne Stockman (2005, Constable)

And the following websites:
saharareporters.com
platformlondon.org
remembersarowiwa.com
wiwavshell.org

The practice of female circumcision, or cutting, known in the UK as female genital mutilation, varies widely in the Niger Delta and is mercifully reducing thanks to the efforts of local and international activists such as Juliana Okoh and Comfort Momoh. Young women from towns and cities describe female circumcision as dying out, and hardly ever talked about. However, it is estimated that between 20 and 50 per cent of girls in Nigeria still undergo the procedure, and this figure is up to 80 per cent in some rural areas.

Female genital mutilation is a violation of human rights. It needs to be talked about. An estimated 10 per cent of girls die following the procedure due to short-term complications, and a further 25 per cent die in the long term, mainly as a result of complications during labour. Here in the UK, up to seven thousand girls are thought to be at risk of female genital mutilation every year.

For further information I recommend *Female Genital Mutilation*, edited by Comfort Momoh (2005, Radcliffe Publishing). To get involved please contact Forward (forwarduk.org.uk), which is an organisation dedicated to the health of African girls wherever they live.

ACKNOWLEDGEMENTS

Grandma's proverbs and stories have come from Motherland Nigeria (motherlandnigeria.com) and the Bayelsa Council for Arts and Culture (bayelsaartsng.com).

Some of the Ijaw words, food and culture are listed in the Ijaw Dictionary Project (ijawdictionary.com) and (ijawland.com).

The birds of Nigeria from (birdlist.org/nigeria) and (africanbirdclub.org).

Thanks go to the following:

For the real work: the remarkable Christine Green, Claire Anderson-Wheeler, Jane Wood, and the teams at Quercus (UK), Other Press (US) and Cassava Republic Press (Nigeria).

For kindness, support and encouragement: Ike Anya and Helon Habila.

For reading and checking drafts, and convincing me that I could tell this story: Mrs Oyintarela Diffa-Umeri, Mr Are Emein, Mrs Doubraebi Emein.

For information about the culture, food and politics of

the Niger Delta: Nene Alokwe, Felix Amoruwa, Ori Ayonmike, Steve Chadwick, Senator Chief Emmanuel W.T. Diffa (Justice of the Peace), Mieske Diri, Tute Ehinlaiye, Mr Egberipan, Kola Grey, Fogho O. Ikede, Nimi Iti, Timi Komonibo, Dr Ebi Komonibo, Achuonye Chidiebere Luckyprince, Kayode Ogundamisi, and the Sahara Reporters, Ken Ofili, Misan Oti-Adams, Chief Oyibo, Basorge Tariah, Kendra E. Thornbury.

For help with the midwifery: Nicky Fisher, Juliana Okoh and Comfort Momoh.

For the first readers: Anjali Joseph, Emma Levy, Justine Mann, Malin Ngoie.

For the lovely UEA people, specifically my workshop group and tutors: Trezza Azzopardi, and Giles Foden, and the RLF fellow, Stephen Foster.

Most of all, I thank those people local to the Niger Delta who took the time to tell me their stories, in order that I better tell Blessing's. I hope I listened well.